THE AIRSHIPMEN TRILOGY

VOLUME TWO

LORDS OF THE AIR

Brigadier General Christopher Birdwood Thomson,
Lord Thomson of Cardington,
Secretary of State for Air.

THE AIRSHIPMEN TRILOGY

VOLUME TWO

LORDS OF THE AIR

BASED ON A TRUE STORY

THE GREAT DUEL BEGINS

DAVID DENNINGTON

THE FULL CAST OF CHARACTERS FOR THE TRILOGY
MAY BE FOUND AT THE BACK OF THE BOOK.

THE AIRSHIPMEN TRILOGY – VOLUME TWO – LORDS OF THE AIR.
COPYRIGHT © 2020 by David Dennington.

This is a work of fiction with both real, historical figures and fictitious characters based on actual events surrounding the British Airship Program between 1920 and 1931. Some events, dates and locations have been changed for dramatic purposes and great artistic license has been taken throughout.

While *The Airshipmen Trilogy—Volume Two—Lords of the Air* is based on real events, characters, characterizations, incidents, locations, and dialogue have been invented and fictionalized in order to dramatize the story and are products of the author's imagination. The fictionalization, or invention of events, or relocation of events is for dramatic purposes and not intended to reflect on actual historical characters, history, entities or organizations, past or present. This novel is not intended to right any wrongs or 'set the record straight' regarding past events or actions, but is intended to *entertain*. Readers are encouraged to research the vast array of books on this subject from which the author has drawn facts as well as the essence of events and characters. In all other respects, resemblance to persons living or dead must be construed as coincidental.

Printed by Amazon.

Available from Amazon.com and other retail outlets.

Also available on Kindle and other retail outlets through Amazon.

DESCRIPTION: This special edition of *The Airshipmen* is now published as a trilogy, (originally published as one volume).

TRILOGY IDENTIFIER: Paperback.

THE AIRSHIPMEN TRILOGY VOLUME TWO
LORDS OF THE AIR ISBN - 9798687361170

BY DAVID DENNINGTON

THE AIRSHIPMEN
(Now also available as a three-part series)

The Airshipmen Trilogy Volume One   *From Ashes*
The Airshipmen Trilogy Volume Two   *Lords of the Air*
The Airshipmen Trilogy Volume Three *To Ashes*

THE GHOST OF CAPTAIN HINCHLIFFE
Based on a true story

For my dear wife, Jenny.

LORDS OF THE AIR

The events so far:

The US Navy sent Lou Remington to England to learn how to fly airships and pick up *R38/ZR-2*. As chief coxswain, he leads his young crew with their dauntless support. That ship breaks in two, killing all but five men. After gallantly saving three of his crew, Lou is hospitalized and he meets the magnificent nurse Charlotte Hamilton and marries her.

After a court of inquiry and a whitewash, it's not long before the British come knocking at his door. With the loss of the flower of their airshipmen in that terrible crash, the British are in dire need of talent and experience.

Lord Thomson, who has been elevated to cabinet level by his friend Ramsay MacDonald, sets up a 'new, improved airship program'— supposedly safer. Two teams have been formed, in ferocious competition with one another. One will fly to Canada, the other to India.

Lou's future shines bright, although Charlotte has grave doubts. Her worry is affecting her mental health. She is trying to conceive, but without success. Lou has become absorbed in his work in coordinating between the two teams, which includes trying to keep the peace!

TABLE OF CONTENTS

VOLUME 2

PART ONE—THEIR TRIALS BEGIN

PART TWO—THE DUEL BEGINS

"Who do I think I am? I'll tell you exactly who I am, sir. I'm the man who stood and watched R38 break in two and blow up, killing dozens of British and American young men, decapitating them, dismembering them, blowing them to bits, drowning them and burning them to a crisp. I'm the man who's trying to avoid more of our boys sharing the same fate. That's who I am, sir!"

Fred McWade, Airship Inspector, Cardington Tower.

Saturday, June 28, 1930.

PROLOGUE

No. 10 Downing Street, London.
Friday Evening, October 3, 1930.

At 10 o'clock, Thomson and MacDonald emerge from MacDonald's study on the second floor, having gone over the agenda for the Imperial Conference of Dominion Prime Ministers scheduled to begin later that month. They stand on the wide landing overlooking the grand staircase. MacDonald puts his hand on Thomson's arm, eyes intense.

"Forgo this trip. I need your wise council for this conference. Do this for me, CB."

"Are you ordering me not to go, sir?"

"No, I'm asking you as my dearest friend."

They hold each other's forearms and Thomson looks earnestly into the Prime Minister's face.

"How can I not go? I'm committed. And besides, the troops are expecting me. I need to rally them." Thomson moves to the top of the stairs. "Don't worry. I'll be back for the conference—have I ever let you down, Ramsay?"

MacDonald's eyes, moist earlier, now glisten. Thomson sees this before he starts down the stairs. When he gets to the bottom, he stares up at MacDonald and waves. Thomson crosses the black and white checkered floor, stopping at the door.

"Farewell, my good friend," MacDonald calls down weakly.

Thomson's voice echoes up the stairway. "Don't look so glum, my dear chap. Don't you remember? Our fate is already written."

MacDonald stands hunched like a man watching his brother going off to war. He wipes his eyes with a handkerchief. "Yes, I do," he whispers. "Yes, I do."

"Ramsay, if the worst *should* happen, it'd soon be over."

As Thomson leaves, the door slams behind him, the sound echoing around the great hall like thunder.

Thomson leaves Downing Street and crosses Whitehall to Gwydyr House. He passes the nightwatchman, giving him a curt nod. His office is in darkness. He switches on the picture light over the huge oil painting of the Taj Mahal and sits down, staring at the airship he'd had superimposed upon it by Winston Churchill. He hopes for some sort of divine affirmation. But he gets none. He gets up and goes to the window and peers out over the river, faintly glimmering under the dim street lamps. The bitter taste and the feeling he has is something akin to buyer's remorse. Brancker's words continue their stinging assault:

I will go CB—and I'll tell you why. I encouraged people to fly in this airship—people like O'Neill and Palstra—believing it'd be built and tested properly. I believed all your rhetoric about 'safety first.' I didn't think you'd use this airship for your own personal aggrandizement, for your own personal agenda, with everything set to meet your own personal schedule. People like O'Neill put their faith in me and my word. I will not abandon them now.

Then he hears the young American's voice like an echo, depressing him further.

You're putting all your chips on black, Lord Thomson... You're putting all your chips on black...

The Taj Mahal, India.

PART ONE

Cardington R101 Over London. October 16, 1929.

THEIR TRIALS BEGIN

Princess Marthe Bibesco painting by Boldini.

1

ENTER THE PRINCESS

July 4, 1929.

It was July 4th, 1929. The rain had stopped. Clouds were dissipating and the sun beginning to show itself after a succession of miserable, grey days. The longed-for moment had finally arrived. The train bearing Princess Marthe Bibesco glided into Victoria Station. As it did, a debate regarding the British Airship Program was raging in the House of Lords. Naturally, Thomson's attendance was required. Six months had passed since Thomson had seen Marthe. She knew he'd be bitterly disappointed, not being able to meet her.

Dust-laden shafts of sunlight, interrupted by clouds of steam, shone down from the skylights onto the platform. The train came to a gentle stop, exhaling a huge sigh. All doors swung open and Marthe stepped onto the platform, preceded by Isadora, her maidservant. A thin young man with a pencil moustache peered at her. She studied him for a moment. James Buck, Thomson's valet, would be meeting her. He wore a green check suit, a yellow tie, and a narrow-brimmed grey bowler, in accordance with the description provided. Not exactly her choice in men's clothing. But this had to be him.

"Princess Bibesco?" he asked.

"Yes, indeed," Marthe said. "This is my maidservant, Isadora."

Buck nodded to the dumpy, non-descript Slavic woman in her fifties wearing a headscarf. She ignored him. She was invisible. Buck turned back to Marthe.

"Honored to meet you, madam. I'm James Buck, Lord Thomson's valet. I trust the journey's been satisfactory?"

Marthe adored his accent. It was what she described as 'upper-class Cockney', and it was amusing.

"It was fine, Mr. Buck. Now, if you'll kindly bring my bags from the guards' van ..."

"Certainly, Princess." Buck summoned a couple of porters. Soon, they appeared with Marthe's luggage piled on a trolley.

"Lord Thomson's limousine awaits you, Princess," Buck said.

"You're most kind," Marthe said, her half smile melting Buck. He led the way to the station entrance where a black Daimler was waiting. The chauffeur opened the rear door and Marthe and Isadora climbed in. Marthe settled down, breathing in the luxurious, beige leather.

Kit's doing well. I'm so pleased for him.

They loaded her baggage into the boot and Buck thrust some coins into the porters' hands. They peered in, smiling and touching their caps.

The British are so decent. Like dear Kit, always anxious to make one comfortable.

The chauffeur got in with Buck beside him. Buck pulled back the glass divider. "The Ritz as usual, Princess Marthe?"

"Yes, if you wouldn't mind, thank you, Mr. Buck."

"No trouble at all, ma'am."

"Can we go by the Palace?"

"Oh, absolutely, ma'am."

Buck closed the partition glass and Marthe relaxed, looking out of the window in the total silence. They entered the main road and moved along Buckingham Palace Road, past Rubin's Hotel. The cobblestone roads glistened, steam rising in the sunshine.

The streets of London washed clean especially for me!

As an acclaimed writer, Marthe habitually documented her impressions of people and places when she traveled. It was one of her passions. She wrote everything down as soon as she reached her destination before her memories faded. She studied pedestrians; most appeared down at heel. Once in a while she spotted a well-dressed, professional type, a lawyer or a politician, perhaps.

Marthe enjoyed London, a bustling city with its red omnibuses and black and blue taxis. Not Paris, but she could get to love this city every bit as much, with all its nooks and crannies steeped in history. Getting to know London would take many lifetimes.

Horse-drawn vehicles laden with goods, building materials, coal, and junk, accounted for the piles of horse manure everywhere. Soon, she guessed, the evil-smelling combustion engines would take over the city and the manure would disappear. The odor was not so unpleasant, unlike foul black smoke emitted from ten thousand tailpipes.

That will be progress. Such a pity!

An old chestnut mare was being allowed to drink at a granite trough. Marthe was thankful. She felt for the poor creature.

At least the combustion engine will spare their suffering.

Her mind drifted to Thomson. She wished she was sexually attracted to him, though that might be futile. She thought back to the time before the war and his mission in Bucharest. Her husband had brought news of her father's death—her greatest hero and friend. The loss, on top of her disastrous marriage, had almost destroyed her. She'd passively given herself up to Thomson. Sadly though, his efforts had been clumsy and lacking in expertise, leaving them both miserable. But despite that, his love and tenderness had carried her through inconsolable grief. He was such a dear man—a wonderful man, whose friendship she treasured.

Yes, no question he was a guardian angel sent to save me and nurse me back to life.

She remembered how Thomson had got her to safety during the German advance. She smiled when she thought of the shoe she'd left in his car in her haste to escape—a delicate, Louis-heeled shoe. She'd been wearing those shoes the night they'd met. He said it reminded him of *Cinderella* from the Italian folk tale. *Cinderella* seemed apt.

Unrecognized, unloved, and lonely at the time—that was me.

He treasured that shoe, keeping it polished and wrapped in tissue paper. He'd still have it somewhere—probably in his top drawer.

Such a small price to pay—that shoe gives him so much pleasure.

The fact remained: no chemistry existed for her regarding the subject of love. He was a gentleman—always attentive and considerate, unlike many of the men she'd had in her life, before and since 1915. But she *had* experienced real passion and sexual fulfillment, thank God, and been deeply in love—but not with Kit.

She remembered how her husband had almost ruined her on her wedding night—her fifteenth birthday—a mere child. Such a brute! The thought of it made her shudder to this day. During her betrothal, she'd had such romantic dreams of marrying her prince and their two aristocratic families being joined. It'd been a fairytale, but one which soon turned into a nightmare. Within weeks of their splendid marriage, the rage of Bucharest high society, he'd gone off with another woman —in fact, many other women, leaving her heartbroken and lonely. And nothing had changed since.

Oh, well, that's George. I don't hold anything against him—he has his good side. Although, it's a wonder I survived to make love ever again.

But she had. In matters of passion, Prince Charles-Louis de Beauvau-Craon was the man who saved her—becoming the love of her life. She thought of the abuse she'd suffered, when compared to Charles-Louis's magnificent, loving treatment of her.

If my body were a Stradivarius, then Charles-Louis was a maestro. He taught me about sex and love. Oh my God, those nights with him were pure ecstasy! For him, I would've given up everything.

Marthe had been madly in love, but his mother had put her foot down, refusing to allow him to marry a divorced woman.

And thank God she did! I should hate to be living in abject poverty now. Sex and love are all very well, but ...

No man had abused her since her marriage. In fact, during her numerous affairs she'd tantalized many a man for her own amusement. Marthe wondered about the future. She was still a beautiful woman, adored and pursued by powerful men.

She thought about this visit and supposed she'd have to succumb to Thomson's advances at some point. Maybe she could manage to hold him off until the last night. She usually did. This naturally left him thirsting for more. Sex with him was a chore to be endured, but thank God, always soon over. But he really was such a dear, dear man though! She told Thomson she'd been totally ruined on her wedding night. He thought of her as a passionless, injured flower. All he ever wanted to do was protect and nurture her.

Bless his heart!

Isadora would play her part. She'd taken care of Marthe in Romania since the age of ten, as her surrogate mother. Isadora certainly cared for her as much as Marthe's mother—probably a lot more—and Marthe adored her. But Marthe couldn't be too hard on her mother. The poor woman was in a perpetual state of grief over the loss of her only son, Georges, to typhoid fever and then later, of Marthe's older sister to cholera. After her father's death and Thomson's departure for Palestine, her younger sister killed herself. Soon after that, both her mother and favorite cousin also committed suicide. Marthe had been very much alone in the world, but for Isadora.

Soon after Marthe's marriage, Isadora had nursed her through near-death during childbirth. Thank God for Isadora! There were two people Marthe kept no secrets from—her priest and Isadora. She and the old Slav woman laughed together and cried together—in private. In public, she became her maidservant, rarely noticed—never heard.

Marthe was terribly fond of the old priest. He was the second pillar in her life. He'd converted her to Catholicism as a girl of twelve, after she'd been sent to Paris by her father. He instructed her in the faith, becoming her confessor and spiritual adviser. He was modern, open-minded and witty, especially for a priest. That chubby little man in his threadbare habit, living a life of poverty—except for the good food and wine lavished upon him by doting parishioners—was extraordinarily well-read. She told him about all the goings on in her life, including details of her affairs, and he usually chuckled. He advised against divorce—under no circumstance would he approve contravention of God's laws, except when violence played a role.

The Daimler passed Stable Row on the palace grounds, where the king's horses were kept. At the top of Buckingham Palace Road, they turned in front of the palace. Marthe was thrilled at the sight of the mounted King's Guard on its way from Wellington Barracks on Birdcage Walk. They looked so fine in their red tunics, gold tassels swinging from side to side. The horses glistened beautifully, like the soldiers' boots and the wet tarmacadam streets. Police held up their limousine as the riders turned and entered the palace gate. Outside the iron railings, Marthe witnessed the changing of the guard.

Such timing! Such splendor! A perfect start to a pleasant interlude in England.

After the horsemen had passed, the police allowed them to proceed around the Victoria Memorial and up the Mall. Soon they turned on to St. James's Street, passing St. James's Palace. The car moved up the hill, in front of Boodle's and White's gentleman's clubs, well known to Marthe. Some of her male friends were members. How she wished she could set foot inside them. Now, here was Brooks's conservative club on the left. Kit wouldn't be a member, but he'd certainly have been invited as a guest. At the top of the street, before entering Piccadilly, the car drew up outside the Ritz. It was immediately descended upon by hotel staff.

The hotel manager escorted Marthe through the marble hall to the lift and up to room 627, a magnificent suite furnished with Louis XV1 antique furniture with a balcony overlooking the Royal Gardens in

Green Park. As soon as the door swung open, she was enveloped by the scent of roses—*Variété Général Jacqueminot*—in cut glass vases placed around the room.

"Lord Thomson came this morning, Princess, to inspect the flower arrangements," the manager gushed. Excited, Marthe went to the vase containing the largest and most beautiful bouquet, placed on the round table at the center of the room. She plucked out the envelope wedged between the stems and removed the engraved card.

"Ooo la la!" she exclaimed.

> *Welcome back to England, my dearest Marthe.*
> *Our special roses come with my deepest love.*
> *Until eight, tonight—Your ever devoted Kit.*

Thomson arranged for flowers to be placed in her room every time she returned to London, but like a young girl, she always expressed surprise and appreciation. He'd certainly out-done himself this time, though. She called for Isadora. A scented bath would help soothe her for a couple of hours before he arrived.

2

THE WRATH OF LORD SCUNTHORPE

July 4, 1929.

Thomson was indeed vexed. He hated not being at the station to meet her. It was such a thrill when her train came steaming in, her face at the window, her uplifting smile. Alas, today it couldn't be helped—the debate in the Lords concerned the future of the airship program and his presence was of paramount importance. Many on both sides were bitterly opposed to 'lighter than air' and out to sabotage the program. They'd cut funding given the slightest opportunity. He must fend off attacks—give them some stick. There were rumors of a showdown.

Thomson entered the magnificent chamber of the House of Lords, which formed part of the Palace of Westminster. The King's throne, the highest seat in the room was modeled on the fourteenth century coronation chair in Westminster Abbey. The area was shrouded by a canopy clad in gold and supported by ornamental columns. Oil paintings, depicting Britain's glorious past, hung above the throne up to the ceiling. The rest of the walls, clad in Elizabethan paneling, ran up to the Gothic stone window surrounds just beneath the beamed roof. Stained-glass leaded windows lent a holy atmosphere. The great space was lit by gold chandeliers hanging from the roof and by candelabras on ornamental columns in front of the throne.

Visitors and the press, which included reporters who'd attended Thomson's first press conference at Cardington, stood on the high gallery running around the room. Today, more than a dozen were present, including George Hunter from the *Daily Express*. As Thomson strode in, he listened to the chatter of finely dressed, white-haired lords. They twisted and turned in their red leather banquettes and leaned over chairbacks, talking. Thomson knew they liked fireworks. They wouldn't be disappointed.

He took his seat in the front row, on the left side of the Lord Chancellor's empty chair. Despite the charged atmosphere, Thomson was preoccupied with thoughts of Marthe—thoughts that gave him butterflies. Everyone stood as the Lord Chancellor entered through the ornate doors. He strode to his seat in front of the throne and sat down. The lords sat down in unison.

After preliminary remarks, the Lord Chancellor indicated Lord Scunthorpe would speak first. Lord Scunthorpe, an imposing man in his sixties, heavily jowled with flowing, white locks had taken his name from the city south of Howden, which was also his family name —making him Lord Scunthorpe of Scunthorpe. He stood up and glared in Thomson's direction for a long moment, before speaking.

"I've never flown in a dirigible and I never will …that is, whilst I'm still in my right mind!" he boomed in his heavy Yorkshire brogue. A chorus went up and many of the heads of white hair shook from side to side.

"Hell would freeze over before that 'appened!" he added.

"Hear, hear!"

"Nor I!"

"Airships are the *devil's* 'andiwork in defiance of God's laws and we should avoid them like the plague!"

"Quite right!"

"Where in the world are we going to find people crazy enough to fly in these diabolically dangerous contraptions? From which lunatic asylum will they be dragged?"

Lord Scunthorpe stared at Thomson as the jeering and heckling continued. Thomson's face was expressionless. Inside he seethed.

"This is not a matter of party politics—of left versus right. It's a matter of common sense verses *sheer stupidity*. A matter of *life and death*. What we're dealing with 'ere is a *flight of fantasy*!"

"Hear! Hear!"

"I agree!"

"Now, let us examine the Air Ministry's achievements to date and the track record of these floating 'ydrogen bombs. We'll start with the *R33*, although there are of course, many earlier horror stories. That airship cost three 'undred and forty-six thousand pounds and blew away to Germany—luckily, no one was killed in that one."

Thomson had seen the newsreels. The ship had been torn away from its mooring in Norfolk and blown to the Continent. It limped all the way home flying backwards after the storm.

"The *R34* cost three 'undred and sixty thousand and was scrapped after an argument with the Yorkshire Moors and getting blown out over the North Sea."

This infuriated Thomson. Scunthorpe failed to mention the ship had made a historic return flight to Long Island, New York in 1919 (with Scott in command).

"Now let me see. The *R35* cost three 'undred and seventy thousand and ended in disaster. While 'undreds were 'oldin' 'er down, she took off with scores of men still clinging on. Men died that day—*for absolutely no good reason whatsoever!*"

"Shame! Shame!"

Thomson remained stony-faced.

"This brings us to another monumental failure—the *R37*. It cost three 'undred and ninety thousand pounds and was smashed into the shed by the wind, destroying the airship and the shed. Luckily, 'undreds of men escaped injury or death."

Thomson folded his arms.

How much longer must we endure this?

"Now we come to the *R38*." Lord Scunthorpe stopped and gazed around the chamber at the faces. No smiles now. Lord Scunthorpe's accusing eyes burned into Thomson.

Carry on, you visionless-fool.

"Yes, we all remember *R38*, don't we? That miracle of British engineering cost a whopping five 'undred thousand pounds. And that's not all it cost—it cost forty-four men their lives. That monstrosity broke in 'alf, exploded in flames and crashed into the River 'Umber." He raised his hands to the heavens as if imploring the Almighty. "I seem to remember after that little mis'ap we all said, 'Never again!' Didn't we? ...Well, *didn't we?*"

"Yes, we did!"

"We did!"

"Now, we mustn't forget our American friends—yes, they 'ave their share of great 'visionaries' too, wanting to build airships as big as their egos. After *R38,* in 1922, the *Roma* went down in Virginia. Thirty-four men got roasted alive in that one. In 1925, the *Shenandoah* broke to bits in a storm over Ohio, costing fourteen more lives. The same thing 'appened to the French *Dixmude*. That thing blew up and fell to pieces in a storm over the Mediterranean with the loss of another forty-four men. It's obvious to me these ridiculous machines are even more useless in bad weather and, I submit, we will *always* 'ave bad weather!"

"Of course we will!"

"Yes, indeed!"

Scunthorpe peered round the chamber with his hands on his hips.

"India ..." The word trailed off into silence, his timing impeccable. He stared up at the chandeliers, shaking his head, his lips pursed. Everyone waited. "...you know ...I think ...you've got more chance of flying to the moon on a *witch's bloody broomstick!*"

The chamber erupted. The Lord Chancellor banged his gavel.

"Order! Order!"

"Ha, ha!"

"Stupid fools!"

"They've got no chance!"

"Let us turn our attention to the Air Minister's *latest folly.* The engineering feat he calls the *Cardington R101,* designed by 'the experts' at Cardington, has been under construction for five years now, costing the taxpayer four 'undred and sixty thousand pounds, which by any stretch of the imagination, could not take to the air *this year* ... *next year* ...or *the year after that!*"

The chamber was now bedlam. Members stood banging the banquette chair backs while the Lord Chancellor furiously hammered his gavel. "Order! Order!"

When order was restored, Lord Scunthorpe resumed softly.

"Finally, I have just one question. When will the British Government come to its senses and put an end to this madness and *stop pouring money down the drain!*"

This crescendo exhausted him. With a red face and bulging veins, Lord Scunthorpe sank into his seat. All eyes turned and rested on Thomson, who remained motionless for what seemed ages, glaring at Lord Scunthorpe. Eventually, he rose and the room fell silent.

"The honorable gentleman may mock ...but God gave men vision to better their lot—to use logic and reason and engineering skill to overcome the obstacles of gravity and distance—and yes, *weather.*

God did not give us brains for us to behave like *shrinking violets*! Men shall break the bonds of earth and take to the air to fly like eagles, despite what the honorable gentleman from the North would have us believe. The trouble with the noble lord is ...he doesn't get out of Scunthorpe enough!"

It was the turn of the supporters of the program to jeer and for Thomson to give Lord Scunthorpe a withering glare.

"All the brave pioneers in aviation who lost their lives shall not have died in vain. From the ashes of *R38* these mighty airships shall rise like the phoenix—*bigger* and *stronger* and *safer*—capable of flying enormous distances in *any kind of weather*. Airships are the wave of the future and they'll forge air routes around the world, binding our empire and improving the lives of millions. Mark my words, sir. Mark my words!"

Thomson bowed to the Lord Chancellor and marched stiffly from the chamber.

3

BITTER SWEET

July 4, 1929.

W hile Thomson was doing battle with Lord Scunthorpe at the House of Lords, Marthe was being bathed by Isadora in the magnificent, marble bath. After sending her away, Marthe allowed herself to soak and contemplate for an hour in the warm, perfumed water. She thought about the roses.

So many this time! He's always generous, but is there more to it?

She hoped not.

By 8 o'clock Marthe was well-rested and Isadora assisted her in putting the final touches to her makeup, hair and dressing. She wore a black chiffon dress and black goatskin shoes. To complement the dress, she wore a magnificent string of pearls given to her by Kronprinz Wilhelm of Germany, an ardent admirer for years. She twirled in front of the mirror like a dancer. At forty-three, she looked as beautiful as the day Thomson had first seen her in Bucharest: her skin still smooth and white as china, without the first sign of a wrinkle; her hair, rich, dark brown with highlights of red, shone with health. Tonight, as on the first night he'd met her, she had her hair fastened up and drawn tightly to the back, accentuating her bone structure and slightly hollow cheeks.

There was a knock at the door. Isadora opened it. Thomson stood dressed in a black evening suit, winged collar and bow tie. He'd known Isadora since 1915. She never changed. She appeared old to him then. Always silent. *Sullen* he thought. She annoyed him, but he knew it was unreasonable to feel that way about a servant. She seemed constantly present.

"Ah, good evening, Isadora," Thomson said. "May I come in?"

Isadora stepped aside without a word, allowing him to enter. Marthe appeared from her bedroom, smiling. Isadora hovered.

"Kit!"

Thomson was overjoyed and rushed forward. She allowed him to kiss her on both cheeks and to kiss her hands. He longed to take her in his arms and kiss her lips, but now wasn't the time. Each time they were reunited he had to court her all over again. He was resigned to the fact that Marthe was not a passionate woman—she'd always been that way; affectionate and friendly, but never *passionate*.

"God, I've missed you, Marthe," Thomson said, clasping her hands.

"Thank you for all these lovely flowers. You shouldn't have gone to so much trouble."

"It gives me great pleasure, my dearest," Thomson beamed.

"We must go if we don't want to be late," Marthe said.

Isadora removed Marthe's evening coat from the closet and held it up. He let go of Marthe's hands.

They were driven in Thomson's limousine to His Majesty's Theater in the Haymarket where 'Bitter Sweet,' an operetta by Noël Coward, was playing. Marthe had expressed an interest in seeing it and Thomson had obtained the Royal Box. The musical was popular and the theater filled rapidly. Marthe appreciated the building, admiring the burgundy walls and fluted columns with gold relief. She slipped into one of the red velvet chairs with Thomson beside her. He was in heaven.

'Bitter Sweet.' How appropriate.

If only he were able to freeze these moments and relish them over and over. "I dreamed about you again the other night, Marthe."

"And what did you dream this time?" she said with a teasing smile.

"The same dream. You are as lovely tonight as the first time I saw you on Rue de Rivoli in that fine, white carriage. You're the girl in my dream."

"And what year was that?" she said with an artful stare.

"1902."

"My dear Kit, I've told you a dozen times. That girl wasn't me. I would've only been fourteen!"

Thomson knew this wasn't an excuse, but didn't argue. "Then you more than fulfill that vision of beauty I've carried with me all these years, dear heart."

He held her hand throughout the evening and they enjoyed the play like a tender, young couple. On arrival back at The Ritz, Marthe said she was tired and after escorting her to her suite, Thomson left. It'd been an enchanting evening, though frustrating. He'd need to exercise patience.

The next day, Thomson took Marthe to Wimbledon for the ladies' finals. They watched Helen Wills Moody beat Helen Jacobs in two sets. Their arrival had created mild interest. People suspected they were 'somebody,' but not sure who. Tennis bored him. Heads turned back and forth like a thousand metronomes, but not Thomson's. Only Marthe was on his mind. He stole discreet looks at her throughout the afternoon.

The following day, they drove to Heston Aerodrome where they watched sky racing around pylons. This was one of Marthe's husband's favorite pastimes. Thomson studied her reaction feeling a stab of jealousy. She obviously found it exciting, spending much of the time on her feet. At the end of the races, Thomson presented silver cups to the winners.

They spent the next few days visiting and dining with friends at their country estates. Marthe was wonderful to be with on these occasions and Thomson was happy, except for the gnawing deep inside that grew painful as time wore on—she'd soon be gone. One sunny afternoon, Thomson took Marthe to visit his chambers in the House of Lords and to pick up his dispatches. He'd taken her to the main chamber before, but now he had his own office. The room was ornate, smelling of wood and leather— 'wonderfully masculine,' she told him.

Marthe kicked off her shoes and sank into a leather armchair opposite his desk, curling up like a kitten, delighting him. After studying the surroundings, she stared at him coquettishly while, like a schoolmaster, he studied his papers through half spectacles.

"Look at you, Kit. Lord Thomson of Cardington, Minister of State —so aristocratic, so royal!" she said.

"Splendidly put, my dear princess."

"All those years ago in Romania, who could've pictured *this*?" she marveled.

Thomson got up from his chair.

"Come, let's walk to the lake. The ducks are waiting."

Thomson had bread in his pocket; he'd made sure Gwen put some in a bag. He'd planned this stroll in the park for weeks and waited for a beautiful afternoon. He felt certain this was the right moment. They left the House of Lords. Thomson was unable to resist taking Marthe through Westminster Hall, forming part of the Palace of Westminster, on the way.

Their footsteps echoed across stone paving in the cavernous building. Thomson always waxed poetic here, seeming to have a spiritual connection with the place.

"Do you know this is my most favorite Gothic room in all England, Marthe?" he said, staring up at the massive wooden roof beams which rested on stone abutments.

"I should, Kit. You tell me each time we pass through it!"

"This is where they tried King Charles the First," he said. He'd told her this many times over the years. In his mind he was now back in January of 1649. "You can just see it, can't you, Marthe? King Charles standing there on a platform, his once pristine white, ruffled shirt, scruffy and dirty, his head held high, despite being tried by a filthy mob led by that scoundrel, Oliver Cromwell, thirsting for his blood—and his throne." Thomson waved his arms grandly. He sensed the crowd around them and now so did Marthe. She became distraught.

"Before they dragged him away and chopped off the poor man's head! Oh Kit, this place gives me the chills. It reeks of despair. Let's get out of here!"

Thomson was surprised—she hadn't acted this way before, but she was right. No question, this place carried an aura of death. They stepped out into the sunshine to stroll arm in arm, enjoying each other's company. On reaching the Horse Guards Parade, they crossed the road and admired the two mounted guardsmen in gleaming, thigh-length, black boots, crimson coats and black capes that fell across their horses' backs.

Marthe made a fuss of the horses before they ambled into the cobblestone yard and across the gravel parade ground toward St. James's Park, where indeed, the ducks *were* waiting. Thomson fished around in his pocket for the brown bag of bread while the ducks watched in anticipation. Together, Thomson and Marthe threw bread into the pond and the splashing birds fought noisily for it. They chatted idly until the bread was gone. When calm was restored on the water and the greedy ducks had disbursed, Thomson became serious. The moment had come.

"Marthe, I have something to tell you which is very hush-hush."

"What is it, Kit?" Marthe asked, alarmed.

"Ramsay is going to put my name forward to the King for consideration for the post of Viceroy to India. Most likely, I'll be offered the job."

"Oh Kit, that's wonderful! I am so proud of you. Congratulations." she said, kissing his cheek.

Thomson was disappointed at Marthe's reaction. Unless …

"Perhaps he's asking rather a lot of … us … Don't you think?"

"What's the difference? I can always visit you in India," she said, with an encouraging smile. "That would be rather fun."

She was too flippant.

"I thought this might be an opportunity for us to be together … perhaps … permanently."

"*Whatever* do you mean?"

"I thought maybe we might … marry."

"But you know I'm *already* married."

That was cold and sarcastic, not the reaction he'd hoped for.

He plunged on. "In my position, I think we'd get Rome's blessing."

"*Rome's blessing!* For what?"

"An annulment."

"I'm married because I *choose* to be married. In *my* position, even an annulment wouldn't be acceptable to society—I'd become an outcast!"

"Marthe, you cannot live your whole life just to please society."

"I live my life the way I *choose* to live it," Marthe snapped.

"How can you go on being married to a man who doesn't love you?"

"This may sound strange, but he does love me—in his own way."

"You lead separate lives. He has a mistress whom you tolerate."

"I'd do nothing to hurt or embarrass him. He's like a brother to me."

"And *I* want to be a *husband* to you!"

"Look, I don't blame him—and what's more, neither will *you*."

"I'm not blaming anyone. I'm simply asking you to end this arrangement and enter a normal loving marriage with *me,*" he said.

"Enough!" Marthe cried.

Totally deflated, Thomson stared across the pond, and after a long pause, spoke softly. "Marthe, I've waited fifteen long years ... and now, perhaps, we have the opportunity."

Marthe was silent. Thomson sensed her pondering the possibilities, perhaps for the first time. He waited patiently.

"At the moment, all this is mere speculation," she said.

Her tone had the air of finality and Thomson knew to press no more.

After two weeks in England, it was almost time for Marthe to return to Paris. The second week had been strained. For the first time in their relationship, there'd been awkward moments. Thomson's proposal hung over them like a black cloud. The day before Marthe's departure, they had tea on the terrace of the House of Lords with the Prime Minister. MacDonald had invited them so he could meet the woman who'd had such an effect on Thomson for so many years. Thomson had been longing to introduce Marthe to him.

"Prime Minister, may I present Princess Marthe Bibesco," Thomson said.

MacDonald's eyes lit up on seeing Marthe, and she appeared to be just as delighted.

"Prime Minister, it's such a pleasure," she said, her long eyelashes fluttering.

MacDonald took her hand between his and delicately raised it to his lips, kissing it as though it were fine china. Thomson closely watched their every movement and expression, remembering distinctly the night, he himself, had fallen under Marthe's spell at the foot of the staircase in Cotroceni Palace. He felt a twinge of jealousy.

"You don't know how long I've wanted to meet the darling of Paris," MacDonald said.

"Prime Minister," she purred.

"Please call me Ramsay; all my closest friends do. CB is one of them and now I hope you will be, too."

Thomson remained silent. This was a meeting of intellectual Titans.

"You're so kind, Ramsay," Marthe said, gracing him with one of her most gorgeous smiles.

"If I say I'm honored, I mean it. For me to meet as talented a writer as you is a great thrill. I know you're the toast of the salons of Paris. Even Monsieur Proust himself heaps lavish praise upon you."

"Oh, they exaggerate, Ramsay."

"No, no. I've read *Catherine-Paris* and *Les Huits Paradis* and the critics praised you as a delicious and learned writer—and I can attest to both. No wonder Thomson's in love with you. Everybody is!"

"You yourself are much accomplished. I've read your works, and although I may not agree with some of the principles of your political thought, there's so much I *do* agree with," Marthe gushed.

Thomson couldn't help but marvel. He knew Marthe to be conservative through and through, but here she was displaying her humanitarian side, which he knew MacDonald would find irresistible. She'd never mentioned reading MacDonald's writings—and neither had he, hers—that was new and interesting. He could see MacDonald was enchanted.

They took their seats around a wooden table overlooking the Thames and chatted for half an hour over cream tea and buttered scones. There were no references to the future or their relationship. It was a pleasant interlude and Marthe was thrilled to meet the man who currently managed the greatest and most powerful empire on earth, with a yearly budget greater than the United States, Soviet Russia and Germany. Finally, MacDonald stood up and graciously bid Marthe farewell with a courteous bow and a kiss on each cheek.

"When you come back, you must both come to Chequers. The gardens are beautiful. I know you'll enjoy them. When will you come?"

"I am not sure, Ramsay—perhaps not until next year."

MacDonald chuckled. Thomson knew Marthe was admiring his stature: his shock of white hair, like an old lion's mane, and the bushy white moustache that gave him character and made him so striking.

She studies people intensely. It's the nature of writers—Marthe especially; she's like a sponge. Nothing escapes her.

"That's a pity. I'm not sure I'll be in residence at Chequers by then, Marthe."

"Oh yes you will, Ramsay," Thomson said, turning to Marthe. "He always cracks that joke. He'll be spending weekends at Chequers for years to come."

"Then we shall see. But I'd like you to come. Both of you," MacDonald said.

"Yes, and during Marthe's next visit we'll dine at my flat," Thomson said. "You must bring Lady Wilson."

MacDonald hurried off to attend to matters of state.

"What a wonderful-looking man. He has such charisma!" Marthe exclaimed, watching MacDonald striding away.

"Thank you, Marthe. You made him feel special today. He loved you."

"You're such a good person, Kit. I can understand why you're such close friends. Does he see much of Lady Wilson?" she asked, looking away across the river.

The next day, Thomson took Marthe to Victoria Station to catch the train to Dover. From there, she'd take the ferry to Boulogne. They walked down the platform in silence, amid hissing steam and the echoing of slamming doors. Isadora trailed at a discreet distance.

Thomson was depressed. Everything seemed different. To make matters worse, after her meeting with MacDonald, he felt diminished. Marthe was difficult to read at the best of times. Perhaps he'd pushed her too hard. He'd lain awake all night alone in his flat thinking of what to say this morning.

At the assigned first-class carriage, Thomson went on board and stashed Marthe's hand luggage on the overhead rack. From there, he went back to the platform and stood at the door. Isadora disappeared down the corridor out of the way. Marthe stood at the open window above Thomson. A picture of unattainable beauty.

"Think about what I said," Thomson said.

Marthe stared down like the Sphinx. Suddenly, there was the guard's deafening whistle screaming in his head, signaling loneliness and grief to come. As the train began to move, she put her hand to her mouth and cleared her throat. She spoke softly.

"All right, I will," he thought she said.

He looked at her, unsure; it was hard to hear over all the damned noise in the station. With a half smile, she moved away from the window and sat down. He watched her departing train until it was out of sight, before trudging away with that familiar sinking feeling in his stomach.

What did she say? All right, I will—I will what?

Her muffled words kept going round in his mind on the way back to the flat. He'd need to write and find out exactly what she meant, but it might take weeks to get an answer, if then.

4

GAS BAGS & ENGINES

August & September 1929.

T
he dreaded engine trials began in August—dreaded because they were both absurdly dangerous and unnecessary. Barnes Wallis stood at one end of the shed with his bullhorn. The three engine cars had been attached to the underside of the airship's hull. Each car housed two reconditioned Rolls-Royce Condor engines in tandem, totaling six and the gas bags, having a total capacity of almost six million cubic feet had been charged with hydrogen. The more expensive helium—not available in Europe—was a safer gas, but produced less lift, making it less effective. Lou often thought about this—helium hadn't helped Josh aboard *Shenandoah*.

The installation of the gas bags and their charging by the hydrogen plant had been a massive and expensive undertaking. Wallis, the absolute perfectionist, had supervised the operation himself, with assistance from Norway, Lou and Teed, as well as the drawing office and technical staff.

Lou and Charlotte traveled up on the motorbike and stayed at Charlotte's parents' house in Ackworth. Ironically, Jessup had also been summoned to assist, joined by his two Yorkshire cohorts, now recovered. On the road north, the three had flashed by at high speed, passing too close, after swerving around Lou and Charlotte at the last second. Charlotte was shaken. Jessup would require further reining in.

Wallis showed signs of stress; often irritable, his eyes heavy due to vicious migraines. Lou realized this wasn't just about having Burney for a boss, nor the sheer enormity of his task. It came down to his nature—the need for absolute control.

During the gas bag installation, Wallis's booming commands filled the shed. Things had gone perfectly until the last bag suffered a small tear, not bad, just a few inches long. The shed became filled with

Wallis's fury. Lou took no notice; he knew the performance of all concerned had been practically flawless.

The gas bag installation and filling operations occurred during a two-week period when Molly was absent (the family having been wisely sent away). During that time, Wallis, Teed, Norway and Lou went over to Wallis's bungalow for tea, lunch and dinner. Often Burney and his perfumed, powdery wife knocked on the door, itching to be allowed in. On spotting the troublesome pair, Teed would wedge a pencil behind the doorbell, while Norway turned up the wireless. After a few minutes leaning on the bell and thumping furiously, they gave up and trudged away.

Lou and Charlotte visited John and Mary Bull during their time up north. News of Lou's promotion made them proud. Charlotte saw the promise of a successful future for Lou, but potential danger overshadowed everything. Charlotte also visited Fanny, still pining for Lenny. Charlotte doubted she'd get over the loss. Billy had done well at Howden and was highly thought of. His future looked bright. He'd be posted to Cardington after the engine tests and promoted to 'rigger' within a couple of months. Lou arranged for Billy to be billeted with Freddie's family for a reasonable price for bed and board. Lou thought it'd be good for Billy to be with a family, with a boy his own age.

Lou rewarded Freddie and his family by getting him a place in the ground crew. Freddie's father had already been a casual member of walking parties for previous airships over the years, including *R38*. In that position, Freddie would graduate toward becoming a crewman one day. For now, he'd work in the walking party when time came to launch and assist in mooring operations.

During their time up north, Lou and Charlotte had dinner with Mr. Shute at the Brown Cow. As soon as they sat down, Norway stunned them.

"Wallis is l-leaving us," he said.

"What do you mean?" Lou asked.

"Switching to aeroplanes."

Lou's jaw dropped and Charlotte gasped, putting her hand to her chest.

"I thought he was committed to airships," Lou said.

"I think he still is, but he'll do anything to get away from Burney. Things are pretty bad."

"That's a damned shame," Lou said.

Then Norway dropped the other shoe. "Burney's now written a book, which in essence says these two airships as designed are a lost cause," Norway said. "I'm not sure if it's to annoy Wallis or Thomson, or if he truly believes it—all three most likely."

"Sounds like they're both baling out," Charlotte said.

"No, Burney's not b-baling. He's suggesting designing elliptical shaped ships, which is a damned neat concept, actually," Norway said.

"So what's Wallis gonna do?" Lou asked.

"Design aeroplanes. He's moving to Weybridge."

"Wow! How long before he goes?" Lou asked.

"I think he'll be here until this ship's launched. He told me he definitely wants to make the trip to Canada, though."

"Which I guess'll be sometime next year," said Lou.

"It turns out that for the past year Wallis has been visiting a workshop in Brough, just up the road from here. There's an engineer building a great big seaplane and Barnes is completely taken with it. Of course, he says they don't know what they're doing, but now he's all fired up about aeroplanes."

"Rotten traitor!" Charlotte said suddenly.

"Gives him a second string to his bow," Lou said.

"If airships don't work out, he's got another avenue," Norway said.

Charlotte, said nothing. She stared down at her Dover sole.

Perhaps he's come to his senses.

She felt empty. She'd thought these men knew what they were doing and they'd get things right. Now Wallis was abandoning them and Burney was questioning the basic designs.

Why?

To her, 'If airships don't work out' meant: 'If they crash and burn, again'. Lou lifted his glass showing no feelings of betrayal. "Here's to Barnes Wallis and to his future endeavors—whatever they may be."

"Yes, to a great engineer," Norway said. They raised their glasses.

"You don't seem bothered in the least," Charlotte said, glaring at Norway.

"No, he's happy about it—*he's* moving up. He'll be the new chief, right, Nev?" Lou said.

"Could be, but I tell you this: Wallis needs to get away from here. His health has suffered terribly. The migraines are killing him. But I have more news," Norway said with a toothy grin.

"What?" Charlotte asked.

"They liked *our* last book *So Disdained*. It's coming out this year."

"Congratulations, Mr. Shute!" Lou exclaimed.

"Thank you both. You don't know how much you've helped me."

"Okay, put our cut toward another wheel for that car of yours."

"And when you're famous, I want to be your editor—don't forget," Charlotte said.

"I'll drink to that," Norway replied.

Wallis lifted the bullhorn to his mouth. "Okay, start engine No.1."

Lou stood in the Howden shed beside engine car No.1. Norway was at No.2. Lou watched the engineer start the engine through the car window. Once they were running, the noise was deafening. The bullhorn now became useless. Wallis put it down. After that, everything was done by hand signals and thumbs up or down. Each engine was run for two hours forward and thirty minutes in reverse.

The eighteen-foot propellers whirled two feet above the concrete floor, causing the airship to surge forward and up and down due to air currents generated—like a massive fan. Lou knew their lives would never be in greater peril. If the restraining cables gave way it would mean certain death for all, not to mention complete demolition of the seven acre shed. Lou looked at the engineer in the car next to him. The man gave him a beaming smile and a thumbs-up. Lou smiled back.

This is so damned phony. No one's fooling anyone.

He hadn't told Charlotte about the danger and when the tests were over, he was glad he'd kept his mouth shut. Engine trials were completed within three days and were a total success. To Lou, the whole exercise was sheer madness and he thought a much safer method could have been devised.

He and Charlotte headed south to Cardington for more of the same in Shed No.1. Similar trials were conducted on the *Cardington R101* engines with Richmond and Scott in attendance, assisted by Lou and Rope. Everyone cheated death once more, and Lou again said nothing to Charlotte. He figured he'd used up two more lives—if he were a cat, he had three left.

5

THE QUARREL

September 1929.

Lou spent less time up at Howden now the gas bags were installed and the engine tests completed. *Howden R100* floated in her shed, her suspension wires slack. Bedford Hospital offered Charlotte a nursing position and she was happy to go back to work. She hoped this was temporary, still desperate for a child. She and Lou kept trying, although Lou became increasingly wrapped up with his job. This sometimes irritated Charlotte. He didn't understand —having a baby was the most important thing in her life. He was either at the shed or studying at home.

Things erupted in September. Lou was at the dining table poring over navigation books loaned by Johnston. Charlotte came up behind him, leaned over and put her arms around his neck. "Lou," she whispered.

He felt her warm breath on his neck. "What d'you want, Charlie?"

"You."

She bit his ear, playfully. He felt her tongue slide invitingly into his ear. It felt good, but this wasn't the time. He had too much on his mind.

"Charlotte, I've got to study this stuff. It's important. You don't want me to get lost over the Atlantic, do you?"

"Come to bed, Remy," her voice husky and seductive.

"Not now. I must finish this. Johnny's gonna test me in the morning."

"*Saturday!*"

"So?"

"Come to bed."

"Look, I've got to do this and I'm really tired, honey."

Charlotte leapt back and straightened up. "Damn! All you care about is that bloody airship. I'm sick and tired of it!"

"That's not true."

"We were so happy up north. Now it's all about the airship. You don't care about me."

"Stop being melodramatic. I have to work on this."

"For all your dead buddies—including Josh of the 'Good Ship Shenandoah'! Right?"

"That's enough, Charlotte!"

Her eyes blazed. "Sometimes I feel like I'm living in a house full of *dead people!*"

"Will you shut the hell up!"

"I'm alive. You should care about your *wife!*"

"Look, I can't help it if you can't get pregnant."

"Perhaps you're just not *man* enough!"

"*I said*, it's not *my* fault you can't get pregnant."

"How do you know that? You won't go to a bloody doctor to find out!"

"Dammit Charlotte! You never stop. There's no need to behave like a damned prostitute in the back bar of some Yorkshire dockside pub."

"You rotten bastard! How dare you!"

Lou swung around in his chair to get up. Charlotte drew her arm back to slap his face. He grabbed her wrists. "Stop it, you bitch!"

She broke free and stormed out, slamming the door, causing a framed photograph of Candlestick Cottage to fall to the floor and break into pieces. Lou cleaned up the glass and tried to go back to studying for his test, but it was impossible. He lay down on the couch, refusing to go up to the bedroom. He slept fitfully until awakened by Charlotte's voice. He'd no idea how long she'd been sitting next to him in the dark, but he was glad. She took his hand.

"I'm sorry, Lou. It was all my fault. You didn't deserve it. Please forgive me. I don't know what's the matter with me. There's so much hurting me deep inside and I worry about you all the time … and I want a baby so much and—"

"Honey *what's* hurting you?"

She didn't answer. She sat looking down shaking her head. Lou knew he'd gone too far last night. He'd been a brute.

"Charlie, I'm sorry for what I called you." He screwed up his face, unable to believe he'd said those things.

"I deserved it. I was a perfect bitch."

"Don't say that … but you're right about one thing. I do much of it for *them*. It seems crazy, but it tears me up to be the one left alive. When I survived the war, it was the same. The chaplain told me my life had been spared for a reason and it was up to me to discover that reason. So, I do this, thinking maybe this is why. Charlotte, I can't let them down—remember that."

Charlotte put her arms around him, drawing him close. "I do understand, Lou. I'm a mess, too. I get so desperate. Sometimes I think this is the day it's gonna happen—I'm gonna fall. It's a hundred million-to-one chance, and I hate to see the moment slip away."

Lou looked at her questioningly. Was there more to all her sadness? Something deeper. He was at a loss. "We'll keep trying," he said finally.

"I thought you were going to see Johnny this morning."

"I didn't finish. I'll see him later."

Charlotte put her hand to his face running her fingertips down his scar. "I'm sorry."

"Don't worry, baby."

Charlotte's face brightened. "I want us to have a big launching party."

"You don't have to do that, sweetheart."

"They'll be pulling it out soon, won't they? I want to have a really big bash. We'll invite everyone. We'll have Walter and Sammy Church and Irene, and Joe Binks and Ginger Bell and their wives – I don't know their names—and Freddie and Billy and Cameron and his dear wife—if they're still speaking—and Dizzy and Polly and Mr. Leech and his wife, he's married isn't he? And …"

"Charlie, these are folks we have round all the time."

"I know, but I want this to be really special—a big celebration. We can get Captain Irwin and Olivia—if they'll come—and Mr. Atherstone and his wife and Johnny Johnston, oh I do like Johnny, and he can bring his wife—what's her name?"

"Janita."

"Oh, and Major Scott—thank God for Major Scott—and we'll get Inspector McWade. Oh, I do like that man, thank God for him, too!"

"You're forgetting Wing Commander Colmore—my boss—he's the most important guy in the joint!"

"Oh yes, and him, too. And your friend the steward who likes you."

"What about Lord Thomson, you're leaving him out," Lou said, chuckling.

"We'll invite him, too, if you want. Do you think he'd come?"

"Yes, and he'll bring Princess Marthe Bibesco and Prime Minister MacDonald, no doubt. Charlie, Charlie. You're being silly."

Lou led Charlotte to the bedroom.

"I'm loopy aren't I," she said.

"No, you're not loopy."

As she lay down she said, "Lou, we will have that launching party, won't we? I'll bake a cake and you can play them some of your mountain music and some of your own songs. You can sing the one you wrote for me—"Oh Charlotte, My Charlotte"."

"Yes all right, we'll invite them all, but it's a bit short notice. I doubt the Prime Minister will be able to make it."

"Oh Lou, I do love you so."

6

LIGHTEN HER LOAD

September 1929.

Later that morning, not wanting to appear rude, Lou went to Cardington House and found Johnston in his office. "Hi, Johnny, I'm real sorry about this morning. I had trouble studying last night and then I couldn't sleep," Lou said.

Well, technically it was true.

"Don't worry, Lou. We'll do it when you're ready."

Lou went and stood by the window. He could see a lot of activity beyond the Cardington airfield. There were countless trucks laden with metal parts being unloaded by dozens of people.

"What the heck's all that metal framing for?" Lou asked.

"It's the fair. They always come to the village in the autumn. It's good timing. There'll be thousands of people here for the launching—they'll make a few bob."

"What's the latest?" Lou asked.

"We should have the temporary permit to fly this week. The launch is set for Thursday, subject to weather. They're desperate to get her out before Howden."

"The race is on!"

"Silly buggers!" Johnston sneered.

"Charlotte wants to have a launching party."

"Good. I hope she'll play the piano. I like a good old singsong—presuming I'm invited!"

"Of course you are. I'm sure she'll play all your favorites."

Johnston sang a verse of "Yes Sir, That's My Baby" and jigged around the office.

"Johnny, you're a star. But don't give up your day job, ol' buddy."

Lou left and as he walked past Richmond's office, someone called his name. He poked his nose around the door. Rope and Colmore were standing at the drawing board with Richmond.

"Ah, come in, Lou," Richmond said.

Lou gave a polite nod to Richmond and Rope and smiled at Colmore.

"Morning, gentlemen," he said.

"Rope and I have completed our calculations. As you know, we've been doing lift and trim tests all week."

"How's it look?" Lou asked.

"Our suspicions have been confirmed, I'm afraid," Richmond said.

Colmore looked grim. "We have thirty-two tons of useful lift," he said.

"And we're supposed to have sixty, right?" Lou queried.

"Quite," Richmond said.

"We've made a list of dispensable items," Rope said, handing Lou a sheet of paper. He began reading.

"Servo assistance, bunks, lavatories, windows, ballast tanks …"

"We'll reduce the number of cabins from twenty-eight to sixteen, remove some washing facilities, and replace the glass on the promenade decks with Plexiglas," Richmond explained.

"And the ballast tanks?"

"We think we can dispense with two of them. We're also looking at loosening the gas bag harnesses—in fact they've started that," Richmond said, pausing for Lou's reaction.

"That's risky! The gas bags'll get torn up," Lou warned.

"It's damned risky!" Colmore muttered. "I don't like it."

"She's 106,000 cubic feet short of the five million we designed her for," Rope said.

"How much do you expect to gain by letting out the harnesses?" Lou asked.

"We'll pick up another 100,000 cubic feet," Richmond answered.

"Won't the bags chafe?" Lou asked.

The topic was depressing Colmore, who was chewing his fist.

"We'll need to make sure they don't. Simple truth is: without radical changes, a voyage to India will be *completely* out of the question," Richmond said. At least they were facing the truth. Lou was relieved about that.

"What do you propose to do now, sir?" he asked Colmore.

"We'll do some test flights after the launch and then reassess the situation."

"We'll find out if she's manageable without the steering servo. If so, we'll remove that, too," Rope said.

"If these changes are made, we'll increase lift by 6 tons—not enough. Damn! I wish we'd made her a bay longer. We had room in Shed No. 1." Richmond said.

"Maybe it's not too late," Lou said.

Billy arrived from Howden the following day, now assigned to Cardington. Lou met him at the station on the motorbike and took him home for a few hours to see Charlotte before delivering him to Freddie's. Charlotte made a fuss of the boy and gave him a Sunday roast dinner. He was now sixteen, tall and wiry like his dad. He was also smoking Woodbines like his dad.

"Seen anything of Mr. Norway and Mr. Wallis?" Lou asked over lunch.

"We see quite a bit of Mr. Norway, but Mr. Wallis hasn't been around. They say he's working at Weybridge now," Billy replied.

"How's your mum? Hope you've been taking good care of her," Lou asked.

"She's all right. We've been staying with me nan."

"Now you're a working man, I expect you've been helping her out a bit, eh?"

"Nah, she's all right. She's workin.' How's *your* mum? Are you takin' care of her?" Billy asked with a sly smile. Lou knew Billy was joking, but the jibe stung. He'd conscientiously written every week but, thanks to Billy, realized he'd neglected his mother. He knew his brother and sister were still at home and they'd make sure she was all right. It gave Lou license to do as he liked, but he wasn't proud of that. He pondered the idea of getting down to Virginia on the train, if fortunate enough to be chosen for the Montreal flight. He'd work on that idea.

"Yes, Lou, we should go to see your mum one day," Charlotte said.

"She'd love to meet you, honey. You know she always goes on about you in her letters."

"I'd love to see Virginia."

"God's country!" Lou said.

"Well, I'll be ...I've never heard you say that before," Charlotte said.

7

THE SIGNAL

October 12, 1929.

It was 3:30 a.m. and very dark. This would surely be the most wonderful day in Freddie Marsh's young life. Here he was on the corner of Crawshay Road on the outskirts of Bedford with a hundred other men ready to form part of the walking party. The group looked sadly pathetic, with Freddie and his father no exceptions—down and out like the rest, dressed in rags and old overcoats, cloth caps and worn out boots.

The British economy, like that of the United States, was in dire straits. The men were hunched on this damp street corner smoking cigarettes. They desperately needed work. Their breath came out in smoky clouds under the streetlamp, their nervous eyes darting back and forth to the sky. They were waiting for the confirmation signal. The previous night, the searchlight beam lit up the sky, indicating a walking party would be required at dawn. Three short bursts this morning would be confirmation. They'd been on standby the last two nights for an early morning launch, but stood down due to increasing winds both mornings. Things looked good for a launch today; the sky was clear, wind dead calm. Freddie was keyed up.

"Relax, son," his father said. "We'll see it in a minute, don't you worry."

At 3:40 a.m. a beam of light shot into the sky over Cardington, prompting a cheer from the men. This happened three times—three short blasts, three cheers. They'd earn a little money today—enough to put food on the table for a day or two.

"There it is, Dad!" Freddie exclaimed.

"Take your time, son. I'll go and get seats. Remember, easy does it." Freddie's father rushed off to one of the five waiting buses to save two seats. Freddie limped after his father at his own pace.

Lou got to Cardington at 3:00 a.m. in his newly-issued, dark blue uniform (his with U.S. Navy insignia). The other officers would be dressed similarly. On his way to the shed, Lou glanced at the fair, which had been going all night. Its colorful flashing lights, carousel steam organ, and carnival atmosphere, spilled over the new chain-link fence, across the aerodrome, creating a mood of gaiety and celebration. Newspapers said people were traveling from all over the country to witness the launching of the world's greatest airship.

Thousands had been at the fence when Lou left last night and thousands more had shown up overnight. They kept vigil, all eyes glued on the shed doors. Would they open to reveal the shed's secrets for the first time at daybreak? Spectators watched ground crewmen and airshipmen going to and fro all night. No one wanted to miss this historic event—the first sighting of the mighty *Cardington R101*.

Lou made his way to the control car. Irwin and Atherstone had already arrived. Above, in the chartroom, Johnston leaned on the rail. Lou gave him a wave. He responded with a grin. There were no journeys to be plotted, but everyone was on board and ready, just in case the ship should break away. It would be disastrous to be aloft involuntarily without charts, a navigator, sufficient crewmen, or fuel. Lou knew that feeling first hand from the *R38* accident, as did Sky Hunt and Capt. Booth after *R33* had been ripped from its mast and blown away to the Continent a few years previously.

Airships can be unpredictable creatures.

Lou recalled the thrill of flying in *R38* those first months—feelings of elation during the flight over Yorkshire; the wonder of looking down at the world in miniature; living, eating and sleeping in the clouds. It'd been a whole new way of life with its own terminology. Even small things—the smell of a new airship and the antics of the ship's cat, Fluffy, intrepid rat and mouse killer—had sparked excitement in him. And then came the crash. It'd been eight years. Would those good feelings ever return? He was skeptical.

"Good morning, sir," Lou said, looking at Irwin.

"Morning, Commander," Irwin said with a nod.

Lou smiled at Atherstone. "Today's the day!" Atherstone said.

"I'm early, sir. All right if I go ashore for a while? I'd like to see what's happening on the field," Lou said.

"Sure you can. It's organized chaos out there," Irwin replied.

He got outside in time to see Scott give the order to shine the searchlight into the air to signal the walking party groups around the region. A cheer went up at the fence. Many had been on the field since Thursday night and were now confident they'd catch a glimpse of the ship today. Lou studied the faces; in addition to genuine excitement, he perceived hope.

The transport of five hundred men by bus and positioning them on the field would take a good hour or two. Lou hung around near the front of the shed where Scott stood with a bullhorn in one hand. He was giving orders to two gangs engaged in opening the shed doors, which stood over a hundred and fifty feet high. Six men pulled ropes turning two capstans, easing the doors open, inch by inch. As the gleaming ship's bow was revealed, another louder cheer went up. A steel curtain was opening on an exciting drama—a contest of leviathans! Scott appeared pleased with the crowd's reaction, as though he were some great conductor.

Lou scanned the field. White lines had been painted on the grass as guidelines for the walking party to follow from the shed to the tower. Down the field, a man on horseback was driving a flock of sheep into a nearby pasture. Lou smiled.

The captain was right. It's chaos all right!

Around the fence, car headlights illuminated people boiling up water for tea on primus stoves and cooking eggs and bacon—it was like camping out. For others, it was too early; they slept under blankets in the backs of cars, snoring with their mouths wide open. Not everyone cooked for themselves. Vendors had set up along the fence, roasting chestnuts and potatoes. Others sold cheese sandwiches, bread and dripping, and cups of tea or cocoa. Hawkers yelled enticements to the crowd to buy souvenirs commemorating this day; postcards, photographs, flags and trinkets were all on sale at inflated prices. In the distance, the brightly lit Ferris wheel slowly turned, while sounds of the carousel organ drifted their way.

"Morning, sir."

Lou spun around to see Billy behind him.

"Ah, Billy, you're bright and early. What are you up to this morning?"

"The foreman told me to muck in with the walking party when it gets 'ere and then 'elp out the ground crew."

"Good. Have you had something to eat?"

"Yes, I 'ad a bacon an' egg sandwich before I left Freddie's."

"They taking good care of you?"

"Yes, they're nice to me, especially his mum."

"Good. You're gonna need them muscles this morning, kid."

"Yes, sir."

"I'm taking some of the crew to the fair later. Why don't you and Freddie come."

Billy broke into a grin. "Oh yes, Lou. We'll come, all right."

Thirty minutes later, at 5:00 a.m. a convoy of buses drew up to the gates and hundreds of men poured onto the field and ambled toward the shed, among them Freddie and his father. Another cheer went up from the crowd and Lou spotted a black limousine approaching, followed by three other official-looking cars. The windows of the limousine were open and the interior lights on, allowing the crowd to view the occupants. The motorcade moved toward the tower, and when it stopped Lou saw Thomson, Brancker and Knoxwood climb out. He realized they must have stayed overnight at Cardington House. Lou had to give the old man his due. He took a personal interest in the program he'd put in motion. He was also a master at managing public relations—and this was an opportunity not to be missed.

By now, ropes had been stretched out by the ground crews from the pulling rings on the airship and laid across the grass along the lines toward the mooring tower. Scott addressed the walking party.

"Good morning, gentlemen," he boomed. "I want you to form four lines across the field. Space yourselves six feet apart. The rest of you take up the lines at the stern and along the port and starboard sides as she comes out."

The men took up their positions, most of them old hands. Lou walked along the line to where Thomson stood. Brancker poured coffee from a thermos flask into a cup held by Thomson. Next to them was a BBC van and a radio announcer. Lou listened.

"This is Donald Carpenter, speaking to you from the airfield at Cardington, home of the giant airship *Cardington R101*. This is an historic occasion indeed, for today she'll be pulled from her shed where she's been under construction. Beside me, I have the architect of the British Imperial Airship Program, the honorable Lord Thomson of Cardington. Sir, this must be a very proud day for you?"

"Yes, indeed it is. The fine people of Bedfordshire have toiled with great dedication for five long years—since I announced the beginning of the airship program in 1924—and we are about to see the results of all their efforts ..."

As a brass band struck up "Soldiers of the King", Lou decided to return to the ship and marched briskly to the shed. He'd heard all this stuff before. It was still flat calm and cool—about 50 degrees—just right. He climbed the ladder into the hull and made his way to the control car. Nothing had changed there. The skipper was still standing with his hands tucked in his jacket pockets. Atherstone held a mug of coffee. Cameron was on this watch as height coxswain. Another man was on the rudder wheel. Providing there were no mishaps, neither coxswain would be required to do anything. The men in the control car peered forward as dawn began casting its eerie glow over the field. The four columns of ant-like men waited for orders. Lou spotted Freddie behind his father, forward of the control car.

Scott put the bullhorn to his mouth. His orders echoed across the field and into the shed. "Take up the ropes." Men in the walking party reached down and grabbed their ropes. "Take the strain." The four lines became taut. "Forward march on the count of three …slowly … one …two …three!"

The columns moved as one, expertly in step. The airship, floating in well-balanced equilibrium, moved gently forward. At the first movement, there were cheers and applause and then the sound of car and truck horns from around the field. The din got louder with every step as the airship, almost the size of *Titanic,* was drawn from her shell, like a great sea creature. Once clear of the shed, the noise rose to a crescendo, drowning out the band, except for the thump, thump, thump! Ropes were attached to all sides and stern, and the crew held them tightly, keeping them taut to prevent the ship moving in the wrong direction, should there be an unexpected puff. These men were also there as ballast to prevent the ship lifting into the sky, should a sudden change in temperature cause an increase in lift. (This, as Lord Scunthorpe had eloquently pointed out in the House of Lords, hadn't always worked out for the best!)

Within minutes, the ship had been walked to the center of the field and tethered to mooring rings set in the ground. From there, she was allowed to rise to eight hundred feet by dropping water ballast. The shining, silver ship floated in the sky for all to see for two hours, after which time, she was winched down and moved to the tower, where she was attached to the mooring cone at the top of the mast. Irwin had posted a watch list for a skeleton crew of ten men to remain on board at all times. He included himself on the ship's first watch. Lou, Johnston and Atherstone disembarked with the crewmen.

8

THE GYPSY FORTUNE TELLER

October 12, 1929.

Later that morning, Lou met some of his crewmen at the fair. After the success of the launching, everyone was in high spirits. First, they rode horses on the carousel and then they split up. Lou took Billy and Freddie on the Ferris wheel—it was all they could talk about. Binks, Church and Cameron made their way around the attractions. Disley and Potter grabbed a hot dog.

From high atop the wheel, Lou and the two boys admired the scene. They got a good view of *Cardington R101* at the tower and the aerodrome surrounded by sightseers. Lou noticed Binks and company had found the coconut shy and had made it their mission to dislodge the big hairy nuts. When the ride was over, they joined the others. Binks and Church were very upset.

"Better luck next time boys," the fairground attendant said to Binks with a smirk.

"Yeah, right! Don't give me all this 'better luck next time' bollocks."

"They've got them things glued in," Church yelled. He had one foot on the top rail about to jump over and prove his point.

Lou grabbed him by the arm. "Steady on there, Mr. Church."

"We've hit the coconuts six times and they won't budge," Binks said.

"Calm down, guys. Come on, let's go this way," Lou said. Freddie spotted a clown's head lit up in a glass display case on a stand. He went over to it and the others followed.

"Look at this," Freddie said. "He looks real. Er, maybe he *is* real!"

The clown's eyes were closed, but then he opened them briefly and blinked a couple of times. He had long white hair, a bald head and a bulbous red nose planted on his vivid white face. The lips were open, revealing a row of yellowed teeth. The caption read:

PUT A PENNY IN THE SLOT & MAKE HIM LAUGH

Freddie stood, fascinated. "Go on, Freddie, put a penny in then," Church said.

Freddie hesitated. Lou figured the kid only had his bus fare in his pocket and handed him a penny. Freddie inserted it in the slot. They heard it drop. The clown suddenly came alive and Freddie jumped backwards in shock. Its bloodshot eyes opened wide, glaring at him, and then the head tilted back and its mouth exploded into crazy laughter. Everybody, save Freddie, joined the clown's frivolity. The boy was visibly shaken. Lou put his arm around his shoulder and gave him a little shake. "Hey kid, don't worry about it. It's just a machine," he said.

After they'd watched the clown, Billy came rushing up. A sign outside a red tent had caught his eye. "Hey, sir, I'd like to go in," he said, pointing at the sign.

LET THE WORLD'S GREATEST CLAIRVOYANT

MADAM HARANDAH

THE ROMANIAN GYPSY

TELL YOUR FORTUNE

PSYCHIC READING

PALM READING

TAROT CARDS

3d EACH

Lou chuckled. "Come on then, guys."

They piled into the gloomy tent, which smelled of damp grass and cow manure. Lou was last one in and smiled on seeing the reactions of his crewmen. Binks peered suspiciously up at the ceiling and walls. "This tent's a lot bigger than it looks from outside," he said. "It's kinda strange!"

Freddie, still visibly shaken by the clown's head, stood at a table covered with a green, baize cloth, peering at a collection of items: a polished wood block cradling a crystal ball, a rabbit's foot, a deck of tarot cards, and a china bowl with burning incense. "Blimey, this place gives me the creeps," he mumbled.

"Don't be silly. It's only a witch's tent. Oh look, there's her transport," Billy said, pointing to a broomstick hanging over them next to a dim, red bulb dangling from an electric wire. Wisps of smoking incense in the eerie glow added to the weirdness. Lou laughed. Madame Harandah was obviously a joker—or was she? He didn't have to wait long to find out.

Church, Disley and Potter gathered under a photograph of a beautiful woman in a blue headscarf hung on the fabric tent wall. It'd been colored and touched up by hand.

"She's a smasher! Wonder if that's her," Church said.

"It's me if you wanna know," a voice growled from behind a black curtain. Billy was in the act of reaching out to touch the rabbit's foot. "Don't touch that, you little bugger!" the voice bellowed, scaring the life out of the boy.

A scruffy woman suddenly burst through the dark curtains. She seemed caught off guard by so many entering her tent. The crewmen were speechless, trying to take in this vision. Her eyes were glutinous, black pools set in a sea of bright blue eye shadow, glowering at them from under ridiculous, false eyelashes. Her eyebrows had been plucked out entirely and repainted in thin black lines, at once comical and frightening, and her puffy cheeks were rouged in a red blush almost as bright as her thick, ruby lips. Shiny, silver bangle earrings dangled from her lobes, as large as those on her wrists. She wore a purple headscarf from which graying, auburn hair sprouted and hung in ringlets to her waist. Her well-worn clothes—a ruffled, dark green blouse and an ankle-length black skirt—reeked of eau de cologne, cigarettes and mothballs.

"*Gordon Bennett!*" Binks exclaimed.

"What d'you lot want?" the woman demanded.

"We thought this was where you got your fortunes told," Church said.

"You've come to the right place," she bellowed.

"'Ere, you ain't the gypsy in that picture! Where's she?" Binks demanded.

"I certainly am! That was taken in Southend-on-Sea ten years ago. Any objections?"

"Forty years ago, more like," Disley grumbled.

"Next you'll want to see me bleedin' birf certificate!"

"We thought you were supposed to be Romanian," Potter said.

"I'm from the Elephant and Castle. Me dad was from Bucharest. So that makes me a Romanian gypsy—all right? If you don't like it, you can sod off—the lot of yer!"

"Keep yer bleedin' wool on, lady," Binks said.

"Okay, if you're stayin', that'll be sixpence each. Show me yer money."

"The sign outside says threepence," Freddie objected.

"All right, all right! Give me one and nine pence."

"We should get a discount. You ought to do us all for one and six, the lot," Church said.

"All right, all right! One and six. Put it right here," she demanded, her craggy hand with long, purple fingernails outstretched.

"Oooh, cross me palm with silver," Binks said.

Lou was thoroughly enjoying himself. He pulled out a shilling and a sixpence and put the coins in the old hag's palm. They all held back while she sat down.

"Okay, whose gonna shuffle the cards?" she said.

"Give 'em to Sammy," someone said.

Church went into action, his hands a blur, cutting and shuffling, cards flying from one hand to the other. Everyone whooped and whistled until the old dear was thoroughly irritated.

"All right! All right! That's enough!" she shouted, grabbing the cards back.

"Go on Dizzy, you go first," Church said. Disley slipped into the chair opposite Madam Harandah, who spread her cards into a fan on the table.

"I see you're going on a journey," she said.

"Ooooooh, you don't say," Binks said, eyeing Lou's uniform.

"Shut up, Joe. Let her tell me."

She turned over another card. "I see you high in the sky."

"This woman's *bloody amazin'*!" Church said.

She turned over another.

"Ah, you're the cool one. Electricity is your friend. You will deliver a message when the great game is over. Next!"

Disley screwed up his face in annoyance.

"What the hell does that mean, 'Deliver a message when the great game is over'? What *great game*? Is that all I get for thra'pence? What a bloody swindle!"

"Come on, let me have a go," Freddie said. Disley reluctantly got up out of the chair, shaking his head.

"Now you! You need to be more careful, Sunny Jim," the gypsy said, poking Freddie in the heart with a long, skinny finger. "You know what I'm talkin' about, doncha?"

Freddie became sheepish. "S'pose I do."

"You've had big ideas coming in your silly little 'ead lately, haven't you, son?" He glanced down at the table, unable to look into her all-seeing eyes. "You need to be careful. Electricity is not *your* friend. So stay away from it! Now get up and let him have his turn," she said pointing to Church. Church slid into the seat. Madame Harandah turned over more cards.

"Ah, here's a boy lucky in love," she purred. She smiled for the first time, revealing two rows of sparkling white dentures. The boys jeered, making Church blush.

"It's true love I see, all right. But I feel such an ache in my heart. Like him over there," she said, pointing at Freddie. "So you better settle down, my lad, and be good to your lady. Stay home! If you don't, she'll marry another. And she *will* do that I promise you—do you hear me?"

Church had heard enough. He got up from the table.

"No flying around for you, Sammy, me old cock-sparra!" Binks crowed.

She looked up at Binks. "The one who's always late—thirty days late being born. You must've given your mother a right fit!"

"Me mum said I was late."

"Better late than never! Ah, and you're an artist. And I see you have the gift, like me. But you've always got far too much to say for yerself, 'aven't yer," she said with a sneer. "Hmm, I see you walking through fire, rain and fog."

"Walking through *fire, rain and fog*? Sounds bloody daft, if you ask me," Binks said.

"Well, I ain't askin' you, am I? But you remember this—'ee who hesitates, is *not* always lost. Next!"

"What's she talkin' about?" Binks moaned.

Billy was standing next to her. She took his hand.

"Now, here's a young man whose father follows him around everywhere. Do you know that, son?" Billy pulled his hand away, rattled.

"He does *not!* Me Dad's dead, so how could he?"

"He might be dead to you, sunshine, but he ain't no more dead than I am! He wishes you well and says 'Go and break a leg, my darlin' boy'," the gypsy said.

Billy became infuriated. "That's rotten. You're makin' all this up."

Lou had listened intently. He'd talk to Billy later. The gypsy peered up at Cameron.

"Come on, Gunga Din, sit down." She spread the cards again. Cameron gingerly did as he was told. "It's very sad …she's a silly little cow, and she'll pay the price—and so will 'ee. My 'ead explodes at the thought of it!" she said, melodramatically throwing her hands from her head into the air as if it'd exploded all over the tent. No one spoke. Cameron jumped up and went outside in a fury. Everyone turned to Lou.

"Come on, sir, it's your turn," Potter said.

"What about you?" Lou said.

"No. I don't wanna know," Potter said. Lou understood perfectly.

"*No, you don't!*" the gypsy snapped, glaring at Potter, her dreadful eyes blazing like fire.

Lou eyed the woman carefully as he sat down and rested his hands on the table. Madam Harandah briefly held both his hands in hers and closed her eyes. He felt his hands tingle. She then took the cards, shuffled them and laid them out in a fan again.

"Ah, I see you have an evil twin. You'd better watch out for that one. You're a lucky man though—like a cat. Six times you've been lucky I see. Question is: Will your luck 'old out? And are you lucky in love? We'll have to see about that, won't we? I see here in the cards you believe there's something you must do. Do you know what it is? You *think* you know—don'tcha? But you've got a lot of questions hanging over you." Lou smiled, giving away nothing. "I'm gonna tell you just this, mister—you're in grave danger of losing everything you 'old dear."

"Well, tell him what you *mean* then. You talk in *bloody riddles*, woman!" Binks growled.

"Come on boys, let's get the hell out of here," Lou said, getting up. They moved out to join Cameron who was still agitated, smoking a cigarette. Lou sensed the gypsy's knowing, black eyes on him and turned to look back at her.

"We'll meet again soon," she said.

"If you say so, lady."

"That woman of yours has some real issues you know—*deep issues!*"

Lou hesitated. What was the old crone talking about now?

"And *try* to keep that bunch out of trouble," she added with a crafty smile.

Outside, Lou and the boys walked straight into Jessup and his pals. On seeing Cameron, Jessup sniggered. Cameron rushed at him, grabbing his throat and leaning him over a chestnut fence, which promptly collapsed. They fell in a heap. Jessup's face turned red and he was having trouble breathing. His five friends grabbed Cameron by anything they could, and pulled. Lou and his crew did the same till everyone was pulling on somebody and throwing punches.

Lou stepped back. "Okay, all of you. That's enough!" He grabbed two of Jessup's gang and pushed them away. "Walk that way, all of you. You and I will be talking, Mr. Jessup."

Jessup and his cronies slunk away.

"Okay, lads. Charlotte's launching party's tonight. Make sure you're all there," Lou said.

"Yes, sir, we'll be there," Potter said. "We're going back in the fair, for a bit."

"Starts at five. Come on Billy and you, Freddie. Charlotte needs our help." They ambled off toward the sheds and the airship floating at the tower.

"Just look. What a sight," Billy said.

Lou turned to him. "So, what did you think of the fortune teller?"

"Didn't like her. She was daft."

"Why?"

"Talkin' about me dad like that."

"Perhaps she *was* able to see him. Maybe he *is* still around you."

"Nah! It's a lot of nonsense. Saying he wishes I'd break me leg. That's silly."

"Billy, it's just an expression." Billy looked puzzled. "When you tell someone to break a leg, it means you wish them good luck," Lou said.

"How could it mean that? If I broke a leg it wouldn't be good luck, would it?"

"I don't know, but it does. Billy, your dad thought the world of you."

"Yeah, I s'pose you're right. I miss 'im."

"He was a brave man. He suffered real bad in the war. I never heard him complain once—*ever*. Remember—he did it all for *you*, kid"

It all came down like a flood on Billy. "Yeah, I know. I wish he was still 'ere." He began to sob. They heard running feet behind them. It was Binks and Church, laughing like madmen. Church had something under his arm.

"Here, look. I told you they was glued in sir. I told yer!"

"He jumped over and knocked it loose with a chunk of wood," Binks said. Church held a coconut high above his head in two hands. They all laughed. Lou turned to Billy and Freddie.

"Come on let's go. Charlotte's waiting for us."

9

A WORD WITH MR. JESSUP

October 12, 1929.

At the crew's locker room, Billy and Freddie showered and got changed for the party. Lou went to the officers' locker room where he changed out of uniform and put on work clothes. He then went to the crewmen's locker rooms to pick up the two boys. Jessup and his gang had finished changing and Jessup was looking into a mirror over the sink, combing his lank, greasy hair. On seeing Lou, fear clouded his face, though his eyes harbored bitter hatred. He looked more brutish after having his jaw wired up and reconstructed. Lou stood behind him, blocking his escape. He glanced into the mirror and for a split second thought Jessup's reflection was his own. It brought out irrational anger in him.

"Okay, you lot—out! Jessup and I need to have words," Lou said. Jessup made a move to leave. "Stay right there, Jessup," Lou snarled.

The other five left without a fuss.

"Don't you touch me," Jessup whined, not turning around.

"I told you, you were on probation. I see you're up to your old tricks again. I don't think you took me seriously." Lou grabbed Jessup by the back of the neck and slammed his head into the mirror. His face was flattened, his breath steaming up the glass.

"I did. I did."

"You've been messing around with people's wives. You think you can go around doing this stuff and get away with it?"

"I don't know wocha talkin' about." Jessup had difficulty speaking. Spit was running out the corner of his mouth and down the mirror.

"I see you're drooling again, Jessup—not becoming a gentleman. I'm talking about *Cameron's wife*! It's common knowledge. You go out of your way to humiliate the man."

"What are you, the bleedin' judge and jury? You told me to stay away from Charlotte and I did. You didn't say anything about other people's wives, didya?"

"You really are a piece of crap. I'm gonna have to kick it out of you. Since they made you a rigger, you've gotten back to your cocky self again."

Lou pulled Jessup away from the mirror and pushed him across the room. Jessup saw his chance to escape and rushed full speed into the metal lockers, causing a deafening crash.

"You stay away from me. I'll report yer. I'll have you up for assault, I will. You have no right ...I can see whoever I want. It's a free country."

"I'll be watching you, Jessup. Now get lost!"

Jessup bolted from the room as Billy and Freddie came out of the showers. Billy looked questioningly at Lou, but Lou said nothing.

"We heard him talkin', Lou," Billy said.

"What'd he say?"

"He said you thought you'd got rid of 'im, but you aven't."

Freddie cut in. "He stood right there combing 'is hair and 'ee said, 'I'm gonna kill that bastard one day. I swear on my father's cold, dead eyes. You just see if I don't.' And then 'ee said, 'My daddy'll be right proud o' me then'."

10

CHARLOTTE'S PARTY

October 12, 1929.

Lou, Billy and Freddie arrived at the house as a man from the local off-license was delivering dozens of wooden crates of beer. Charlotte came to the door in her apron and stood aside while they carried the crates inside.

"Ah good, now you lads can move the furniture for me. We need to make lots of room," Charlotte said, after kissing Lou.

They followed her down to the kitchen, where the women had been working furiously. Olivia Irwin, the captain's wife, had made a pile of small, triangular sandwiches of fish-paste and watercress and Mrs. Jones, the neighbor, had made a stack with egg and cucumber. On the table was a large, square cake Charlotte had baked and just finished icing with a picture of an airship on top.

"Hey, look at this!" Freddie said. "What's the fish on top for?"

Billy rushed over. "It's not a fish—it's the *R101*, you daft sod."

"Looks like you ladies've been busy. Mind if we have a sandwich? We're famished," Lou asked.

"Lou!" Charlotte exclaimed.

"Launching airships makes a man hungry," Olivia said. "Come on, help yourselves."

Charlotte pointed at Freddie. "Watch out for this one, he'll eat 'em faster than you can make 'em," she said. She put her arms around him and squeezed him tight, making him blush. "I'm only kidding, Freddie. I love you, really," she said. "He's such a lovely boy, isn't he!"

"I'll pour you boys some tea," Mrs. Jones said.

"How did it go, love?" Charlotte asked Lou.

"Everything went without a hitch. She's up there, floating at the mast. The crowd's going nuts. I took the lads over to the fairground for a while afterwards," Lou replied.

"How smashing!" Charlotte said.

"You're good to the crewmen," Olivia said.

"Yeah and we 'ad our fortunes told by a gypsy," Freddie said.

"You did? Oh, *I* want to go! What did she say?" Charlotte asked, excitedly.

"She talked a lot of nonsense. Said my dad keeps following me around and 'e wishes I'd break me leg," Billy sneered.

"How weird," Charlotte said.

"She could be right. Perhaps he does follow you about. Them gypsies have special powers. Very psychic, they are you know," Mrs. Jones said.

Charlotte was filled with curiosity. "Tell me what she said, Lou."

"Hmm. I've forgotten already. I wasn't paying attention. It was just a lark, that's all."

"Come on, Lou, tell us," Olivia said.

"Oh, I remember, she said I'm lucky—" Lou said.

"She said six times he's bin lucky—" Billy interjected.

"Yes, that's about it," Lou said, glaring at Billy, who took the hint.

"Promise you'll take me after church tomorrow. I love fortune tellers," Charlotte pleaded.

Lou knew exactly what was going on in Charlotte's head. "You mustn't let those people mess with your mind, Charlie."

"I know how you feel, Charlotte. I can never resist myself," Olivia said. "My husband won't go anywhere near them. Well, I'd better go home and get changed. I'll be back with my Blackbird later. We won't be able to stay long. We've got three launching parties to go to. I hope you'll play for us, Charlotte."

"Of course I will. Thank you for all your help."

"Bird loves Al Jolson. Will you play "Blue Skies" for him?"

"If he'll sing it, I'll play it," Charlotte promised.

Lou was setting up the bar in the living room when Charlotte came down from the bedroom. He handed her a glass of sherry and she took a good sip. She wore a black chiffon dress in the latest fashion, skinny at the waist and delicate.

Freddie was swept off his feet. "Oh, Charlotte, you do look smashin'!"

"He's got a right crush on you, Charlotte. Lou's gonna have to watch out," Billy said.

Charlotte drank the rest of her sherry and put the glass down. It was making her woozy. "Come here and give me a big hug you beautiful boy," she said. Lou laughed as Charlotte gathered Freddie into her arms and squeezed him to her bosom, making him blush and sweat all over again.

"It's your birthday on Wednesday and I've got a present for you, Robert …er, Freddie," Charlotte said, becoming flustered and then, "Come with me."

Lou pretended not to notice Charlotte's gaff. Billy whooped as Charlotte led Freddie up to the bedroom. She went to the wardrobe and took out a brown paper bag and handed it to him. "Here, something you need, now you're a fine, working man," she said. "Try them on."

Freddie opened the bag to find a pair of black boots. After she'd bought them, Charlotte had taken them to a shoe-mender and had them soled and heeled, asking the cobbler to make the sole thicker on the right shoe. She said nothing to Freddie about that. "They're second-hand. I found them in the market, Freddie," Charlotte said.

"They're smashin'," he said, after slipping them on. They fit perfectly and he was thrilled. When he walked around, his limp was less noticeable. Freddie was pleased, but also puzzled.

"Why did you call me Robert just now?" he asked.

Charlotte shook her head, slightly embarrassed and a little light-headed. "I'm going to let you into a little secret. I met a soldier once. His name was Robert. And you remind me of him, that's all."

"Did you love him?"

"Oh no. I only knew him for one day—but he was very, very nice."

"What happened to him?"

Sadness swept over her. "I don't know. I expect he was killed. Our little secret, right?"

"Yes, yes. I won't say anything to anyone, Charlotte, honest."

When they got downstairs, he kissed Charlotte's cheek and thanked Lou with a handshake.

By the time the crewmen and regular crowd trickled in, Billy and Freddie had put a sign up in the living room, which they'd colored with kids' crayons. Everyone admired it, and though child-like, the sentiment was right.

GOOD LUCK CARDINGTON AIRSHIP R101
LAUNCHED OCTOBER 12th 1929

Some brought bottles of beer and wine and boxes of chocolates. Many drank tea, ably served by Mrs. Jones and her husband. Johnston, the navigator, and his wife came in around 6 o'clock and had tea and sandwiches. The crewmen were on their best behavior and took turns playing darts in the garden where they started a competition. Church turned out to be the expert, winning every game and taking everyone's money. They stood around, relaxed, chatting and sipping drinks. At 7 o'clock Capt. Irwin and Olivia arrived. Most were informally dressed, but well turned out. After the sandwiches were gone, they made a big fuss while Charlotte cut the cake and they enjoyed a slice for good luck.

"Come on, Charlotte. Play for us," someone said.

Charlotte went to the piano and burst into "Toot, Toot, Tootsie, Goodbye." Everybody joined in, Johnston singing the loudest. At the end of the song, Olivia made her own request. "Can we have "Blue Skies" please," she called.

Charlotte obliged, while Lou strummed the guitar and Potter played his accordion. It seemed the perfect tune for a perfect day. Everyone sang along. While they were singing, Doug Cameron and Rosie showed up. Their presence made others uncomfortable. The couple were at odds, not looking at each other or speaking.

About half an hour later, Scott, carrying a bottle of gin, arrived with Fred McWade. Lou was surprised, but thought it a nice gesture. Scott, already 'well on the way', happily joined in the singing. Shortly after, Capt. Irwin and Olivia expressed their thanks and bid everyone goodnight. By nine, the alcohol had run out and the gathering dispersed. Scott said he'd another party to go to and he and the Atherstones went off together, leaving Disley finishing a chess game with Ginger Bell. McWade stayed on a little longer and Charlotte made a big fuss of him.

Later, while Charlotte was lighting a candle before slipping into bed she remembered something. "What happened to your chief steward friend? I was looking forward to meeting him."

"Oh, sorry, I forgot to ask him, honey," Lou said, as they snuggled down.

"You forgot Lord Thomson and the Prime Minister, too, I suppose?"

"Yes, my love I plain forgot," he answered.

"Okay, but just don't forget about the gypsy tomorrow," she said.

"Charlotte, let's think about us," he said, gently lifting her so she was straddling him.

"Yes, yes, all right, my darling. I can do that," she whispered, settling over him.

He loved to see her like this in the candlelight, smiling down at him, hands behind her head, hair tumbling around her shoulders to the waist. She began to writhe.

"I can certainly do that …" she said, closing her eyes.

"It was a wonderful party, Charlotte. Thank you."

"You're very welcome, my darling."

"I'm the luckiest man in the world," he said

"Yes, you are, and just don't you forget it, Lieutenant Commander Remington."

At times like this, Lou felt really and truly blessed to have Charlotte as his wife.

11

ST. MARY'S - BLESSING & HARVEST THANKSGIVING

October 13, 1929.

T he next morning, everyone, with the exception of Rosie Cameron, attended St. Mary's Church. Her absence didn't go unnoticed. Lou wondered if she was with Jessup. All officers and crewmen of *Cardington R101* were in their smart, new Airship Service uniforms. This was a special service to bless the airship and to give thanks as part of the Harvest Festival. The church, with the aroma of a garden market, had been decked out in a colorful display of locally-grown fruits and vegetables: sweet onions, cabbages, huge, polished marrows, potatoes and carrots scrubbed clean; all collected and donated by school children, later to be given to the poor.

On their way to the old, brick church, worshipers lifted their eyes in wonder to the airship tethered to the tower, glistening in the sun. They trooped into the church to thank God and ask for His protection. The organ played softly while everyone took their seats in wooden pews, which smelled of lemon polish. They sat with their heads bowed amid hushed whispers. A baby cried in the rear of the church, close to Freddie and Billy. Charlotte waved to them and Lou gave them a nod as they passed before sitting down toward the front.

Suddenly, the organist became energized and the congregation stood for the singing of "All Things Bright and Beautiful"—the cue for the vicar, choir and assistants to file down the aisle toward the altar, holding their hymn books high in front of them as they sang. Lou and Charlotte sat in a row near the Atherstones, Irwins and Johnstons. Scott and his wife sat in front of them with Wing Cmdr. Colmore, recently promoted from Assistant Director to Director of Airship Development. Colmore's wife sat proudly beside him. They looked at each other fondly from time to time, like sweethearts. The Richmonds sat nearby with Rope and his wife. Lou was struck when Richmond turned to acknowledge them, by how much he'd aged this past four years. Scott appeared jaded, but no doubt he'd recover by noon.

Staff from the Royal Airship Works design offices and machine shops sat in nearby pews, intermingled with strangers—here for the launch. By the time the vicar started the service, the church was full. During a long pause after prayers, the sound of children mumbling to their parents and people clearing their throats echoed around the building. Irwin got up and moved to the front of the church. He climbed the pulpit steps to the lectern, where an enormous Bible lay open with the lesson marked. He read beautifully, in his rich Irish dialect, the opening passages of 'Jonah and the Whale'. The captain's soft voice was mesmerizing, gently floating around the church as he related the story of Jonah disobeying God's commands and fleeing aboard ship. In an ensuing violent storm, the crew, blaming him for bringing bad luck upon them, cast him into the sea.

" *...Then Jonah prayed unto the Lord his God out of the fish's belly and said, 'I cried by reason of mine affliction unto the Lord and He heard me; out of hell cried I and Thou heard my voice. For Thou had cast me in the midst of the seas; and the floods encompassed me about and Thy waves passed over me ...*"

Lou glanced at Charlotte. He wondered if he had a connection to this story. By Charlotte's returning stare, she was wondering the same thing. He squeezed her hand.

"...but I will sacrifice unto thee with the voice of thanksgiving; I will pay that that I have vowed. And the Lord spake unto the fish, and it vomited out Jonah upon the land."

To Lou, the text chosen by the vicar was ironic—perhaps too ironic!

Maybe that whale out there's gonna swallow us all and spit us out!

Irwin reverently closed the Bible and returned to his seat. The vicar moved to the center of the church to face his flock. "Tomorrow is an important day in our lives—the maiden flight of our great airship. I want you to remember the words read to you by Captain Irwin.

Remember always that in times of trouble, you must pray to the Lord and ask for his help and deliverance. At this wonderful time of Harvest Thanksgiving we now see the fruits of all your labor—*Cardington R101* floats out there at the mast for the world to see. Similarly, we experience the fruits of the labor of our farmers and those who tend our fields and gardens. The harvest has indeed been bountiful. Let us give thanks to God and ask Him to bless this airship and all those who fly in her." The vicar signaled for the congregation to kneel and began his prayer. "Oh, Heavenly Father we thank You and humbly beseech You …"

The faint sounds of the carousel and the girls' screams from the fairground drifted from across the road behind the graveyard. Lou looked at Charlotte, who seemed far away in a dark place—a place she inhabited too often these days. He wondered where her mind was at times like these.

She noticed him studying her and returned from her brooding. Lou winked and she forced a smile. He took her hand, signaling, no, he hadn't forgotten—they'd walk over to the fair and see the damned gypsy. The organ struck up again for the last hymn—a rousing one to lift all spirits: "Jerusalem."

> *And did those feet in ancient time*
> *Walk upon England's mountains green:*
> *And was the holy Lamb of God*
> *On England's pleasant pastures seen!*

Lou made a point of looking at all the faces, particularly the ones he knew. Everyone sang, except poor Cameron. Even Binks seemed to be taking things seriously for once. Freddie and Billy, were giving it their very best.

> *Bring me my Bow of burning gold;*
> *Bring me my Arrows of desire:*
> *Bring me my Spear: O clouds unfold!*
> *Bring me my Chariot of fire!*

The organist at this point, pulled out all the stops, giving it everything. The church came alive, the enthusiasm tangible—the usual Sunday morning drowsiness swept away with everyone singing at the top of their lungs. The vicar and his brethren marched out grandly, uplifted.

I will not cease from Mental Fight,
Nor shall my sword sleep in my hand:
Till we have built Jerusalem
In England's green and pleasant Land.

Lou and Charlotte followed Irwin and Olivia down the aisle.

"That was some hymn, Charlotte. I've never heard it before," Lou said as they filed past the vicar, smiling and shaking his hand at the door.

"The hymn is fairly new, I think. There's something magical about it," Charlotte said.

"Is there a story behind it?" Lou asked.

Overhearing, Olivia turned to them. "'Jerusalem' is about the legend of Jesus' lost years. They say He came to England during that time and went to Glastonbury," she said.

"Wow! Interesting to think He may have walked this 'green and pleasant land.'"

Outside the church, Lou and Charlotte socialized for a short time, but Charlotte was anxious to get over to the fairground. As they strolled along Church Lane, Lou couldn't resist pulling her leg. "Out of the church and into the soothsayer's tent! It all seems a bit sinful, if you ask me, missus!"

"Oh Remy, it's just a bit of fun, love."

"I'm sure there's something in the Bible about fortune tellers," Lou said. They turned into the gap in the chestnut fence and walked toward the Ferris wheel.

"Do you want to go on some rides first?" Lou asked.

"No, I want to see the gypsy!"

"All right, this way." Moments later, they were outside the red tent where Madam Harandah stood at the entrance. Charlotte studied her, suddenly unnerved.

"Waiting for us?" Lou said, smirking.

"Yes, I was. Come in, my dear. My, what a lovely girl you are. You *are* a lucky man," she said looking from Charlotte to Lou. Inside, Lou took out a shilling and put it in the old woman's hand. He was about to sit down.

"You'd better go for a walk, young fella," the gypsy said.

Lou was surprised. He glanced at Charlotte.

"Oh Lou, do you mind? Do as she asks, please, my darling."

Lou left the tent. He regretted bringing Charlotte now.

Oh Damn! This was a mistake.

He hoped the gypsy didn't upset Charlotte; that was all he cared about. He walked over to the chestnut fence and bought the *Sunday Pictorial* from a paperboy and a coffee from a vendor. He sat down in the sunshine to read about the launching and drink his coffee—which tasted like crap. The article told how wonderfully advanced the Cardington airship was; how much like an ocean liner; the wave of the future; blah, blah, blah; a good write-up—propaganda, nonetheless.

Charlotte appeared forty minutes later. She seemed more cheerful.

"There you are," she said.

"How did it go?"

"I couldn't understand half of it."

"She talks in confusing riddles. That's her technique," Lou said.

"But she did say I'd have a child. In fact, she said 'You *will* have *children.*' But she said I needed to get my house in order first. There are things I must do."

Lou frowned. "Like what?"

Charlotte looked away, evasive.

"Well, she could be right… You might and you might not," Lou said.

"No. She said *I would,* one day." Her eyes brightened at the thought.

"Yes, I'm sure you will, Charlotte … I'm sure you will."

He swallowed the last of his coffee and stared across the field at the airship.

Let's hope they're mine.

12

OVER LONDON

October 14 & 16, 1929.

T he next day, with her blessing bestowed, *Cardington R101* rose into the air in perfect weather conditions, watched by an enthusiastic crowd and a friendly press. The ship, under the command of Capt. Irwin and his officers, Lt. Cmdr. Atherstone, Flying Officer Steff, Johnston the navigator and Lou as third officer, made a short flight around Bedford and then on toward the outskirts of London before returning home. When the airship passed over Bedford, Charlotte came out into the street with dozens of other nurses to catch a glimpse. To most of those who saw her, the airship appeared as a thing of awesome beauty.

Cardington R101 had proved she could fly. Thomson was invited to make a flight two days later. As with the launching, Thomson, Brancker and Knoxwood stayed overnight at Cardington House so they could be at the field early next morning. At 6:30 a.m. the crowd cheered Thomson as he climbed out of the car. This event, seen as the 'official' maiden flight, appeared as a bright spot on the otherwise chaotic, depressing world-wide economic front and spectators made the most of it. Thomson waved to the crowd and then marched along the line of ground crewmen to the tower, nodding and smiling to each man. He noticed Freddie standing next to Billy.

"My, my, you've been working hard on those boots, young man," he said, placing his hand on Freddie's shoulder. "Good work, son."

Thomson knew the boy must have spent a lot of time the night before polishing those old boots. They shone like black-gloss paint. He took pains to notice things like that. When he reached Irwin, waiting at the foot of the tower, he took his hand between his and greeted him warmly.

"My dear Captain Irwin. This is a momentous occasion."

"Welcome aboard, sir." While the captain shook hands with Brancker and Knoxwood, Thomson stepped back to look up and study the gleaming airship. "Give me a moment," he said.

"Please, take your time, sir," Irwin said.

Freddie and Billy followed Thomson at a discreet distance and stood watching and listening. After a few minutes, Thomson turned to them and smiled again.

Two young lads witnessing history in the making—future airshipmen of the fleet!

Thomson and his party squeezed into the elevator and the operator closed the accordion gates. There was a stiff breeze at the top of the tower and, although sunny, it was chilly. Thomson was glad he'd worn his overcoat. He stood for a moment taking in the scene across the field toward the sheds and beyond to Cardington House. He held onto his hat as Irwin allowed them to go aboard. Church stood rigidly to attention inside the entrance ramp and as Thomson passed he greeted him with a polite half smile.

"Good morning, young man," he said.

Thomson and his group were led by Irwin along the catwalks from the rounded bow. Crewmen and engineers had been posted at intervals. He passed Binks, who stood ramrod straight.

These chaps are not military and here they were doing their best to appear so.

This showed respect and he liked that. He wore his benevolent headmaster expression as he moved along. Disley stood at the door of the electrical room. He nodded to Thomson.

Not so servile, this one. Probably intelligent!

Then there was Sky Hunt, the chief coxswain. Thomson had taken the trouble to find out who was who. He'd heard about Hunt's no-nonsense reputation and his bravery concerning the *R33* breakaway, for which he'd earned the Air Force Medal. Thomson reached out and took Hunt's hand, surprising and pleasing the man. Thomson moved on, noting the areas leading to the passengers' section were somewhat spartan. This would need to be a topic for discussion.

Not as luxurious as a real ship, but we'll soon fix that.

Colmore, Scott, Richmond, Johnston, Rope and Lou, all in uniform, waited for Thomson in the lounge in a line with eight well-dressed civilians from the Royal Airship Works and the Air Ministry. As Thomson entered, they broke into applause and he went down the line shaking hands, saying a few well-rehearsed words while they praised him as the great architect of it all. Colmore and Scott took over the handling of Thomson from Irwin, who went to the control car with Lou to join Atherstone. Thomson was led out to the promenade deck where he could appreciate the extraordinary view and witness take off from the enormous windows.

In the control car, Irwin picked up the phone and gave orders to the tower crew foreman to be on standby for cast off.

"Is everybody ready in the control car?" he asked.

"All ready, sir!" Cameron, on elevators, and Potter, on rudders, answered together.

Irwin turned to Lou. "Let's pull up the gangplank and close the forward hatch."

Lou picked up the speaking tube to Church. "Bring in the gangplank and close the hatch."

"Right away, sir. Yes, sir!" Church answered in Lou's ear.

Lou glanced up at Johnston, leaning over the chartroom rail, who winked and smiled. Irwin turned to Lou again.

"Start engine Nos. 1 and 2 and idle."

Lou passed this order to the engine cars via the telegraphs. They rang faintly below in the cars. This was followed by puffs of smoke from the starter engine exhausts. As the diesel engines kicked over, the propellers began to turn after slight hesitation. In a few moments, plumes of black smoke and diesel fumes spewed from the engines and drifted down the field. Moments later, the engines settled down and ran smoothly.

"Engines 1 and 2 are idling, sir," Lou said.

"Start engines 3 and 4," the captain ordered.

Lou went through the same process until all four were running.

Irwin picked up the phone to the tower again and held it. "Be ready on ballast. Ready on rudders. Start engine No. 5."

"Ready on ballast. Ready on rudders, sir," Atherstone repeated.

"Starting engine No. 5," Lou said, relaying the order to Binks and Bell, who were anxiously standing by. Lou caught a flash of Binks five years ago standing at Cardington gate, cap in hand. He'd come a long way.

Mr. Humble Pie!

Lou smiled. A puff of smoke came from the exhaust and the propeller started moving. The critical moment had arrived. Irwin put the phone to his mouth.

"Standby to slip."

Lou was impressed with Irwin. He'd studied him closely on Monday's short maiden flight. "Ready on reversing engine No. 2?" Irwin asked.

"Ready on No. 2, sir!" Lou confirmed.

"Be ready to increase revs on No. 2 to four hundred."

Irwin spoke loudly into the phone. "*R101* ready to slip." He listened for a second, then spoke again forcefully. "Slip now! Thank you, Cardington Tower."

The bow dipped after disconnection from the tower. The ship did nothing for a few moments, being suspended in air.

"We're free and clear of the tower, sir," Atherstone announced.

"Okay increase revs on reversing engine No. 2 to four hundred."

Lou passed the order to the engineers in No. 2 and the revs went up. The ship pulled back, her nose down.

"Increase revs on No. 2 to six hundred. Dump two tons at Frame 4," Irwin ordered. Atherstone released water ballast. The bow came up. Not nearly enough.

"Shut down reversing engine No. 2 and increase revs on the rest to six hundred."

"Shut down reversing engine. Increase revs all engines to six hundred, sir," Lou repeated.

The power on the four forward running engines increased and the ship turned smoothly away on a starboard tack toward the perimeter fence. She cast a giant shadow over the crowd gathered a hundred feet below, nose still dangerously low, wallowing like a whale in the shallows.

"Drop emergency ballast. Now!"

Lou grabbed the speaking tube to Church at the bow.

"Drop emergency ballast. *Right now!*"

Water cascaded from under the ship's bow and even though the amount of water was small, the effect was dramatic. The bow came up, but still not enough. The crowd below got soaked. The ship lumbered on, hovering over the country road toward a school where children waved handkerchiefs and scarves as the great monster approached. Still she wallowed. More water ballast was dropped from the forward frames. This time the children got wet, but it did nothing to dampen their spirits—quite the opposite; this was a wonderful game. They ran off screaming and laughing in all directions. The bow came up, at last, until she was flying straight and level.

On the promenade deck, Thomson was in good spirits. He and his entourage waved back at the crowd at the fence initially, and then to the children in the schoolyard. He was elated, relishing Irwin's maneuvering, which he presumed to be flawless.

"Superb getaway! Well done, Captain Irwin," Thomson exclaimed.

"Hear, hear!" Brancker and Knoxwood seconded. Not everyone was so sure. Some mumbled under their breaths. "We're too close to the damned ground for my liking," one R.A.W. engineer grumbled.

"I'd of thought we'd be a lot higher by now," another complained.

Scott peered out the window, his expression sullen.

The airship slowly gained altitude and, after reaching eight hundred feet, turned toward Bedford to show herself a second time. So many in this city were counting on the success of this vessel. Thirty minutes later, they turned south toward London. The chief steward approached Thomson.

"Good morning, sir. Breakfast will be served in the dining room in ten minutes, if that suits you, my Lord." He addressed Thomson a little more tenderly than he would've preferred.

"Splendid," Thomson said with a weak smile. "All this excitement makes one very hungry."

After a delicious breakfast of ham and eggs and freshly ground coffee, everyone gathered on the promenade deck to get a good view of the London skyline from a cloudless sky. The ship, now at twelve hundred feet, approached from the north, passing over Lord's Cricket Ground, close to Regent's Park, and then followed Edgeware Road along the edge of Hyde Park, bursting with vivid, autumn colors. At Hyde Park Corner, the ship turned toward Buckingham Palace. Its rooftop flag was absent.

The effect the ship had on the streets below Thomson thought was magical. Traffic came to a halt. Open-mouthed Londoners stopped in their tracks. *Cardington R101* traveled over Birdcage Walk to

Westminster Palace, the heart of the British Government. The panorama was a beautiful sight: Westminster Hall, the House of Commons and Big Ben, now striking the bottom of the hour—8:30 a.m. Thomson gazed at the House of Commons. He thought of Lord Scunthorpe and his scathing remarks.

Now we shall find out who's right.

He didn't dare crow, even to himself. He wondered what Scunthorpe would think if he came out of the House of Lords at this moment and looked up.

Would he be inspired? No. Of course not!

Thomson glanced down at the spot on the quadrangle where he and Marthe had recently had tea with MacDonald by the river. Seeing that place was gut-wrenching. Everywhere he turned was a reminder of her. The ship made its way along Whitehall, over the Horse Guards Parade, on to St. James's Park Lake, and the Ritz Hotel. He'd requested they pass over these landmarks. For him it was enjoyable, masochistic torture. They traveled along Piccadilly to Piccadilly Circus. During this time, Thomson and Brancker stood together, separate from the others. They'd often talked about Marthe—not in depth as he did with MacDonald—but Brancker was aware of Thomson's devotion. Brancker had met Marthe a few times at the Ministry.

"I wish Marthe were able to witness this," Thomson confided.

"All in good time, CB. No doubt, she'll be impressed."

Brancker, in a well-cut, pinstripe suit today, appeared refined, not his usual rustic, country-gentleman self. He leaned on the promenade deck rail, monocle planted in his left eye, voice deep, accent rich and upper-class, toupée smartly combed and greased down.

"It's been a long time coming, but worth the wait, CB. You must feel very, very proud indeed," Brancker said.

"I do. I can't help myself. It's unjustified. I've had so little to do with it all really."

"You had *everything* to do with it."

The ship pressed on over the Strand, along Fleet Street, home of the British press. Thomson had an idea. Press photographers were out in droves this morning; he'd made sure of that. Tomorrow there'd be photographs of *Cardington R101* over every landmark. Sunday newspapers would be full of it, with whole pages and center spreads devoted to her maiden flight.

Marthe will read about it soon enough.

Thomson decided to address the Lord Scunthorpe situation head on. He beckoned everyone over. "Gather round. I have an announcement." He held his hand out toward the press buildings below as they formed a circle around him. "I hope after today we'll get full support from the Government and the press," he said.

"I should jolly-well think so, sir," Scott said.

"I want to announce that we're inviting one hundred Members of Parliament to make a flight in this airship," Thomson said. Everyone was surprised and most faces lit up.

"What a splendid, original idea," somebody said.

"A hundred MPs over how m-many flights, sir?" Richmond stammered.

"One, of course! That ought to shut the critics up," Thomson replied.

"Are you sure about this, CB?" Brancker asked, taking down his monocle and polishing it thoughtfully.

"Don't worry; nothing like a hundred will take us up on it. But our confidence will speak volumes!" Thomson noted Richmond doing his best not to appear negative, while Colmore, by his demeanor lacked confidence in the idea.

Damn, that man is weak!

"Trust me. This'll be a good move," Thomson assured them. The airship passed by St. Paul's, Tower Bridge and the Tower of London. The time was nine-thirty. Having seen the sights, and London having seen the sight of her, *Cardington R101* headed over northeast London toward the Essex countryside, then Cambridge and Sandringham. Thomson had looked forward to spending time on the airship, working on his papers.

"There are some matters of state that cannot wait," he said grandly, excusing himself. "Come Knoxwood, we must earn our keep."

They headed to the promenade deck on the starboard side where a privacy curtain had been hung across the opening to form a makeshift office with an imposing desk and a leather executive chair.

13

SANDRINGHAM

October 16, 1929.

While the ship cruised silently at twelve hundred feet, Thomson sat and read through the papers in his dispatch box and ministerial files, glancing up every so often to appreciate the countryside. The surroundings and the silence made him calm and confident—just how he'd always imagined it. Knoxwood sat at a table preparing documents for Thomson to sign. He got up and brought them to Thomson.

"Can't beat this, what?" Thomson said.

"Smoother than a liner, sir," Knoxwood replied.

"This makes the perfect office, such peace and quiet."

While Scott and Richmond chatted with the rest of the VIP's, Brancker and Colmore paid a visit to the control car, where they found Irwin and Lou with two coxswains. As Brancker entered, he threw up his arms in exultation.

"This is magnificent!" He ran his hands over the hardwood and his eyes over the instrumentation. "The workmanship and finish are extraordinary. We should call her HMAS *Victory II*, or HMAS *Queen Victoria*, or some such splendid thing!" After a few minutes, Brancker, an experienced pilot, couldn't resist. "May I?" he asked.

"Of course you can, sir," Irwin replied. He instructed both coxswains to leave the control car and for Lou to take over the elevators. Brancker took the rudder and turned the wheel gently around from port to starboard. He then turned the ship through twenty degrees, the massive bulk, moving like a great sea galleon under canvas.

"I say, she seems responsive. What do you say, Irwin?"

"She's responsive to the helm all right, but she's underpowered and grossly overweight." Colmore sighed in exasperation. Irwin was confirming everything Richmond and Rope feared—but were things even *worse* than they thought?

"You mean *seriously* overweight?" Brancker asked.

"Fully loaded, this ship wouldn't get off the ground, sir."

"Hell, you don't say!" Brancker exploded. "He's all set to go charging off to India before Christmas!"

"That'd be suicide. This ship's quite unserviceable at the moment, sir," Irwin replied.

Lots of questions went through Lou's mind.

Would the lightening help to any significant degree? Would they need to push for an extra bay? Even then, would that really be enough?

Irwin's pronouncement was devastating to Colmore. Brancker raised his hand, indicating Thomson's location on the promenade deck above them.

"We'll need to keep his Lordship in check somehow. We must develop a strategy for dealing with the problem before things get out of hand. Damn it all! He's talking about inviting a hundred politicians to go on a flight *next week.*"

"Oh dear," Colmore said, his sad eyes searching the countryside.

After circling Cambridge University for ten minutes, the airship sailed on toward the North Sea coast and by 11:00 a.m. they'd arrived at the King's country home at Sandringham, a magnificent red brick house, quoined in white stone, set in manicured gardens. While gardeners raked the lawns, pleasant smells of burning autumn leaves wafted heavenward, permeating the airship.

The ship was flown slowly in wide circles, showing herself to the King and Queen who had emerged from the French doors onto the stone terrace. The royal couple slowly walked down the steps to the gravel path and stopped. The Queen waved a red silk handkerchief, while the King stood motionless at her side, his right hand raised. Thomson was thrilled they'd been noticed by the royals.

"God save the King!" he exclaimed.

"God save the King, indeed, sir!" Brancker echoed, and then under his breath to Lou, now at his side, "God save us all!"

After a final wave, the King and Queen made their way unsteadily back up the steps and re-entered the building. The airship was turned toward the bay of the North Sea. Twenty minutes later, they crossed the water and traveled toward Boston and Nottingham.

A luncheon of tomato soup, Dover sole, gooseberry tart and custard was served in the dining room at noon, accompanied by a Beaujolais '22. Thomson was conservative in his drinking, especially during the day. After two or three glasses of wine, Scott requested brandy and after one or two of them he stood up. "Would anyone care to join me in smoking a fine cigar in the smoking room? We can find out if it's air-tight," he said with a broad grin.

The chief steward wasn't amused, but Thomson's face also broke into a grin. "What a smashing idea, Scottie. I find the idea of lighting up and smoking a cigar, surrounded by five million cubic feet of hydrogen, quite *irresistible!*"

The stewards looked from one to the other.

"Can we bring you coffee, gentlemen?" the chief steward asked.

Thomson stood. "Yes, please. And lead us to the smoking room. We'll take coffee there. That room needs christening."

The chief steward looked down his nose. "Very well, sir. Follow me."

He led the way with Thomson, Brancker and Scott, close behind. Only one of the R.A.W. people joined them. Knoxwood excused himself, saying he had more work to do. The rest returned to the promenade deck to admire the view of Nottingham.

Thomson was a little disappointed once in the smoking room—depressing without windows and not terribly well-lit. He thought now perhaps his own bravado had been overdone. The chief steward poured coffee and then brandy from a drinks trolley. He then brought drinks on a silver tray. He passed round a box of Cubans. Each man solemnly took one, as if it might be his last, cut the end with the cutter and lit up with a lighter, (prudently chained to the trolley). The room soon filled with smoke, which the extractor fan fought bravely to overcome.

"You may leave now, steward, if you like," Thomson told him.

"It's quite all right, sir. I'll be here, if you need anything," the chief steward said between coughing fits. He then slunk away and sat on a chair in the corner. Thomson suspected the poor man was afraid to open the door. The truth was that Lou had instructed him to stay and keep a watchful eye on the smokers.

While Thomson smoked his cigar, Lou inspected the ship, running into Sky Hunt as he moved along the catwalk.

"Hi, Chief, what do you think?" Lou asked.

"It's flat calm out there, even so, the bags are rubbing. Let me show you," Hunt said. He led Lou to the stern and from there, they moved down the length of the ship to the bow. Hunt pointed out locations where gas bags were in contact with the ship's frame.

"In rough weather, they'd really be getting ripped up," Hunt said.

"I think she's getting heavy," Lou said.

Hunt gestured toward the bags. "Here's the reason: the bags are getting full of holes and the valves are discharging gas—she's losing lift all the time." They walked past the hissing gas valves and Hunt continued. "I'm not happy with these valves. In bumpy weather they'll be discharging even more gas."

Richmond appeared. "Discharging! What do you mean?"

"Gas. Lots of it, sir, from the valves and the bags," Hunt explained, but obviously Richmond already knew. Lou returned to the control car.

Later, Thomson and the cigar-reeking smokers returned to the promenade deck. The chief steward immersed all their cigar butts in a bowl of water before allowing them out. By now, Richmond was back from his own inspection.

"Well, as you can tell, the smoking room experiment was a complete success," Thomson declared as he rejoined the others. "Where are we now, Richmond?"

"Leaving Leicester and approaching Birmingham, Lord Thomson."

Over Birmingham the passengers peered down at the tight-knit masses of tiny houses. Once again, traffic came to a halt. Elated citizens got out and waved and honked their horns.

14

MISHAP AT CARDINGTON TOWER

October 16, 1929.

S oon, they were over Northampton, heading toward Bedfordshire. At 2 o'clock passengers were served afternoon tea, digestive biscuits, and Thomson's favorite cucumber sandwiches. They were nearing Cardington. In the control car, with Atherstone and Lou at his side, Irwin was becoming concerned. Lou had briefed him on Hunt's comments.

"She's getting heavy and losing gas doesn't help. It's happening so rapidly," Irwin said.

"Do you want to dump ballast yet, sir?" Lou asked.

"Yes. Dump five tons from Frame 2 and five tons from Frame 8."

"Right you are, sir," Atherstone said, grabbing ballast release valves.

"I'm going to drive her hard and keep her nose up. Increase all engines to eight hundred."

"All engines to eight hundred, sir." Lou sent the message to all cars and the engine notes increased.

"How are we off for fuel?" Irwin asked.

"We got plenty. Enough for eighteen hours," Atherstone replied.

"Dump water ballast on Frames 3 and 6," Irwin ordered.

"Dumping ballast on 3 and 6, Captain. We're down to five tons of water ballast," Atherstone said.

"Save that. We might need it at the tower. Damn. She's sinking like a rock. Dump five tons of fuel from Frame 5."

"Did you say *fuel,* sir?" Lou asked.

"Affirmative. Start dumping *fuel.*"

Atherstone carried out the order. From the control car they watched diesel fuel cascading over the fields.

"That's good for the animals and crops," Atherstone said.

"Can't be helped," Irwin muttered.

Lou imagined what the farm would smell like when the cows came home tonight. Soon, they were within three miles of Cardington at an altitude of four hundred feet. They were surprised by a voice from above.

"Okay, I'll take over now," Scott shouted from the chartroom, his speech slurred. Lou, Irwin and Atherstone stared up in disbelief.

"Steer off forty degrees—" Irwin began.

"Steer straight in from here," Scott barked. "Don't you change course!"

"I was planning to avoid the fairground, sir," Irwin said.

"No, we've got plenty of height. Go straight across the fairground to the tower. We can't mess around. Daft place for a fair anyway."

"But sir, that would be—"

"Just do as I say, Irwin," Scott hollered, bounding down the stairs. "Make room, Atherstone. Go upstairs and wait for my orders." Atherstone reluctantly did as ordered, mounted the stairs and stood with Johnston at the chartroom rail.

"Cut power to dead slow all engines," Scott ordered.

"Dead slow all engines," Lou repeated looking to Irwin for confirmation. The captain merely nodded. Lou relayed orders to the four forward driving engine cars, 1, 3, 4 and 5, via telegraph.

"Start reversing engine No. 2 to idling speed," Scott shouted. Lou relayed that order. Potter on rudders instinctively steered away from the fairground. Scott leaned across and grabbed the wheel. "Hold your course I told you!"

"Yes, sir," Potter mumbled. A few minutes later they were over the fairground. The music drifted up to the control car. Lou glanced down and saw the gypsy at the opening of her tent. She stood looking up, her hands on her hips. He didn't know if she could see him, but felt her eyes on him. Moments later, she'd disappeared. He thought perhaps it'd been his imagination. The people at the fairground were thrilled at the spectacle, waving furiously. Those on the Ferris wheel yelled like crazy people, from what appeared to be eye level.

"Okay, increase revs on reversing engine No.2 to four hundred," Scott ordered. "Cut all other engines to dead slow."

"They're already at dead slow," Irwin said.

"Er, right. Continue on. We'll coast in from here."

The airship passed over the Cardington fence where the crowd had doubled in size since morning. Cars sounded their horns; flags, handkerchiefs and scarves were waved, resembling a soccer crowd. The ship wasn't aligned with the tower and their altitude had been misjudged.

"We're not gonna make it. We'll have to go around again, sir," Irwin said.

"Er, yes. I think you're right, Irwin. That coxswain messed up. Get us out of here. We'll start over."

Irwin took a deep breath. "Go to full power on 1 and 3—cut power on 2!" The ship swung away from the tower and, when safely clear, Irwin fired up engines 4 and 5 to bring the ship up with dynamic lift. They climbed to four hundred feet and traveled toward the east, making a huge circle in preparation for another attempt.

Twenty minutes later, they were in position to try again. As soon as Irwin had the engines set at the right revs, Scott stepped in again and took over. Precisely the same thing happened and again they had to start from scratch. After dumping more fuel, the third attempt went slightly better, and as they approached the tower, Irwin gave instructions for the mooring line to be dropped. Lou communicated with Church at the bow.

"Church, drop the mooring line."

Church shouted a 'Yes, sir' back to him. Lou knew he'd have the hatch open, ready to drop the line. The ground crewmen were also at the ready. Then Lou saw Freddie, like a sprinter coming out of the starting blocks. He'd never seen the boy run before. He seemed to hop and run at the same time, but even with his limp, he was swift. Freddie raced under the airship toward the bow, where he knew the line would be dropped. Lou saw the other crewmen running after him waving their arms frantically—to stop him. Freddie turned, and seeing the others chasing him, ran all the harder, throwing back his head and laughing hysterically. Lou couldn't hear them; Freddie's laughter and their warning shouts were drowned by the engines, carousel music and spectators. The frustrating scene was like a hideous mime on some great stage. Lou saw the line thrown down and Freddie, like a whippet go for it.

Why didn't anyone tell the kid to use the damned mat!

As Freddie grabbed the line, an arc of static electricity hit him and his body arched. He stiffened and fell backwards, striking his head on the ground where he lay motionless. Lou had seen everything. He was totally distracted.

Damn, is he dead? Oh, no, please!

He was jarred back by Irwin's voice.

"She's sinking fast! Dump the last five tons of ballast at Frame 7 and five tons of fuel from Frame 8!"

Lou hesitated for a second, looking at Irwin, questioning his order.

Surely not. We can't dump fuel and water on Freddie!

"Do it! *Right now!*" Irwin yelled. Lou came out of his stupor and grabbed the ballast discharge valves. Scott did the same with the fuel dump lever. Freddie lay on his back, eyes wide open, legs spread apart. Water ballast and diesel fuel cascaded over his body, fresh, young face and shiny boots.

"Pay attention, we're closing in," Irwin said.

"I'm going to the bow to direct the operations," Scott said, climbing the stairs. "Atherstone, you come back down to the control car."

Docking and locking onto the tower took another hour, due to Scott's continued meddling. Lou watched the ground-crew foreman yelling at his men to get away from Freddie and attend to lines dropped from the ship.

On the promenade deck, Thomson was oblivious to the calamity below, but suspected the docking operation wasn't going well. He calmly addressed the Royal Airship Works staff standing stiffly before him, while the ship lurched and bumped against the tower. They looked uncertainly at Thomson in the surreal lighting emanating from the fairground.

"I want to congratulate you, Colmore, and your staff, for the successful culmination of all your years of hard work. This has been a great day. This is the beginning of a new era in British aviation ..."

From the control car, Lou watched an ambulance draw up alongside the airship. Freddie's body, draped with a sheet, was placed on a stretcher, carried to the ambulance and loaded into the back. Lou winced as the ambulance men slammed the doors, guilty that he'd got Freddie the job in the ground crew. This was bizarre. He couldn't understand it. And how the hell was he going to break the news to Charlotte?

The ship was locked onto the tower just after 6 o'clock. The throbbing engines were shut down and the sounds of shouting and confusion grew faint, allowing the carousel organ and screams from the rides to wash over the field. Lou and the other officers went ashore where Thomson was already speaking to the press, surrounded by R.A.W. personnel. As soon as the elevator doors had slid open, flashbulbs had popped. Thomson was delighted the journalists had turned up on schedule.

"How was your flight, Lord Thomson?" a reporter called.

"I must say, I've rarely had a more pleasant experience than I've had today—with a feeling of safety and well-being. We've all been comfortable and dined like kings amid luxurious surroundings. I spent some hours working in peaceful seclusion. This has been a wonderful day, gentlemen. The views from the ship have been magnificent. We even watched a fox hunt—and what a colorful sight that was!"

"Do you look forward to going on a voyage soon, sir?"

"I'm hoping to make the trip to India during the Christmas recess and that, I can tell you, will be a welcome interlude, where one can relax and read, or work with the comforts of an ocean liner."

"You said Christmas, sir? Did you mean this coming Christmas? That's less than three months away."

"Look, there are more trials to be done and all sorts of tests. I refuse to put any pressure on our Cardington team. I want to make one thing perfectly clear. As I said in 1924 when I introduced the program, no long distance flights will be undertaken until the staff is ready and testing is complete. I said then: *'Safety first and safety second, as well.'* We shall live and die by that policy. Good night, gentlemen."

An unknown reporter shouted from the back of the group.

"Sir, are you aware that a young ground crewman died this evening?"

Thomson's pleasant mood was shattered. This would put a damper on the weekend newspaper stories. He looked round helplessly at his people.

Damn, why didn't someone tell me!

They shuffled around in embarrassment.

"What happened?"

"We believe he was electrocuted, sir."

"My goodness. Er, …this is the first I've heard of it. I'm deeply saddened. My condolences and my prayers go out to the young man's family."

Lou watched Thomson walk to the car, his pain evident. It all seemed such a shame after what had appeared to be a good day—except for Irwin's reservations (also unknown to Thomson, as yet). Thomson climbed into the car and the door was slammed shut. Everyone dispersed.

Lou went home. Behind him, the carousel music played on, the girls on the Ferris wheel squealed with delight and the hideous clown in its glass box threw back its head and laughed hysterically.

15

BLACK TUESDAY

October 29, 1929.

Freddie was buried in St. Mary's graveyard on October 29—a day of misery that became known around the world as 'Black Tuesday.' The American stock market crashed almost as soon as Wall Street opened and panic ran its course. There were stories that afternoon of people throwing themselves out of high-rise windows in New York.

Burial had been delayed due to the requirement of an autopsy—Freddie's death occurring in unusual circumstances, they said. Attendees were not concerned with world finance, but it added to the mood of despair; their focus was on Freddie's poor family. The funeral was heavily attended with crewmen, officers and their wives present. Freddie's grave had been dug at the back of the cemetery, farthest from the road, almost in the shadow of Shed No.1. The higher echelon of the R.A.W. didn't attend, in case the program garnered too much adverse publicity. Billy stood in the drizzle with Lou and Charlotte, still badly shaken. The boys had become inseparable. Billy, though traumatized, decided to remain at Freddie's home for the time being, since his presence gave the family some comfort.

Lou had entered the house around 7 o'clock the evening Freddie died. He walked into the living room, his face ashen. Charlotte looked up from her sewing and knew instinctively something was seriously wrong. She jumped to her feet.

"Lou. What's the matter?"

"Freddie."

"What's happened to him?"

"He's dead."

"Oh, my God, no!" she sobbed. "What happened?" Her voice trailed off in despair.

"He ran and grabbed the mooring line and fell down dead."

"No!" Charlotte sank back onto the couch again, screwing up her face.

"It made no sense. None of us could understand it. I feel terrible."

"Damn these airships!"

"Joe Binks told me later Freddie had a weak heart."

"Damn these *rotten, bloody* airships!"

"He should never have been in that crew. That family kept his condition from us."

"That ship is cursed!"

"If I'd known, I swear he'd never have been on that field."

"And this *city* is cursed."

"Charlotte, please don't."

"And now *we're* cursed, too ...Don't you see that, Lou?" she said, as though entranced.

"It was just unfortunate—nothing to do with the airship."

"Just unfortunate! *The boy's dead!* He was here with us in this room only last week. Poor Freddie ...oh, that poor boy, he was just a child. I loved him so much." She was inconsolable and floods of tears flowed down her cheeks. Lou felt wretched and powerless. Freddie had become like her own child.

"You came in the door with that same look on your face when Josh died. How many more times do I have to see it? I can't take this anymore!"

Lou sat beside her and put his arm around her. "Charlotte, Freddie had a bad heart, my darling."

"What about Billy? He'll be next. I shouldn't have allowed you to bring him into this dreadful business. That ship is cursed!"

"It's not *cursed.*"

"Oh, it's cursed all right. They're *all* cursed!" Charlotte sneered. Everything was crystal clear now. Only hell lay ahead. She stopped crying, wiped the tears and stared out the window into the darkness. After a few moments, she got up, left the room and went upstairs.

Charlotte took to her bed, where she stayed for three days, unable to return to work. The morning of the funeral she put on the black frock Freddie had admired at the party and a black, heavy topcoat with a matching hat, lent by Mrs. Jones. It was cold and windy at the grave site. She was chilled to the marrow and practically catatonic. Freddie's father told her they'd dressed him to look nice in the clothes she'd bought him, including the boots. He thanked her for being kind to him.

The following week, ill and deathly white—accentuated by her black mourning garb—Charlotte trudged to Putroe Lane in the rain and knocked on the Irwins' door.

"Olivia, may I come in?"

Olivia held out her arms and hugged Charlotte. "Oh, Charlotte, you poor dear. Come in and sit down by the fire. Give me your wet things."

Charlotte took off her coat and headscarf. Olivia hung them over a chair to dry by the fire. "Here, sit and warm yourself. I'm going to make you some coffee," Olivia said.

While Olivia was in the kitchen, Charlotte sat staring into the flaming coals. Soon, Olivia reentered the room with a tray of coffee and homemade cake.

"I needed someone to talk to," Charlotte said.

"I'm glad you came."

"I've been so miserable."

"Poor, wee Freddie. *Everybody's* sick about it."

"I'm so worried, not just for Lou—but there's Billy, my best friend's boy—and everyone else. We've got to know everybody here now."

"You're worried about the airships?"

"Yes, of course, aren't *you?*" Charlotte asked, in disbelief.

"Freddie's death wasn't due to the airship. Bird said Scott made a balls-up of the mooring, but none of that had anything to do with the poor, wee lad's death."

"People said he'd been electrocuted," Charlotte said.

"Bird told me there's always a kick of static electricity, but not enough to kill anyone. They're trained to stand on a rubber mat when they take hold of the line so they don't feel it. Freddie had a weak heart. They did an autopsy. Chasing after the line must have killed him. He wasn't even supposed to touch the line—it wasn't *his* job. They said he bashed his head when he fell down, too. Someone even said he broke his neck."

Charlotte wasn't listening. "I don't think these airships will ever be safe, Olivia."

"I'm *sure* they will, dear gel."

"How do we know that?"

"Bird isn't satisfied, but he thinks they'll get the problems sorted out, eventually."

"*Eventually!* A man was on the radio this week talking about an article in the *Aeroplane* magazine saying these airships are experimental and we must *expect* many more disasters."

"There're always going to be naysayers forecasting doom and gloom, pet. We must look on the bright side. We're officer's wives. We've got to give them our support."

"Yes, I know, but ..."

"You seemed so happy at the party. Then you went to see the gypsy, didn't you?" Charlotte looked sheepish. "What did she tell you?"

"She didn't say, exactly."

"But she's upset you, hasn't she?"

"I suppose she has. She gave me a bad feeling about the airship— as if she knew something. She kept talking about 'their big game' and said there'll be no winners—only *losers*."

"She gave you the impression something bad would happen?"

"Yes. Perhaps it's already happened with Freddie dying—or maybe this is only the beginning ...Oh, Olivia, I don't know ..."

"She's told you nothing really, has she? Now you're worrying yourself to death."

"That's not all. She told me I would have a baby ... one day."

"Well, that's good, isn't it?"

"In a way, yes, I suppose. She gave me the impression this would be after my life had changed ...after huge things happening ...after all the things making me miserable were resolved ...the decks cleared ...when all things unspoken were spoken ...when I'm *free* ...I will become whole again ...and only then, will I conceive." Charlotte shook her head from side to side. "I don't know how any of *that* can happen ...there're just too many things! ...I'm at my wit's end."

Olivia, although obviously burning with curiosity, didn't press it, lest she upset Charlotte further. "My poor, wee bairn. You need to get away for a rest. Couldn't you go to your mum's place for a while?"

"I thought about that. Lou even suggested it. He's going to be away a lot doing tests."

"Then you must go. I'll come with you to the station. They already know you're sick at the hospital. You need rest. You're drained."

16

OVER YORKSHIRE

November 1929.

Two days later, Olivia put Charlotte on the train to Wakefield, where she made the connection to Ackworth. While she recuperated at her parents' home, Lou took part in test flights aboard *Cardington R101*. The weather was perfect for these tests and, although pleasant, not useful for testing her durability.

The engines proved troublesome on two trips, but not as troublesome as Scott during docking operations. His ham-fisted interference created havoc, causing them to run into or over the tower several times. On a couple of occasions, he dropped ballast without Irwin knowing, sending the bow shooting upward. The officers grew sick and tired of him and by the end of the fourth test, were showing signs of strain. Any one of these botched attempts at docking could have easily resulted in the loss of the airship and everyone on board.

The Air Ministry also caused unnecessary stress by insisting they take government officials, MPs and civilian VIP's for pleasure trips around the countryside. These flights were intended to give the public the impression that the Cardington airship was *'as safe as houses'*—a phrase bureaucrats liked to bandy about. Once, they carried forty-four crew and forty passengers, plus the additional weight of a wet cover from the previous night's rain. This broke all records for being the largest number of people ever carried in the air, a fact proudly reported in the newspapers the next day. During the flight, *Cardington R101* flopped around the vicinity, barely able to stay afloat. Lou credited Irwin's flying skill and good luck for their safe return. Its confidence bolstered, the Air Ministry decided to go ahead with Thomson's plan to take a hundred MPs on a 'demonstration flight,' scheduling it for November 16th.

Ten members of Parliament on board for one of these joy rides had a serious scare one afternoon. No one knew the lift and trim equipment at the mast was out of adjustment. After casting off, the bow shot skyward at twenty-five degrees, and VIPs seated in the dining room ended up with their lunch in their laps. The sound of breaking crockery frightened them out of their wits.

That same week, a storm hit Bedfordshire without sufficient warning to get the ship put away in her shed. Lou was on board with the watchcrew while 80 mph winds battered the ship. Many thought she'd be wrenched off the mast and blown away, as R33 had been from Pulham. She remained, held fast by the mooring gear—a credit to Scott, who'd designed it. Officials were pleased with the ship's performance, but disappointed when they discovered the state of the gas bags. Adding to their dismay, the valves had expelled gas at an alarming rate, while the cover leaked like a sieve.

The night before the ship was to carry the hundred MPs, the weather deteriorated and the trip was postponed until the following week. In the meantime, *Cardington R101* sailed off to carry out her thirty-hour endurance test. The pleasure of it was that they were unburdened by politicians or Air Ministry bigwigs and able to consume the food and drink put on board for the MP's flight. With no one aboard to impress, Scott behaved himself most of the time. Lou witnessed Irwin make the best take-off so far without any drama. The weather, once again perfect, caused minimal gas loss from the valves, but the bags were still full of holes. The flight took them up the east coast over Lincoln, Darlington, York and Durham.

Over Yorkshire, after passing Scunthorpe, Scott came down to the control car. He called up to Johnston for the bearing to Howden. Johnston checked the map. "Three hundred and twenty degrees. About fourteen miles, sir," he replied.

"Okay, let's drop in on our friends at Howden," Scott said.

Capt. Irwin turned to the rudder coxswain. "Steer three-twenty."

The ship veered to port. Irwin raised his eyebrows to Lou.

"We'll show them what a real airship looks like," Scott said with a crafty smile. "Bring her down to six hundred feet, five miles out and then bring her down till you can see the whites of their eyes!"

Lou glanced at Scott before he disappeared upstairs. He didn't think Scott was being malicious—mischievous perhaps, reckless certainly—probably hoping to tweak Burney's nose. It made Lou uncomfortable.

The sky was clear and soon Howden Air Station loomed in the distance. They'd reduced altitude and were still descending. Lou, although pleased to see the old place, worried that the appearance of *Cardington R101* would infuriate Wallis—like a detested neighbor showing up on his doorstep uninvited, but a whole lot worse. When he raised his binoculars, his fears were realized. As they approached the dilapidated shed at 400 feet, Norway came out and stood at the doors in his tweeds, hands on hips. Wallis joined him, followed by *Howden R100's* Capt. Booth. Norway showed no emotion, except wonder, perhaps. He held up one hand, shielding his eyes, clenching his unlit pipe between his teeth. His mouth was set in that peculiar grin he wore when concentrating. Wallis scowled up at them, rubbing his temples. Lou knew he'd take this as a personal insult—which, of course, it was.

His migraine's gonna get a whole lot worse!

Norway removed his pipe and shouted something above the noise, cupping his hand over Wallis's ear. Wallis nodded his head vigorously up and down and replied with a grimace. Lou could see Wallis was seething and wondered what Norway had said to him.

I must remember to ask Nev when I see him.

Scott and the R.A.W. staff were content to sail on, confident they'd annoyed the hell out of their rivals in their own backyard. Lou knew Colmore wouldn't have allowed this stunt. It was bad form, and he, too, much of a gentleman. Richmond would've felt the same. Both men were busy at Cardington House, working on a report to present to Thomson, addressing the ship's weight problems. This 'in your face' detour had been childish and fate-tempting. Repercussions would be *incalculable.*

Why go out of your way to make enemies?

Irwin grinned at Lou. "They've had their bit of fun. Now it's our turn." Lou was puzzled. The captain glanced up at Johnston leaning on the rail above. "Johnny, give me the bearing for Low Ackworth."

Lou understood. Seeing that beautiful place from the air in perfect weather would be a treat, but hoped it wouldn't upset Charlotte.

"Two hundred seventy-five degrees," Johnston called down. "Nineteen miles, Captain."

"Do you think they'll mind upstairs?" Lou asked Irwin.

"I don't suppose they'll notice. They're too busy tucking into the caviar and champagne," Irwin replied.

Twenty minutes later, the airship was cruising at six hundred feet, closing in on Ackworth Village and its three collieries, each with its own coal mountain. The fields, rivers and pastures appeared as beautiful as ever, even in November with the trees almost bare. Soon they were nearing Station Road. Many residents, hearing the engines, had come out and stood in the street. Lou spotted the obelisk and St. Cuthbert's through his binoculars—and then Charlotte's house. He smiled when he saw a wisp of smoke coming from the chimney. It was a sure sign.

Somebody's home!

"There's her house," Lou said, pointing. "Over there."

The door opened and Charlotte ran out into the front garden.

"Ah, look now, there's your missus," Irwin said.

Charlotte was followed by her parents and then Auntie Betty. Johnston came down to see for himself. "I think she's pleased to see you, mate!" he said. Lou's heart skipped a beat. He slid the window open, took out his handkerchief, and waved it. She spotted him and pointed. He felt relieved. She was looking better and blew him a kiss. As they sailed on, he watched Charlotte until she was out of sight. He hoped she'd come home soon.

The rest of that flight was uneventful, passing over many parts of England, including York and Newcastle, then Edinburgh and Glasgow in Scotland, and Belfast and Dublin in Ireland. Irwin took a detour of his own, steering the ship over his hometown of Bray, on the coast south of Dublin. They returned to England and thick fog over Stafford. Scott didn't interfere and landing was accomplished without mishap. Reporters were waiting when the officers disembarked. Scott was happy to give them a statement.

"This has been a magnificent flight. Everyone's been most comfortable. We've been doing rigorous turning exercises in the air and she's been behaving splendidly."

Scott was trying to say that this airship wouldn't break in two like *R38* had done. He didn't say the ship was overweight and the gas bags were full of holes. That would be broken to the public on another day perhaps—perhaps not.

Charlotte returned to Bedford a week later and went straight back to work. She pushed the worry and grief over Freddie under the surface where it lay with her other torments. At last, it was time for the MP's flight, or in Johnston's words, *'the flight of a hundred old men.'* Although the forecast wasn't favorable, the Air Ministry refused to postpone again; Thomson kept bringing it up. There was no way out.

On the morning of the flight, Lou attempted to climb out of bed, but Charlotte pulled him back. "Stay awhile, love," she implored.

"Let me check the weather first, honey." Naked, Lou climbed out of bed and while Charlotte laid back on her pillows admiring him, he went to the window overlooking the garden. Rain was coming down in torrents, wind howling.

"Great! I don't think anyone'll show up in this weather. I can spare you half an hour." He slipped back under the warm covers and took her in his arms.

"You cheeky dog. I need you for at least an hour," Charlotte said, pulling him closer.

"God, you feel so good, Charlie. Let's make it two."

"See what happens when I'm not around."

"It's been too long, my darling. Much, much too long," Lou whispered.

17

ONE HUNDRED MPs & AN ULTIMATUM

November 23, 1929.

Lou put on his waterproofs and drove to Cardington in driving rain two and a half hours later. When he arrived, *Cardington R101* was rolling gently around on the tower while an army of men serviced the ship from below. Hydrogen was being pumped aboard and would continue to be until the last moment before takeoff. Boxes of food and drink were being carried up the tower stairs. Lou stopped Bert Mann to ask why they weren't using the elevator. Mann told him it was broken. Lou climbed the stairs as usual.

This won't please the old boys—if they bother coming.

He went to the control car. "Sorry I'm late, sir. Something came up," Lou said.

"I'm sure it did …nice having the missus back, I expect. No need to worry yourself. Maybe no one'll show up," Irwin said, checking his watch. "Hmm, ten minutes to ten. Boarding's at eleven. *Oh, Jeez.* Will you look at this!"

Lou glanced at the road. Two limousines were driving up to the gate.

"What are you going to do?" Lou asked.

"She's already as heavy as old Sister Malone's heart. Tell Sky Hunt to drain off half the fuel and ballast. Let's hope the weather gets worse," Irwin said, peering at the waterlogged field. "It's beginning to look like Lake Superior out there—I guess they'll be comin' in two by two."

Lou went and found Hunt and relayed Irwin's message.

"Are they gonna fly in this?" Hunt asked.

"Doubtful, I reckon," Lou replied.

"Major Scott might have other ideas," Hunt scoffed.

Half an hour later, twenty more black cars had appeared at the gate. At 10:45 a.m. the gates were opened and they drove across the sodden field to the tower, where ground crewmen in raingear directed MPs to the customs shed. No one was deterred by the weather or the broken elevator. Lou went to the bottom of the stairs to check conditions and attitudes. Waves of huffing, puffing, determined, old men on walking sticks made their way into the tower to begin the slog to the top.

Lou went into the customs office—where many were getting checked for lighters and matches—before the climb. One of the men, a little rotund, fifty-something, Lou recognized as Winston Churchill. He was in the act of removing a leather cigar case from his raincoat and counting his cigars. Lou politely stopped beside him. He peered up at Lou defiantly.

"Sir, you won't be lighting those, will you?" Lou asked

Churchill gave him a haughty stare, mouth drooping, chin out.

"And who the blazes are you?"

"Commander Remington, sir."

Churchill glanced at Lou's insignias. "United States Navy?"

"Affirmative, sir."

Churchill's attitude softened. "Ah, the American." He stuck out his hand, smiling broadly. I'm honored to meet you. I know these things are deathtraps, but I don't intend to prove it—not today."

One or two MPs shuffling past gave Churchill a filthy look.

"Glad to hear that, sir. What's up with those folks?" Lou said.

"Don't worry about them. Not fans of mine, or my party."

Lou grinned. "And you don't have any matches, or lighters, sir?"

"Absolutely not. I've already been interrogated by this bunch."

"Good. Thank you, sir," Lou said. Churchill pulled up his collar and started up the tower stairs beside Lou. He shouted above the drumming rain.

"I hear there's a smoking room on board?"

"Yes, sir."

"Thomson told me he's already christened it, personally."

"That's true. He did."

"He's hung some fifth-rate oil painting on his office wall done by some daubing fool—probably a painter and decorator! He's asked me to brush in an airship for him. God knows why. Anyway, I thought I'd better come here and see the damned thing for myself first.

Lou laughed. "You picked a good day for *that*, sir!"

A massive wind blast made the tower shudder and rattle and rain showered down on them through the open sides.

"Do you think there'll be a flight today in this lot?"Churchill asked, eyeing the weather. Scott, in civilian clothes, was on his way up the stairs.   "Indeed there will, Mr. Churchill," Scott answered. "Even if Remington and I have to fly the bloody thing ourselves." Scott bounded past them two at a time. Lou gave Churchill a crooked half-smile and cocked his brow. Churchill understood.

"We may need to keep an eye on that one. I hope I can get coffee and some decent brandy on this old rust bucket—then at least I can die happy," Churchill said. They continued their ascent of the never-ending steps.

Less than forty miles away, black and silver clouds rolled like breakers across the skies above Gwydyr House. Rain pounded the Georgian windows in Thomson's office and cascaded down the brickwork. He stood peering out into the mist hanging over the river, listening to the hoots of invisible tugs.

He returned to his desk and sat down while the tugs continued sounding their mournful warnings. He felt the dreary dampness in the air due to lack of heat. Six table lamps lit the room in isolated areas, leaving the rest in gloom. He assumed Colmore and Richmond were waiting outside in the reception office. They'd be nervous and soaking wet.

Good. Let them be.

He sat for another ten minutes planning his attack. Marthe's framed photograph smiled up at him from the half-open desk drawer at his side, while the Taj, in its ornate gold frame behind him, dominated the room. Buck had hung it for him and later he'd had a picture light installed over it. He often sat staring at the architectural masterpiece, meditating. It gave him inspiration. He looked forward to Winston visiting with his paint brushes. Finally, he stood and drew himself to his full height and strode to the door. He threw it open with a beaming smile, putting his hand out to Colmore.

"Gentlemen, gentlemen, good of you to come. Come in! Come in!"

Both uniformed men got out of their chairs and shook Thomson's hand. Their dripping raincoats hung on the coat stand by the door.

"Morning, sir," they said together. Thomson noticed their faces brighten.

They're thinking 'He's in a good mood—things won't be so bad.'

"Oh, you shouldn't have got dressed up. There was no need."

This was all insincere banter, of course. They followed him in, carrying briefcases, wet hats under their arms. There was a sitting area with a low table and a couch and easy chairs set around the unlit marble fireplace. Richmond looked in that direction, but Thomson gestured for them to sit in the upright wooden chairs in front of his desk.

No good you looking over there, Richmond. This isn't going to be a cosy, little fireside chat.

They waited for Thomson to sit down. When he'd done so, they stared at the brightly lit painting of the Taj Mahal behind him, impressed.

"How was your train journey?" Thomson said casually.

"The weather's filthy out there, sir, coming down in buckets," Colmore replied as they sat down.

"Cats and dogs, eh? Same up there?"

"Worse actually," Richmond said.

"Not sure they'll be able to make that flight today," Colmore said.

Typical Colmore!

"Why the hell not?"

"Might upset the passengers," Richmond said, not touching the real reason.

"A spin around Bedford'll do them good—blow the cobwebs away! How many showed up?"

"When I spoke with Scott on the phone, he said forty-four had arrived," Colmore said.

"*Forty-four!* We must take them up if they've gone to the trouble of showing up in such foul weather. Excellent. They're as keen as mustard!"

"Forty is the maximum we've carried so far, sir," Colmore said weakly.

"Well, here's the chance to break your own record, man!"

Richmond rummaged around in his briefcase, bringing out a file.

Lou got back to the control car where Irwin was still eyeing the weather.

"How many are there now?"

"I just counted forty-eight. And more cars are arriving."

"Did you talk to Sky Hunt?"

"I did, sir. He's draining down fuel and ballast per your orders."

"It's getting worse," Irwin said.

Atherstone entered the control car. He looked worried.

"I've just looked this boat over from stem to stern," he said.

"And?"

"The canvas cover's leaking and breaking down. I could see daylight in a lot of places."

"What about the bags?"

"They're rubbing all right, sir."

"And leaking?"

"Oh, *yes!*"

"Lou, keep an eye on the passengers and keep a count. We're getting dangerously overweight. Keep me informed every fifteen minutes," Irwin said.

Lou checked his watch. It was 10:30 a.m.

Thomson still appeared amiable and his two airshipmen had achieved a reasonable comfort level. Thomson picked up a sheaf of papers and waved it in the air.

"I read your report. Seems this airship of yours is too heavy?"

"Yes, sir. Heavier than expected," Colmore answered.

"You may remember at the briefing in June I touched on the subject, sir," Richmond said.

"I do remember—and *you* made light of it! How much lift do you have?"

Richmond hesitated. "Around thirty-three tons."

"A bit shy of sixty, isn't it!" Thomson said. He glared at them in silence, while the wind screamed around the rumbling window frames. "It doesn't look as though we'll be getting to India any time soon, does it?"

He let the sense of failure hang in the air.

"The schedule will be delayed, I'm afraid, yes, sir," Colmore said.

Thomson stared at them, saying nothing. During these silences, the ticking of the pendulum clock on the mantel sounded as loud as Big Ben.

"'The schedule will be delayed.' You speak as if we have all the time in the world, Colmore."

"Sir, we deeply regret the delay, but we'd like to discuss solutions," Richmond said.

At this, Thomson brightened and smiled pleasantly.

"I must point out we followed the rules rigidly, especially regarding safety. And we've been innovative to an unprecedented degree. The Howden ship will be using highly flammable petrol, whereas we'll be carrying much safer diesel fuel."

"Yes, yes, you said all that before, Richmond. At least *they'll* have enough lift to carry fuel."

"Sir, we have options."

Thomson thought for a moment. "How much lift does Burney have?"

Richmond looked pained.

"They're saying they've got over fifty-three tons," Colmore answered.

"I doubt that's true," Richmond bristled.

"If *Wallis* is saying it, it probably *is* true, and we're going to look pretty damned silly," Thomson said.

Lou entered the dining room where the stewards had laid out a light buffet of starter dishes and snacks with tea and coffee. MPs were helping themselves, chatting happily, well into their cocktails. Lou counted twenty-three in the dining room, mostly standing. He went to the lounge—another thirty-nine. On the promenade deck on the port side there were eleven and on starboard, eight. Eighty-one total. He wrote it down. He spotted the chief steward.

"Chief, see Mr. Churchill over there, with the cigar?"

"Yes, I do indeed, sir. He's a scary one, that one—like *a ruddy bulldog!*"

"Tell the stewards to keep an eye on him—just in case."

"Ooooh, believe me, sir, we're watching him like a hawk. He makes me very nervous. I'm the nervy type."

"I see, well, I'm sorry to hear that," Lou said.

"Commander, I prefer to be called Pierre if you don't mind—it's Peter really, but I like it the French way, you know..." He smoothed a lock of hair back over his ear. Lou suspected he was wearing an expensive hairpiece.

"Okay, *Pierre* it is."

"How many more should we expect, sir? They're coming on board by the dozen."

"I'm not sure. You got plenty of chow?"

"Enough to feed the five thousand," Pierre answered.

Lou hurried off to the control car.

"How many you got now?" Irwin asked.

"Eighty-one and counting."

"How's Hunt doing?"

"Fuel and ballast drained as instructed, sir."

"There's no sign of a break in the weather. We'll give it thirty minutes. Anyway, make sure our passengers are comfortable."

"Aye, aye, sir."

Thomson leaned back in his chair. "Tell me about these solutions," he said, his tone reasonable.

"I'm proposing we lighten her, as I said in the report. We made a list of items we can live without ...it was in the report."

Thomson showed them a look of disgust. He'd studied it.

"You intend to remove cabins and bunks and bathrooms—most disappointing!"

"We've already increased the capacity of the gas bags."

"How did you do that?"

"We slackened the harnesses, sir."

"The harnesses holding the gas bags in place?"

"Yes, sir."

Thomson tried to comprehend this. It was confusing. He glared at Richmond."Why weren't they adjusted to give maximum capacity in the first place?"

Richmond looked uncomfortable. "It's not the ideal situation, sir."

This part Thomson hadn't properly understood in the report.

"I see," he said vaguely.

"And finally, I'm suggesting we add another bay," Richmond said.

An expression of well-planned incredulity came over Thomson's face. "Just how in the world would you do that?"

"It's in the report, sir. We'll need to part her and insert an extra bay which will carry another gas bag—giving us a further nine tons of lift."

"By 'part her' you mean cut the thing in two pieces?"

"Yes, sir, we'll build an extra section and insert it."

Thomson let them see he was irritated now. "Do you have any idea how embarrassing this is to the government and to me *personally*?"

Lou returned to the dining room. The place was heaving now, the plates picked clean. Tea and coffee were still being served by the stewards, but gin and whisky were in greater demand. In the lounge, Churchill sat with the unlit cigar in his mouth, removing it to take a sip of cognac or coffee once in a while. He looked up at Lou with a precocious smile.

"You see I'm behaving myself, Commander."

"It's much appreciated, sir," Lou responded.

"Besides, you've got all these people in white coats watching me!"

Lou laughed, continuing to count heads. He returned to the control car.

"Eighty-two on board now, sir."

"And they're still coming," Irwin said, pointing at the gates.

"Who was it said 'Nothing like a hundred would show up'?" Atherstone said. More cars were arriving and ground crewmen were escorting occupants to the tower under umbrellas.

Thomson had turned up the heat.

"We certainly do realize it's embarrassing and we sincerely apologize. But please, with respect, sir, understand that the design of this airship is entirely new—much of it experimental," Colmore said with uncharacteristic boldness.

"But *Burney's* people seem to be doing so much better, do they not?" Thomson snapped.

"They don't have the glare of publicity like we do, sir. We are trapped by it."

"So, it's all this publicity that is causing the airship to be so overweight, is it? Don't be ridiculous, man. I'm required to play the press every day like a damned Stradivarius—justifying your existence. Now, I'm forced to go before the House, cap in hand, and explain why it's necessary to tear the damned thing apart and rebuild it!"

"But sir, all this is easily explainable—" Richmond began.

Thomson's face became contorted with anger.

"I've favored you people from the start, giving you every advantage. Despite that, it looks as though the Howden ship is still the superior ship."

"We don't know that yet, do we, sir?" Colmore said, his face showing hurt.

"If that ship rolls out and flies rings around you, we're all going to have egg on our faces," Thomson snapped.

"I'm sure that won't happen," Richmond said.

"When is it coming out?"

"Howden's ready to launch now, sir," Colmore replied.

"If I secure funding, how long will these modifications take?"

"Three months, sir," Richmond said.

"We'll need time for testing after that," Colmore reminded them.

Thomson calmed down. "The Prime Minister's Conference is scheduled to begin next October. I want to make the trip to India and arrive back in time for that."

Thomson noticed Richmond's eyes dart back and forth to the painting of the Taj behind him. He seemed mesmerized by it. But overall they seemed to be getting comfortable again, believing the worst was over.

"That ought to be do-able, sir," Colmore said, now actually smiling.

"The Commonwealth Prime Ministers will have traveled for weeks to get here. I intend to demonstrate how airships will improve their lives and the lives of their citizens."

"I understand, sir. And you will be demonstrating your point brilliantly. It will be a major coup on your part," Richmond said. The meeting had gone according to plan, but Thomson wasn't quite done with them yet.

The weather conditions at Cardington had worsened, with winds up to 60 mph. Rain continued pounding the airship, but still more MPs arrived. By 11 o'clock, Lou had counted one hundred. He returned to the control car, where Scott and the captain were in a heated discussion. Atherstone was also present, but saying nothing. Irwin looked round at Lou.

"What's the count now?"

"One hundred, sir, plus forty-eight crew."

"I'm well aware of the count. I've given orders not to allow any more on board. Now, are you ready to depart?" Scott asked.

"This flight's canceled. The weather's worsening and we're overloaded."

"This flight certainly is *not* canceled, Irwin," Scott shouted angrily.

"I'm the captain of this ship and it will *not* be taking off today."

"Now you see here. I'm your superior and I demand you prepare for take-off."

"Indeed you are my superior, sir, but you are not the captain of this ship. *I am!*" Irwin and Atherstone stood shoulder to shoulder facing Scott, their arms folded, guarding access to the ship's wheels. "To take off in this weather with a hundred and forty-eight people on board would be suicide—unless, of course, it's your intention to wipe out half the British government in one fell swoop. I suggest, sir, with the *greatest* respect, that you return to the dining saloon and have yourself another drink with the other gentlemen." Irwin's words sank in. Scott, his face red with fury, was beaten. He turned abruptly and headed back upstairs. Irwin turned to Lou again. "Tell Hunt to drain off half the fuel and half the ballast we have left. And tell him to make sure and keep the gas bags charged all afternoon. Then instruct the chief steward to serve lunch."

"Aye, aye, sir!" Lou said.

Thomson stared at Colmore and Richmond for some moments, reminiscing and carefully considering his words. He was going to enjoy this.

"I'm going to tell you a story, gentlemen. During the Boer War, we received a message: 'CLEAR THE LINE IMMEDIATELY. I AM COMING THROUGH. I knew who 'I' was—it was Lord Kitchener. Now I realized, 'doing my best' would not be good enough. Saying 'I tried' wouldn't work either. Clearing the line and getting him through would be the only measure of success. I assembled a force of a thousand men and personally supervised the pulling of twenty railway cars off the tracks onto their sides. Kitchener got through, and from that day forth, he never forgot my name."

Thomson got up from his chair and, resting his hands on the desk, leaned over Colmore and Richmond. His piercing eyes bore into them.

"*Kitchener* did not recognize the word 'impossible.' *Kitchener* did not accept the concept of 'failure' …and neither will I. Your mission is set in stone. Do I make myself clear, gentlemen?"

Thomson stood up straight. Colmore and Richmond jumped up and came to attention. "Yes sir, very clear, sir," Colmore answered.

"Perfectly clear, sir!" Richmond echoed.

They froze as the telephone rang. It was Thomson's private line. He picked it up and listened. "Yes." A look of disbelief came over his face followed by fury.

Am I surrounded by fools?

"What time was this? On whose order? Find out and let me know."

He replaced the receiver and glared at them. "Someone up there has canceled the flight. I want to know *who* it was and *why*. There was a lot riding on this. Now, in front of the Government up there, we're being made to look weak—a if airships can fly only in good weather. They must be shown to be capable of flying in *any* weather! Got that?"

"Yes, sir!"

Thomson nodded for them to leave and sat down. No handshakes. He was done with them for now.

After Lou informed Pierre that the ship would not be leaving the tower, within minutes, an army of stewards laid out a lavish buffet on silver platters with every conceivable type of British food, only seen on the aristocratic tables of the finest houses and restaurants: pheasant, duck, grouse, turkey, chicken, beef, lamb, pork, baked potatoes, mashed potatoes, Brussels sprouts, peas, broccoli, carrots, runner beans, turnips and parsnips. And to go with that, an array of complementary sauces: white sauce, cheese sauce, mint sauce, Oxo gravy, Bisto gravy, cranberry sauce. The collection of wines available was worthy of a fine French restaurant.

A line formed and everyone attacked the buffet then made their way to the lounge to sit. They enjoyed themselves immensely and, although the ship was being buffeted by sixty mph winds, she was very stable. The cover leaked badly, but buckets were strategically located above the passenger area ceilings to catch the water, and efficiently rotated and emptied by crewmen. Lou prayed no one would fall through the ceiling onto the diners.

After lunch, a variety of exotic desserts was served: crème brûlée, chocolate soufflé, honey wine pears, and sherry trifle, as well as some not-so-exotic: spotted dick, date pudding, jam roly-poly, bread and butter pudding, rhubarb and custard. A handful of MPs went to the smoking room, including Churchill, where they smoked their Cubans. Lou saw to it that this operation was supervised by Pierre as before, keeping the door locked from inside with finished cigars properly doused. Lou made observations and reported to the captain every fifteen minutes, as instructed.

The feast was over by 4 o'clock and passengers began leaving. Irwin stood at the exit door of the lounge with Lou and Scott, who was in the same state of inebriation as their guests. Lou and Irwin felt Lady Luck had been kind and they were relieved it was over. The MP for Staines shuffled up to Scott with a group of other gentlemen. They shook hands.

"Thanks for a splendid flight, old man."

"Didn't feel a thing."

"Smooth as a baby's bottom, sir."

"I'll definitely fly with you again."

"If this is a sample of the food you'll be serving on these voyages, you can put my name down, Captain," the MP for Barking said.

Irwin grinned.

"Let's have some pretty gals on board next time, what!"

"Yes, wonderful."

"Reserve me a berth on the first India flight."

"Yes, and me, and me …"

Scott's replies were just as daft and incoherent. Irwin and Lou shook their hands, all the while trying not to collapse with laughter. The flight of 100 MPs had been *a smashing success!*

PART TWO

Howden R100 flies over Howden Minster. December 16, 1929.

THE DUEL BEGINS

18

THE LAUNCHING OF HOWDEN R100

December 16, 1929.

It was ten minutes past two. The air over the Howden shed was dead calm, the sky, deep midnight blue, fading to black at its outer edges. Lou stood at the shed doors studying the full moon and scattered stars. He never failed to be amazed. He wondered where the animals were tonight. His question was answered by an owl tawit-ta-wooing off somewhere in the distance, followed by a chilling vixen's scream. Even after all these years, this place still had a magical, almost holy feel. He reminisced, recalling his first visit in '21 with the Navy, and then his many subsequent visits in the middle of the night, leaving Charlotte sleeping peacefully in their bed. Once here, he'd communed with nocturnal animals and ghostly memories of his dead buddies, to whom he felt he owed a heavy debt. Footsteps behind interrupted his thoughts.

"What are you up to, Lou?"

"Ah, Nevil."

"Barnes got back last night."

They glanced across the frost-covered field toward the bungalows. All the lights were on; everyone was up and around. Lou had traveled up by train with Billy the day before, having received word from the Cardington meteorological office that the weather would be settled enough for launching. When Norway met them in his three-wheeled sardine can, they squeezed into the thing and drove to the shed where cots had been set up for them to sleep in Lou's old office.

The works canteen would be operating during the evening and throughout the night. There'd be plenty of cold, hungry people around in the coming hours. Lou called and spoke to John Bull who agreed to pick up Billy's mother, Fanny, in Goole at 3:30 a.m. and bring her to see Billy off. John told Lou there was no way he'd miss out on seeing the launch of *Howden R100*.

After the flight of the 100 MPs, *Cardington R101* had remained on the tower under a condition of 'Storm Watch.' Due to windy conditions, it'd been impossible to walk her into her shed until the end of November. *Howden R100*, although completed and ready since early November, couldn't be launched until the Cardington tower was available.

The weather had remained unsettled until today: 16th December, 1929. A whole contingent of R.A.W. people, including Colmore, Scott and Inspector McWade, traveled to Howden and were ensconced in the Railway Station pub and one or two bed and breakfast establishments around the village. The ship's officers, Capt. Booth and Capt. Meager had been in Howden for over two months.

Out of the darkness, John Bull's Humber came chattering across the gravel driveway, up to the parking area beside the shed. Another car followed, carrying George Hunter and a photographer from the *Daily Express*. They also had a reporter from the *Hull Times* with them. After saying hello, Lou found Billy and sent him to the canteen to bring tea and toast for John and Fanny.

He then took John and Fanny to the office for half an hour, where it was warm. Norway disappeared on board the airship with Booth and Meager. The aerodrome was coming alive. Two buses arrived with the crew of riggers and engineers. Shortly after that, another, smaller bus with Cardington R.A.W. staff appeared. Next came a convoy of twenty-two buses from the barracks in York, carrying five hundred soldiers. The narrow road leading to the air station became choked with traffic.

John and Fanny retreated to the edge of the field and stood with the tiny crowd from surrounding areas. The hundred and fifty foot high shed doors were opened, revealing *Howden R100's* silver bow in the arc lights. Soon, Molly Wallis came and took John and Fanny back to her bungalow, out of the bitter cold for more hot drinks. Wallis, in a smart black overcoat, entered the shed to prepare for the extraction with Capt. Booth and the riggers ballasting up. Though gaunt, Wallis looked in good spirits and greeted Lou warmly.

"How are you, sir?" Lou asked.

"Wonderful, thank you, Lou."

Norway had told Lou that Wallis had been in Harrogate with Molly trying to relax, but had been suffering, not only from migraine headaches and insomnia, but also nausea and lack of appetite.

"I just had a huge breakfast, and once the birth of this creature is over, I shall feel even better," Wallis told him.

The R.A.W. officials gathered in a group at the front of the shed where they were joined by Wallis, Norway and Lou. There were no pleasantries, no handshaking, no attempts at cordiality; they merely swung their arms trying to keep warm and ignored each other. They had reached a critical period in the fight to the death between the dueling airships—a moment of truth. Lou wondered would this ship fail its initial tests, too.

Unlikely!

The ground rules were laid down by Scott, in charge of the operation on behalf of the R.A.W. However, he'd allow Wallis to oversee the removal of the ship from the hangar before taking over. Wallis and Scott met with the army colonel and a sergeant to discuss the formation of the walking party. Scott set things up as he'd done at Cardington in October.

The crew of ten riggers, including Billy and Jessup, six engineers, and three ship's officers, one of them Lou, climbed on board through the control car. Norway followed and went upstairs to the observation windows. Lou remained in the control car, which was much larger than that of *Cardington R101,* since the chartroom formed part of the control car itself.

Everybody was in position. Wallis gave the order through the bullhorn for the soldiers to take up the ropes. Floodlights made the scene surreal; clouds of exhaled breath from straining shadows and silhouettes; ten thousand footprints in the frost. The ship, over two football fields long, was eased out into the darkness to weak cheers. It was 6:20 a.m.

Once the airship's stern had cleared the doors, Scott took command, directing soldiers in lockstep to pull her out to the middle of the field. Wallis stalked off to one side where he watched them manhandle his creation. The bow was turned from the shed and pointed toward the open fields.

Molly rushed forward from the crowd and hugged Wallis, kissing his cheek, while people clapped and cheered. He showed no emotion, except embarrassment. They stood together for a few minutes, surveying the magnificent, silver structure, like its womb, overwhelming and gargantuan, gradually becoming bathed in the rising sun's glow.

The soldiers formed a line around the perimeter, keeping hold of the ropes while Scott checked the ballasting of the ship. The engines were started and warmed up. When Scott was satisfied, he stepped aboard, beckoning Wallis to join him in the control car. Wallis left Molly with a brief nod and trudged to the ship. Before disappearing inside, he turned and waved to her and at that moment, the cheer of approval rose to its loudest. Lou smiled at Wallis and shook his hand as he came aboard.

How proud they are of this man—and rightly so.

Wallis and Scott remained in the control car.

"Are you ready, Captain Booth?" Scott asked.

"Yes, sir."

"Then let's get the hell out of here!" Scott grunted.

Booth opened the sliding window and instructed the sergeant to be ready to cast off and then to Lou, "Drop half ton at bow and stern simultaneously, Commander Remington," he ordered.

"Aye, aye, sir," Lou answered. Water gushed from the outlets of the ballast tanks, causing soldiers to scatter and the ground to become slick. The ship was immediately drawn upwards by invisible forces.

"Let her go now!" Booth called. "Thank you, sergeant; thank you all."

The soldiers cheered and shouted up to them.

"Hooray!"

"Good luck!"

"God bless!"

Howden R100 lifted into the pale blue sky. All faces on the ground were raised heavenward in wonder.

"Go to slow ahead on Engines 1 and 2," Booth ordered. With increase in momentum, the elevator coxswain eased her bow up to six hundred feet. The rudder coxswain, following Booth's orders, circled over the village of Howden as they gained height. Lou admired the old minster in the early sunlight—a stunning sight from the air.

"How's she feeling on the wheels?" Booth asked.

"Light as a feather, sir," the rudder coxswain replied.

"Like silk, sir," the height coxswain confirmed.

Lou looked at Wallis and Scott. They must have heard this, but their faces remained impassive. Lou would tell Norway when he got a chance. His calculations concerning steering assistance must have been on the money.

Thank God! I guess ol' Nevil ain't as dopey as he looks!

Booth called back to Johnston at the chart table. "Johnny, what's the bearing for York?"

Johnston looked at the chart. "Steer three hundred and forty degrees and look out for a big cathedral," he said.

Twenty minutes later, they were over York, flying at an altitude of thirteen hundred feet in a radiant, clear blue sky. People on the ground were excited and waved at the ship. After a salutary thirty-minute flight, Booth came back to Johnston.

"We need the heading for Bedford now, Johnny."

Johnston already had the answer. "Steer due south for now. I'll give you corrections on the way."

Wallis stirred himself. "I'm going for breakfast."

"Good idea. I could use some coffee," Scott said. He turned to Booth before mounting the stairs. "Send me word of any problems, Captain Booth."

"Yes, sir," Booth replied. "Why don't you join them, Lou? Captain Meager and I'll be fine."

People from the R.A.W. and the Howden team filed into the dining room and sat down to breakfast in two separate groups. The atmosphere was cold, with no attempt at communication beyond icy stares. The journey south was uneventful. Lou spent much of the time with Wallis and Norway on the observation deck. Though it was winter, the views of the pastures and towns of England were truly beautiful.

Charlotte expected Lou home for dinner and for Norway to join them. At noon, she went to the butcher's at the parade of shops and bought a loin of pork. As she left, a milkman was unloading crates of milk and carrying them into the dairy. Irwin, who'd stopped in to buy cigarettes at the corner store, walked out, bumping into Charlotte.

"Charlotte—how nice to see you."

"Oh, hello, Captain Irwin," Charlotte said. A droning in the sky in the distance interrupted them and they glanced up. The milkman put down the crate and dashed to the door of the corner store.

"Alan, the other ship's 'ere, come and see!"

The butcher, in his bloodied, blue and white apron, also came running out to join them and so did the owners of the dairy and greengrocer's. The sound of four of the six crackling Rolls-Royce engines got louder as the airship approached from Bedford.

"Now here comes trouble, eh, Captain?" the milkman said, looking at Irwin, who was getting his first glimpse of the Howden airship.

"I wouldn't say trouble, no," Irwin said. "She looks like a very fine ship to me."

The kids poured out from the school across the street. They crossed the road toward the shops and gathered around Charlotte and the shopkeepers, staring at the airship, jabbering with excitement.

"It's the other ship from up north," a kid yelled. The airship roared directly overhead. "That's *my dad's* airship. He's going to fly in that one," another shouted in a north-country accent.

"It's not as good as *my dad's*."

"My dad's is *bigger*."

"No, it's not, *my dad's is bigger!*"

"And my dad's is *faster!*"

"*My dad* says that one's going to crash and burn like this," one kid yelled gesturing with his hand, showing it crashing into the ground. "Boom!" he yelled. The first kid jumped on the other's back and they rolled on the ground in a fierce fight, the rest urging them on.

"Stop that, immediately!" Irwin shouted, grabbing them both by the scruff of the neck. One boy's eye was puffed and closing up. The other's nose was dripping with blood.

"You should be ashamed of yourselves. Don't *ever* talk like that!" Irwin scolded.

"See what I mean?" the milkman said. "It's been bad around here lately and it's getting worse. Those Yorkshire crewmen have been causing a lot of trouble in the pubs and the kids are fighting in the schools."

"Now be careful what you say, mister! I'm from Yorkshire. There's been a lot of bad feelings on all sides," Charlotte snapped, her own accent loud and clear.

The milkman held up his hand. "Sorry, miss, no offence. I meant nothing by it."

"All this conflict has spilled out of the offices and into the streets and schools," Irwin said to Charlotte.

"It's sad, if you ask me. I'd better go. I've got more shopping to do," Charlotte said, trying to force a smile.

"See you again, Charlotte. I'll tell Lou when I see him, not to be late home."

She went to the greengrocer's further along the parade to buy Lou's favorite roasting vegetables, tears running from her eyes as she went. After that, she went into the off-license for wine.

Lou was much later than he should have been. It took three hours to dock the ship, mostly due to everyone's inexperience with the mooring gear, but Scott's interference made matters worse. It reminded Lou of Freddie. They were forced to make multiple attempts at landing, leaving the mast and flying out and returning three times. When they finally docked, Wallis left the ship immediately and was driven to Bedford Station. A meeting had been prearranged for five thirty to assess the flight and schedule another test.

Since they'd time to spare, Norway asked Lou to show him *Cardington R101.* Lou was happy to oblige, interested himself to see how the lightening operation was going. Upon entering Shed No.1, they ran into Richmond. Surprise and contempt for Norway showed in Richmond's face.

"May I ask what you're doing in this shed?" he demanded.

Lou thought Richmond must be embarrassed—'caught in the act' by his rival. "You know Nevil Norway, Assistant Director of Engineering at Howden," Lou said. Richmond glanced at Norway. Norway stuck his

hand out. Lou glared fiercely at Richmond, daring him to be rude. After a brief hesitation, Richmond begrudgingly shook Norway's hand as though he were infected with 'Spanish Flu'.

Perhaps this visit wasn't such a good idea.

"I was going to show Nevil around—unless you have any objections, of course?"

"Er, I suppose, if you must. But don't be long. They'll be shutting down for the day."

"That's aw-awfully g-good of you," Norway said. Richmond smirked and hurried away without another word.

"What's the matter with him?" Norway asked.

"You'll see," Lou said. "Don't worry. We'll take a quick gander."

The ship had been handed back to the Cardington works staff. She'd been degassed and her gas bags removed. The hangar looked as though a bomb had dropped—parts and pieces everywhere. Glass removed from promenade decks was propped against the shed walls. A line of workmen, carrying toilets, lavatory basins and bunk beds, filed past Lou and Norway. The first one, carrying a toilet on his shoulder, smiled and winked at Lou, did a little jig, and broke into song. "Oh, we puts the toilets in, we takes the toilets out, we puts the toilets in and we shake 'em all about, we do the Hokey Pokey, we turn around and that's what it's all about—oi!"

Norway looked around, puzzled, but didn't comment. Lou called across to the shop foreman and waved. The foreman nodded. They had no beef with Lou.

"How's it going, Ronnie?"

"Oh, same ol' same ol'."

"You know what you're doing?" Lou said, grinning.

"Yeah, we gotta get the fat lady's weight down."

"We're just going to take a quick look, if you don't mind. You're closing up in a few minutes, right?" Lou asked.

"Not any time soon, no, sir."

Lou and Norway spent thirty minutes wandering around inside the ship. They went through the passenger quarters, the dining room and the sitting areas. Norway's eyes scanned everything. He admired the gold-leafed columns and other finishes, nodding his head in approval. During their tour, Norway inspected the servo assistance mechanism and frowned.

"That looks damned heavy," he said.

Later, by the light of the rising moon, they walked over to Cardington House. With the exception of Capt. Meager who was on watch, the key players gathered in the conference room. These included Scott, Colmore, Richmond, Inspector McWade, Irwin, Atherstone, and a few R.A.W. staff members. The day's flight was dissected and a list of defects drawn up: a leaking cylinder on one engine, a possible big end problem, and a vent that allowed in too much air, causing the gas bags to blow around. That would be sewn up. It was agreed that if these issues could be dealt with tonight, another test flight would take place in the morning, meaning they could take advantage of the favorable weather. In less than an hour, Lou and Norway headed home for dinner on Lou's motorbike—Norway looking like cartoon character in a furry, fleece-lined 'teddy' from the ship.

19

HOME FOR DINNER

December 16, 1929.

Delicious aromas wafted up from the kitchen to greet them as they walked in the front door, just after 7 o'clock. Norway had brought a bottle of Scotch. He handed it to Charlotte.

"Ah, there you are. Thank you Nevil," she said as he kissed her cheek. "Dinner's been ready for some time."

"Sorry we're late, honey. We had to go over the flight at a conference," Lou said, giving her a hug and a kiss.

"That's okay, you're here now. It's a bit dried out, I'm afraid."

"I've got to take Nevil back later. He'll be working most of the night."

"I've made a bed up for you in the spare room, if you need it," Charlotte said.

"I'll have a snooze in one of the cabins, if I get a chance," Norway said.

Charlotte had laid the dining table on the middle level beside a blazing coal fire. She struck a match and lit the candles. "Sit down. I'll bring dinner up. Lou, there's a bottle of Claret on the sideboard if you'll open it, please," she said.

Lou did as he was asked and Norway sat down. Charlotte made a couple of trips bringing up the meals on a tray. The meat was dry, but Lou and Nevil were too hungry to notice. Lou suddenly put his hand to his head and laughed.

"There's something I've been meaning to ask you, but forgot, Nev."

"What?"

"When *R101* flew over the Howden shed, you and Barnes stood there gnashing your teeth … Remember?"

"How could I not? It was a pretty poor show."

"Barnes looked like he was about to blow a gasket."

"He was damned annoyed."

"What was it you shouted in his ear?"

Norway put down his knife and fork, casting his mind back. "Hmm. Ah yes, I remember. I said, 'Methinks they bite their thumbs at us, sir!'"

"What the hell's that all about?" Lou asked.

"It's Shakespeare—Romeo and Juliet," Charlotte said.

"Look, I'm just a dumb country boy. Did Barnes know what you meant?"

"Of course he did."

"And what did he say to that?"

"He shouted 'Let them bite them till they bleed!'"

Lou got the picture. "That's all he said?"

"Actually, no. Barnes is a religious man, but I've never heard him use such foul language before. Words I couldn't repeat in front of a lady," Norway said, eyeing Charlotte.

"Enemies for life?" Lou said. Norway nodded.

Charlotte refilled their glasses. "This is all going to end in tears," she said.

"So, what the heck's going on up in that shed, Lou?" Norway asked.

"They're removing stuff to lighten her."

"That's why he got so nasty?" Norway said.

"You caught Richmond with his pants down. He was humiliated."

"I can see that. But I'll tell you this—the work I saw in that shed, was magnificent. Puts *us* to shame," Norway said.

"Oh, how he'd love to hear that."

"Was Barnes on the flight down with you?" Charlotte asked.

"Yeah, but when we landed he got out of town immediately," Lou answered.

"I cooked enough food in case you brought him home."

"He wants to get back to his aeroplanes," Norway said.

"And Molly?" Charlotte asked.

"Yes, and Molly. He's been spending too much time away from her lately."

"Not good," Charlotte said.

"All he wants to do is organize Christmas with family. He loves Christmas," Norway said.

"Good for him," Charlotte said. "I'm *not* looking forward to Christmas—not one bit." She looked away into the flickering flames in the fireplace. Lou noticed.

"The docking took far too long today," Norway said.

"That gear will work okay once everyone learns how to use it—as long as Scott stays out of it," Lou told him.

"They seem to have too many experiments going on at the same time. Everything's complicated. They've got too much money at their disposal," Norway said.

"So were you pleased with the way she behaved, Nevil?" Lou asked.

"She was splendid. I was relieved about the servo gear."

"Barnes didn't say a word," Lou said.

"Oh, I can tell you he was pleased all right. That ship flew just the way he intended. I *know* he was satisfied."

"So do you think he'll make the trip to Canada?" Lou asked.

"I know he wants to go, certainly," Norway replied.

Without a word, Charlotte got up from the table to clear things away.

About 9 o'clock, Lou took Norway back to the mast to supervise the minor repairs. A huge amount of activity was taking place, both on board and on the ground. The gasbags, fuel tanks and ballast tanks were being topped up for next morning's flight.

Lou returned home, thankful to be with Charlotte and not on that frigid airship. He was due on watch at 6:00 a.m. When he reached the chilly bedroom, he saw the candle was lit on Charlotte's beside table and she was sleeping. He smiled as he stripped off his clothes and, with his teeth chattering, carefully lifted the bedclothes and snuggled down against her warm, naked body. She felt wonderfully comforting.

"Man, I'm so lucky," he whispered.

"You're bloody freezing. Don't you *dare* put your feet on me!"

By the time Lou went aboard the ship next morning, Norway and his mechanics had made the repairs. Norway was nowhere to be found. He'd crawled under some blankets in one of the cabins in his teddy.

Speed trials had been planned during this flight test, but in one of his in-flight inspections Norway had discovered a loose sealing strip across the rudder hinge, causing the cover to flap. Speed trials would have to wait and more repairs made. *Howden R100* was brought back to the mast in the afternoon in freezing fog without fuss. She was then walked to the shed and put away for the Christmas holidays.

When they were leaving the hangar, Norway came up with a brilliant idea—at least *he* thought it was brilliant. And the more Lou thought about it, the more he liked it. Norway said he was thinking of asking his girlfriend, Frances, to go skiing in Switzerland for Christmas and suggested that Lou and Charlotte join them. "You can be chaperones," Norway said.

"We can be your *cover*, you mean, you dirty dog!" Lou said.

"No, I d-don't mean that at all. Come on, it'll be fun."

"I like the idea, Nev. It would be a nice break for Charlie. We haven't had any get-togethers since Freddie died. I know over Christmas she's gonna sit around moping."

"So you'll come?"

"Yes, I expect so, but there's one proviso: no screwing around. No creeping about in the middle of the night—you got that?"

"I'm sh-sh-shocked you'd even s-suggest such a thing!"

Since it was dark, Lou couldn't see Norway blushing from ear to ear.

20

HOLIDAYS IN SWITZERLAND & PARIS

Christmas 1929.

Five days later, after rushing around to get Charlotte a passport, all four were in Murren, Switzerland having a wonderful time. Most importantly for Lou, Charlotte got back to her old self. They'd traveled through France by train, during which time, she'd became more subdued. But once they'd crossed the border into Switzerland, the sheer beauty of the place took her breath away and her mood changed. Throughout the days after that, Charlotte was in high spirits, especially when learning to ski (much of the time on her behind). On the last night, she played the piano in the hotel and a group of vacationers gathered around for a singsong. It was the best vacation Lou and his party had ever had, and they said so. For Lou and Charlotte, it was like a second honeymoon. It lasted ten days.

When the holiday was over, Norway was happy to get back to work, resuming the tests on his airship. Lou had mixed emotions. He saw the pain the Cardington people were going through. He also knew Charlotte's mood would likely falter.

Just after the New Year, Thomson moved into a larger flat in Ashley Gardens with room for a study. He took on a parlor maid, to complement his present staff. Naturally, Sammie the cat went, too. Thomson sat at the credenza in the living room from where he usually wrote Marthe, her picture positioned in front of him, as always. Outside, the weather was foul; wind shook the window frames and rain beat on the glass.

Dearest Marthe,

Being a bone fide Englishman, naturally, I must talk about the weather. The New Year has burst upon us with a vengeance, with howling wind and torrential rain. I apologize for not replying sooner, but my schedule has been quite muddled. I'll be in Paris on Tuesday of next week on the pretext of attending a dinner at the Chamber of Commerce. This is a blatant lie, of course. My reason for being in Paris is to be with the woman I adore.

Fondest love always and forever,

your Kit.

The following week, Thomson set off in high spirits for Paris aboard an Imperial Airways flight, with thirteen other passengers. It turned out to be a bumpy ride and an even bumpier landing. On approaching Paris, they ran into impenetrable fog and had to turn back over Beauvais Ridge where they were violently buffeted about. One poor soul bumped his head on the ceiling. They landed safely in a field near Allonne with several mighty thuds.

A local man, with other peasants, led the passengers and crew to their humble cottages and gave them shelter. Eventually, a car took Thomson to Beauvais Railway Station and he made it to Paris from there, arriving at Marthe's apartment four hours late. Marthe had gathered a few mutual friends from Bucharest to see him. The trip turned out to be pleasant and successful regarding his official duties and his romantic ambitions.

Thomson spent four blissful days with Marthe, strolling the streets and parks of Paris. They walked along the bank of the Seine, crossing the bridge to Notre Dame, where Marthe prayed fervently and lit four candles—for her father, her maid, her priest, and one for someone else —she wouldn't say who. Thomson hoped it was for him. She knew he was wondering and looked at him with that maddening half smile. Did he detect a trace of guilt, too? He wasn't sure.

They climbed the hundreds of steps to Montmartre and went into Sacre-Coeur Basilica, where Marthe prayed again. They had splendid meals, some simple, some lavish. A whole day was spent in the magnificent Musée du Louvre, soaking up its treasures. In all that time, although he longed to, he never brought up the subject of his marriage proposal. He stayed at the British Embassy for one night and the rest of the time at Marthe's apartment at Quay de Bourbon. After these few days, which filled Thomson's soul with almost total contentment, it was time to get back to the daily slog of helping MacDonald run the Empire, and to continue driving the Airship Program forward. He left Marthe a note before departing.

Dearest One,

My sincerest appreciation for your gracious hospitality. As always, you have encouraged me to carry on in the fight we call 'life.' These days with you have been magically calming and I'm ready to carry on and meet the challenges that lie in wait. Again, I thank you, darling Marthe. I hope you are able to come to England for Easter.

Au revoir.

My eternal devotion,

Kit.

21

BACK TO WORK

January 1930.

Upon his return to London, Thomson went to the House of Lords to make his report. He'd be breaking the bad news during this speech. He hoped the hostile lords would either be absent, or not pick up on all his statements. He spoke as softly as he could, since most were deaf.

"I'm here to deliver a progress report concerning the Airship Program I introduced in 1924," Thomson said. Aggressive mumbling and sneering began around the chamber. Smirks appeared on jowled faces. "I must remind you, we never claimed to be building two airships that would take to the skies and circumvent the globe immediately. No, that wasn't the case at all!"

"*I* thought you did," someone muttered.

"What *did* you say, then?" asked another.

"What did he say? I can't hear him."

"If any blame is to be cast concerning the lateness of these projects —I stand here ready to accept that blame. Please understand such aircraft are experimental and cannot be rushed. Overseas testing is due to begin this year with *Howden R100* flying to Canada in June and *Cardington R101* flying to India in September after insertion of an extra bay ..."

There was silence in the chamber until that sank in.

"Extra bay!"

"What extra bay! What's that for?"

"What's he up to now?"

"More expense!"

"Good money after bad!"

"What did he say? Speak up man!"

Jeering broke out on all sides as Thomson attempted to justify his policies. It became deafening when he announced how much more money would be needed to continue the program.

The weight reduction of *Cardington R101* continued and as soon as the weather allowed, resumption of flight-testing *Howden R100* began. But before that, all remedial work had to be completed. The major issue was the repair of the outer cover securing system. It was found that the wires holding the cover in place chafed on the traverse girders, causing them to break and the cover to become loose and flap around. This meant the wiring had to be replaced and rerouted and the cover had to be laced up again. It was a massive task, but a vitally important one. On Norway's birthday, January 17th, Lou called him in York, where he'd returned for a break.

"Happy birthday, pal! You need to get your ass back down here pronto. We're taking your big balloon for a ride tomorrow morning. You need to be here by 5:00 a.m. sharp."

"Oh, bugger! The weather's bloody awful."

"It'll be calmer than a monk on morphine in the morning, 'ol buddy—first time in weeks."

"All right. I'll be there," Norway said.

"They're leavin' with you, or without you," Lou told him.

"Let Burney know—he wants to go."

By the time Norway got there, *Howden R100* had been pulled out and moored at the mast. Norway had bought himself a newish car, a Singer Coupe. It was covered in ice, inside and out, and so were Norway and his passenger, a calculator from Howden.

"Oh crap, Nev, look at you!" Lou exclaimed.

"The weather's been atrocious—ice and freezing fog all the way. We've been driving at twenty miles an hour all night," Norway said.

"Well, at least you've got *four wheels* now. You're late, but don't worry. They were two hours behind schedule walking her out."

They went to the tower and boarded the airship where Norway thawed out in the dining room with Burney over breakfast. The usual unfriendly R.A.W. officials were on board. A top speed requirement was stipulated in the contract and Cardington was anxious to find out if the airship could meet that requirement. Half an hour later, the captain gave the order to slip and they climbed above the fog into clear blue sky. Airspeed indicators had been set up and during the course of the day Booth pushed the ship to full speed. Scott appeared displeased. They were well over the speed requirement.

"What's the reading?" Burney asked.

"Eighty-one miles an hour," Norway called back.

"Must be something wrong with the instrumentation," an R.A.W. official said.

Scott scowled. "Something strange is going on with this cover. Look at it!" The cover was fluttering. They peered at it though the windows.

"I'm sure this isn't anything serious," Burney said.

"She must be under a lot of stress, I'd say, looking at that," Scott grumbled.

"Nevil, get some riggers and inspect this ship from end to end," Burney instructed.

"There's something seriously wrong with this airship," Scott persisted.

"Now steady on. Don't get carried away!" Burney cautioned.

Norway climbed about inside the airship with a gang of riggers, including Nervous Nick. They checked every inch of the structure and Norway determined that under full power no part of the airship became overstressed. Lou, McWade and Atherstone and two other R.A.W. officials joined them for the inspection and they, too, agreed. When they returned to the control car with their findings, Scott still wasn't satisfied.

"What we h-have is a har-harmonic con-condition caused by the eddying w-wind currents at high speed. It's n-nothing serious," Norway explained.

"As far as I'm concerned, this airship is substandard," Scott snapped.

Burney had the answer. "This is easily solved. We're ten miles an hour over specification requirements. By the way Scott, while we're on the subject: what top speed did your ship reach?"

"You have no business asking such questions," Scott snarled.

"Here's what we'll do. I'll instruct my team to put restrictors on the throttles so she'll only be able to reach a maximum speed of seventy, in accordance with the contract requirements. At cruising speeds up to seventy, the cover is completely normal with no signs of fluttering."

"You'll do *no such thing*," Scott growled.

"There's nothing wrong with this airship and you're trying to make out there is—and I wonder why!" Burney said. "We've met our obligations—which is more than I can say for you people at the Royal Airship Works!"

The final acceptance trial for the Howden airship began on January 27th and lasted until January 29th, amounting to fifty-four hours of continuous flight. The designated *Howden R100* flight crew was on board, including Jessup and Billy as riggers. Lou, since his promotion, served on both ships as third officer. Sky Hunt also flew in both on an 'as needed' basis.

Howden R100 left the mast around 8:00 a.m. in mist, which turned to rain with winds over fifty-five mph. These were the worst conditions Lou had flown in to date, but he didn't find the motion of the ship unduly worrying. She pitched slightly, but behaved obediently to her controls. They traveled to Oxford, unable to see the ground, and then toward Bristol and down to the southern tip of Cornwall.

Some hours later, they flew over the Channel Isles toward the North Sea, where they spent the night cruising around in the dark. A four-hour watch-keeping routine was in place, and Lou got plenty of rest in a comfortable cabin. He slept for much of the night over the North Sea and found they were crossing the coast over Norfolk on their way to London when he emerged for breakfast. Over London, they peered down into thick, greasy fog. It cleared for a minute, revealing Tower Bridge and the Tower of London. They headed south again for Torbay in Devon. In the vicinity of Eddystone Lighthouse, turning trials were carried out on both port and starboard helm, using the light as a point of reference. They spent that night cruising the English Channel between England and France, traveling to Portland and then on to the Scilly Isles in the Atlantic.

In the morning, Lou was in the control car as the ship traveled over Cornwall, the south-west peninsula of England. It was a beautiful sunny morning—a delightful contrast after so much lousy weather. Mist floated in the valleys like fluffy clouds in varying colors of white, gold and pink. Lou wished Charlotte could see it. Over the Bristol Channel, they traveled through more rain squalls. By afternoon, they were back in Cardington, moored to the mast. Lou and Norway were home at a reasonable time for dinner with Charlotte.

Norway was able to stay the night this time and they spent the evening together. However, the happy mood Charlotte had exhibited in Switzerland had disappeared. She'd returned to her moody self once the ships had taken to the air again.

Trials were concluded and *Howden R100* officially accepted by the Air Ministry, whereupon the penultimate stage payment of forty thousand pounds was paid to Vickers. The final payment of ten thousand pounds would become due after a successful voyage to Canada. After more visual inspections in the air, the fluttering cover wasn't mentioned again. *Howden R100* was put into her shed for more remedial work and maintenance. There she would remain until May.

22

THE DINNER PARTY

April 1, 1930.

A t the end of March, Princess Marthe returned to London and Buck drove her to her favorite suite at the Ritz, where more of Thomson's special roses waited with a card of greeting.

Beloved Marthe,

I am sorry I could not meet you and that I'm unable to be with you this evening. Cabinet meetings till late, I'm afraid. Tomorrow I'll send the car to pick you up at six-thirty to bring you here for dinner with our distinguished guests. I am longing to see you. Until tomorrow evening then,

My deepest love,

Kit.

The following evening, Thomson, dressed in a black, woolen overcoat and matching trilby, waited in the shadows outside his apartment building in Ashley Gardens, close to Westminster Cathedral. Big Ben began striking seven. His breath came out in white puffs and he had heart palpitations. Bitterly cold, he rubbed his hands together. Presently, he spotted the headlights of his limousine and edged to the curb. The car drew up and Thomson opened the passenger door. Marthe, swathed in mink, eased her way out. He took her hand.

"My dearest Marthe."

"So lovely to see you, Kit," Marthe responded, her cheek pressed to his, her French accented whisper warming his frozen ear and arousing him. He kissed her delicate hand.

"Come, dear lady, let me take you to my new flat. Our dinner guests are waiting."

He led Marthe through a marble entrance hall to a small elevator and they traveled up to the flat. Daisy, the new parlor maid, opened the door. The princess swept into the reception room, pausing for Daisy to remove her furs. Underneath, Marthe wore a pale blue, narrow-waisted, chiffon dress, which almost reached her silver, open-toed shoes. Deep red nail polish perfectly matched her lipstick. Around her neck, she wore a necklace of diamonds, which complemented her diamond earrings. Her shining, dark hair was gathered up tight to the head and crowned by a small diamond tiara.

"You are truly magnificent, darling!" Thomson said, kissing her hand again. He turned to Daisy. "We'll go in now."

Daisy obediently pushed open the double doors, revealing the spacious, bright yellow and white accented sitting room. MacDonald and his companion sat opposite each other on couches positioned each side of a statuary marble fireplace, where a log fire blazed in the hearth. Between them was a coffee table laden with half-finished cocktails. A huge guilt mirror hung above the mantel. Thomson studied Marthe as she briefly gazed at her own reflection as she approached MacDonald, who sprung to his feet. Lady Wilson remained seated.

"Thank goodness you're here at last!" MacDonald exclaimed. "Thomson's been a bundle of nerves—and I can't say as I blame him! You look positively stunning." MacDonald raised her hand to his lips.

"Ramsay," Marthe whispered, her eyes burning into his. "So lovely to see you again."

"You know Lady Wilson, don't you, Marthe?" Thomson said.

"Yes, of course. We're *old* friends," Marthe answered, giving Lady Wilson a sincere smile. After greetings and more cocktails, everyone moved to the dining room where Gwen served a fish starter course.

"I was just admiring your carpet, CB," Lady Wilson said.

"It's precious to me. It was presented to me in Kurdistan," Thomson said grandly.

"The funny thing is—I used to own its identical twin," Marthe said.

Thomson withered visibly. He hated mention of it.

"Really. And don't you still?" MacDonald asked.

"No, it perished in the flames when the wretched Germans burned down my house in Romania during the war."

"Good Lord! What reason did they have to do such a thing?" Lady Wilson asked.

"They believed I was keeping British secret documents there—which, of course, I was. This was in the early days of our friendship, wasn't it Kit?"

"Yes, and very nearly the last!" Thomson said.

"Oh, you poor thing!" Lady Wilson said. "It must have been awful for you."

Thomson appeared sheepish. He wasn't proud of the episode. For years after the war, he regretted storing those documents at Marthe's house. It was foolish and naive. He worried it may have diminished him in her eyes.

"It was a dreadful occurrence. Now, Marthe shares this one with me. It's my talisman. As long as I possess it, Marthe and I shall remain close."

MacDonald lifted his glass. "Then I say God bless you, CB. Guard it with your life!"

"Hear, hear!" said Lady Wilson.

Gwen served duck à l'orange for the main course and Daisy recharged their glasses.

"I'm trying to talk Kit into coming to Paris for Easter," Marthe said.

"Why don't you both come to Chequers? The blossoms will be bursting out in all their glory," MacDonald said.

"I cannot be here at Easter, but will you ask me in July, Ramsay?"

"July! That's a long way off. Do you think I'll still be in office, Marthe?"

"Of course. Tory friends of mine have said so."

"You can't believe a word they say," MacDonald said, with an ironic smile.

Lady Wilson glanced at Thomson. "Tell us about your recent trip to Paris, CB. Did you have fun?"

"Wonderful!"

"Tell them what happened on the way over, Kit," Marthe said.

"We ran into fog and couldn't land in Paris. We ended up having a bumpy ride over Beauvais Ridge, then a rough landing in a field near Allonne."

"How dreadful!" exclaimed Lady Wilson. "Were you all right?"

"You didn't tell me about this," MacDonald said with surprise.

"Oh, everything turned out well. I didn't want to tell you. I know how you worry. And you might ban me from flying—which might be embarrassing for the Minister of State for Air."

"What happened?" MacDonald asked.

"A delightful little rabbit poacher—a Monsieur Rabouille!—came running out of the woods and led us to some old, stone cottages, where these wonderful peasants took us in. What a place! Desolate and unforgiving, but wonderful just the same. He kissed my hand when he saw me. Monsieur Rabouille, the rabbit poacher! Splendid fellow! I hope we meet again, someday."

"So you actually went inside one of the cottages?" Lady Wilson asked.

"Yes, I sat huddled by the fireplace while this wonderful lady kept me plied with wine. What an experience it was! I was so touched by it —those people are the salt of the earth. I pulled out my wallet and said, 'Let me pay you for your kind hospitality, dear lady.' 'Non, non, non. I have had the pleasure of your conversation, monsieur,' she said. Nevertheless, I tucked a franc under the seat cushion for her to find later."

"Oh, that was so sweet of you," Lady Wilson exclaimed.

"'You are the luckiest of folk to live in this place, Madam. You have peace,' I said to her. She just said, 'Plutôt un très grand isolement.' Total isolation, more like. 'I love your people, Madam. This country is so good and so beautiful—someday I shall come here to die,' I told her."

"Oh Kit, how could you say such a thing!" Marthe said, her eyes filling with tears. "You should never speak that way." She looked in desperation at Lady Wilson. "He didn't tell me he'd said that."

Daisy cleared the dinner plates while Gwen served a dessert of rhubarb tart and cream.

"Come, Marthe, let me take you in the other room. You can compose yourself and we can talk," Lady Wilson said.

The two women went into the sitting room while Thomson and MacDonald ate dessert and drank their coffee. After that, they drank brandy and smoked cigars. The ladies' desserts remained untouched.

"I'm astonished it upset her so much," Thomson said.

"She cares about you a lot, you know. I can see that," MacDonald said. Thomson sat in silence, pondering Marthe's emotional outburst—it'd seemed genuine.

Maybe it's time I spoke to her again.

Later, when the dinner guests had gone and the servants had finished clearing away, Marthe and Thomson sat beside the fireplace drinking liqueurs.

"Have you considered my proposal any further, Marthe?" Thomson inquired gently.

"Oh, Kit, you know it's impossible."

"If the voyage to India is successful and I'm appointed Viceroy, anything will be possible, my dearest, I can assure you of that. The viceroy position requires him to be married."

"What do you mean, '*if* it's successful'?"

"Promise me, Marthe, that we'll discuss the subject before the voyage. I haven't spoken of it for nearly a year and I will not speak of it until then."

Marthe sat up and looked directly into his eyes. "Kit, will your airship *really* be safe? Please tell me the truth."

"Marthe, this whole voyage is about my destiny and I hope yours, too, my darling."

He knew power was her aphrodisiac. She turned to him and he took her forcefully into his arms. He kissed her passionately—more passionately than he'd ever done before.

23

THE WHISTLEBLOWER

Sunday June 29, 1930.

The guns raged on both sides. Boom! Boom! Boom! Lou lay there in the darkness alongside twenty-five other combat-weary soldiers.   Boom! Boom! Boom!

Suddenly, a tremendous explosion ripped through their deep bunker, blasting a mountain of rubble, earth, wood whalers and body parts everywhere. He was entombed and couldn't move his legs. A terrible pain in his chest and pressure in his lungs made it hard to breathe and he was freezing cold. He tried to suck in foul-smelling air and smoke, realizing he'd been hit. Reaching into his top pocket, he pulled out his lighter and spun the flint wheel with his thumb. The blessed flame burst before his eyes. He looked down in horror at his chest and watched blood oozing from a gaping hole. It spread over his shredded tunic and over the ground like a creeping red blanket. The torso of another buried man lay across his legs, trapping them. He tried to scream for help, but he had no breath and no sound came. His thin flame was replaced by a bright shaft of light penetrating the dust and smoke. He watched a gloved-hand pulling away rubble from outside his tomb. A grotesque giant fly's head pushed its way through the hole babbling at him in guttural gibberish. As his eyes focused, Lou realized it was man wearing a gas mask with goggles over his eyes and a German helmet. Had he come to rescue him, or to kill him?

Boom! Boom! Boom! There it was again.

"Lou, Lou, wake up, wake up!" Charlotte urgently whispered, shaking his arm. "Someone's banging on the door."

"What? What's happening?"

Lou, unable to move, gasped for breath. He felt sticky, warm blood running down across his stomach and could taste it in his mouth.

"Lou, Lou, wake up."

"What? What? What time is it?"

"After midnight. Something awful must have happened."

Lou opened his eyes, beginning to come round and put his hand to his chest with dread. It seemed dry, but the awful pain remained. He pulled back the covers and, clutching his chest, rolled out of bed. He switched on the bedside lamp and looked at his chest. No blood. He slipped his dressing gown on over his pajamas.

"See who it is, but do be careful."

After switching on the dim landing light, he moved down the creaking stairs, clinging to the banister.

Boom! Boom! Boom!

"All right! All right! Damn it. I'm coming."

Lou, on opening the front door, was surprised to see the rotund figure of Inspector Fred McWade. He was hopping from one foot to the other. He looked frantic. The night was warm. McWade wore what he always wore—white shirt, grey sports jacket, tie, and flannel trousers—held up from his ankles with metal bicycle clips. It looked like he was wearing plus fours, ready to play golf. He pulled off his tweed cap.

"Fred! What ever's wrong?"

"I've got to see you, Lou. It's very important."

"Come in, come in. What's going on?"

"I'm sorry, laddie, I know it's late, but I *must* talk to you," McWade said, pulling out a handkerchief to mop his dripping face and brow. Speech was difficult. He was wheezing and his breathing, labored.

Charlotte leaned over the railing on the top landing in her nightdress. She called down. "Lou, who is it? Is something wrong?"

"It's okay, honey. Fred McWade's come for a chat, that's all. It's only about work. Go back to bed. Everything's all right. Don't worry."

McWade stepped into the hallway. Lou pushed the living room door open. "Let's go in here. You can tell me what's eating you," he said, switching on the table lamps. Fred followed him and Lou silently closed the door.

"I'm sorry to come here like this, Lou. I hope I haven't upset Charlotte, but it couldn't wait."

Lou motioned for McWade to take a seat. "What the hell's the matter, Fred?"

"Lou, you're special," McWade said, sinking into an armchair. "I saw it ever since we pulled you off that wreck in the river up north. Someone upstairs thinks you're special, too."

"Charlotte?"

"*Almighty God!*"

"Oh, …yeah, right."

"I don't want to see anything happen to you, especially after what happened over the Humber. I want you to get out!" The more agitated McWade got, the thicker his Glaswegian accent became. Lou went to the sideboard and poured two full tumblers of Johnny Walker.

"Fred, you're gonna have to talk a bit slower for me." He handed the Scotch to McWade.

"Oh, thank you, son. I need this."

"Now calm down, Fred. What's up eh?"

Charlotte had slipped silently down the stairs and was now sitting on the bottom step. She could only make out odd words here and there, but what she heard alarmed her. She felt a desperate need to run out the front door. To be swallowed up by the darkness.

"Take the advice of an old man who's been in airships all his life. Get out of this business, fast." McWade pointed toward Cardington. "That thing up there is *a bloody deathtrap!*"

Lou knew McWade was one of the most experienced men in the country. He'd trained at the School of Military Engineering and joined the School of Ballooning in the Royal Engineers before Lou was born. He'd worked on airship construction for government for years, becoming a senior man in the Airship Inspection Department—the A.I.D. Lou sipped his whisky and peered into his glass.

Both ships had been laid up in their sheds for most of the winter and into the spring. *Howden R100* had problems of her own, but fixable. The cover leaked. Water had shorted out the electrical systems and damaged the gas bags. The tail structure needed rebuilding after collapsing during one of her endurance test flights, and the second-hand engines caused trouble—just as Wallis knew they would. They'd need replacing.

By early summer, some modifications to *Cardington R101* had been completed, though not all. The rotting cover had only partly been removed and insertion of the extra bay hadn't even begun. Padding where gas bags rubbed against the structure had been attempted, haphazardly. In places where the cover hadn't been replaced, reinforcing strips of canvas had been glued over weak, friable areas, giving the ship a 'patched up' look.

Under the pretext of testing the ship after weight-reducing modifications, *Cardington R101* had been rushed out of her shed in questionable weather. In reality, she'd been brought out to participate in a publicity stunt. That June, the Royal Air Display took place and Air Ministry big shots thought it'd give the public a boost if *Cardington R101* came out and did a party piece in front of the King.

The airship was moored at the tower and immediately a ninety-foot tear was discovered on the starboard side and a forty-five-foot tear on port. Riggers dangled on ropes for hours in wind and rain in soft-soled shoes with needles and thread making repairs.

That week, the ship made several flights. Lt. Cmdr. Atherstone had gone to Canada to make preparations for *Howden R100's* arrival. Capt. Booth and Capt. Meager covered for him while Maurice Steff acted as second officer. Lou was on board for all these flights. It proved to be an unnerving experience, especially for Booth and Meager, not being used to *Cardington R101's* unpredictable behavior.

McWade had been on board with the A.I.D. and Lou could see he was unimpressed. On practice day, with Booth acting as first officer, Lou watched in horror as the ship, required to come in low over the crowd and dip her nose to the royal box, almost collided with an adjacent building. Cameron, the height coxswain, lowered the bow in salute, but it continued to drop sharply and he had difficulty bringing her back up. The journey home had been grim, the ship becoming increasingly heavy and uncontrollable. Irwin managed to get back to the tower by dumping fuel and water ballast as he'd been forced to do the year before.

The following day, Lou was on board with Meager as first officer this time. They needed to be over Hendon Aerodrome at 3:50 p.m. After spending several uneventful hours over London and Southend, Irwin brought the ship through rain showers to Hendon for the display, where Cameron managed to perform the salute to the Royal Box over a crowd of a hundred thousand people. It had been touch and go. Lou thought diving to within five hundred feet and pulling up sharply in front of the King was sheer lunacy—a stunt which could have easily resulted in catastrophe for the nation.

The homeward journey turned out to be as bad as the day before. As they passed through rain squalls, the bow kept dropping without warning. Water ballast and fuel were dumped all the way home. Irwin, Meager and Lou knew something was radically wrong. The loss of lift was dramatic—even after burning two tons of fuel, it was still necessary to drop another ten tons of ballast. In this condition, lightened or not, this airship could never make it to Egypt—let alone India.

Lou took another sip of whisky. "Fred, I can't just up and walk away. I represent the U.S. Navy. Besides, I couldn't leave the men, or Captain Irwin."

"Och, Lou, we fished you out of the bloody river once." He took a gulp of his drink. "You might not be so lucky next time. You should take Charlotte and go back to America." McWade put his hand to his head. "Oh, I'm sorry, that's none o' my business."

"And what about *you?*" Lou asked. "You'll be flying in both ships —to Canada and then India."

"It doesn't matter about me. I'm old. It's all those young boys I'm concerned about. I don't want them on my conscience."

"Look, Fred, I think you're just upset. Granted these flights this week didn't go so well—"

"Go so well! They were *a bloody disaster!* She nearly dived into the ground nine times by my reckoning. I don't know how that boy held the damned thing up. I've had enough—something's got to be done. You're the only person I can talk to." With that, McWade took out a white envelope from his inside pocket and held it up. Lou figured it must be his resignation.

Ah, this is why he came at this ungodly hour!

"I want you to read this," McWade said. "I finished it half an hour ago."

He leaned forward in his armchair and held it out to Lou. Lou switched on the table lamp behind him as the clock on the mantelpiece (a wedding present from Charlotte's parents), chimed prettily. It was 2:00 a.m. He began reading. His eyes widened when he saw the title of the addressee. As he read the beautiful script, Lou heard McWade's broad Scottish accent accompanied by the gently ticking clock.

86, Barmeston Rd.
Bedford.
29th June, 1930.

The Director of Aeronautical Inspection,
Air Ministry, Whitehall,
London.

Re: HMA CARDINGTON R101

Dear Sir,

Owing to the very serious state of affairs concerning His Majesty's Airship Cardington R101, I am forced to write directly to you. On the 26th of June, I issued a 'Permit to Fly,' dated 20th June and valid until 19th July 1930. Due to modifications of the harness system in an effort to increase gas capacity, the gas bags are now tight against longitudinals and rubbing against nuts and bolts and all parts of the structure. In my opinion, these modifications have led to a dangerous situation with thousands of holes being made, causing loss of gas at an alarming rate.

Over the years, padding has been an acceptable method of repair in isolated instances. Padding to the extent required in this case is totally unacceptable. The gas bags in this airship were recently removed and repaired, but after recent test flights, they are full of holes again. When padding is installed, these areas become hidden from view and corrosion of the structure usually ensues, which is another reason why padding is unacceptable.

Until this matter is taken seriously, and an acceptable solution put forward, I cannot recommend to you an extension of the present Permit to Fly or any further Permit or Certificate.

Yours Respectfully,
F. McWade,
Inspector-In-Charge,
Airship Inspection Dept.(A.I.D.)
Royal Airship Works, Cardington.

Lou put the letter down in his lap and rested his head on the back of the armchair. "My God, Fred, you're taking a hell of a risk, aren't you?"

"I know this could cost me ma job and ma pension, but that's nothing compared to the risk they're taking."

"I'm not sure this is a good idea."

"Are you advising me not to post it?"

"No, I'm not saying that. If you feel this strongly, then you must— but understand you will become the most hated man in Cardington."

"I needed your opinion."

"I wouldn't dissuade you, Fred, and I have to say, I admire your guts."

"That makes me feel better, laddie."

"But look, Fred, these men aren't fools. They're gonna add an extra bay. It should perform a lot better then, don't you think?"

"Nay, laddie. They committed a grave mistake when they let those harnesses out. Those valves might become detached. She's unstable now—the bags are surging up and down and back and forth. And adding an extra bay will only weaken her resilience. That ship's damned now. I have to tell you in all candor: these bloody geniuses at Cardington are outmatched." McWade swallowed the remnants of his glass and got up. "I'll be off, then. This letter is going in the post-box first thing in the morning."

Lou smiled weakly. At least McWade would have time to sleep on it. Maybe he'd change his mind by morning. "All right, Fred. Ride home safely. I can take you home on my motorbike, if you like?"

"No, no, son. I'll be fine."

Lou stood at the front door and watched the old man peddle off down the street, wobbling as he went. When Lou got back to the bedroom, he found Charlotte sitting on the bed staring at the floor.

"I thought you'd be asleep, honey," Lou said.

"It didn't sound good. That man is worried sick, isn't he?"

"He'll be all right, once the modifications are done."

"I told you—that ship's cursed!"

They climbed into bed. Lou lay on his back reflecting on their approach to the tower on Saturday, minutes before the arrival of a violent storm. They' d got the ship moored just in time.

When they reached the tower, Colmore was waiting with Richmond, Rope and Scott to make an inspection. Sky Hunt was already on board. Colmore was anxious to know if the modifications to lighten her had made any noticeable difference. During these past few days the ship had no load to speak of, so these flights should indicate clearly if the ship was airworthy. When the extra bay was inserted, the additional lift would be used up by the weight of passengers and extra fuel. If she couldn't fly now, she *never* could.

Once locked onto the tower, the gas hoses were connected to recharge the gas bags and a thorough inspection carried out from bow to stern with everybody in attendance. With the wind blowing a gale and rain coming down in torrents, this was the perfect time. The first obvious thing was that the cover leaked badly. In no time everybody was soaking wet. The damp atmosphere accentuated the smell of cattle's intestines.

As the ship rolled and was buffeted about, deep sighs from the gas valves were loud enough for all to hear. The creaking and squeaking of gas bags rubbing against the structure was no less unnerving. Richmond's face expressed disappointment. He spoke to Irwin first.

"Captain, assuming your calculations are correct, you're losing ten tons of lift every day. Is that correct?"

"Absolutely correct. Commander Remington can attest to that."

"We're pumping in more than 300,000 cubic feet of gas a day just to keep her afloat at the tower," Lou said.

Richmond looked at Sky Hunt for confirmation. "That's correct, sir," Hunt said.

"This is all *very disturbing*, indeed," Richmond declared, glaring at the officers.

Lou saw McWade about to explode.

"It's more than *disturbing*, sir. When you let out the harnesses, you allowed the gas bags to become riddled with holes throughout this airship. That's why you're losing gas at an alarming rate and why she's unstable. This situation is *totally unacceptable!* I cannot allow this."

"What are you trying to say? Speak up, man!" Richmond erupted.

McWade replied as though speaking to a child. "I'm saying that, as far as I'm concerned, this airship is *totally* unsafe."

Richmond was enraged. "Just who the hell do you think you are?"

"Who do I think I am? I'll tell you exactly who I am, sir. I'm the man who stood and watched *R38* break in two and blow up, killing dozens of British and American young men, decapitating them, dismembering them, blowing them to bits, drowning them and burning them to a crisp. I'm the man who's trying to avoid more of our boys sharing the same fate. That's who I am, sir!"

Richmond stormed off down the catwalk. Lou figured he was about ready to break down.

Lou lay in bed with Charlotte beside him. He was sure she wasn't asleep even though she lay perfectly still. He remembered feeling sorry for Colmore; the man's troubles seemed to be multiplying daily. When McWade made his damning statement, Colmore stood there at a loss, water pouring from his hair, running down his face, and dripping off the end of his nose. Scott remained quiet. Rope cradled his chin, deep in thought.

A couple of days after McWade's late night visit, *Cardington R101* was returned to her shed and work resumed on replacing the cover. The question of the holes in the gas bags still needed to be addressed. Lou visited the shed to see how work was progressing. He stopped by McWade's office in the corner.

"Hi, Fred. How're things?"

Fred closed the door, his manner conspiratorial. "I posted that letter," he whispered.

McWade had just brewed a pot of tea and poured a cup for Lou, his chin stuck out defiantly.

"Brave man," Lou said.

"Och, I'm not brave at all. I just don't want to see bad things happen to these men—or this city, come to that."

Lou sipped his tea, feeling awkward and disloyal. Sometimes he knew too much. He wished people wouldn't confide in him, but they did. He'd keep it all to himself and see what happened. No doubt Colmore would bring it up with him.

"I expect you've got Whitehall in a flurry, Fred."

"I bloody well hope so," McWade said.

Lou laughed. "Maybe they'll scrap the whole program, eh?"

"Better now than later," McWade replied. He finished his tea and put down his cup. "I told yer, I've been in airships all my life. The older I get, the more futile it all seems to me. It's all been for nought."

As Lou expected, Colmore confided in him the next day. He told him the chief of the inspection department at the Air Ministry had called him and told him he'd received Fred McWade's letter. They were 'all in a tizzy about it' down there.

"He asked me if this was as serious as it sounded," Colmore said.

"Did you tell him it was?" Lou asked.

"How could I do that? We're our own judge and jury here. How would it look if I said 'Yes, actually, we've built an un-flyable airship.'?"

"Sir, who cares about looks. We're talking about people's lives. Here was a chance to buy more time."

"Easy for you to say. Heads would roll."

"So what did you tell him, sir?"

"I told him it was nothing we couldn't handle."

Lou was frustrated. "How?" he asked skeptically.

"By padding. It's done all the time. And we'll do it again."

"McWade's a highly experienced man. Maybe we should all listen to him."

"Lou, I'm in an impossible situation. Can't you see that? Can you imagine his Lordship—he'd go stark raving mad."

"That would be his problem, sir. You should remind him of his own 'Safety First' policy."

Colmore put his hand to his forehead and sighed. "Lord Thomson told us a story—something that had happened in his early life involving Lord Kitchener in South Africa. I won't go into details, but it was intended as a warning, or a threat—an ultimatum really. I'm haunted by it."

Lou was fascinated and wanted to find out more, but the phone on Colmore's desk rang. Colmore picked it up. "Sir Sefton, how nice to hear your voice, sir ...Yes, hmm, okay ...Yes, I'm sure that can be arranged. Right you are ...Ah yes, I'll bring him along, too," Colmore said, looking at Lou as he hung up. He lowered his voice. "That was the Director of Civil Aviation—Sir Sefton Brancker."

"Yes."

"He's calling a meeting. Very hush, hush. He said Thomson's girlfriend is coming to town next week and they've been invited to Chequers. While he's out of the way, he wants me, Irwin and you, to meet with him at his home in Surrey. He's very concerned about what's been going on this week with the ship—and about McWade's letter."

"Okay, sir. Sure, I'll come, if I can be helpful."

"He thinks a lot of you, Lou. Saturday morning, 9:00 a.m."

"Sir, may I ask you something?"

"By all means."

"Suppose you were asked to judge *Howden R100?* I mean, suppose the ships were reversed and they had *Cardington R101* and you had theirs. What would you do?"

"I'd declare their ship unsafe and forbid them to fly it."

"Then you should do the same thing with your own ship."

Colmore screwed up his eyes and then looked down at his desk. "We're in a box. We're stuck. We have to do as we're told—do our duty."

Lou understood Colmore's dilemma. It would be interesting to see how it played out.

Later that week, Lou was in Shed No.1 again. An Air Ministry dispatch rider came striding into the shed toward him. "I'm looking for a Mr. Frederick McWade, sir," he said, reading from a white envelope. Lou pointed to the end office in the wooden structure in the corner of the shed. He watched the man walk over and knock on McWade's door. McWade opened it, surprised at first. He took the letter and closed the door. A few moments later, McWade came bursting out, his face crimson.

"Lou, come and see this," McWade said, disgusted. They went back to McWade's office and closed the door. McWade handed the letter to Lou. He read the envelope:

Director of Aeronautical Inspection,
Air Ministry, Whitehall, London.

Lou scanned the letter. He read aloud when he reached the heart of it:

" *.....I have discussed the matter you raised at length with the Director of Airship Development, Wing Commander Colmore. Naturally, I understand it is absolutely essential that contact between the ship's structure and the gas bags is eliminated. I am sure you understand it would be quite impossible to change the framing of the airship at this juncture. Therefore, the only solution is to install padding. It will be your responsibility to ensure all points of contact which could cause damage are properly padded."*

Yours Truly - Da-dee-da-dee-da!"

Lou whistled. "Nice!"

"*Bastards!*" McWade whispered.

"You put Colmore in a bind," Lou said.

"He's gutless. He'll go along with anything they say."

"He's in a difficult position, Fred."

"This seals our fate," McWade said, almost to himself.

"What are you going to do?"

"I'll oversee the padding, I suppose. And they'll all be laughing at me while I do it. I'll do everything in my power to make the damn thing safe. I'll not walk away—not yet."

"You're a damned *good man*, Fred."

"Aye, *'damned'* is right!"

McWade was close to tears.

24

CHEQUERS & A MEETING WITH BRANCKER

Friday & Saturday July 4 & 5, 1930.

Marthe returned to London in July and this time Thomson was able to meet her at Victoria. He took pleasure in standing on the platform under his umbrella, waiting for her glistening train to come gliding in. He patiently watched it grind to a halt. Marthe alighted from the train, minus the irritating Isadora. They greeted each other warmly, but formally, and were driven by Buck across London and Buckinghamshire to Chequers. Marthe was in an excitable mood, chattering like a young girl. Thomson couldn't remember seeing her this bubbly for a long time, if ever. She made him feel elated, too. She'd certainly warmed to him this past year.

"There's something special about Fridays, don't you find, Kit?" Marthe said.

Thomson took her hand. "Even for princesses?"

"Yes, I'm happy to be here and I'm so looking forward to seeing your dear friend."

"*Our* dear friend! He's dying to meet you again, Marthe."

Forty minutes after leaving the northwest suburbs, they reached the winding lanes of Buckinghamshire, flanked by hedgerows and swaying beeches, leading up to the imposing mansion. Marthe was in a dream as they entered this magical place—a place where prime ministers relaxed, played and sometimes made policy. This was where they met with the most important men in the world and came to agreements. It was also where they entertained and bedded their mistresses.

Thomson took pleasure in watching Marthe's darting eyes. She took in every detail. Soon she'd be writing it all down. She stared up at the red brick building looming above them. Thomson knew the façade's air of enchantment cloaked an underlying menace. This came from its long history—no doubt bad things had happened within these walls. The car reached the impressive wrought-iron gates and a nondescript man in gray appeared.

"Afternoon, Lord Thomson, nice to see you back, sir," he said in a Cockney accent.

"Hello, Robards," Thomson said.

"Who is that?" Marthe whispered.

"The policeman in charge of the Prime Minister's security."

The gates were opened by two roughly dressed men.

"And here are two more, disguised as gardeners—imported from Lossiemouth," Thomson explained.

Marthe gave him a teasing look. "You British are so cunning."

"I've told him he needs more security out here, but he won't listen."

The limousine cruised slowly past the center lawn and Hygeia, the health goddess, up to the entrance. The gravel driveway crunched under their wheels in welcome. The main front door opened and Ishbel came out to greet them, while the gardeners unloaded their luggage. Thomson kissed Ishbel's cheek and turned to Marthe to make introductions.

"Ishbel, this is Princess Marthe Bibesco. Our lives have been inextricably linked since before the war."

Ishbel was shy. Marthe took both her hands. "Ishbel! What a beautiful name. Oh, I can see a striking resemblance. You are so very lucky—your father is such a handsome man."

This made Ishbel more shy and embarrassed. "Welcome. Please come in and I'll show you to your rooms, Princess," she said.

"Please call me Marthe."

"Very well, Marthe. My father told me which rooms you're to have."

"And you speak just like him. *Captivating!*" Marthe exclaimed, pressing her hands together. Ishbel smiled and led them upstairs and along a wide corridor that creaked underfoot. The walls were decorated in flowery, brown and tan wallpaper. She stopped at Thomson's room.

"Christopher is in here—where he usually sleeps." She moved on to the next room. "And you, Marthe, are in here—the Lee Room— reserved for special guests, or heads of state."

Ishbel gestured for Marthe to enter. Marthe's eyes lit up when she spotted the hand-carved four-poster bed. "I'm so honored," she said.

The room was decorated in floral pink and green wallpaper with coordinating drapes and cushions. Marthe went to the window and looked across the gardens, which were bursting with color. MacDonald had not exaggerated their beauty.

"There are two bathrooms, one each end of the corridor. There's plenty of hot water if you'd like a bath after your journey," Ishbel said.

Thomson and Marthe spent the rest of the afternoon settling in. Marthe relaxed in a hot bath, savoring the place she hoped would become part of her life, as it had for Thomson. She was soon looking her best for MacDonald's arrival and for cocktails before dinner. She wore a long, tan, satin cocktail dress with a subtle, sculptured floral design showing a hint of silver and pale-blue. The dress, from her Parisian dressmaker, was low-key and understated, narrow at the waist and covered her slender neck. She kept with her a designer wrap in a slightly darker shade, to throw around her shoulders later.

Once Marthe was ready, she sat down at a writing table in her room. She wrote down her thoughts in a leather-bound diary, together with vivid descriptions of her observations since arriving at Victoria. She'd use them in a future memoir, hopefully a best seller.

After half an hour, Thomson knocked on Marthe's door dressed in a black evening suit with a pale-blue tie. He kissed her hand. "Marthe you look quite lovely, my dear." He breathed in. "And your perfume is divine."

Just after 5 o'clock, they heard MacDonald's blue Rolls-Royce crackling over the driveway. Marthe went to wait in the reception hall and Thomson joined her. He watched as the butler opened the front door and MacDonald walked in, his face beaming, not taking his eyes off Marthe. He raised her hand and kissed it, looking into her face. Thomson felt quite invisible. MacDonald let go of her hand and she stepped closer for him to kiss her on both cheeks. He, too, breathed in her perfume.

"Dearest Marthe, welcome to Chequers. I am most honored to have you as my guest."

"I've been so looking forward to this visit, Ramsay."

"The feeling is mutual, my dear."

"*And* you're still in office!"

"You bring me good luck, obviously."

Ishbel joined them as MacDonald turned to Thomson.

"Come. This deserves a celebratory drink!"

They went into the Great Room, where they sank into the huge armchairs. Amid the splendid paintings and lofty ceilings they drank cocktails served by the butler, a kindly Scot dressed in black, also from Lossiemouth. The room dwarfed the small party, making them feel out of place. Later they moved to the cosier dining room, where dark oak paneling was brightened by late afternoon sunshine through leaded windows. As in other rooms, original paintings hung from the walls and over the carved mantel. They sat down to a three-course dinner and polite small talk, after which, Marthe faded fast.

"Well, Ramsay, as thrilled as I am to be in your company, I'm longing to climb into that four-poster bed," she said, her eyelids fluttering wearily.

"You must be terribly tired, my dear, after your journey. Be off and get your beauty sleep. Tomorrow we'll take you for a long walk," MacDonald said.

Thomson and MacDonald stood and Marthe kissed first MacDonald and then Thomson. Ishbel excused herself and the two women went upstairs while the men moved to the Hawtrey Room, a comfortable drawing room, overlooking the gardens. The butler brought a bottle of Courvoisier and glasses on a tray, closed the curtains and left.

"Are you making headway, CB?"

"I couldn't be happier, Ramsay. I believe the planets are aligning."

"Good."

"And if it's any indication, Marthe's stopped bringing her confounded maidservant, Isadora. She's left in Paris these days."

"That must be a relief."

"She's like a damned watchdog."

"Any progress on the matrimonial front?"

"Marthe has become closer and more loving of late. I pushed too hard last year, which had a detrimental effect, but she seems to be coming around, although I can never be sure."

"How do you mean?"

"I'm never sure if there aren't others ... well, I know there *must* be, she's such a vibrant woman ... in the *'social sense'*, I mean ... she's been so terribly damaged on the *'physical side'*, if you know what I mean ..." Thomson's voice petered out in embarrassment. MacDonald understood and nodded sympathetically. He frowned, looking up at the ceiling considering what Thomson had just divulged.

"Perhaps the viceroy position will bring things to a head," MacDonald said.

"I'm hoping for her answer before I leave for India in September, but she may not let me know until I return."

"You're definitely going, then?"

"Yes, I am. I must say, I've been rather touched by Marthe's concern of late."

"We're all concerned, CB. Must you really go?"

"I've stated publicly since 1924 that I'll be on *Cardington R101* when she makes her maiden voyage. I *will* go, and by golly, I'm looking forward to it. Please don't worry, Ramsay."

MacDonald left it at that.

The sun shone brightly the following morning and MacDonald and Ishbel were up with the larks. For Marthe, waking up at Chequers seemed like a fantasy. She lay happily in bed, wide awake, studying the room and its floral décor. She enjoyed the aromas and birdsong drifting through her casement windows from the garden—so unmistakably English! How she loved this place. She was aroused from her musing by Thomson's gentle knock and his entrance with a tray of tea and biscuits. He wore a silk dressing gown over his pajamas.

"Good morning, my dear," he said brightly.

"Ah, there you are, Kit."

"I thought perhaps we could spend a little time together before we go down to breakfast," he said coyly as he put the tray down.

The idea was met with coolness.

"I don't think that would be appropriate, or respectful to our host, Kit, do you?"

He was used to being rebuffed.

Later, they came down to the breakfast room looking well-rested, although Thomson didn't quite have the spring in his step that he'd hoped for. The two men ate their bacon and eggs and drank coffee. Marthe and Ishbel had porridge and fruit.

"I'll show you around the gardens this morning, Marthe," MacDonald said.

"I've been looking forward to this, Ramsay," Marthe said.

"I see you're suitably attired for a walk."

"They're her walking shoes," Thomson said.

"I'm a country girl at heart. I love the mountains."

"We used to walk in the Carpathians," Thomson said.

"You must come to the Highlands," MacDonald said.

"Indeed we must," Thomson said. "I remember my first visit to Lossie. I had an affinity with the place immediately."

"Sounds delightful," Marthe said.

"And the house—such peace," Thomson said.

"I built the house for my mother and my dear wife. They both died within the same year. The place brings me solace, but with it dreadful sadness ..." MacDonald faltered, his eyes filling with tears.

"Oh Daddy," Ishbel said, moving toward him. Before she could embrace him, he got up and moved to the window.

"It's a beautiful morning and we must get out there, before it clouds over, as it usually does by midmorning," he said.

"I won't come if you don't mind. I have things to do," Ishbel said.

"Just as you wish, my dear," MacDonald said. "She's a busy girl. Runs this house and Number Ten like clockwork. Heaven knows where I'd be without her."

While Thomson and Marthe were having breakfast at Chequers, Lou and company were traveling to Brancker's home, near Warlingham. The house, a black-beamed, white-stucco Tudor, was situated on a hill overlooking the Surrey woods and pastureland. The imposing, oak-planked, steel-studded front door was opened by a young maid in black with a frilly white apron. She showed them into a spacious study with magnificent views from leaded windows. The room was full of antiques and shelves stacked with books. The walls were filled with framed pictures of aeroplanes, airships, aviation personalities, big game kills in East Africa, as well as aviation artifacts, which included a huge wooden airship propeller, stained and varnished. There was one apparently special picture at center, of Auriol Lee, signed in bold lettering. It read:

'With much love and thanks to my dear Branks'.

Grouped around Auriol were photos of some of the Kenyan big-game crowd. Denys Finch-Hatton and his mistress Karen Blixen with his soon-to-be mistress, Beryl Markham (who would become an aviation legend within seven years), then a shot of Brancker and three shining natives standing proudly beside a slaughtered buffalo. Alongside that, there were photos of Edward, Prince of Wales with Finch-Hatton, who'd taken up promoting the use of cameras for shooting animals instead of guns.

The three men studied it all in fascination. The door flew open and Brancker came bounding in, full of vim and vigor—a vortex of pure energy. He shook hands with each of them.

"Good of you to come. I thought it better we meet here. Too many big ears and wagging tongues in Whitehall—what!" He turned to the maid at the door. "Bring us a pot of tea and plenty of biscuits, Mable, please." Brancker caught Lou looking at a picture of him (much younger) beside a plane. "I made that flight solo to Persia," he said proudly.

"*Solo!* Gee!" Lou said.

"Yes, I followed the railway lines most of the way—excellent navigation tool, my boy. You should remember that. Please sit down. We have lots to talk about."

Brancker went and threw himself down in a worn, brown leather chair behind an ornate desk. They took their places in easy chairs in front of him.

"I got you down here to plan our strategy." He picked up a silver cigarette case on the desk and offered them around. Irwin took one and Brancker lit it for him with a desk lighter. Lou was tempted, but resisted. He'd quit smoking after the war when he joined the airships branch of the Navy. Brancker sat down again and stuck a cigarette in a long black holder and lit up. He immediately started coughing. They waited for him to stop.

"We need to sort things out. I didn't ask Scott—he's not the man he was—you're people I trust," Brancker said. Smoke billowed everywhere.

"Sir Sefton, I ..." Colmore began.

"Yes, Reggie you're in a very difficult position. We all are." Brancker stood up and pushed the casement window open behind him. "We need to discuss our options and use our damned intelligence!" He paused to think. "The situation with that inspector fellow—McWade— he certainly set the cat among the pigeons, I can tell you!"

"He put me in a bind all right," Colmore said.

"I know—but he might just come in useful. Let's start from the beginning. What's the prognosis on the Howden ship?" Brancker looked at Irwin for an answer.

"I've spoken to both Booth and Meager and they're satisfied with that ship—and Lou's flown in both."

"She's well balanced and handles pretty well," Lou said.

"It's got its share of problems though ..." Colmore said.

Brancker looked quizzical. "But not to the degree of being un-flyable?"

"No. I couldn't quite say that. They've had a lot of trouble with the cover and its securing system. I'm still uncomfortable with it. A ship's only as good as its cover, after all."

"Their tail collapsed on her twenty-four-hour test, didn't it?" Brancker reminded them.

"Yes, and we just rebuilt it for them," Colmore replied.

"That's big! We need to play up that issue as much possible," Brancker said.

"How?" Colmore asked. The maid came in with a tray, set it down on the desk and tiptoed out.

"I'll get to that. When is *Howden R100* scheduled to leave for Canada?"

"At the end of this month," Lou said.

"Then we don't have much time," Brancker said. He stared across the room, admiring Auriol Lee for a moment, drawing on his cigarette.

"And you're scheduled to sail in her?" Brancker asked Lou.

"Yes, he is, and so am I," Colmore answered, with a frown. Brancker removed the lid from the teapot and slowly stirred the tea. He banged the drips off before replacing the lid.

"I'll be mum," he said, pouring milk from a jug into flowery, bone, china, gold-rimmed cups. He carefully placed the silver tea strainer over each cup and poured out the tea. Lou couldn't help but smile.

What a character: the toupée, the monocle, the cigarette holder. Hell, this is like the Mad Hatter's tea party!

Although sunny, it was cool. Each wore a sweater. MacDonald led them along a narrow, gravel walk between the house and a high brick wall enclosing the kitchen garden. It contained a variety of bushes, flowering plants and herbs the chef (also from Lossiemouth) used in his dishes. The path was bordered each side by manicured grass. From here, MacDonald showed them the lawn tennis courts. Marthe walked between the two men, slipping her arms into theirs.

"Doesn't he look *divine* in his plus fours, Kit?" Marthe said.

"Why, thank you. I find them most practical," MacDonald said.

"You must get some," Marthe said to Thomson.

"I don't think they'd suit me half as well," Thomson said.

"Ramsay, you're my Lord of the Manor and Kit—he's my Lord of the Air!"

"Come, I must show you our tulip tree," MacDonald said. They went to the entrance court and admired the tree.

"I've never seen anything like it—it's magnificent!" Marthe exclaimed.

"It's actually a type of magnolia," MacDonald said, picking one of the blossoms with a leaf attached and giving it to Marthe.

"Thank you. I shall send this to Abbé Brugnier, my close friend."

"He's Marthe's spiritual advisor in Paris. He's a very fine fellow," Thomson said.

MacDonald picked another and gave it to her. "Then he shall have his own. Send him this one. This tree has deep religious connections," MacDonald said, his eyes full of fun.

"Do tell me more," Marthe said, sensing she was about to be teased.

"I have it on the highest authority that when Eve—in her naked state—was being run out of the Garden of Eden by God's angels, she desperately grabbed hold of the last piece of foliage hanging over the wall from a tree—a magnolia tree identical to this. The leaf she held in her hand was just large enough to cover her private parts and thus, she was able to maintain her respectability."

Marthe giggled. "You're obviously very well-versed in botany," she said.

"Not to mention Eve's private parts. It all comes from the Scottish version of the Old Testament," Thomson told her.

They laughed and then made their way round to the Lavender Terrace on the south side, where Marthe admired a huge lavender bush and commented on its overpowering aroma. Stone steps led down from the terrace to the rose gardens, flanked by perfectly-cut box hedges. Marthe stood, hands on hips, staring up at the ancient, red brick façade.

"This is the stuff of ghost stories, Ramsay. It really is!"

"We should import some ravens from the Tower of London," Thomson suggested.

"We do have our share of ghosts here, you know. You'd better keep your head under the covers tonight," MacDonald said.

Marthe gave him a knowing smile. "Oh, ghosts appearing in the night don't bother me."

"I shall remember that, Marthe," Thomson said.

She caught the scent from the rose beds and breathed deeply. "Mmm, that fragrance!"

"Not quite as nice as our special roses, my dear," Thomson said.

This tweaked MacDonald's interest. He looked at Marthe.

"Kit always buys me very special roses—*Variété Général Jacqueminot.* They're extraordinary. We refer to them as our own," Marthe explained.

"I didn't realize CB was so profound in matters of love."

"Don't give my all secrets away, Marthe," Thomson said.

"Do you send flowers to Lady Wilson?" Marthe asked.

"Once in a while I send flowers to friends, but not such exotic varieties as Thomson's, obviously."

"I thought we might be seeing something of her this weekend," Marthe said.

"We both have busy schedules. Besides, I wanted to focus exclusively on you and CB."

"She is such a lovely lady," Marthe said.

"She is, indeed."

Brancker lit another cigarette and continued, "Okay, first things first. Get Richmond to write a memo to be read by all, saying neither ship has been designed to carry enough hydrogen and therefore neither provides adequate lift. Describe this as a massive safety problem," he said, as he handed a cup to Colmore. "It'll say it's not the designer's fault. The blame belongs with the Air Ministry, since they wrote the specifications."

Colmore stirred his tea. "I had a hand in that," he said, his expression pained.

"Don't worry about that, Reggie—so did lots of *other* people." Brancker held out tea to Lou and Irwin. "I want you to put it out there that not only does *Cardington R101* require an extra bay, but so does *Howden R100*. You can say drawings are on the boards and an additional bay is being designed for both ships, *right now*."

"That's a *very* good idea—after all, we own them *both* now," Colmore said.

"Then I want you to get Rope to write another memo to everyone and his dog, saying the covers on both airships are in terrible shape, making them both less than airworthy. He's to say that it'd be better to postpone the flights for six months—no, make that a year—rather than take unnecessary risks with peoples' lives for no damned good reason."

"They'll gladly comply. It's *exactly* what they think," Colmore said.

Brancker smiled. "I know it is, Reggie." He turned to Irwin. "The next thing I want is for you, Captain, to write a report on the dismal performance of *Cardington R101* this week. That document is also to be read by all and sundry."

"I've already written it, sir," Irwin said.

"*Excellent!*" Brancker responded, rubbing his palms together.

The three companions strolled down to the meadow south of the rose garden, past the gate house and through the five-bar gate, stopping to admire the countryside. MacDonald pointed down the hill.

"We used to own a small house not far from here before I became a Member of Parliament. My wife and our five children used to come up this way for walks to Beacon Hill. I wrote to Lord Lee for permission to cross this land. He was here renovating the house in readiness to make it a deed of gift to the government for the use of future Prime Ministers—"

"Such as yourself!" Thomson said.

"Yes, indeed. He invited us for lunch on the terrace and told us all about it. Wonderful fellow!"

"And now you're enjoying his gift—little did you know!" Marthe said.

"Funny how things work out," Thomson said.

"Now you practically own it," Marthe said.

"Everything's only ever on loan, Marthe," MacDonald said.

Marthe looked back toward the trees. "I could swear I just saw someone up there behind that tree."

"Oh, it's only Robards. He's there to protect me."

"I see, and who will protect *me*?" Marthe asked.

"Why, *CB*, of course!"

They walked along a wide grassy pathway between lines of flowering lime trees. MacDonald looked more serious and stopped. He disengaged his arm from Marthe's and turned to face them.

"Marthe, you know I've asked CB to take up the post of Viceroy to India?"

Marthe beamed. "Yes, Prime Minister, I think it's a wonderful opportunity for him."

"Then you'd support such a move on his part?"

"*Wholeheartedly!* I know he's a great leader of men, and returning to the land of his birth in that capacity would be a huge triumph."

"It's a vitally important position."

"Without doubt," said Marthe.

"He's the one man in Britain most suited to the position."

"A very wise decision, if I may say so, Ramsay."

Thomson said nothing.

"And you'll visit him there, Marthe?"

"Indeed, I shall. What an adventure that'll be! Oh, how I long to visit the Taj Mahal."

"A testament to Shah Jahan's love of his wife, Mumtaz Mahal, who died in childbirth," MacDonald said. Marthe stared at MacDonald, amazed at his knowledge. Thomson remained silent, deep in thought.

My love for Marthe is as strong as Shah Jahan's. And someday I shall prove it.

MacDonald resumed. "Good. Good. I know you love to travel, Marthe."

"She does, she's Romanian!" Thomson said, himself beaming now.

MacDonald chuckled. "You're saying because she's a gypsy. How romantic. Bring on the violins!" He rapidly became somber again. "I shall also visit when I can. He's my wisest and most trusted friend. I'll miss him sorely."

Thomson perked up. "Don't look so down, Ramsay. We'll have a regularly scheduled airship service to India by then. You'll be able to travel in comfort."

"Perhaps one day we shall all visit the Taj together," Marthe said.

"*Splendid!* That's all settled, then. I propose we have a spot of tea on the terrace in the sunshine, followed by a game of croquet," MacDonald said.

"Wonderful idea," Thomson said. They turned back to the house.

Brancker had called for more tea and was pouring them another cup.

"Now there's another little wrinkle. If we can delay parting *Cardington R101* and thereby throw Lord Thomson off his schedule with the Prime Minister's Conference thing, he may let it slide and not care if we postpone her voyage to India till next year. That'd give us time to test these ships and do things right. So, the tactic is for us to hold off parting that ship on the pretext we're holding it in reserve for the Canadian trip. Bear in mind, *Howden R100* has yet to do another twenty-four-hour test since her tail was rebuilt. You never know—she might fail, especially if they have any more trouble with the cover."

"That's unlikely, sir," Irwin said.

"I'm waiting for the official word to begin work on the extra bay," Colmore said.

"I know you are. Don't do anything until you are expressly ordered to. I have someone working with us on delaying that. Unfortunately, the bean counters are with Thomson—they want results, and they want them *now*."

"It'll be tough, but we'll delay things if we can," Colmore said.

Brancker smoothed out his mustache with his thumb and forefinger, narrowing his eyes. "*Delay! Delay! Delay!* It'd be easier if we could get Howden to postpone. That's the goal. It'd take pressure off Cardington to make the India voyage." He looked at Lou. "This is where you come in, Commander. I'd like you to reach out on behalf of your boss, Wing Commander Colmore here—*unofficially*—and request they do the right thing."

"You want me to ask them to postpone their flight, sir?" Lou asked.

"*Exactly!* I know you have a wonderful relationship with Howden. You're a godsend! I want you to set up a meeting as soon as you can."

"I'll be glad to try, sir, but I know Mr. Burney is anxious to fly to Canada immediately," Lou said.

"No more '*Mr. Burney*'!" Brancker exclaimed. All eyes widened. Lou wondered if Burney had been sacked. "He's *Sir* Dennis now—he's just been knighted," Brancker said, laughing. They all rolled their eyes. "Anyway, arrange a meeting as quickly as possible and see if you can pull it off—and don't forget to call him *Sir Dennis*!" Brancker said.

"I won't forget, *Sir Sefton*," Lou said.

"You're going to need to appeal to his better side. I'm sure he must have one. You know: 'We're all in this together, old man' and all that. If none of that works, try telling him that new designs for bigger and better ships are on the boards and Vickers will be expected to play their part. Tell them Brancker very much wants Vickers's involvement. For now, we seek their cooperation, their patience and their understanding. We're all *airshipmen* and we're all *gentlemen* and we'll return the favor and look out for them in the future—tell Burney he has Brancker's word—the word of one knight to another." They all stood up, preparing to leave. "One last thing," Brancker said. "It's important testing is carried out thoroughly—not cut short for any reason *whatsoever.* Be firm. Stick to your guns!"

Lou was dazzled by Brancker's brilliance. But would any of it work? He decided to try and track down Burney as soon as they got back to Cardington.

Nevil will give me his home number.

Tea was served on the Lavender Terrace. They sat round a wooden garden table under an umbrella. Clouds were rolling in and it was getting muggy. MacDonald took off his sweater. After tea, they played croquet until a cloudburst soaked them. They dashed back to the terrace, giggling like college chums.

Later, while MacDonald spent time at his desk in his study, Thomson took Marthe on a guided tour. They went to each room, inspecting the furnishings and paintings. She was especially taken by the oak Regency pedestal table used by Napoleon and with Nelson's watch in a display case. A ring belonging to the great Queen Elizabeth filled her with wonder. Cromwell's death mask she hated on sight— he'd been responsible for the death of so many good Irish people. But the library filled her with joy. As a highly acclaimed writer, she was able to appreciate the first illustrated edition of Milton's *Paradise Lost* printed in 1688. To hold such ancient books in her hands gave her a special thrill.

25

CHEQUERS & A MEETING WITH BURNEY

Saturday July 5 - Sunday July 13, 1930.

As soon as Lou got back to Cardington, he tried calling Norway in York, but got no answer. After an hour, he gave up and went home. He would've preferred to make this call without Charlotte around. On arrival, he found her coming in with some shopping. She didn't look happy. Her mood was always sour these days. After kissing her, Lou used the phone on the small table in the living room. Norway answered.

"Nev, where the hell've you been? I've been calling you for the *last two hours!* "

"I just got home from the flying club. What do you need, old man?"

"I need Burney's number."

"What do you need that for?"

"I want to talk to him."

"What about?"

"Nev, I can't say right now. I'll tell you later."

"Keeping secrets, eh? I can guess … Here it is …"

Lou wrote down the number as Charlotte entered the room. "Thanks, Nev. Look, I'll speak to you later. Okay?" He hung up the phone.

"What's going on?" Charlotte asked.

"I've been asked to talk to Burney and get him to postpone their flight."

Charlotte said nothing. Lou knew she understood exactly what was going on. He picked up the phone and dialed Burney's number. A well-spoken woman answered. Charlotte stood at the doorway, listening.

"May I speak to Sir Dennis, please."

"And who may I say is calling Sir Dennis?" she wah-wahed.

"Commander Remington, ma'am."

Lou heard the woman calling, "Darling … a Commander Remington is on the phone."

A few moments later, Burney came on. "Lou, this is a surprise. What can I do for you, my dear chap?"

"Good of you to take my call, Sir Dennis. I have a favor to ask."

"Of course, fire away."

"I'd like to meet with you. It's important."

"I see. I'm going to the Continent on Monday. I'll be back in ten days. We can meet then, if you like."

"Oh, dear. I'd hoped to see you on Monday."

"Well, if it's that important, I can meet you tomorrow morning in Westminster."

"Splendid, sir. Could you have Barnes and Nevil attend?"

"Don't see why not. I'll instruct them to be there."

"That's awfully kind of you," Lou said, realizing he was lapsing into British jargon.

"What's this all about, Lou?"

"I prefer to tell you tomorrow, if you don't mind, sir."

"All right. 9 o'clock. Sunday morning—Vickers's office on Broadway."

"Thank you, Sir Dennis."

Lou put the phone down. Charlotte looked at him and shook her head sadly. She gave a deep sigh, turned and went upstairs to the bedroom. Lou called Norway back, but didn't say what the meeting was about. He said he'd tell them in the morning.

That evening, Thomson and Marthe sat down to dinner with MacDonald.

"What did you do with your friend's flower?" MacDonald asked.

"I have it pressed in my journal. I'll send it to him next week with a letter describing my delightful stay at Chequers with you," Marthe replied, smiling warmly.

"Will he approve of you sleeping under the same roof as a couple of ne'er-do-well British politicians?"

"I'm sure he would. He's met Kit and loves him to death. Kit took us on a tour of Westminster Palace a couple of years ago."

"He's quite a wit," Thomson said. "On entering the House of Lords, he said he understood why politics is like a religion to us."

"He said that?"

"He said it's because we practice our politics in a cathedral!"

"I'm glad to hear he approves of CB," MacDonald said. MacDonald's observation had implications, but Marthe didn't respond. "What do you think about this proposed flight of CB's to India in September, Marthe?" MacDonald asked.

"He feels it's his destiny. I wish he wasn't going, but I wouldn't try to dissuade him."

"I *must* go. It'll give the troops a boost. Look, when your time's up —that's it. I'm a *fatalist*."

"You mean everything's preordained?" MacDonald asked.

"I told you about the boy at Cardington, didn't I?" Thomson said, looking at Marthe.

"Yes, that was a pity," she said.

"No, you didn't tell *me* about it," MacDonald said.

"Ramsay, I thought you had enough to worry about."

"I seem to have heard that before. What happened this time?" MacDonald asked.

"I met this boy in the ground crew. He stood out. He had this pair of old boots he'd shined like glass. There was something about him. I put my hand on his shoulder and complimented him. He had a beautiful young face—*angelic*."

"So what happened to him?"

"We went out for many hours—marvelous flight! I had a desk put on board and worked up there in perfect solitude. It took ages for them to land at the mast and when they did, that boy ran and grabbed the mooring line and fell down dead."

"My goodness gracious! That's terrible! What happened?" MacDonald exclaimed.

"There's always a burst of static electricity when they throw the line down."

"And he didn't know that?" Marthe asked.

"Well, everyone thought he'd been electrocuted, but it turned out, he had a weak heart and his great run for the line finished the boy off."

MacDonald looked distraught. "That poor, wee laddie."

"The point was, at the time, none of us knew anything about it. The press told me. But when they said it, I sensed immediately who it was."

"You mean he was marked for death?" MacDonald said.

"I'm saying—it was his time."

"Did he know, do you think?" Marthe asked.

"Oh no, he was a happy, young fellow. Dead keen! Very sad. I often think about him."

MacDonald said nothing for a few moments and then, "Perhaps it was his boots that marked him. God must have said, 'Bring me the boy with the shiny boots.' They'd been shined so His angels would know him."

"Oh, that's lovely, Ramsay," Marthe said. "He's such a poet, isn't he Kit?"

The weekend was spent in a state of contentment, enjoying each other's company despite the dreary weather; they were three souls in perfect harmony, at one with the universe. In Sunday morning drizzle, they were driven to St. Peter and St. Paul, the old parish church overlooking the tiny village of Ellesborough. They were greeted by the vicar and exchanged respectful nods and smiles with members of the congregation. Although Marthe found the service different, she enjoyed it.

That Sunday morning, Lou traveled down to London by train, wearing a sports jacket and slacks under his raincoat—this was unofficial business. He arrived at the Vickers offices just before nine. A security man let him in and showed him into an ornately-furnished board room on the ground floor. Soon, Norway came blundering in, out of breath, worried he was late. Wallis arrived a few minutes later, looking fit and relaxed. They made pleasant small talk, reminiscing about the good times at Howden. Punctually at nine, Burney entered the room and after shaking hands, sat at the head of the table.

Burney glanced at Wallis and Norway. "Sorry to drag you fellows out on a Sunday like this. The Commander called this meeting.

Apparently, he has something important he wishes to discuss. Perhaps you'd be good enough to enlighten us, Lou."

"Yes, sir. But first I want to congratulate you on your knighthood. Sir Sefton Brancker mentioned it yesterday and sends his congratulations and kind personal regards." Lou glanced at Wallis who appeared irritated, looking down at his hands on the table. Burney beamed, while Lou continued. "Wing Commander Colmore asked me to make an approach to you, *unofficially*."

"*Really?* How strange," Burney said, appearing puzzled, but obviously enjoying this.

Is he play-acting?

Wallis and Norway remained expressionless.

"He's suggesting both transcontinental voyages be postponed until next year."

Wallis was aghast. "On what grounds?"

"Colmore's view is that both ships haven't been sufficiently tested. He thinks they have flaws, making the risks unjustifiable and doesn't feel comfortable putting men's lives in danger unnecessarily."

"What flaws is he talking about?" Burney asked.

"The R.A.W. is worried about the outer covers on both ships."

"Our cover will be in p-pretty good shape prior to our d-departure," Norway said.

"*Cardington R101's* cover is also being replaced. The tail collapsing on *Howden R100* caused a great deal of concern," Lou said.

"That's been fixed by the Airship Works staff. Nevil will be looking at that on Tuesday when he's there for the preflight conference. I understand the R.A.W. took it upon themselves to redesign the tail section. So there shouldn't be anything to worry about, should there?" Wallis said, without hiding his displeasure at their tampering with his design.

"I think they'd like to see more testing done, just the same," Lou said.

"Lou, we all like you, you know that. But I'm going to cut to the chase, as they say in Hollywood." Burney smiled at his own little joke. "The truth is, it's *they* who don't feel ready, do they?"

Lou paused. This was the crux of the matter. It was time to go into the 'old Sir Sefton routine.' "You're perfectly correct, Sir Dennis." Lou stole a glance at Wallis and saw him grimace. "And quite honestly, I think they'd admit that to you. They're making an appeal to you as fellow airshipmen."

Burney lifted his eyebrows. "It's a bit late for all this old chummy stuff, isn't it?"

"Yes, it is, and that's regrettable," Lou said.

"I told you what was happening ages ago, Lou," Wallis said.

"You were right. But do you really have to put the boot in? It couldn't hurt to be magnanimous, could it, Barnes?" Lou chided him.

"So let us understand this—they're asking us to postpone *our* flight to Canada to allow *them* time to get *their* ship into a flyable condition and in the meantime have the world believe *Howden R100* is in the same pathetic state," Wallis said.

Lou looked kindly at each man around the table in an attempt to appeal to their better sides. "Sir Dennis, Sir Sefton told me that if you do this, Vickers will be well rewarded. He regards Vickers as part of the team—an indispensible part. New designs are on the boards at Cardington for even bigger airships and he says it's *imperative* Vickers plays a major role. He asked me to tell you that, and for the moment, he seeks your cooperation, your patience and your understanding. He knows this project has been a loss for Vickers, but he'll see to it you come out whole at the end of the day. I'll tell you exactly what he said: 'We're *all* airshipmen and we're *all* gentlemen. We *will* return the favor and we *will* look out for Vickers in the future.' He said, 'Tell Sir Dennis they have Brancker's word—the word of one knight to another.'"

Burney seemed impressed. Lou sensed he'd won him over, but Wallis and Norway appeared unmoved. The 'one knight to another' part certainly didn't go down well with Wallis. Norway sat frowning.

Then Burney's demeanor changed. "I'm skeptical for one simple reason. Short Brothers used to build airships. They had a nice little business going until the government decided they'd take it," Burney said.

"What do you mean, *take it?*" Lou asked.

"They nationalized the business and renamed it the 'Royal Airship Works.' It has a nice ring to it, doesn't it? We could do all the right things, and yes, get more airships rolling out of our sheds, and then— *hey, presto!*—we're nationalizing your company! We don't trust these people. It's what they do!"

"Well put, sir," Norway said.

"Maybe the next damned socialist who comes along and can't get himself elected will call himself Lord Karl Marx of Howden!" Burney quipped.

"I can't believe it," Lou said.

"You're an American. Things like that could never happen in America," Norway said.

"There is another way," Wallis said. "They own both airships. We're merely trying to fulfill our contractual obligations. They could instruct us not to fly to Canada—announce a postponement. It's really as simple as that, Lou!"

"Easier said than done. They'd lose face with their masters at the Air Ministry—and with the public, of course," Lou said.

"The main problem is, Thomson's got his own personal agenda and schedule, which shouldn't get mixed up in the development of experimental aircraft," Wallis said.

"Surely, their ship can't be that b-bad, can it? They've removed all the unnecessary weight and they're building in an extra b-bay. That should solve their p-problems," Norway said.

"Let's hope so. But there's still not enough time for testing. Lord Thomson is insisting they leave at the end of September," Lou said, putting his hand to his forehead—he'd lost this battle and his disappointment showed.

"There you have it. They're in a mess of their own making. It's a pity, but I vote *NO* to postponement," Wallis said.

"Hear, hear," Norway said. Lou wished he'd not asked Burney to invite them now. That was a mistake. He may have pulled it off, one on one.

"They must postpone and not fly until their ship has been properly tested—or throw in the towel. It's our judgment *Howden R100* is ready. Remember, government officials were on board for all our tests and accepted the ship. It only remains for us to make our intercontinental voyage and we will have fulfilled our obligations," Burney concluded.

They all got to their feet. There was no animosity, only total detachment between Wallis and Burney. Lou shook hands sadly with each of them.

"I'll see you on board then," he said, looking at Burney and then Wallis. Wallis said nothing. He just smiled. Lou knew Wallis well enough to know there was *more* to that smile.

Lou returned to Cardington and delivered the bad news to Colmore who took it hard, although he wasn't surprised. Colmore had seen to it other parts of Brancker's plan were being put into effect. Richmond, Rope and Irwin would have their reports ready early in the week for dissemination to all interested parties. The only trouble was, there *were* no interested parties that Lou could tell. The Air Ministry didn't want to hear about any more delays, no matter how bad the reports, or who wrote them. The only person who believed the negative reporting was McWade and, as recently proved, his view didn't count for much. Lou was frustrated; the R.A.W. wanted the Howden people to make the move so they'd appear blameless themselves. Howden was having none of that. After the debriefing, Colmore called Brancker to update him. After that, Lou went home and gave Charlotte a sanitized version of events of the past two days. She remained silent.

Thomson and Marthe stayed at Chequers for almost two weeks. They had a lazy time reading and walking the estate or going out in Thomson's limousine for rides in the country. When MacDonald was home, they played croquet or cards and had lively conversations. During this time, Thomson received reports of disturbing rumors. He was also told work hadn't yet begun on parting *Cardington R101*. He decided not to let this spoil his time with Marthe—he'd give them some stick on his return the following week.

26

CANADA PREFLIGHT CONFERENCE

Tuesday July 8, 1930.

Lou was at his desk in his office at Cardington House when he
heard a small plane go over. He went to the window and looked
out.

That must be him.

Lou rode down to the field outside the sheds on the *Brough
Superior* in time to see Norway's plane flaring down onto the grass. It
turned and taxied toward him from the St. Mary's end of the field. Lou
grinned. This man Nevil was 'a bit of a lad', as the Brits would say,
landing here at Cardington like this. Lou had informed Colmore, who
was much too decent to object, but others would be extremely irritated;
no one at the Royal Airship Works could fly a plane. And by now,
they'd heard Colmore's overtures to Howden had failed. Lou strolled
out and cast a skeptical eye over the Gypsy Moth.

"Methinks 'tis made of sealing wax and string!" he said.

Norway scrambled out of the cockpit. "It's lovely to see you, too,
old man," he said.

"They sent me out to meet you," Lou said.

"Have they put out the welcome mat?"

"They'd rather welcome a case of the pox, old buddy."

"Thanks," Norway said.

"You wanna take a look at her rear end first?"

"Okay, let's take a peek."

They rode over to Shed No. 2. Once inside, they walked to the end
of the building and Norway stared up. His jaw dropped.

"Oh, bugger me! That's so b-bloody radical! Wallis will have a f-
fit."

"Don't get your knickers in a twist. It ain't that bad!"

They climbed aboard and inspected the work from the inside.

"Nothing wrong with the workmanship," Norway said. "It's bloody good—much better than ours!"

They drove across to Cardington House where they drank coffee in Lou's office before heading to the conference room. The R.A.W. people were assembled: Colmore, Scott, Richmond, Rope, McWade, Booth, Meager, Atherstone, and about ten others from the design office. Lou and Norway walked in and sat at the table. Lou was surprised at the expressions of pure hatred on their faces. He knew Norway hadn't bargained for this. It was as if Lou had brought in the devil himself. Norway filled and lit his pipe. They didn't like that pipe. They didn't like the Harris Tweed jacket. They didn't like the leather elbow patches. They didn't like the leather edging on his breast pocket. They thought he was attempting to look older than his years, create the impression he was a mature, studious thinker.

Colmore cleared his throat. "We're here to discuss *Howden R100's* flight to Canada. We'll talk about preparations Commander Atherstone has made in Montreal. He'll give us an update later. We'll go over the preparation of the ship—provisioning, fueling, ballasting and gassing up, and the final twenty-four-hour test flight this week. We'll talk about the crew and her officers and their roles." At this point Colmore looked purposefully at Scott before continuing. "We'll go over the intended schedule and routing in detail. This will take three or four hours. We'll break for lunch at 12:30 and resume this afternoon." Richmond raised his hand.

"What is it, Colonel?"

"Before we get into details, I'd like to ask Mr. Norway a few questions, if you don't mind, sir," Richmond said.

"You can—providing Mr. Norway has no objection," Colmore said. No one had been able to bring themselves to look at Norway, but suddenly their accusing eyes were upon him.

Norway removed his pipe from his mouth. "N-N-Not at all."

Richmond stared down the table with contempt. "After the collapse of the tail of *Howden R100* and the subsequent repairs and design corrections done by the Royal Airship Works—are you confident you can make it across the Atlantic, Mr. Norway?" Richmond asked.

Norway swallowed hard, blinking like an owl. "W-We knew there were some p-p-problems with the tail s-section and—"

Richmond rested his elbows on the table and leaned forward holding his head, as though perplexed. "You *knew* there were problems and you brought it to the Royal Airship Works, anyway? I don't understand, Mr. Norway."

"W-We knew we m-may have a p-problem as something had shown up in the testing m-m-model, but we thought we'd r-resolved the issue. But they b-broke down the model b-before we could do more t-t-tests. We—"

"So you delivered an untested airship to the government, knowing there was a good chance it still had structural problems?"

"They weren't m-major—"

Richmond sat back. "I'd call the collapse of the tail in mid-flight a major problem! How do you know other structural flaws won't surface en route to Canada—when it's too late? And what about the wiring system holding down and securing the cover? I hear that was chafing and falling apart."

Colmore was listening intently with alarm.

"We redid all the z-zigzag wiring and remedied the s-situation."

"Remedied the situation! That cover has a very weird look about it, if you ask me."

"There's nothing wrong with the c-cover. We conducted s-six f-flight tests—more than a hundred and twenty hours—c-covering s-six thousand miles, many in adverse w-weather c-conditions."

"And then the tail collapsed. What's going to collapse next? Maybe your ship's getting tired, Mr. Norway. I believe a hell of a lot more testing is necessary."

"I-If that's your o-opinion ..." Norway was struggling for breath, his mouth puckering up like a goldfish, "you should order us n-not to under-t-take this f-flight. The ch-choice is entirely yours, s-sir," Norway said, stabbing the air with his pipe.

This set off much eye-rolling and sighing among the R.A.W. officials, frustrated at being beaten by someone they considered to be a stuttering fool with no airship experience. The audacity of Norway's last statement had surprised and silenced them. Colmore glanced at Richmond. "Any more questions for Mr. Norway?"

"No! We might as well talk to the *wall,*" Richmond said.

"Very well then, let's continue," Colmore said, shaken by this exchange.

At the lunchtime break everyone got up and went to the dining room. No one offered Norway lunch. Lou and Norway were left sitting at the table.

"No lunch invite for you, Nev, old buddy," Lou said, grinning.

"It doesn't matter. I'm not hungry."

"Just as well—it might be laced with rat poison, mate."

"Thanks."

"Come on. Charlotte's got sandwiches and a nice warm beer for us. Let's go."

Fifteen minutes later, they entered 58 Kelsey Street where Charlotte waited. Although very pale, she looked starkly beautiful, stunning in a tight black dress and high-heeled shoes. She was expertly made up. Lou studied her gorgeous face and perfect derriere. She'd made a big effort, probably because Nevil was coming. Even after nine years, she still made Lou's heart race. It'd been ages since they'd made love. He wished he could take her to bed for the afternoon, instead of returning to that oppressive conference room. She kissed Norway's cheek and Lou on the lips. They sat downstairs at the kitchen table looking into the garden.

"How's the meeting going?" Charlotte asked, placing a plate of ham sandwiches on the table.

"Brutal," Lou said. "Look at him—he's black and blue!"

"I think they're warming up to me," Norway said with a silly grin.

"Hell, I must have been in the wrong room," Lou said.

Charlotte poured their pale ales. They were parched after Norway's grilling and took a few welcome gulps before attacking the sandwiches.

"Maybe you can't blame them," Charlotte said, fixing Norway with an icy stare.

"Charlotte, they can elect to postpone our flight," Norway said gently as he chewed.

Charlotte pouted in annoyance, her full red lips emphasizing the whiteness of her skin. She flashed her eyes at him. "Nevil, you're right, but these men have their pride and you people are bloody-well wiping the floor up with them!"

"Not you, too, Charlotte? I'm really sorry, but their fate's in their own hands."

"And what about the fate of *my husband?* How will you feel if anything happens to *him?*"

"But *I'm* going, too."

"And *you're* crazy! The tail might fall off again."

"It didn't f-fall off. It only b-buckled a bit. It's f-fixed now—"

"You're forcing them to fly *their* ship! It's a bloody *deathtrap!* And *you* won't be on that one, will you!"

"Not t-true. We're n-not f-f-forcing anybody to do *anything.*"

"You're like a bunch of school kids. I'm sick of it!" Charlotte said, getting up.

"We'd better get back. We don't want them getting upset," Lou said.

"If anything happens to them all ..." Charlotte began. Lou gave her a disapproving look. She picked up their two empty bottles and threw them in the bin with a *clunk*, turned away and went upstairs without kissing them goodbye. Lou and Norway left the rest of the sandwiches and rode back to Cardington House.

They entered the empty conference room.

"They're not back yet," Lou said.

"I didn't expect them to be, but I'd sooner f-face this lot than your wife," Norway said as he filled and lit his pipe.

"You know Charlotte loves you really, Nev. She's worried, that's all. She'll be all right once these two voyages are over with."

They sat and waited in silence until the R.A.W. crowd filed in. The rest of the meeting went as planned and at the end Colmore passed out sheets of paper. "This is the proposed list of officers and crewmen for the flight to Canada and is subject to the approval of Captain Booth, as *pilot in command,*" Colmore said.

A copy of the list was given to everyone—except Norway. Lou passed one to him. Lou scanned it: Sir Dennistoun Burney ...Barnes Wallis ...Nevil Norway ...Fred McWade ...Billy Bunyan ...William

Jessup and Sqn. Ldr. Archibald Wann, (from *R38*, which came as a big surprise to Lou). Scott's name was at the very bottom.

"*Howden R100* will be under the command of Captain Booth, with Captain Meager as first officer. Flying Officer Steff will serve as second officer and Commander Remington as third officer and American Observer." Colmore paused to glare at Scott. "Major Scott will be acting Rear Admiral, a ceremonial role limited to issues concerning routing and scheduling and nothing more." This last statement was lost on most people in the room, but to Lou, it was telling—Scott couldn't be trusted. Lou glanced at Scott who as clearly furious. "This meeting is adjourned," Colmore announced.

There were no pleasantries when Norway left. Booth and Meager trooped down to the field with Lou and Norway to see him off the property. A few *Howden R100* crewmen joined them, including Nervous Nick. They stood around chatting for a while before Norway set off.

"They're all up at the windows watching you, Nev," Lou said indicating Cardington House behind them with a sideways nod.

"Perhaps they'd prefer to remember me as 'C-Crash-and-B-Burn' Norway."

They all thought this was pretty funny. Nervous Nick gripped the propeller and Norway gave the word to swing. The engine caught and he turned the plane out to the center of the field. Soon he was bouncing along and lifting off.

"He's a brave soul," Booth said.

"Sooner him than me in that thing," Meager answered.

A few minutes later, Norway was at two thousand feet and making a banking turn toward them. He roared over their heads, waggled his wings and disappeared into the clouds.

"Well, if they weren't mad before, they will be *now,*" Lou said.

Two days later, another small plane, this one bearing Brancker, piloted by one Miss Honeysuckle, dropped in on Cardington. Brancker loved having this leggy blond as his personal pilot and chauffeur. Brancker showed Miss Honeysuckle around Shed No.1 with Colmore and Lou for half an hour. Brancker hadn't popped in for the sake of a jaunt.

"What about a spot of tea, Reggie? Anything doing?" he asked.

"Of course, sir." They left the shed and walked to Cardington House.

"I was sorry to hear about their damned poor attitude, Lou," he said.

"I did my best. They were nice and very polite, actually," Lou said.

"It's a shame. Thanks for giving it 'the old college try.' I'm grateful to you."

"They're businessmen," Lou said.

Brancker stared through his monocle at the sky, as if that thought had never crossed his mind. "I suppose you're right." He turned to Colmore. "When we get to your office, I want you to track Burney down."

"He's away on the Continent this week, sir," Lou said.

"We'll need to find out if he left a contact number."

When they got to the building, Miss Honeysuckle was left in the grand reception hall, Brancker telling her he'd be in conference. The three men went to Colmore's office, a suite with a secretary's office leading into his. He had a large room overlooking Cardington Field. Colmore closed the outer door to the corridor and spoke to his secretary. "Doris, I want you to get hold of Sir Dennis Burney. Try the London office first," he said. "Please arrange for tea to be sent to Miss Honeysuckle and we'll have some, too. Thanks."

They went in, closed the door and sat down. Doris soon came on the line on the speaker. "Sir Dennis is out of the country and cannot be reached."

"Hmm. All right, try and locate Mr. Barnes Wallis. Not sure where he's based these days," Brancker said.

"Right sir. The tea lady's here."

Ten minutes later, Doris came on again. "I managed to locate Mr. Wallis, sir. He'll be on the line in a moment."

The speakerphone crackled. "Hello, Wallis here."

"I have Sir Sefton here and Commander Remington," Colmore said.

"Good afternoon to you all," Wallis said.

Brancker leaned forward in his chair. "My dear Barnes, Sefton Brancker here. As you might have guessed, this is a follow up to your meeting with the Commander, which he kindly conducted on our behalf. I've been discussing the issues concerning both airships with

Wing Commander Colmore—you know, the covers on both, the structural issue with the Howden ship, the weight issues with the Cardington ship. I think it would be beneficial to all parties if we came together as a team and recommended postponement. Then all these things can be resolved, and we can move forward knowing we've done *absolutely everything* in our power to ensure both ships are perfectly safe."

Wallis's tone was cool. "As far as *Howden R100* is concerned, I can say the problems have been minor in nature and everything's been rectified."

"But I don't feel these ships are ready. They're not fully tested, are they?"

"It's not actually up to me to make that judgment, Sir Sefton. I don't know whether you've heard, but I'm based at Weybridge now, working on aeroplane designs."

"Not officially, no. I thought this was just in the interim between airships," Brancker said. "You know we have plans to get going on more designs for much bigger airships."

Colmore was itching to speak. "How do you feel about crossing the Atlantic, or making the voyage to India in one of these airships, old man? I don't think they've proven themselves yet, do you?" he said.

"You're asking me, as the engineer of *Howden R100*, if I am confident in the ship I've designed. I have complete confidence in that airship. She has more than fulfilled my expectations and met every requirement of the contract."

"So, you're one hundred percent confident in making the Atlantic crossing in her, then," Colmore asked. There was a long pause at the other end and they took it to mean that *maybe* he wasn't.

Wallis eventually responded."Actually, I won't be going."

This came as a horrible blow to Colmore who was unable to conceal his shock. He looked betrayed.

"What! Why ever not?"

"I wish I could."

"What do you mean?"

"I'd love to go, but I'm forbidden to fly in airships by the chairman of our board."

"Why? You're on the list of passengers!" Colmore exclaimed.

"Apparently, my safety is of paramount importance to the company."

There was a long, awkward silence and Colmore looked sick.

"Barnes, will they consider holding off for a spell?" Brancker asked.

"I don't think they'd entertain the idea for a moment, Sir Sefton—and why should they, after the way they've been treated by Cardington all these years?"

The following Sunday afternoon, Buck drove Thomson and Marthe from Chequers to the Ritz, where Marthe was dropped off. She had much writing to do. Thomson returned to Ashley Gardens. He usually found Sunday evenings depressing at the best of times, but tonight it was worse. After such wonderful company, he felt lonely. He played his gramophone and sat on the chaise longue studying his ministerial papers in preparation for a busy week. Time was slipping away. He needed to get after Colmore.

He shut his eyes, soothed by the sounds of Mozart's *Don Giovanni* and Sammie's purring. He soon dozed off and found himself wandering the rues of Paris, searching for the girl in the white carriage. The streets were empty.

27

ENEMIES IN THE CAMP

Monday July 14, 1930.

The next morning, Thomson went to Gwydyr House. After his initial snooze on the chaise, he'd stumbled off to bed, but couldn't get back to sleep. He'd spent a sleepless night stewing about *Cardington R101*. All his personal plans depended on that ship being ready for the India flight. He instructed Knoxwood to call Colmore to Whitehall immediately. Colmore, rather shaken, arrived before lunch and was led into Thomson's office. He had no idea why he'd been summoned. He'd explained to Knoxwood he wasn't in uniform and was told it didn't matter.

"Just get down here, at once, Weggie," Knoxwood had said.

As soon as Colmore walked in, Thomson calmed down. The man was harmless; no point in scaring him to death. But he did want to confront him.

"I got you down here—and thank you for coming, by the way—as I've been hearing things which give me cause for concern. I thought it best to talk to you directly." Colmore gave a start. "Rumors are circulating of a concerted effort to delay the airship program."

"Er, h-how, sir?"

"They're trying everything in their power to postpone both voyages." Colmore swallowed hard and his eyes bulged. "A series of memos and reports were written and disseminated by people in your organization last week suggesting neither airship is ready for their flights."

"It's true reports were issued by—"

"I'm aware of who wrote them, Colmore, and what they say," Thomson snapped.

"Yes, sir."

"We have enemies in the camp. I trust you're not playing a double game—not part of a conspiracy, are you?"

"No, sir."

Thomson paused, his eyes fixed on Colmore. "I'm sure I know where this originated—it's coming from right here in this building, isn't it? Tell me who it is!"

"I don't know anything."

"No one has approached you?"

"No."

"I *will* find out. And you'd better *not* be involved."

"No, sir. *I'm* not involved."

That had to be a slip right there!

"You're not involved in *what*?"

"I've never heard of any conspiracies."

Thomson sat and stared at Colmore again. "I understand one of the inspectors has been stirring up a lot of trouble?"

"I wouldn't say that. He's concerned the gas bags are full of holes."

"And are conditions so serious to warrant him writing letters directly to the Air Ministry—going over the heads of you and your staff?"

"He's a bit of an alarmist, that's all."

"He wasn't put up to it by you, or someone else in this building, was he?"

"No, sir, absolutely not!"

"This problem he talks about—can it be rectified or not?"

"Oh, *definitely*, sir.

"He's not part of a conspiracy?"

"Oh Lord, no, sir, *certainly not*."

"I understand you've put him in charge of correcting these deficiencies?"

"Yes, it'll be his responsibility to oversee and inspect the work."

"Good. Perhaps it'll make him feel important."

"Quite, sir."

"That'll keep him quiet. Has work begun on the extra bay?"

"Er, no, sir."

Now there was an edge of menace in Thomson's voice. "And *why* is that, Colmore?"

"I haven't received instructions from my superiors to proceed."

Thomson studied Colmore with suspicion, his eyes narrowing. "I see."

Colmore went on. "It's my vague understanding the Cardington ship is being held in reserve until *Howden R100* completes her final test—in case she fails. Then *Cardington R101* would be available—"

Thomson looked incredulous. "To fly to *Canada?*"

"That's my understanding, yes, sir."

"To hell with the Canadian flight. You're not making any sense, Colmore. They're not going to fly to Canada in a ship in need of an extra bay. That's all hooey!"

"I think they were trying to maintain flexibility, sir. Then *Howden R100* would be available for the flight to India, if necessary."

"What is my name and title, Colmore?"

"Lord Thomson of Cardington, sir."

"I'm not Lord Thomson of *Howden?*"

"No, sir."

"I do not want to arrive in India in a ship constructed by the Vickers Airship Guarantee Company in Howden."

"I understand completely, sir."

"Nothing must delay my flight to India in *Cardington R101* built by the *Royal Airship Works!*

"Yes, sir."

Thomson spun round in his chair to face the painting of the Taj Mahal on the wall behind him. He raised his hand grandly to it, as though talking to a schoolboy. "The *India* flight, Colmore! Do you understand? *India!"* He turned back to face the beleaguered man. "*Got that?*"

"Yes, sir," Colmore said weakly, staring with dread into the Indian summer heat—but then noticing the airship, his eyes opened wide with surprise. Thomson smiled inwardly. Churchill had done a nice job. The man was quite a painter—for a *damned Tory!* It had certainly spooked Colmore.

"Make it happen! Everything clear?"

"*Perfectly* clear, sir. Yes, sir."

"Don't fail me. All right, get out."

Thomson was more convinced than ever that his suspicions and the rumors had been correct.

Thomson and Marthe spent the remainder of their time together enjoying London and their friends, with trips to country houses and dining in fine restaurants. Thomson usually went to the Ministry in the mornings, while Marthe worked on her writing in her hotel suite at the Ritz.

They spent many pleasant hours walking the streets of the West End, visiting museums and parks, their favorite being St. James's, where they fed the ducks. Like other things, this had become a ritual in this special place, the discord of last year forgotten.

Thomson didn't bring up the subject of marriage. He'd wait until just before Marthe's departure on Monday. As the week went by, he sensed this time she might give him a positive answer—she'd been exceptionally sweet this visit. On the last Saturday morning, since the weather was nice, they drove to Lord's Cricket Ground where Marthe made an effort to understand and enjoy the game.

While Thomson and Marthe were at Lord's, Lou was traveling back from the Scilly Isles in the Atlantic Ocean aboard *Howden R100*, completing her final twenty-four-hour test. The ship had behaved perfectly. Shortly after she returned to Cardington, her departure for Montreal was confirmed for 3:30 a.m. Tuesday morning.

Lou and Charlotte had seen little of one another over the past few weeks. She'd been on night duty at the hospital and asleep during the day. He was awakened by her in the mornings as she climbed into bed just before dawn; usually tired and irritable. She rarely spoke. Lou had been working long hours, getting the airship ready for the twenty-four-hour final test and the flight to Canada. In the evenings, he arrived as Charlotte was leaving. They gave each other a smile and a peck on the cheek, like passing strangers.

Charlotte had lost weight and settled into a never-ending state of despair, speaking in monosyllables, if at all, her vitality gone. There was no animosity between them and Lou was patient and affectionate. He remained convinced Charlotte would snap out of it once the two ships had made their intercontinental flights and were up and running, confident their closeness would return.

Charlotte still kept the house immaculate and the kitchen cupboards well-stocked. She'd put his things together for the Canada voyage and his side trip down to Virginia to see his family. Lou got the impression she was glad he was making the effort to see them. Pity she couldn't be with him. They'd love her. Still, there'd be plenty of time for that. Perhaps they'd make a trip to New York next year—he'd suggest they start planning as soon as he got back.

When Lou returned from the final test on Saturday evening, Charlotte was home. She appeared brighter. She told him she had time off to help him get ready for his departure on Tuesday. "Does your family know you're coming?" Charlotte asked.

"I sent them a telegram," Lou replied. "I expect they'll be at Union Station." The atmosphere was difficult to comprehend; although she was more communicative, there remained a distance between them as wide as the Atlantic Ocean. They'd become polite strangers.

"I've washed plenty of socks, pants and shirts for you. And your spare trousers are on the bed. Shall I put them in your kit bag?" Charlotte asked.

"No, no. I can do it."

"It's no trouble."

"If you could dig out one or two photos of yourself and of us together, I'd like to show them to my parents," Lou said.

"I'll put some on your bedside table."

"Thanks, honey."

"I put a book there for you — 'Great Expectations.'"

"Dickens. Super! I'll read it on the ship. Thanks, love."

"So, it's definitely on for Tuesday, then?"

"Yes."

"What happened with Fred McWade and all that late-night carry-on?"

"Things blew over. I told him they would."

"So everything's all right now with the Cardington ship?"

"Yes. I expect it'll be fine. Fred's overseeing the problem now—he'll make sure things are done right." As he said this, Lou wondered if any of Brancker's tactics had worked.

Nothing had been started on extending the ship. He thought someone had to be pulling strings to prevent Colmore moving ahead. It was mystifying. He assumed the reports written by the R.A.W. team had fallen on deaf ears, since he'd seen no reaction from any quarter. If ordered to insert the extra bay, would they still be required to meet Thomson's schedule? If so, they were losing valuable time for testing. Irwin had drawn up a comprehensive schedule of tests to be done after modifications were complete. Lou had never told Charlotte about any of this, knowing she'd worry herself sick. He had to admit it worried him, too.

"And they're putting in an extra bay—shouldn't be any problems then," Lou told her.

"What about the Howden ship? Were your tests okay?" Charlotte asked.

"They went without a hitch. She's a good ship. The flight to Canada will be as easy as pie."

"I expect you'll be glad to see your family. That'll be nice. How will you get down to Virginia?"

"I'll hop on a train in Montreal. It'll take me through New York to Washington. They'll know when we arrive. It'll be big news. God, I wish you could be with me, Charlie. Next year, perhaps, huh?"

Charlotte gave a half smile. "It's been a long time. I hope they're okay. Things are very bad in America." This made Lou pause—he hadn't given the American economy much thought. "When you're with them, perhaps you might decide to stay there," she said.

Lou grabbed her shoulders and looked into her eyes.

"Hey, don't talk like that. You know I'll come back. I love you, Charlie."

She looked away as if she hadn't heard.

"The time will fly by. I'll be back in no time flat," Lou said.

"Yes, I expect so."

28

TIME TO SAY GOODBYE

Monday & Tuesday July 28 & 29, 1930.

Thomson and Marthe sat on the terrace waiting for afternoon tea. It was sunny, with a delightful breeze off the river. Buck waited in the limousine on the quadrangle with Marthe's luggage stowed in the trunk. Thomson needed to be available. An important vote was coming to the floor. Prematurely, the newspapers were full of the story of Thomson's selection as next Viceroy to India. This gave him satisfaction, though he hadn't formally accepted—that could wait until his return from India. He still needed Marthe's decision. A waiter arrived with a tray of tea and cakes and set them on the table. He poured their teas and left.

"The newspapers are full of it today," Thomson said.

"This will be your crowning achievement. After that, who knows what the future may bring? Perhaps *even* higher office someday," Marthe said.

Thomson didn't want to concern himself with that today, although the thought had often crossed his mind. "I'm still uneasy about leaving Ramsay to deal with the radicals in the party. It's a lonely life being Prime Minister. Our talks give him solace. It's all perhaps too much to ask for the sake of what—*ambition?* Five years is a long time to be away—*"

He was cut off by one of the ushers from the chamber rushing up and the sound of Big Ben striking the half hour: five-thirty.

"Lord Thomson—it's time to vote, sir."

Of all the times!

"Marthe, wait for me. We must talk before you go. I won't be long."

"Don't worry. I'll be here. Go and cast your vote."

"I'll meet you in the Hall in twenty minutes," he said, glancing at his watch.

Thomson set off for the House at a brisk pace. Marthe strolled down to the river wall and peered at the rippling water, lapping the embankment. A tug hooted as it passed, towing empty barges toward the docks. She was jarred back from her reflections on Thomson's overtures by the pitiful calls of a seagull which landed on the wall beside her.

A warning?

She turned away from the river and headed for the lobby. Once inside Westminster Hall, she glanced across the flagstones to the spot where Charles I had been sentenced to death through Cromwell's treachery. She thought of his horrible death mask at Chequers.

Go away morbid thoughts!

"This is the place where they bring the dead to lie in state," Thomson had told her once.

She shuddered and went to the wall to study a picture of the beleaguered King in a gilt frame, his head still defiantly on his shoulders. Wherever she stood, his accusing eyes followed her. She was disturbed by the sound of someone entering at the bottom of the hall. The crash of doors echoed across the space a hundred feet away. She turned to look, hoping it might be Thomson, but it was a paunchy, old gentleman with long, white hair who strode toward her.

"I'm sorry. I thought you were somebody else," Marthe said.

"Who are you waiting for? Perhaps I can be of assistance," the man said.

"Lord Thomson."

"Ah, you must mean our precious Lord of the Air!"

Is this man being sarcastic?

"Er, yes."

"If I were you, Madam, I'd talk him out of all of his grandiose schemes. It can only end in disaster. It's all just an *impossible dream*, you know."

"And who are *you*, sir?"

He raised his hat. "Lord Scunthorpe at your service, Madam. Good day to you."

He walked off toward the north entrance. Thomson entered from the other end, carrying his hat. He noticed Marthe looked ruffled. "Did that man speak to you?" he said.

"Oh, he just asked if he could be of assistance, that's all."

"Did he say anything else?"

"Nothing *important*."

They walked across the room and he stared up at the ceiling as he always did.

"Yes, I know, it's the most magnificent Gothic room in all of England," Marthe said. He smiled. They stopped for a moment at the center, his eyes earnest. "Marthe—"

She raised her hand to stop him.

"Kit, I've given the matter a great deal of thought. Your voting gave me a final moment to reflect." She placed her hand on his arm. "Fly your airship to India and on your return, I promise, you shall have my answer."

Thomson was disappointed, but perhaps a triumphant return aboard *Cardington R101* would seal things. When they reached the exit doors, they kissed cheeks and said their goodbyes. He led Marthe to the curb, Buck opened the car door and Marthe slipped into the backseat. They exchanged waves and smiles through the window as Big Ben was striking six, Thomson watched her driven away. The car turned onto Parliament Square and disappeared on Victoria Street. He put on his hat and walked back toward Westminster Hall.

As Thomson and Marthe were saying their farewells, Lou was checking progress at the tower for *Howden R100's* departure next morning. The area around the tower swarmed with ground crewmen pumping gas, water, petrol and carrying provisions on board. Since the ship had behaved flawlessly, no repairs were required.

Lou spoke with Capt. Booth and First Officer Meager who told him to go home and be with his wife— *'everything was under control.'* Norway confirmed the same thing, saying he planned to stay on the ship all day and through the night until departure. He sent his love to Charlotte. Lou went to bid farewell to Irwin and Atherstone in Shed No.1 and find out if there were any new developments on their front. Lou entered the shed as a commotion started.

The works foreman stood in the corner yelling. "All right, you lot." The men shuffled toward him. "Okay, boys, it's time to cut the lady in half."

"Oooo-bloody-ray!"

"It's about bleedin' time!"

"Been standin' around 'ere for weeks waitin'."

"Bunch o' wankers!"

Lou normally would've smiled, but morale and discipline had slipped steadily over the past few weeks—not so much with the Howden group, but it was out in the open in Shed No.1. They were looking in his direction.

"Not this bloke. He ain't a wanker," one said.

"What? The commander? No, he's all right."

"This bunch 'ere don't know if they're comin' or goin' half the bloody time."

Hundreds of men gathered equipment and wheeled scaffold into position, ready to break the ship at its center. Utilities and controls inside the airship would need to be detached, lengthened and reconnected on completion—itself, a daunting task. Workmen climbed aboard to get started. Other crews were getting ready to detach the exterior cover.

Lou knocked on Irwin's door and went in. Irwin appeared gaunt. Atherstone sat behind a dilapidated desk in the corner. He looked just as weary. Irwin stood at a high table reviewing drawings for the modifications.

"Looks like something's happening out there, sir," Lou said.

"They just got word," Irwin replied.

"They've been hanging around for weeks without pay," Atherstone said.

"At least someone made a decision," Lou said.

"Now it's gonna be *rush, rush, rush*," Irwin grumbled.

"There'll be plenty of overtime," Lou said.

"For them, it's feast or famine," Atherstone said.

"I want to make sure this ship gets tested properly when they're done," Irwin said. "I heard your test went well, Lou?"

Lou nodded.

Irwin stuck out his hand. "Charlotte okay?"

Lou pursed his lips and waggled his head from side to side. "Not really."

"I'll make sure Olivia keeps in touch with her. Lou, have a safe flight."

"Thank you, sir."

"Good luck, Lou," Atherstone said.

Lou returned to the shed floor, running into Ronnie the works foreman and McWade.

"They're happy now, aren't they?" Lou said.

"This lot's *never* 'appy."

"At least they're back to work."

The foreman shook Lou's hand. "Best of luck, sir."

"Thanks, Ronnie."

"You'll be all right," Ronnie whispered.

"You're still coming right, Fred?" Lou asked.

"I suppose I am," McWade answered.

As Lou was leaving, Potter, Binks, Church and Disley gathered round him. They shook his hand, wishing him a safe journey. Cameron arrived, out of breath.

"What's up, Doug?" Lou asked.

"I've just been told I'm going to Canada."

"You lucky devil! What happened?" Binks asked.

"Their coxswain's gone down with mumps."

"Well, don't look so bloody miserable, mate," Church said.

"It's money in yer pocket, ain't it?" Binks said.

Lou glanced at Cameron, understanding his dilemma. He hurried home to Charlotte.

The day was hot. Lou sat outside on one of the deck chairs he'd bought the previous summer. Fluffy lay lazily in the shade beside him. Charlotte brought out corned beef sandwiches and a beer for Lou.

They sat listening to the insects buzzing around Charlotte's flowers, conversation impossible.

Later, Mr. and Mrs. Jones popped their heads over the garden fence and spent a few minutes wishing Lou a safe voyage. Sensing tension, they didn't linger. When they'd gone, Lou and Charlotte resumed their awkward silence. In the end, they went to the living room on the second floor and Lou read the newspaper. Fluffy followed and sat on the couch beside him. After twenty minutes Charlotte went to the kitchen to prepare dinner, peeling potatoes and carrots. When Charlotte had left the room, Lou rested his head back while he stroked Fluffy.

"You want to come for a ride in an airship, Fluff? The cat mewed softly, jumped down, and went out. "No, I don't suppose you do—sorry puss, I forgot," he said.

This was all too painful. Lou wished he was on the airship over the Atlantic—anywhere but here right now. That wasn't fair. He knew how Charlotte would feel as he drove off on his motorbike in the morning.

She'll be damned lonesome.

They ate dinner and went to bed early. Charlotte did something she hadn't done for a long time. She lit the candle on her bedside table. He made love to her. She wasn't responsive, nor was she cold, just preoccupied—in some other place. She let him do whatever he wanted. He took pleasure in re-exploring every curve of her beautiful body. How long had it been? Weeks—perhaps months. He couldn't remember. After an hour, he cradled her in his arms until it was time to leave. He got up and washed and put on his uniform. He went downstairs and left his kit bag by the door. Before going back upstairs, he took the framed photograph of Charlotte from the mantelpiece in the living room, wrapped it in a shirt, and slipped it into his kitbag. He searched for Fluffy, but she was nowhere to be found. He opened the back door. She wasn't there.

Charlotte got up and put on a long, white, silk nightdress and came to him at the center of the bedroom. She stared at him and put her arms around his neck. She kissed his lips slowly and deliberately, seeming to savor the moment. He held her and took a handful of her hair, running it through his fingers at her back. She gazed at him with those huge, blue eyes, as if for the last time. He sensed she believed she'd never see him again.

God, you're so beautiful!

"Oh God, I love your hair," he said softly.

"Make the most of it," she whispered.

"I *am* coming back, you know—I promise you."

Doubt showed in her eyes.

"Better go," he said, letting go of her.

She slowly removed her arms and followed him down to the door. They embraced and kissed again on the recessed front porch.

"See you in about three weeks, honey," he said. "I love you."

Her voice was barely audible. "Goodbye, Lou."

He descended the steps to his motorbike, fastened his kit bag on the luggage rack and kicked it over. He climbed on and turned to Charlotte standing in the doorway, her long, white nightdress backlit by the overhead light. She looked like an apparition of a Greek goddess, her flowing, black hair shining in the moonlight. He felt sick leaving her now, and guilty. He wished he could stay another hour, or just not leave at all. He bowed his head to her and waved. She didn't move or make any gesture. Like a statue. He drove away believing he could never feel more miserable than this. But he was wrong.

PART THREE

Howden Airship R100 Approaches Montreal. July 1930.

CANADA

29

LIVERPOOL

Tuesday July 29, 1930.

Lou arrived at the Cardington tower at around 2:00 a.m. The place was a hive of activity; gear, mechanical parts, gas valves, fuel tanks and ballast tanks had to be checked and rechecked. Ground crewmen carried luggage and last-minute items aboard while the gas bags were given a final top up. A crowd of two thousand spectators watched the floodlit ship from the fence. Lou's mood lifted. Next to their black Austin, Meager kissed his wife and small son goodbye. Mrs. Meager laid the child on the back seat and got in, blowing a kiss as she drove away.

Lou noticed Jessup assisting the ground crew, carrying boxes of provisions to the elevator. He gave Lou a hateful glance over his shoulder. Lou climbed off his motorbike as Binks came up.

"What's *he* doing over there?" Lou asked, nodding toward Jessup.

"He's working with the ground crew."

Lou was puzzled, but said nothing.

"Shall I take care of the bike, sir?" Binks asked.

"That'd be nice of you, Joe, thanks. Leave it over by the admin office. Oh, I've another favor to ask." Lou pulled out a brown envelope from his kit bag containing a flat box. "Would you mind putting this in the postbox next Monday? It's a birthday card for Charlotte. Her birthday's on the sixth of August. I'd like it to arrive the day before."

Binks tucked the envelope inside his coat.

"I'll do that with pleasure."

"Thanks, Joe."

"I wish I was coming with you, sir."

"Won't be long now. We'll all be off to India in *your* ship soon."

Binks climbed on the *Brough Superior*. "Good luck. I'll be right here with your bike when you get back, sir," he said.

Lou headed toward the customs shed for clearance before boarding. Colmore got out of the Works' Humber in front of the building, dressed in a sports coat, collar and tie. He'd had his hair cut for the trip—an extreme short back and sides. His face had a grey pallor, matching his jacket. He looked sick with fright.

Lou went over to him. "Is everything all right, sir?"

Colmore raised a trembling hand, wiped his forehead and grunted. Lou put his kitbag over his shoulder and took Colmore's small suitcase from the driver and walked with him. Inside, crewmen and a few civilians were being checked for prohibited items. On the wall was a notice with red lettering:

ABSOLUTELY NO MATCHES OR LIGHTERS ALLOWED

WEIGHT RESTRICTIONS:

Passengers and Officers 30 lbs
Crewmen 15 lbs

Lou stood at Colmore's side. When asked questions, Colmore answered in monosyllables. Scott appeared behind them, tapping Colmore on the shoulder. Colmore's face brightened slightly and he let out a deep sigh.

"I came down to get you, Reggie. You'll be all right. It'll be a lovely trip, you'll see. The views along the St. Lawrence will be spectacular," Scott said.

Lou emptied his kitbag for the customs officer and was surprised to find a black leather writing case at the bottom. Charlotte must have put it in there. After clearance, he walked with Colmore and Scott to the tower elevator.

"Coming?" Scott asked.

"No, I'll take the stairs, sir," Lou answered.

Lou was glad to get away to his assigned cabin in the officers' section. He hated to see men of high rank paralyzed with fright—he'd seen plenty during the war. The passenger section accommodated one hundred, with eighteen four-berth cabins on the upper level and fourteen two-berth on the lower level. Cabins were situated above the crew's quarters over the control car. The officers' cabins were grouped together—small but comfortable, measuring seven feet by eight, with paper-thin, beige, fabric walls.

Lou's narrow bed, tight to the wall, consisted of stretched canvas over aluminum framing and beside the bed, a writing table against the head wall—both immovable. On the bed was a 'teddy' and a Sidcot flying suit with a fur collar, neatly folded beside them, a sleeping bag, a blanket and a sheet.

A curtain concealed a small closet in the corner with two shelves. Lou removed the framed photograph of Charlotte from his kit bag. He'd taken the picture in Switzerland at Christmas: she posed beside a snow-laden fir tree wearing her ski outfit and a big smile. He studied her suntanned face. She'd been happy on that trip. He carefully placed the frame on the bedside table next to his binoculars. He emptied his kitbag on the bed and picked up the writing case. He flipped it open. Inside he found a leather-bound diary embossed with gold lettering and a pad of fine, white writing paper, together with a pen, but no inscription or note. Charlotte must have wanted him to keep a journal.

A nice going-away present. Good girl. Great idea!

He placed it on the writing table with *Great Expectations* beside her photograph. He suddenly had a horrible sinking feeling. Those old feelings of panic and depression swept over him. She was his rock. He didn't want to leave.

Damn, I miss her already.

Lou took the shirts and hung them in the closet with his work clothes and stowed his socks and pants on the shelves below. He heard a nervous cough outside and then that familiar voice.

"Hello, *Lou?*"

"That's me."

Lou opened the curtain. Norway stood there grinning, his unlit pipe clamped between his teeth.

"All set?" he inquired.

"I guess."

Norway showed Lou where he was berthed. Burney was in the next cabin. He came out and shook hands with Lou.

"You still want to do this, Sir Dennis?" Lou said.

Burney didn't say much—perhaps he'd got the jitters now, too, Lou thought. Along the corridor, Scott stood at Colmore's door. Hopefully, Colmore was feeling better. When Scott saw Norway's pipe, he charged down the corridor and gave him a shove.

"Get rid of that damned thing!" he yelled.

"It's not lit," Norway protested.

"I don't care, just get rid of it!" Scott grunted.

Norway put the pipe in his inside pocket and wandered back inside his cabin.

"He's right, Nev, you'll scare everyone to death," Lou called after him.

Scott took Colmore's arm. "Come on, Reggie. Let's go and get some coffee in the dining room, shall we?" he said.

There were half a dozen passengers in and out of their cabins, getting settled in along the corridor, including R.A.W. officials. Inside some berths, people snored, a few having come aboard early and retired. After chatting for a few minutes, Lou made his way to the control car, passing McWade, whose face was like a mask. Since McWade had received the letter from the Ministry, neither of them had mentioned his late-night visit again. Lou was sure he was frustrated and highly embarrassed. Lou reached the wireless room above the control car and poked his head in on Disley, who glanced up.

"Evening, sir."

"How you doing, Dizzy?" Lou said.

The meteorologist's room was next door and occupied by Mr. Giblett, whom Lou had met at Cardington House a few times. Giblett was working on weather maps and data. Lou descended into the spacious control car incorporating the chartroom, passing Johnston, busy with his charts. Capt. Booth and Capt. Meager stood nursing mugs of coffee, waiting for the last passengers to arrive. The two coxswains were stationed at their wheels.

Lou smiled at the officers. "Good morning, Captain," he said, nodding.

"Morning, Lou. I'll take the first watch until 6:00 a.m. We'll rotate in four-hour stints throughout the voyage. We've got a lot of experienced officers on board. We can split some of these watches up."

"Very good, sir."

Giblett entered the control car holding up a sheet of paper. "I've just finished the weather chart. As I said earlier, a small depression is centered over the north of Ireland. If we work our way around to the north, we'll pick up a favoring wind that'll push us west."

"*Excellent!* Exactly what we need," Booth said.

"That won't last, but I'm working on another system over the Atlantic, which might come in handy."

"Keep us posted." Booth turned to Lou. "Ask the chief coxswain to let us know when everyone's aboard. We're ready to cast off."

"Aye, aye, Captain," Lou said.

On his way to the stairs Johnston looked up. "Hey, Lou."

"This is the *India* flight, right?" Lou said.

"Oh, non, non, non. You're on der wrong sheep," Johnston said, chuckling. "Dis sheep is for Montreal, *French Canada!*"

Lou headed to the central corridor and found the chief coxswain, who reported they were still waiting for one R.A.W. official. All first watch crewmembers were at their stations. Second Officer Steff was in the main corridor with a crew of riggers ready to set the gas bags on take-off. As the ship ascended, the gas would expand and bags would need careful repositioning to prevent damage to them. The rest of the crew sat in their quarters drinking coffee, or slept in their bunks. Lou returned to the control car and relayed the information to Booth.

"We'll give that man ten minutes," Booth said.

They stood around waiting until the chief coxswain called down. "Everyone's aboard, sir, save the one. Thirty-eight crewmen and six passengers present and accounted for. Crewmen are at their stations awaiting orders!"

"Then we shall wait no longer. Start engines and pull up the gangplank," Booth ordered.

Lou wondered what had happened to the R.A.W. guy. Perhaps he'd got cold feet. He remembered his engineer Wiggins who missed *R38* when his car broke down.

That was Wiggins' lucky day! Is this the 'Wiggy thing' all over again?

Engines were started and in no time they'd slipped the mast. In the half darkness, the ship floated upwards. Booth gave instructions for ballast to be dumped at the stern to bring the tail up. There was just enough light to make out the fields and the roads below. They heard cheers from the ground crewmen on the tower and on the field through the open windows. The ship turned slowly and cruised very low across the front of Shed No.1, while *Cardington R101* crewmen and construction workers stood at the doors shaking their fists at them.

Booth smiled. "Now it's *their* turn. And they don't like it."

"Do we bite our thumbs at you, sir? *Damn right we do!*—I've been polishing up on my Shakespeare," Lou said, smiling at Meager, who laughed.

Booth ordered more power and the ship ascended to one thousand feet. They turned toward Bedford. Lou was able to make out Kelsey Street and then their house, which was in total darkness. He presumed Charlotte had gone back to bed. He thought about how lovely she'd looked on the front step in the moonlight. Already, he couldn't wait to get back home to her.

I'll make it up to you, I swear.

After passing over Bedford, Johnston called out the heading for Liverpool and they were soon at fifteen hundred feet and on their way, riding smoothly on three engines at forty-five knots. Lou was tired. He went to his cabin, changed into his work clothes and lay down, covering himself with the sleeping bag and blanket. The ship was eerily quiet, seeming perfectly still—the engines far enough aft of the control car to make them completely silent. Before drifting off, he thought of Charlotte, then *R38* and his dead crewmen, and then Josh and *Shenandoah*. It all seemed so long ago. He slept while the ship cruised across Midland towns toward Liverpool.

Lou was awakened just before 6:00 a.m. by music from the gramophone in the crew's quarters below. They had the volume low—at least they were being considerate. At first, Lou had no idea where he was. He listened to the music for a few minutes, looking at Charlotte's photograph on the bedside table. He hoped she was okay and able to sleep.

Although still tired, he went to the toilet room and washed his face in cold water and brushed his teeth. A steward brought him hot water in a tin can for shaving. The floor of the washroom was covered in brown linoleum and echoed hollow underfoot. There were two small shower stalls with a sign 'Please Conserve Water' and in a separate area, two WCs with privacy curtains and an extractor fan in the ceiling. By the smell, they had already been used extensively.

He looked in on the control car where Meager had just taken over the watch from Booth. They passed over the Roman-Saxon town of Chester. Off to starboard, they saw the smoky haze over Liverpool and turned toward it. The ship flew directly over the impressive, white city hall building and then the sandstone cathedral. As they went over, train whistles, car horns and steamer sirens in the port, wished them well.

30

THE IRISH SEA

Tuesday July 29, 1930.

They left the English coast at Formby Point at 6:20 a.m. and headed out into the Irish Sea toward the Isle of Man, passing Morcambe Lightship on starboard. Lou decided to stretch his legs before breakfast and climbed to the upper deck.

From there, he could look down onto the promenade decks, equipped with loungers, wicker seating and matching low tables. He turned and went to the center and leaned on the white railing around the perimeter of the forty by forty foot, two-story dining room below. It was bright and airy with windows allowing plenty of natural light— a departure from previous airship design. This room was the largest space on the ship, seating fifty-six.

Stewards, in white coats and black trousers, were serving breakfast. The chief steward, Pierre, looked up at Lou and smiled. Lou gave him a nod. He admired the tablecloths and flatware—not as expensive as the other ship's stuff. Not the Ritz exactly, but not bad—a reasonable restaurant in town, perhaps. The room was busy with a buzz of whispering, punctuated by clattering plates in the galley. The smell of eggs, bacon and coffee wafted up—it all seemed surreal, hovering above the Irish Sea like this.

He returned to the control car as they entered a heavy rain shower and flew blind for a few long moments. When they came out, a mountain on an island appeared dead ahead.

"What's this island, sir?" Lou asked.

"It's Isle of Man and *that* is Sugarloaf Mountain—which I think we should take pains to avoid," Meager replied. They altered course to fly along the coast of the island toward the point of Ayre Lighthouse and Scotland beyond. The green hills of the Lake District lay to starboard.

"I'm going for breakfast. Do you need anything?" Lou asked.

"Johnny and Steff are relieving me at eight. I'll join you then, thanks."

Lou went to the dining room where Colmore sat with Scott and Sqn. Ldr. Archie Wann and a couple of R.A.W. officials. Colmore looked more relaxed. McWade sat at a table with Giblett the meteorologist. Lou nodded to McWade and went over to Wann, who got up from the table to greet him. Lou hadn't seen him to speak to since leaving him in the control car on *R38* just before it broke in two and fell from the sky. Lou had been down to visit Wann in the intensive care ward just before he left the hospital, but Wann was swathed in bandages, unconscious. He was surprised how much Wann had aged, his hair now pretty grey. They shook hands while everyone looked on, understanding their connection. It was a touching moment. Neither man spoke. Lou left Wann and went and found an empty table. They'd talk later.

Lou felt drained due to lack of sleep and worry about Charlotte. It'd been a wrench leaving her. He'd burdened himself with all her emotions and added them to his own. It felt like a hangover. Norway entered the dining room as Lou was finishing breakfast. He was smiling and pretty jazzed.

"You're looking mighty pleased with yourself there, buddy," Lou said.

"I just s-saw the lighthouse at P-Point Ayre. It's b-blowing a gale out there."

The steward came to take Norway's order.

"I'll have c-coffee and the f-full English breakfast and t-toast p-please," Norway said. "And yes, I'm very p-pleased with the sh-ship."

Meager appeared and joined them. The steward looked at Meager.

"I'll have what he ordered. Sounds good to me," Meager said.

"We've a long way to go yet. Don't get too cocky," Lou cautioned.

Lou glanced around the room as though appraising it for the first time—for Norway's benefit. "It looks pretty good, I suppose," he said.

"You slept well?" Norway asked.

"No complaints."

"An airship is the best place in the world to fall asleep," Meager said.

"What happened to our friend?" Lou asked.

"Who?" Norway asked.

"Jessup. I saw him at the tower, but I haven't seen him since."

"He got the b-boot."

"Who by?"

"Captain Booth."

"Why?"

"Someone told him Jessup was a b-bad lot," Norway said.

"Who told him that?"

"Me." Norway grinned.

"You!"

"Yes. I didn't want to d-deal with that n-nut. We've got enough to worry about."

"We can do without that," Meager agreed.

"Who broke the news to Jessup?" Lou asked.

"Sky Hunt. He said he was p-pretty annoyed."

"He'll blame me for it. Not that I care," Lou said.

The steward arrived with a plate of eggs and bacon in each hand. Norway and Meager began eating.

"I'm starving," Meager said. "I'm going to take a look on top later. You might as well come with me, Lou."

"I've got to pump petrol first. Can we do it after that?"

"Sure."

Norway looked envious. "Should I c-c-come, too?" he said.

"No, no need," Meager answered.

"All right, I'll take a look round inside then," Norway said, disappointed.

After breakfast, Lou went with Norway to transfer petrol with hand pumps to the gravity tanks above the engine cars. They were assisted by Billy, Cameron, Nervous Nick and Disley. Everyone was expected to do his part and Lou thought he might as well get used to it. There'd be plenty of this grunt work to be done if they wanted to reach Canada.

"I can't believe you people were too cheap to install a couple of damned electric pumps," Lou grumbled. "And you didn't put pumps in the WC's either did you? It's gonna get pretty nasty in those rest rooms, mister."

Norway grinned his silly horsey grin. "We didn't have money for luxuries," he said.

Later, Lou followed Meager up the cat ladder to the forward hatch on the roof.

"Keep your eyes open for damage to the cover. If the rain gets in, you know what happens to the gas bags," Meager said.

"Yes, sir."

"Hold on tight. Let's go."

They climbed out of the envelope onto the twelve-inch-wide reinforced catwalk on the roof, holding onto a bitterly cold, steel cable. The cable stretched over seven-hundred feet from bow to stern, lying alongside the catwalk. The conditions were blustery and cold, and they were surrounded by scattered, swirling clouds.

"Where are we?" Lou shouted.

"Over the Mull of Galloway."

Lou looked out to the starboard side and saw the rugged terrain of Scotland in the distance.

"Come on, follow me!" Meager yelled above the howling wind.

They crawled on their hands and knees up the slope of the never-ending catwalk, making their inspection. Lou thought of Charlotte; if she could see him now, she'd die! He wondered how many airshipmen had been lost doing this. If they were blown away, no one would even know. They'd just be unaccounted for. When they reached halfway, violent squalls peppered them with showers of hail, which felt like razor blades on their faces and hands. It was as if Mother Nature was trying to pry their hands off the cable. By the time they reached the stern, they were soaked through and chilled to the marrow. Neither of them had spotted any damage to the cover or intakes. Meager opened the trap door and they climbed down, their hands so numb it'd become almost impossible to hold on.

"Well, that was invigorating!" Lou said.

"Let's go and dry out," Meager said.

They returned to their cabins and changed into their second set of work clothes. Lou put on his teddy, which was aptly named. They took their wet clothes to the cook in the galley for him to dry. Pierre admired Lou's outfit.

"Very nice, my dear. *Very cuddly*, if you don't mind me saying."

Meager roared with laughter. Lou went off to look for Norway and found him amidships.

"You look sweet," Norway said.

"Now don't *you* start!"

"How's everything on the roof?" Norway asked.

"Bloody freezing! But everything looked good. No leaks—*yet*."

"I'm going to take a gander at the engines," Norway said.

"Come on then, let's go."

They climbed down the ladder to each of the three nacelles, the menacing, grey Atlantic only twelve hundred feet below. Lou admired his friend, who showed no fear. Climbing down was no problem for Lou, but once inside the engine car, he felt uncomfortable. His heart rate accelerated and he began to sweat. He kept an eye on the exit to reassure himself there was a quick way out.

In each of the three cars were two, brand-spanking new Rolls-Royce Condor IIIB liquid-cooled, V-12, 650 bph engines, in tandem—a total of six. They were barely broken in, having been installed only recently for the final test flight. The Air Ministry had decided, without fuss, to change the reconditioned engines Burney had forced on Wallis.

To a mechanic, or anyone with a love of engines, these monsters were impressive and sounded sweet. After a few hand signals between themselves and the engineers, they left the engine car and went to the ladder, where they paused to look at Rathlin Island on port. It looked wild and remote in this force eight gale. They climbed back into the hull. Norway went to his cabin to write up his log and Lou changed into his uniform, ready for an early lunch, before going on duty.

Lou returned to the empty dining room. One steward stood by the wall, his arms folded. Pierre greeted Lou with a welcoming smile.

"It's lovely to see you again, sir," he said.

"Thank you," Lou said, sitting down.

"You look much smarter in uniform, Commander, but I must say I *did* like you in your teddy."

Lou nodded modestly, noticing the other steward scowling.

Pierre put a jug of water on the table. "We have beer, if you prefer?"

"No, I'm going on watch. Water will do."

"For lunch we have mushroom soup, beef stew, mashed potatoes and peas."

"That'll be fine, thank you."

Pierre hurried off to the kitchen with the steward following him. After hearing raised voices and grumbling, the sour-faced steward returned and placed a bowl of soup and a basket of bread in front of Lou without speaking. Lou got started.

Pierre reappeared as Lou was finishing his soup. He picked up the plate and empty soup bowl. "Was the soup to your liking, sir?"

"Yes, thanks."

"I was on the promenade deck earlier looking at the Scottish scenery. It's lovely. Have you seen it?" Pierre asked.

"Yeah, I saw it from the roof when I was up there."

"You were on the roof! Oh my goodness, you must be *ever so* careful."

"I was holding on, don't worry."

"I'd love to go there. I've never been," Pierre said.

"On the roof?"

"Oh no, no, silly! *Scotland*."

"Scotland, yeah, right."

"I expect you must be missing your wife, sir. I heard you were married to a most *beautiful* lady."

Lou cleared his throat, pretending not to have heard. He picked up his glass and swallowed a mouthful of water and Pierre scurried out. The steward returned, carrying Lou's stew on a tray. He set it down and disappeared. Lou stared after him as Pierre reentered the room. He noticed Lou's expression.

"Oh, don't worry about him. He's got the 'ump," and then conspiratorially, "He can be a right little 'you-know-what' sometimes!"

Lou finished his lunch and Pierre returned.

"For dessert today we have greengages and custard," he said.

Greengages and custard!

"I'll take a pass on that."

"I thought you would," Pierre said, puckering his lips.

Hell! Now what have I said!

"Oh, I do love your accent—I could listen to it *all night*," Pierre said.

Lou raised his eyebrows, but didn't respond.

"If I can do anything to make your voyage more pleasurable, I'm at your mercy ... er I mean at your *service,* er sorry. My name's Pierre, but you know that. If you're in need of anything, I mean *anything*, please let me know ..."

Lou got up. "That's very kind of you, Pierre. I don't anticipate anything, but thank you just the same."

"What about *coffee?* Aren't you staying for coffee?"

Lou made his escape.

Lou reported for duty at 11:45 a.m. in the control car with Cameron and one of the regular ship's rudder coxswains. They'd picked up the favorable winds promised by Giblett around the Head of Islay and were heading due west along the last stretch of Ireland's north coast. They'd stopped the aft engines and were now cruising on three at forty-five knots. With the favoring wind, the ship's ground speed was now sixty-five knots. Steff and Johnston stayed with Lou and the two relief coxswains for ten minutes, lingering to look at Tory Island, five miles in the distance, before going for lunch.

"Say goodbye to the Emerald Isle, lads," Johnston said, putting on an Irish accent. That's the last dry land you'll see for seventeen hundred miles—'til we reach Newfoundland."

Johnston turned one of the clocks back one hour to 11:00 a.m.

"We just entered Greenwich Mean Time, Zone One," he said.

When they'd gone, Lou looked down at the ocean ahead. It was foreboding. He felt fear in the pit of his stomach, which caught him by surprise. He looked at the two coxswains. He knew they'd be having similar thoughts.

"You lads okay?"

"Yes, sir," Cameron said gloomily.

Lou wasn't convinced.

"Fine, sir," the rudder coxswain said more brightly.

31

THE ATLANTIC

Tuesday July 29, 1930.

Lou returned his gaze to the ocean below. They were so low—at times it felt as though they were actually on the water. It looked pretty damned desolate and unfriendly out there. He wondered if they could've made it to New Jersey in *R38* if she hadn't broken in two.

That's a good question.

And what happened to that pilot and the heiress who'd attempted to make this crossing in a small plane? Lou had met the guy in Cardington with his wife, there to ask for assistance from the Meteorological Office. That was when Lou had first met Giblett, the weather guy. After the pilot and his wife had discussed weather patterns over the Atlantic with Giblett and Johnston, a whole crowd had gone with them to the Kings Arms pub. It was like a celebration—a send-off. Pretty soon the pilot and Richmond got into a dust up about whether planes or airships would prevail.

Not long after that, the pilot and his heiress copilot took off from Cranwell Aerodrome and disappeared. The newspapers had been full of it and the public became totally engrossed. It was a weird story. Following their disappearance, the pilot's wife went on a crusade in a bid to end the airship program—supposedly put up to it by her dead husband. Lou glanced at the whitecaps below and shook his head.

Crazy people! What was their name? Hinkley? ... Hinchliffe—that was it!

Lou heard footsteps on the stairs. It was Scott and Colmore.

"How's everything, Commander?" Scott asked.

"Everything's fine, sir. We've a following wind now, giving us a boost. Should last for a couple of hours. We're running on three.

"Three? Excellent! Any problems?"

"Everything's fine at the moment, sir."

Colmore stood motionless, his face frozen, listening to the howling wind. Lou guessed Scott must've brought him down to make him feel at ease, but it was having the opposite effect. Colmore's eyes darted around the perimeter windows. The craggy cliffs on Ireland's northwest coast were rapidly disappearing behind them. Ahead, an endless, angry, grey sea.

Colmore peered up at the hull above them. Its dull silver cover reflected the sun intermittently as they ran through the underside of swirling black cloud. He stared down at the engines suspended in space behind them.

"You don't want to visit the engine cars, eh Reggie?" Scott said, winking at Lou.

Colmore ignored Scott's silly joke. "Let's go back upstairs," he mumbled.

"Okay, Reggie. Keep up the good work, Commander. Let me know if anything needs my attention. I've done all this before, you know!"

"I most certainly will, sir."

The two men began climbing the stairs. "You need a strong Bloody Mary, Reggie. Come, it'll settle your stomach," Scott said, as they went.

Lou and Cameron exchanged glances.

"I could do with one of them myself," Lou said.

The two coxswains remained silent.

An hour later, Norway appeared, with mugs of tea for Lou and the coxswains. "Here. I mustn't stay long or I'll be in trouble with ol' Captain Bligh up there," he said, putting the tea tray down.

"I was just thinking about those two people in the plane who attempted this flight—you know Hinchliffe and the chick—whatsaname—the heiress?" Lou said.

"Elsie Mackay. She was a corker!"

"I'll take your word for it."

"I must admit, I used to have those grand notions of trying it myself, once," Norway said.

"We'd have been reading your obituary, too, pal."

Norway studied the ocean again. "Yes, from here—it looks like sheer madness."

"I guess there were a lot of bucks riding on it?"

"Enough to retire on, I reckon."

"A lot of people tried it," Lou said, after a swallow of tea.

"Many died in the attempt."

"His wife's still campaigning to stop the airship program with messages from the grave."

"She's often in the newspapers and on speaking tours. She's got no chance. After this voyage and the India trip—airships will be part of everyday life," Norway said confidently.

Lou finished his tea.

Norway squeezed past Giblett on the stairs.

"It's bad luck to pass on the stairs," Giblett said.

"Don't be s-superstitious, Mr. G-Giblett. All will be w-well."

"Don't listen to him; he's just the design engineer," Lou said.

"I'm a man of science, too, and I *am* superstitious," Giblett answered.

"Do you have good news?" Lou asked.

"A high pressure area has developed in the Atlantic to the south. We need to head in that direction to get another favoring wind. I'll ask Johnny to work out the new heading."

"Thank you. I'll brief the captain when he comes on watch," Lou said.

The rest of Lou's spell on duty was uneventful. After giving Booth the information, he went to the dining room for tea and sandwiches. He sat talking with Wann, Colmore and Scott. Alcohol had calmed Colmore down to some extent. They didn't mention *R38,* not wishing to upset him again.

After tea, Lou went to lie down. The crewmen below were playing the gramophone, louder this time. Strains of "Can't Help Loving That Man O' Mine" came up through the floor. Lou gazed at Charlotte's photo—the blues seemed fitting. He listened, remembering the songs she liked to play. She hadn't played for ages; Freddie's death had put a stop to the parties. As sad as Freddie's death was, the grief *had* to end. Fun and laughter must be brought back into their house. Children would bring joy back into her life. Yes, children were the answer. The song ended and Al Jolson sang "Blue Skies" in his upbeat vamping style. Lou spoke out loud, not caring if anyone heard him. "That's right, Mr. Jolson. You sing it! It's gonna be blue skies from now on, ol' buddy."

During the next two days of the crossing, Lou had an epiphany. His spirits rose and he became euphoric. This voyage had given him time to reflect in solitude. Whenever he came to rest, or attempt to read the book Charlotte had given him, he had similar thoughts.

How could I have been so thoughtless?

Everything became crystal clear. He'd selfishly put his career above all else—while she'd met his every need. He'd failed her miserably! He knew what he must do on his return. They'd begin the adoption process, but beforehand, he'd get checked out. He'd stubbornly refused before, hoping for a miracle. He dreaded being found to be less than a man.

Lou's love for airships returned during the crossing and this flight proved airship travel could be safe. It'd certainly go down as a landmark flight. The ship had behaved magnificently with only a small repair necessary to one engine. Lou was glad he'd stuck to his guns, sure Charlotte would come around, especially after they'd made a few intercontinental flights. Perhaps, one day he'd be able to take her to America by airship—a pleasant three-day voyage!

On Wednesday morning, Colmore invited Lou to join him on the promenade deck. They sat at one of the wicker tables in comfortable easy chairs, encompassed by the sea. Colmore appeared fairly relaxed, well-scrubbed and shaved, his graying hair slicked down and shiny; he was well-dressed as always—sports jacket, collar and tie. He ordered tea. Lou ordered coffee.

"I'm going to confide in you, Lou. Hope you don't mind."

"Not at all, sir."

They were interrupted by people gathering at the windows, watching a whale ploughing through the waves, water spouting from its blowhole. Lou and Colmore got up and joined them for a few minutes to enjoy the awesome sight. The massive creature disappeared and they returned to their seats. Pierre set down a tray of tea, coffee and biscuits.

"I wasn't always like this, you know. Oh, always nervous about flying, but not this bad. I got on with it—strange thing for the Director of Airship Development to admit, eh."

"We can only admire your courage, then, sir."

"It's ridiculous. I get so annoyed with myself," Colmore said, sipping his tea.

"Regardless, many think you're the best man for the job."

Colmore sighed. "I hope so. My fear got worse after Captain Hinchliffe's wife came to Cardington with Sir Arthur Conan Doyle last year."

"What happened?"

Lou picked up his coffee and Colmore offered him a biscuit.

"She claimed she'd had messages from her husband—the pilot lost with Elsie Mackay—right out here, somewhere." Colmore waved his hand vaguely at the foreboding sea.

"What did she say?"

"The Airship Program was too dangerous and would end in horrible disaster."

"I expect she was upset after losing her husband, sir."

"She and Doyle showed up after the briefing—you know when Lord Thomson came up after he got back in office. They were in the garden when Thomson gave his speech."

"Yes, I remember. I couldn't figure out what was happening. We couldn't hear—someone switched off the mic. It looked like she was making some sort of protest," Lou said.

"She asked a lot of embarrassing questions."

"Lord Thomson looked irritated," Lou said.

"It was astonishing how much she *knew* about the Airship Program —top secret technical stuff. Lou, it was *unnerving!*"

"I bet."

"But you see, it made the woman *so bloody credible*."

"But it's a bit weird, sir. Conan Doyle has a reputation for being an eccentric—what with the fairies and all that stuff."

"Yes, but how the hell did she know so much?"

"People talk. They find out things. I shouldn't worry about any of it, sir."

"She has a lot of powerful people on her side, you know."

"Well, there you are. They probably fed her the information. Poor woman was being used. It's all politics."

"I'm sure you're right," Colmore said, his smile half-hearted.

"Sir, may I be blunt?"

"Please do, dear boy."

"If you're not sure the ship's ready, regardless of how well *Howden R100* does, you must put your foot down, be strong and stand up for what you believe. *Postpone* the voyage to India!"

Colmore looked frightened by the prospect. He scratched his chin and gazed at the surrounding ocean. "We'll have to see, but I do value your council, Lou. You know that."

Lou drew a deep breath. "I've cheated death a few times. I guess I was spared for a reason—but when our time's up, that's it. We meet our Maker—but I think we must do all we can to prevent that day coming *prematurely!*"

"You're lucky. You're *bloody fearless!*"

"I wish that were true, sir."

"Somehow, you always manage to make me feel better, Lou," Colmore said, pausing to watch a rusty freighter heading in the opposite direction. "And you give me much to ponder."

"You started telling me about Lord Thomson and his experience with Lord Kitchener."

"Oh yes, I did."

"I'd love to hear that story."

Colmore smiled fully for the first time and Lou listened in fascination to the tale of Thomson's ruthless obedience to Kitchener's orders during the Boer War, as well as his recent threats. By the end of the story, Colmore was back in the doldrums, and Lou understood why.

It was important for the officer on watch to be a skilled navigator and, during the crossing, Meager and Johnston gave Lou instruction. All he had learned in books over this past two years, he put into practice. He accompanied both men when they took sun sightings with the sextant on the roof. They left him to calculate their latitude using these observations. Sometimes, if the stars were visible, they showed him how to fix their position by taking astronomical sightings. They also taught him to use the Pole Star to ascertain their latitude.

Lou was shown how to make drift, wind speed and directional calculations using targets dropped on the water from the control car. During the day, they used 'dust bombs,' small boxes filled with aluminum dust, which exploded when they hit the sea, leaving a perfect sighting target. At night, they dropped calcium flares, which burst into flame on contact with the water.

The aspect of navigation Lou found most interesting was the use of ships at sea. During the crossing, Lou sent a signal to the *Montclare*, which sent *their* position and the airship's bearing back to the airship. Moments later, the same information was received from the *Caledonian*. By getting two bearings at almost the same time, they determined the 'cut' and hence their own exact position. At that time, they were at fifty-three degrees north—twenty-one degrees, zero minutes west. Lou believed he'd be a competent navigator by the end of this voyage, having been instructed by the best.

Norway out-did himself on Wednesday afternoon. Meager was on watch and the ship was now positioned seven hundred miles east of Belle Isle, where the St. Lawrence enters the Atlantic, about a thousand miles south of Greenland. After visiting the engine cars with Lou, Norway decided to go up to the roof. Lou followed him. Norway opened the bow hatch and popped his head out. The rushing, damp wind hit them full force. They were making fifty knots and Norway, in his Harris Tweed jacket and green woolen polo-necked sweater, clambered onto the roof and sat down. Lou stuck his head out.

"Icebergs!" Norway shouted, pointing into the distance.

"Some of them are huge," Lou said, looking southwards. "I guess the Titanic must have hit one somewhere south of here."

"Over there in iceberg alley. Four hundred miles off Newfoundland," Norway said. They both stared at the inhospitable landscape. Norway began crawling away.

"Hey, where the hell d'you think you're going?" Lou yelled after him.

"I'm going to see if I can make it to the stern!"

"What are you, crazy? Stop! It's too dangerous."

Lou stood on the top rung of the cat ladder and watched Norway inch away on his belly along the narrow catwalk up the incline, holding the steel cable. After Norway had gone about a hundred feet, Lou was astonished to see Nervous Nick heading toward them from the other direction. He wasn't crawling, but walking upright with his hands in his pockets, leaning into the wind. His lips were pursed—he was whistling!

Now what?

When Nervous Nick reached Norway, Norway looked up, startled at first. Then he turned sideways, making himself as small as possible. Nervous Nick stepped over Norway without breaking stride and on toward Lou. He grinned. "Afternoon, sir," he said on reaching him.

"Out for a stroll?" Lou asked.

"Just getting a little air, sir, are you going?"

"Not today," Lou said, climbing down the ladder to allow him to get down. "You've progressed a bit since we first met, Nick."

"Oh yes, sir—thanks to you. I love this job!"

"I take it everything looks good on the roof?"

"No serious damage, sir, but I think those intakes might be leaking."

Lou made a mental note to pass that on to Meager and moved on to make an inspection of the structure and gasbags. He'd check on Nevil later. Amidships, he ran into Wann.

"Good afternoon, Commander. Working on anything special?" Wann asked.

"Just a routine inspection."

"Then I'll join you. I could use the exercise. It's damned boring around here. *No crises.*"

"I don't think we need *another* crisis, do we?"

"I apologize—stupid joke. Boring is *always* best."

They progressed along the catwalks, peering up at the helically wound girders. "Pretty damned impressive," Wann said.

"Barnes Wallis," Lou said.

Wann nodded approval. "I'm surprised he's not on board."

"Vickers wouldn't allow it."

"Very wise of them."

They reached the stern and found one of the riggers making repairs to a small chafe in the cover on one of the fins. They watched him for a few minutes. After complimenting him on his work, they moved on.

"They're a conscientious lot, this crew," Wann said. He stopped and turned, holding onto the rail. "How are you, Lou? Have you got over that bloody catastrophe?"

"I guess, but it took a while," Lou replied.

"Some of us were spared. God knows why. I never got over the guilt of that," Wann confessed.

"I saw the control car lying in the water. I didn't think anyone could've survived."

"They say everything happens for a reason."

"There's the rub," said Lou.

"Do you know your purpose?"

"I *think* so."

"Good. You're lucky. I heard your testimony in court was excellent," Wann said.

"Oh, I don't know—"

"You saved the commodore's reputation."

"I just told it the way I saw it."

"I'm not sure he deserved it. You were very gracious." Wann said as he stared up into the ship's structure. "We continue to believe in these damned things—or pretend to."

"I think we're getting them sorted out," Lou replied. He suddenly remembered Norway. "Oh hell! I'd better go up and look for Norway. He went on the roof. I'd better make sure he hasn't been blown away."

"Yes, you better had," Wann said. "The R.A.W. would *never* get over the loss!"

Lou made his way to the stern hatch cat ladder, climbed up and opened the hatch. He was disturbed by what he saw. Norway stood fifty feet away, arms outstretched, facing the horizon, hair blowing riotously around his head. He reminded Lou of the Christ the Redeemer statue under construction in Rio de Janeiro.

The master of all he surveys! Dumb S.O.B!

"Nevil! What the *hell* are you doing? Get back down here. Right now!"

Norway turned around slowly, as though coming out of a trance.

"Ah, Lou."

Norway walked carefully toward Lou at the hatchway.

"*Exhilarating!*" he shouted.

"Life's dangerous enough without you pulling a silly stunt like that."

"It felt so good and I wanted to prove I could do it," Norway said.

"If you fall off, there'll be a lot of disappointed readers out there."

"I can just see the headlines. 'Hated airship designer mysteriously disappears over Atlantic. Royal Airship Works staff helping with enquiries.'"

"*Very funny,*" Lou said smiling.

Norway looked at his watch. "Come on, Lou, it's time to pump petrol."

"It's time you pumped the toilets out, too—they're getting pretty smelly, pal."

Later that day, Lou made an entry in the diary Charlotte had given him:

Wednesday July 30th 1930.

Saw icebergs this afternoon. Some of them collapsing. Awesome sight. All I could think about was the Titanic. I thought about that beautiful ship on the bottom, not far away. And all those poor, wretched souls! Sad to think about. Was it an iceberg that killed them, or someone's stupid pride?

32

NEWFOUNDLAND

Wednesday July 30, 1930.

It was 9:45 p.m. Wednesday evening—Meager's watch. Lou Johnston, Booth and Wann had gone down to join him. Johnston spotted it first. On the port bow they saw a flashing light—the lighthouse on Cape Bauld on the northern tip of the island of Newfoundland.

"I see a light!" Johnston shouted.

Everyone rushed to the windows at the front of the control car.

"Yes, there it is!" Lou confirmed.

"The crossing from Ireland to Newfoundland has taken ..." Johnston hesitated carefully reading his watch. "Thirty-seven hours and forty minutes or ..." He looked out into the darkness. "Forty-six hours and twenty-eight minutes from Cardington."

The officers shook hands and smiled gleefully.

Within half an hour, they were passing directly over flat, scrubby Belle Isle. Gradually, fog closed in as they traveled along the Belle Isle Strait. Below, they heard plaintive foghorns. The fog cleared when they reached the Gulf of St. Lawrence. Low clouds impeded visibility, but once in a while they spotted a ship moving smoothly through the black water and later, a pod of glistening blue whales breaking the surface in the moonlight.

By the midnight to 4:00 a.m. watch (now Thursday), the cloud cover had gone and it became beautiful and clear. Giblett warned these conditions wouldn't last, and as usual, he was right. Next watch, Scott being anxious to get to Montreal before dark, they put on two more engines. They ran on all six engines, though not at full power, at fifty-eight knots, bumping against headwinds, which reduced their ground speed to thirty-six knots.

Lou visited the control car at 4:00 a.m. They'd reached well inside the Gulf of St. Lawrence, between Anticosti Island and the coast of Quebec. At dawn, with the sun coming up on the water, the scene was spectacular, with quaint fishing villages set in treed hillsides along the riverbank. Lou spent much time studying the landscape through binoculars. That morning, he wrote in Charlotte's diary:

Thursday 31ˢᵗ July 1930.

What a great place the Gulf of St. Lawrence is! Teeming with wildlife. Saw a black bear at the water's edge with her cubs this morning. She stopped to look up. I wonder what she thought of us. We've also seen blue whales and bright, white belugas, elk and moose (good swimmers). No icebergs. Wish C was here to see this.

Later in the day, two magnificent steamships, their hulls stately dark blue, topsides gleaming white, moved majestically along the seaway below toward Montreal. Disley entered the control car, waving two wires.

"We have two messages. The first is from the *Empress of Scotland*, the second the *Duchess of Bedford*. Both captains send their best wishes and congratulations." The ships sounded their sirens as they passed over, their decks lined with madly waving passengers. Freighters and fishing boats, swarming with seagulls, joined in, adding to the fuss, and then came the roar of engines, as a Canadian flying boat came by to make its own inspection.

"It's getting busy around here. Show these to Captain Booth. I expect he'll send a response," Lou said, handing the messages back to Disley.

A damper was put on all things when the chief coxswain reported gas leaking from bags seven and eight. With Johnston left in control, Booth, Meager, Lou and Norway went to investigate, after easing off the power. The riggers, led by Nervous Nick and Billy, clambered around on the radial wires making an inspection, without the possibility of using safety harnesses. They found six slits in each bag, three inches long, some out of reach. Booth ordered the ship up to three thousand feet to make the bags move toward the riggers as the gas expanded. That worked, and Nervous Nick completed the repairs. About that time, Disley brought another message.

Montreal Police Department Montreal, Canada.

Understand your position to be 50 miles from Quebec. Please advise us of your ETA so that we can manage the traffic and welcoming spectators gathering at St Hubert Aerodrome. Sincerely Chief of Police Montreal.

Meager asked Lou to show the message to Booth, at lunch in the dining room.

"This wire just came in from the Montreal Police, Captain," Lou said laying the wire on the table. Booth read it. Scott was sitting on another table nursing a brandy.

"What have you got there?" he grunted. Booth showed him the message. "Tell them we'll arrive before sunset." Then, checking his watch, "One-thirty. What's our speed?"

"Fifty-eight knots."

"Right, crank 'em all up to full power."

"I don't think that's wise, sir," Booth warned.

"*Just do it!* We need to get our skates on to make it before dark."

"I don't like it. It'll put unnecessary strain on the ship. She's already taking a pounding. We're up against a twenty knot headwind, sir."

"Maybe that's not a good idea, Scottie," Colmore said.

"Reggie, we've got to push on. Booth, just do as I say, there's a good chap."

McWade, who'd been sitting with Giblett, got up and left the dining room shaking his head. Lou returned to the control car with Booth.

"*Damn!* He's not supposed to give orders," Booth said.

"What do you want to do, Captain?" Meager asked.

Booth looked at Lou. "Do as the man says. Full power, all engines."

Lou relayed instructions to the engine cars and within a few minutes all six engines were up to full power, slogging against the wind. Lou and Meager left Booth fuming in the control car with Johnston. Meager went to inspect the gas bag repairs. Lou went to his cabin and wrote in his diary:

Thursday July 31ˢᵗ 1930.

It's a beautiful day with a clear blue sky. Coming up to the Saguenay River, which flows out of the spectacular Laurentian Mountains on the north side. Engines on full power against 20 knot wind on the nose. We've been ordered by Major Scott to reach Montreal before dark. Saw steamers today. What a sight! Decided this is definitely the way I'll bring Charlotte when we come by sea. Then from Montreal to Washington by train. She's gonna love it!

Lou lay on his bunk while Mr. Jolson belted out his song for the umpteenth time. He thought about Charlotte until he drifted off to sleep. He dreamed she was holding up a baby's shawl she'd made and was looking at it, her face like alabaster. There were tears in her eyes and they were running down her cheeks. He woke with a start with the sickening smell of mothballs in his cabin. After that, he couldn't get the baby clothes out of his mind. She hadn't made any for a long time, nor had she opened the 'baby drawer', where she kept them wrapped in tissue. He assumed they must still be there.

Charlotte, I promise you, your labor of love will not be for nothing, my darling ...

He fell into another deep sleep.

At 2:40 p.m. Lou was dumped out of bed. The ship was slammed by what felt and sounded like a freight train. The gargantuan *Howden R100* had rolled onto her side and was rolling back upright as Lou came round. He struggled to his feet, the ship pitching wildly up and down and yawing to and fro. He staggered into the corridor holding onto the railings and grab bars. The dining room was in total disarray —cups, saucers, plates, bottles of ketchup and sauce, cutlery and food scattered all over the floor, chairs and tables overturned. Pierre was distraught.

"Whatever is happening?" he cried.

At that moment, Lou felt real sorry for him. "Don't panic, Pierre. It's just turbulence, that's all," he assured him in the most calming voice he could muster. People emerged from all corners of the ship with the same question, many of them, like Lou, having been catapulted out of bed. As he ran into the control car, he felt the power easing off. Booth and Johnston held on, looking stupefied.

Booth yelled at the rudder coxswain, "Steer to the opposite shore. Cold air's spilling out of this valley." He pointed to the Saguenay River valley where the mountains each side reached four thousand feet. The coxswain swung the wheel, turning the ship away from the disturbed air and the turbulence gradually eased, then ceased completely. The starboard engine car telegraph bell rang, followed in quick succession by the aft car.

"Lou, go and find out what their problem is," Booth ordered.

In the corridor, Lou ran into Norway who tagged along. Lou climbed down into the starboard engine car. The engineers pointed up through the window at the rear fins, where the cover was torn up and flapping. Lou bounded back up the steps. Meager had now joined Norway.

"Cover's all torn up on the starboard fins," Lou shouted.

They rushed along the corridor to the stern, led by Meager, with Wann, Nervous Nick and Billy in tow. Along the way, other riggers joined them. They examined the bottom fin first. Not so serious: three tears about three feet long. Meager left Wann to supervise two riggers making repairs while he, Lou and Norway climbed a transverse girder to the starboard fin. There was more damage there, but no reason to panic. A split in the cover ran along the outer fin edge about twelve feet long. Two riggers were sent with needles and thread to make repairs, with Norway assisting.

Lou and Meager moved to the fins on the port side, although they'd received no reports of damage from the port engine car. They climbed along the cruciform girder to the port fin to make an inspection. They were shocked by what they found. The fabric to the underside was in ribbons, flapping around a gaping hole about fifteen feet square. Meager sent Lou to inform the captain.

Lou climbed down and went to the speaking tube in the stern corridor and signaled the control car. It was 3 o'clock. Booth answered and Lou explained the situation. Booth sent the chief coxswain and ten more riggers to assist. Meanwhile, Booth made the ship stationary, positioned near a small island, head to wind, with just enough power to maintain their position. Lou returned to the riggers. While they worked, they heard what they thought was the howling wind on the opposite shore. It turned out to be wolves howling in the canyons.

The chief coxswain showed up with an army of riggers and a roll of canvas he'd stashed away. They were joined by Norway and his men from the starboard side, their own repairs satisfactorily completed. They stretched a system of cords over the opening, forming a mesh as a foundation. New canvas was laid over them and lashed down. It was like watching tightrope walkers at the circus, balancing on wires—their only means of support. Meager nagged the riggers to keep their safety lines fastened. The riggers were unfazed by the thousand foot drop and the bobbing Belugas breaking the surface and staring up at them. They joked that the Belugas wanted to mate with the big silver whale in the sky. The repairs took two hours.

At 5 o'clock, during the dog watch, His Majesty's Airship *Howden R100* resumed her journey, but with less haste. They proceeded toward Quebec at fifty knots against the same headwind. As they approached the city, Meager decided to inspect the top of the ship for damage, with Lou and Norway assisting. Leaks in the cover had been discovered in the past few days, requiring repairs to the gas bags.

Before going to the roof, Lou went to his cabin for his Sidcot suit. It'd be chilly up there. The room was still a mess. While picking everything up, he was upset to find Charlotte's picture lying underneath his clothes, its glass smashed, her face no longer visible. He laid it face-down on the bedside table.

At 6:00 p.m., Lou climbed the cat ladder to the roof with Norway. Meager had gone before them. They were over the city and heard the commotion below: ship's sirens, train whistles, car horns and people cheering. While Meager and Norway made their inspection, Lou waited at the hatchway, his attention fixed on the sky directly ahead. It was an alarming sight. A fifteen-mile squall of sparkling, copper cloud, like a line of fire with ominous blackness beneath, stretched across their path. Above the wall, raging cumulonimbus cloud formations reached up to the heavens.

When Meager and Norway returned to the hatchway, Lou gestured toward the storm. Meager's face showed concern. They made their way to the saloon, where Scott was drinking sherry with Burney and Colmore while stewards busily laid out a buffet on tables pushed together. Everything was spic and span once more. The meal looked delicious, with soup, salad and assorted cold cuts. Bottles of wine, stacks of plates, bowls and wine glasses sat nearby.

"There's a bad storm ahead, sir," Meager said, almost casually.

Scott sounded bored and dismissive. "Yes, they've already sent us details from Montreal advising us to go around, but we don't have time for that."

"We should discuss this with the captain. I'm about to go on watch."

Irritated, Scott drained his glass and plonked it down on the table. He strode off toward the control car. Norway and Burney went to the promenade deck to see what they could see from there. Lou and Meager followed Scott to the control car where they found Booth and Johnston standing with Giblett, studying the squall line dead ahead. They were alarmed.

"I think we need to avoid this, sir. It looks bad," Booth said grimly.

"I must agree," Giblett said.

Scott's face was as black as the storm. "Well, *I don't!* We've already lost too much time."

"What's the point? We're not going to make it before sunset anyway," Booth argued.

"A fifty-mile detour for safety's sake might be worth it," Johnston said.

"There are thousands of people in Montreal waiting for us!"

"I don't think it's worth the risk, sir," Booth said.

Scott became more irritated. "We can't bugger about. We're already late and we'll look ridiculous."

"At least we'll arrive in one piece," Booth said.

"It's just a rainstorm—nothing to be frightened of."

"But—"

"Hold your course, Captain. That's an order!"

Scott turned abruptly and when he got to the stairs he stopped.

"Let me know if you run into difficulties requiring my attention."

He went upstairs.

"That man is a *bloody* menace," Booth muttered.

"*Reckless!*" Giblett agreed.

The five men stared through the windows straight ahead. Night was falling fast as they approached the black wall.

At 7:40 p.m. they felt the first tremors under their feet. It was completely dark.

"Hold on boys. This is it!" Booth shouted.

The storm struck with a blast, rocking and shaking the ship. It was accompanied by shrieking winds, heavy rain and hail beating the windows. A mighty gust lifted the bow and ran under the ship to the stern, as though it were a paper cup, tipping the nose sharply downward. Cameron, on the elevators, did his best to counter the effects, turning the metal wheel one way and then the other, to no avail.

"*I'm losing her! I'm losing her!*" he screamed.

The altimeter dial that read thirteen hundred feet spun to three thousand in a matter of seconds. Her nose, which was pointing at the ground, slowly came back up. A few moments later, they were hit by another, even more violent updraft. Again, the ship went shooting toward the heavens tail first, and again, the altimeter spun wildly, now to five thousand feet.

Adding to everyone's distress, all the lights went out, except those on the control panels.

"Oh, bugger!" Meager said.

Lou thought of Josh and Zackary Landsdowne in *Shenandoah*.

Is this what it had been like for them?

Charlotte's alabaster face came back to him and her solemn goodbye.

Perhaps she was right. Maybe she knew I wasn't coming back.

Other thoughts raced through Lou's mind in milliseconds: Richmond's strident words shouted at Norway about the structural integrity of his ship, and then the 'Wiggy thing' clinched it. Something dripped on Lou's nose. He wiped it with his finger. In the glare of the instrument lights he could see it was red.

Blood? Someone upstairs must be badly cut.

He sniffed at it.

No, it's dope! Thank God.

The riggers fixing the canvas had left a drum of dope open up there somewhere.

Silly fools!

"Look, we're done for!" Cameron screamed, his voice breaking in fear. Everyone peered at the black horizon. A massive cross shone in the sky.

This must be Heaven!

"Okay, settle down, boys. We're not dead yet! It's the cross on Mount Royal," Johnston boomed from the back of the control car.

"Ease her gently down to fifteen hundred feet, coxswain," Booth ordered.

"Yes, sir," Cameron said, steadying himself.

Booth issued further instructions. "George, go and survey the damage. Lou, get hold of Disley and get the lights back on."

"Aye, aye, sir."

"Johnny and I will remain here. Oh, and if you run into Major Scott, inform him we ran into a little difficulty—in case he hadn't noticed."

"Right, Captain," Lou said.

"We're through the worst of it. The cross tells us we are," Booth said.

"I think I'm going to convert," Johnston said.

"So you should, Johnny!" Lou said.

Lou got Disley working on the electrical breakers and then went to the dining room, which once again resembled a bombed out ruin. He found Colmore sitting in the dark, surrounded by the buffet strewn across the floor, with broken plates and wine glasses from one end of the room to the other, and down the corridor to the bow.

Pierre sat in the corner sobbing. "Oh, my Lord. Whatever is going on? Look at my beautiful buffet ... Oh my Lord ... Twice in one day ..."

"Pierre, it's all right. It's over now. Come on, pick everything up, there's a good fella. Everything's going to be fine," Lou said, offering his hand. Pierre allowed Lou to pull him up, whereupon he put his arms around Lou and hugged him tight, his head on Lou's chest.

"Oh, my dear Commander, what would I do without you? You're such a comfort in these perilous times."

Lou glanced over Pierre's shoulder at Colmore slumped in a chair, holding a flashlight in one hand and an empty brandy glass in the other. Lou broke free from Pierre and went over to him. Colmore was badly shaken. Scott was nowhere to be found.

Probably crashed in his bunk.

"Are you all right, sir?" Lou asked.

"What can I say? I'm at my wit's end. But I suppose if we can survive this we can bloody-well survive *anything!*"

"Quite right, sir."

"I'm off to bed. If we were going to die today, we'd already be dead," Colmore said, struggling to his feet. He staggered down the corridor toward his cabin.

"Goodnight, sir. Try and get some rest," Lou called after him.

The lights came back on.

Meager, Lou, Wann and Norway walked the ship with flashlights. The repairs made to the fins had held up pretty well, but the underside of the starboard fin had sustained further damage: two twenty-foot tears this time. A gang of riggers was assembled and patching started.

Howden R100 limped into Montreal at midnight and flew over the magnificent city of a million lights until dawn, weaving her way around numerous localized thunderstorms. At first light, Booth steered straight for the tower at St. Hubert to a cacophony of sounds. A loud brass band couldn't be drowned by a cheering crowd of ten thousand who'd waited patiently through the night. When the sun came up, the size of their welcome became apparent: flags and bunting flew everywhere, huge placards of greeting, advertisements for beer, chewing gum and motor oil posted on every available surface. All roads to and from St. Hubert were jammed. The journey from Cardington had taken almost seventy-nine hours. This was indeed a moment for celebration—and relief!

PART FOUR

TROUBLE IN
AMERICA

33

EZEKIAH WASHINGTON

Friday August 1, 1930.

Lou boarded the *Washingtonian* from Montreal Station the day the airship landed at St. Hubert. This had been a day to remember, but hectic and tiring. He felt glad to be alone, at last. Everyone on the airship had been treated like royalty, from the officers, to the engineers and riggers. They weren't used to being fussed over back home. The men sensed a lack of rank and class—that stuff didn't seem so important here.

Lou got the film star treatment. Girls gathered around him, some actually swooned—highly embarrassing but, he had to admit, a little satisfying. The press knew he was on board and anxious to meet the 'American hero' who'd survived the *R38/ZR-2* disaster. It was a great angle that'd sell newspapers. One reporter told him, "Son, you should take your handsome looks and fame to Hollywood. You'd be a sensation!"

Lou just laughed. He answered their questions with patience and good humor, making it plain he didn't like the hero label. On this ship, they were all heroes; he wasn't special. This made him even more popular and everyone wanted their picture taken with him. Lou was glad to get away; the focus needed to be on the British crew and the ship's designers, including his good friend 'Mr. Shute' and 'Mr. Shute's' boss, Sir Dennis, who got into top gear the moment he stepped off the ship. *Howden R100* was *his* idea, *his* design and *his* airship. As soon as Lou could escape, he sent two wires. The first to Charlotte in Bedford:

My darling Charlotte Arrived safely Thinking of you STOP Heading south today by train STOP Will wire later Love you Lou

The second went to his family in Virginia:

Dear All Landed Montreal Arriving Union Station 8 am Saturday August 2 Love Lou

When he got close to the train, a portly steward studied him from beside the door. He was dressed in a crisp, white jacket and well-pressed black trousers. He bowed his domed head that shone like a clarinet, perfectly matching his patent leather shoes. He rubbed his huge hands together.

"Good afternoon, sir. I'm honored to have you aboard my train," he said, taking Lou's kit bag. He led Lou to a luxurious sleeper suite. Lou glanced at the couch, the writing table and the pull-out bed.

"There must be some mistake—this isn't for me."

"Oh, it most certainly is, sir, yes indeedy," the steward said, flashing an enormous smile, his perfect teeth as white as his jacket.

"But—"

"My name is Ezekiah Washington the Second and I'm here to take care of you," he said, busily stashing Lou's bag in a closet.

"I can't accept this."

"Why not? The train's half empty and we've got to take care of our people—especially, *you*, sir."

"*'Our people'?*"

"Our brothers ...our brothers-in-arms." Ezekiah Washington's wide, black nostrils flared for a second. "I know you were at the Front." He pointed at the newspapers on the table. "I have the *Washington Post* and the *New York Times* here for you," he said, his huge, brown eyes shining and radiating warmth.

"How did you know who I was?"

"You're wearing the uniform of a lieutenant commander in the United States Navy—previously of the United States Marine Corps, sir —Belleau Wood right? I know exactly who you is," he said, his voice gravelly and coarse. Lou appeared disappointed. "Don't you worry, sir. I won't tell a soul. I'm a veteran, too."

"Army?"

"New York 369th. The Harlem Hellfighters, yes sir!"

"France?"

"The Argonne Forest. We were the first colored outfit in there."

"Oh, yeah, I know. You guys took a hell of a beating!"

Ezekiah beamed with pride. "The French were good to me—awarded me the Croix de Guerre with gold palm. Even General Pershing said nice things about us. I was one of the lucky ones. Still am."

"I'm proud of you, man. And you made it back!" Lou said, nodding.

"Yep, in one piece. My Lord and Savior Jesus brought me through. I was lucky to get my job back on the railway. The rest of 'em ain't looking so good."

"Why, what's happening to them?"

"Thousands are down in D.C. You'll see 'em when you get there. It's a cryin' shame, is what it is. They're camped out down there in that bog hole, tryin' to get the money the government promised 'em."

"What money?"

"When they came home they were given government bonds, promising to pay 'em a bonus for their service to the country."

Lou remembered. He'd received bonds when he got back, but since he joined the Navy almost immediately, he'd stuck them a drawer in his mother's chest and forgotten about them.

"What about you?" he asked.

"Yes, I got some, too. But I'm okay. I've got this job. The rest of our brothers are starving. They're *desperate*." Ezekiah's eyes glistened now.

Lou rested his elbow on the window ledge and looked out. This was truly depressing. He hadn't realized things were this bad. He wished he'd taken more interest.

"What about everybody else?"

"The country's in a terrible mess, millions out of work, thousands losing their homes. Banks a' takin' everythin'—hundreds killin' 'emselves. It's *pitiful!*" Ezekiah said. Tears ran down his cheeks.

A commotion started up on the platform: Whistles blew, doors slammed, multiple voices yelled "All aboard!" The train lurched forward. Ezekiah cleared his throat and wiped away the tears on the back of his hand, recovering his demeanor.

"They'll be serving afternoon tea and sandwiches, if you're hungry, sir," Ezekiah said. "I can reserve you a place in the dining car, if you like."

"That would be great. I'll come down, shortly. I'm starving."

" 'Bout half an hour then, sir. I'll have you a seat."

When the steward had gone, Lou picked up the *Washington Post*. The headlines confirmed what Ezekiah had said.

The left-hand headline read:

TEN THOUSAND MARCH ON CAPITAL

The right-hand headline:

BONUS ARMY REFUSES TO GIVE UP

There were photographs of men in rags, marching on the streets of Washington, waving banners. BONUS NOW, read one. WE ARE YOUR SOLDIERS DON'T FORGET US, read another. Lou studied the article with concern for his home town, his veteran brothers-in-arms and his country. He wondered how his parents were faring.

They must be okay, surely?

His eye skipped to the bottom of the page. A small headline caught his eye and then a photograph of himself outside the Howden Court in 1922. He remembered them taking that picture. He'd been standing with Potter, but they'd cropped *him* out.

Virginia Welcomes Favorite Son

Hero of the ZR-2 due to arrive at Union Station

Lt. Cmdr. Louis Remington is expected to arrive at St. Hubert's, Montreal early today aboard one of the largest airships ever to fly, British airship, Howden R100. Remington is serving as third officer on board and will play the same role aboard Cardington R101, another monster dirigible under construction by the British government. Remington has been serving as a special assistant to the Director of Development of British Airships at Cardington in Bedfordshire on behalf of the U.S. Navy throughout design of both airships. Remington is known for his bravery as chief petty officer aboard U.S. ZR-2 when that airship crashed into the River Humber in Yorkshire, in 1921, killing all but five of the British and American airshipmen on board.

The flower of the British Airship industry was lost that day and due to his valuable knowledge and airship experience, Remington was seconded as a liaison officer by the British and attached to the Royal Air Force. The Lt. Commander was born in his grandmother's farmhouse in Great Falls, Virginia in 1898. Remington is expected to arrive in the U.S. in the next day or so.

Lou scratched his head in embarrassment. He went to the dining car for tea and ham sandwiches. He studied the other travelers. No one appeared happy. Some glanced at him and smiled, seeming to recognize him, but respecting his privacy. He supposed they were Americans returning from business trips, or visiting relatives. The American immigration officer politely welcomed him home.

Later, Lou returned for dinner, where he had a decent steak. He struck up a conversation with a Canadian lumber salesman. "The U.S. economy is in dire straits," the man said. "These are desperate times we're living in. And it's all Hoover's fault!"

Lou returned to his car and sat on the couch, put his feet up, and read the rest of the newspapers. The steward reappeared and offered him a drink. He ordered black coffee and a Jack and Coke. It felt good to be home, but he found the news troubling. He slept well, lulled by the rocking motion and clicking wheels over the long North American tracks.

Lou was vaguely aware of coming into New York's Penn Station, disturbed by slamming doors and the general bustle of hundreds on the move. He faded in and out until the train got underway again. He slept deeply until there came a gentle tapping on the door. He woke up confused and disappointed, expecting Charlotte to be lying beside him.

"Sir, it's six-thirty. They're serving breakfast now," Ezekiah called.

Lou sat up. "Thanks. I'll be right there."

He got up and washed his face in the sink. An hour later he sat with his kitbag, ready for Washington D.C. The train began slowing down as Ezekiah came in.

"The train always stops here for ten minutes—sometimes longer, going into Union. You might as well relax, sir," he said.

As they came to a halt beside a stationary freight train, two men chased down and cornered two filthy wretches beneath Lou's window. He watched in horror. Despite their pleas, they were beaten mercilessly with billy clubs until blood ran from their heads and down their faces. Ezekiah stood at the window beside Lou.

"It ain't right what they do to our brothers. Look at 'em. It's disgusting."

"Who are they?"

"The ones with the clubs are railway police. They're just thugs is what they is."

"What the hell is going on in my country?" Lou said, jumping up. He rushed to the door, jumped down from the train into the gravel, and ran over to the men with the clubs. "Leave these men alone," he shouted.

"Get back on the train, sailor. We're railway police," one said holding up a badge.

"And these men are veterans. Leave them alone." Lou turned to the men on the ground. "Where you guys tryin' to get to?"

"Anacostia, sir."

"These here men have been ridin' the rails *illegally*. They're under arrest." Lou stepped forward to help one of the beaten men to his feet.

"Step away," the one with the badge ordered, drawing a gun.

Lou jumped him in a flash, putting his arm in a lock. The gun fell from his hand and Lou wrenched it upwards and bent the fingers of the gun hand backwards, breaking them. He then methodically yanked the man's thumb out of its socket.

"Ah, Jeez!" the man screamed. His partner froze.

Lou dumped the first man down like a sack of turnips and moved toward the other man.

"I don't want no trouble, mister," the second man pleaded.

Lou picked up the gun, emptied the bullets on the ground, and threw it across the tracks. "Back up, right now!" Lou shouted.

The man obeyed. Lou pulled the two veterans to their feet.

"D.C. right?" Lou asked.

"Yes, sir."

"Get on that train."

Lou led them to the door where Ezekiah waited to give them a hand up. He took them to a quiet car and gave them wet towels to clean up the blood. Lou pulled the train door shut and on cue, the train moved forward.

34

UNION STATION

Saturday August 2, 1930.

The *Washingtonian* rolled into Union Station and, after trying to give Ezekiah Washington the Second a crisp dollar bill, Lou hoisted his kit bag onto his shoulder and marched down the platform with the two veterans he'd rescued. He tried to spot his brother within the crowd gathered at the barrier. Some were dressed in business suits. Many others were in tatters and disheveled—homeless perhaps. Lou assumed they were waiting for a congressman or a senator. Then he heard shouts.

"Look, this must be him!"

"Yes, that's him."

"I see him."

The ticket collector glanced at the two scruffy veterans with Lou, about to say something. "These men are with me. Any problem?" Lou said.

"Go right ahead, sir. If they're with you, that's good enough for me," the man said, waving them through.

The small crowd broke into spontaneous applause and a few cheers. A couple of men in trilbys were holding Speed Graphics. Flashbulbs went off. Lou couldn't understand what the fuss was about.

They must think I'm someone else.

Then he remembered the newspaper article. Standing apart from the crowd, he noticed two people beside a column. They looked familiar. She reminded him of his mother.

Oh my goodness, it's Anna and Tom!

The crowd swarmed around Lou before he could get to them. Reporters peppered him with questions. "Are you home to stay, Commander Remington?"

"How was your airship flight, sir?"

"How long are you here for?"

"We read you got married in England."

"Tell us about your wife."

"Have you gotten over the crash of *ZR-2*?"

"Can airships really ever be safe?"

"Are you going back to England?"

"What do you think about the Bonus Army?"

"D'you think they should get the money?"

One of the men in rags stepped forward. He reeked. People backed away in disgust, screwing up their faces.

"Lou, d'you remember *me*?" he asked, his voice plaintive.

Lou studied him. He was about his own age, but in poor physical condition; his face was filthy, hair long and greasy, a front tooth missing, the rest discolored and about to fall out.

"It's me, Henry—Saint-Mihiel—*France!*"

Good God, it's Henry Faulkner! He was behind me at Verdun somewhere in that last attack.

He hadn't seen Henry since that horrible morning of eleven, eleven. Lou had been taken to a field hospital. It was all a blur; chaos had followed the official ending of the war at 11:00 a.m. He assumed most of his buddies were dead. Lou took the man's grimy hand.

"Yes, of course I remember you, Henry. I thought—"

"No, I survived, but we might as *well* be dead. We need your help, sir—real bad."

Henry thrust a piece of scrap paper at Lou. "I've written down where you can find us—Tent City in Anacostia. Just ask for me. We *must* talk to you."

"I'll come. I promise," Lou said.

"There's so much you can do to help us, Lou."

Lou pointed to the two men he'd brought with him on the train. "Henry, do what you can for these two men," he said, slipping a few dollar bills into his hand.

The crowd listened in rapt attention, while reporters scribbled madly.

"I must go. My family's waiting for me," Lou said, raising his voice.

"Where are you staying, sir?" a reporter called.

Lou didn't answer. He smiled and moved toward his brother and sister.

"You won't *forget* us?" Henry shouted.

"I'll come as soon as I can," Lou yelled back over his shoulder.

Before Lou got away, a man and a woman stopped him. They were about fifty-five, dressed casually, but decently. The man put his hand on Lou's arm. "Excuse me, Commander Remington, I'm Daniel Jenco —Bobby's father—*Bobby Jenco*—you remember our Bobby, don't you?"

Lou's heart skipped a beat. This was exactly what he'd always dreaded.

"Bobby was on *ZR-2* with you," the man said, his eyes sad and penetrating. Lou could see the resemblance to Bobby. The crowd closed in around them once more, the reporters wide-eyed, eager like wolves.

"Josh Stone told us what you did—how you threw Bobby your own parachute …"

"Oh, er, Josh, well—"

"We came down from Baltimore to personally thank you for trying to save our boy."

They put their arms out and hugged Lou. He suddenly remembered the two pregnant girls at the court of inquiry. "Did you know you have a grandchild?" Lou said. They looked stunned and thrilled at the same time.

"No, nobody told us—"

"I talked with your son, just before the ship broke up. He told me he was going to ask the girl to marry him that same evening—a nurse."

Overwhelmed, Bobby's mother began to cry.

"The child would be about eight or nine now, I guess," Lou said.

"What was the girl's name?" Bobby's mother asked, her eyes pleading.

Lou thought for a moment. "It was *Elsie*. Write to Hull Infirmary. They'll help you. You can contact me at the Royal Airship Works in Cardington if you need to."

The couple was thankful for the information. Bobby's father wrote down their address and gave it to Lou.

"I must go. My folks are waiting." Lou left them knowing he'd given them something precious—something from Bobby. Their eyes shone with hope.

Lou broke away from the crowd, finally reaching Tom and Anna. Tom, now 26, was a couple of inches shorter than Lou, with the same broad shoulders and muscular arms, obviously put to good use. Tom's hair was already starting to recede like their Dad's. His bone structure was also similar, chiseled, and his eyes as intense. He was a man, not the boy Lou had last seen. Anna was a couple of years younger than Tom, with long, light brown hair, most of it hidden under a floppy, yellow sun hat. She wore a long, white, cotton skirt and a pale blue blouse. Her eyes were ice blue and wider apart, similar to Lou's—a younger version of their beautiful mother.

Anna put her arms out and Lou embraced her, feeling her tears on his face. He turned to Tom and hugged him, too, though he sensed Tom was distant. Tom led the way out of the station. Lou put his arm around Anna and they followed. They walked toward a crowd of Army veterans, who watched them with doleful eyes. They stopped and Lou gave them all the money he had in his pockets and in his wallet. Tom appeared sullen and unimpressed.

They had an old pickup truck parked outside the station.

"Thanks for meeting me. You got my wires okay?" Lou asked.

"No, we didn't get any wires," Tom answered.

"How did you know I'd be here, then?"

"We read it in the paper—you're famous. They said you were on the airship," Anna said with a giggle.

Tom went to the pickup and pulled back the ragged canvas cover.

"This is Granddad's old Buick from the farm!" Lou exclaimed.

"Yep. A bit rusty, but still rollin'," Tom said curtly.

He threw Lou's kitbag in the truck-bed beside the shovels and picks and covered it with the canvas. It was sunny, not yet too hot. They climbed in the cab, with Lou in the middle, and Tom drove out of

Union. Along the sidewalk, a crowd of several hundred waited beside a line of empty tables.

"What are they waiting for?" Lou asked.

"*Food!* That's a soup line. They're waiting for it to arrive," Tom replied. Lou detected sarcasm. He looked around, speechless.

Goddammit! What the hell's happened to my country?

Tom drove along Louisiana Avenue and on to Constitution, heading west toward Virginia, about three miles off. There were groups of men everywhere with placards and mounted police watching from a distance. On the surface, everything appeared peaceful. Lou studied their hopeless faces.

"Looks like everything's gone to hell in this town."

"These men are coming from all over, many of them with wives and kids," Tom answered with resignation, as if *Lou* had something to do with it.

"I feel so sorry for them," Anna said.

"I saw them on the railroad tracks," Lou said.

"It's a bad situation. They should give 'em the damned money," Tom snarled. They drove in silence for some minutes, until Lou spoke.

"How are Mum and Dad?"

Silence.

"*Well?*" Lou asked.

"They're okay, but you'll notice a change—especially in Dad—but don't worry, they're fine. They've both gotten older, that's all," Anna said. She sounded weary.

"We *all* have, I reckon. I'm ashamed to say it's been ten years," Lou said.

Tom smirked, but remained silent, keeping his eyes on the road. Lou was disappointed at Tom's off-handedness. He hadn't expected it —but perhaps he should've. It was only natural. Big brother back on the scene. It might take a few days.

Anna studied Lou, trying to ease the tension. "You look wonderful, Lou," she said. "If you weren't my brother, I'd take a fancy to you *myself.*"

They drove past the Smithsonian Museum of Art and along the tree-lined mall. Lou thought back to when his Mom and Dad used to bring him here to see the paintings.

"We've all missed you," Anna said, her eyes resting on him again, but seriously now. "Aren't you coming home soon … for good? You really should, you know. God, we so much want you home, big brother."

Tom showed no reaction.

"Well I'm …" Lou began, but Anna knew what was on his mind.

"I'm sure you and Dad will get along. He's pretty mellow nowadays. He's a big softie. Bring Charlotte. We'd love to meet her. She looked so beautiful in the wedding photo."

Lou looked down. It was gut-wrenching to hear. "I'd love to bring her over to meet you all. I miss you, too," he said. He looked across the open lawn toward the White House in the distance. "And she'd love to come."

"Then bring her!" said Anna.

"I'm dying to see Mum and Dad, and of course, Gran. Tell me about them."

"They've been getting ready for your homecoming since 5 o'clock this mornin'," Tom grunted. He turned off the main road and onto the George Washington Parkway, the scenic country road along the Potomac River toward Virginia.

"Where you goin'? We live that way," Lou said, pointing back at the main road.

"Actually, we *don't*—not anymore," Tom said. He seemed to be enjoying this.

"What d'you mean. Did you move?"

"Yeah, had to," Anna said.

"Why?"

"They took the house," she said.

"What do you mean *they* took the house? *Who* took the house?"

"The bank," Tom said.

This was like a jab in the guts.

"They also took the car," Anna said.

"Dad's Ford?"

"Bank took everything. Everything they could get their hands on," Tom said, his eyes narrowing.

Shattered, Lou put his hand up to his forehead, unable to breathe.

"Lou, it could be worse. Dad lost his job, but—"

"That was *ages* ago!" Tom sneered.

"Dad lost his *job!* Things could be worse! How could they be *worse?*"

They motored along the high, winding road overlooking the glistening river. It was beautiful, but Lou hardly noticed.

"Dad had been with that firm for what ...twenty years?" Lou said.

"Twenty-three, actually. But they shut down. Like thousands of other companies," Tom said bitterly.

"So, where are you now?"

"We're all back at Gran's place, like the old days. Gran doesn't owe anyone a dime. They can't touch her," Anna said.

"Why wasn't I told about any of this?"

"They didn't want you to worry, dear brother," Tom replied.

"So, what do you all do for money?"

"We do jobs. Dad and I work at Arlington Cemetery sometimes, or he did 'til recently. Jeb helps me nowadays," Tom answered.

"Doing what?"

"Digging graves, doing landscaping and stuff," Tom replied.

"*My God!*"

"Lou, we're lucky. Millions are out of work. Millions are starving," Anna said.

"You just saw the soup lines, didn't you," Tom said.

"We grow stuff. We've got rabbit, deer, squirrel, bear, possum, ground hog. We'll *never* go hungry!" Anna said.

"We opened a couple of fields Gran had left fallow. We're growing tobacco for Gran, like always, and old Jeb and I are growing a stack of potatoes and carrots and peas and beans—you name it. And grain o'course. We sell some and we give a lot away. Jeb takes a load to his people in D.C. every week," Tom said.

"Plus we trade in a little of the old '*you know what.*' We like to keep the Army and the Navy and Congress happy," Anna said with a wink.

Lou smiled.

"Which brings us to another sore subject. More trouble," said Tom.

"What kind of trouble?"

"The Klan," Tom said.

Lou stared out the window at the forest. This was like walking into a hailstorm. "What the hell are those idiots up to?"

"They're enforcing Prohibition," Tom answered.

"How?"

"They're running around in bed sheets burning down bars and destroying stills all over the place," Anna said.

"And *lynching blacks*, I suppose," Lou said.

God, he wished he were here to help deal with this crap. They traveled up the Georgetown Pike. As the day got hotter, the cicadas in the trees got louder.

What a racket!

It was a screaming whine. He'd forgotten that sound.

"When you left, Gran let old Jeb build a shack down by the creek. The family's always taken care of Jeb and he does a lot for us. After Granddad went, he tended the still. He's a good man—and his whisky's every bit as good as ol' Granddad's," Anna said.

"His wife's okay, too. They ain't no trouble," Tom said.

"They have two beautiful children. A boy and a girl," Anna said.

"So, tell me what's been happening?"

"The boys in white have been around, looking for the still. It's been drivin' 'em crazy," Tom said.

"But they didn't find it?"

"Not yet. But I'm sure they will. They're determined," Tom replied.

"They've been threatening Jeb. He's terrified," Anna said.

"Poor old Jeb. I love that man," Lou said.

It was Jeb who'd taught him to fish on the river in the skiff and to beware of the current rushing to the falls. He'd taught him to shoot and skin a rabbit, expertly wring a chicken's neck with minimum suffering to the creature, plant beans, and set up and run the still, which Grandfather—known locally as 'the man from Moray'—had passed on to Father and Jeb.

"Their threats are gettin' worse," Anna said.

"They'd better not lay a finger on him," Lou said.

"What are *you* gonna do? You can't mess with the Klan," Tom sneered.

"Do you know who these men are?"

Tom hesitated.

"Tom!"

"I've got a good idea," Tom said, waving his hand dismissively.

"Good. Then you'll tell me and I'll pay them a visit."

"*What!* Don't get crazy," Tom said.

"Tom, only cowards hide under bed sheets."

They pressed on along the pike, up winding hills and down through valleys between wooded banks toward Great Falls.

"Charlotte would love it here. It's so much like England," Lou said. "I'd forgotten."

"I reckon you did," Tom said.

Soon, they came to an opening in the trees on the right marked by two massive boulders. His grandfather had placed them to mark the entrance to the farm, meaning to build two fine stone pillars one day, but there'd always been too many other more important things to do. Lou wondered again how his grandfather got those boulders there in the first place. Now he'd never know. Someone had put up a sign.

REMINGTON'S FARM

"That's new," Lou said. "I like it."

35

REMINGTON'S FARM

Saturday & Sunday August 2 & 3, 1930.

They followed the winding trail through the forest for three quarters of a mile. These familiar surroundings Lou found magically calming. Although the property belonged to his grandparents, he'd lived here for many years. When Lou was twelve, his father had saved enough to put down a deposit on a home in Fairfax, and he and his siblings had been sorry to leave this place.

Presently, the Virginia, black stone farmhouse came into view among the towering oaks. Lou's grandfather had built this house in the 1870's after leaving Moray, Scotland fifteen years earlier, at age twenty-five. The roof was clad in gunmetal grey, standing seam metal, complete with snow-guards. The second story was sheathed in white clapboard. Operable green shutters set off the small-paned, double-hung sash windows. It was a Virginia classic.

As the pickup rolled around the dirt driveway, chickens kicked up a fuss and dogs barked. The arrivals got out of the pickup and the dogs, a gold Labrador and a black mutt, came with their tails wagging to welcome Lou. He patted them.

"The Lab's 'Tobacca' and the black one's 'Moonshine'—she's a sweetie," Anna said. The screen door flew open and banged shut, and Lou's mother, Violet, rushed out. It opened again, more slowly and was closed carefully by his father. Following him came Gran in her long, white kitchen apron. Then Jeb emerged from the path leading up from the river—tall and stooping, his hair and mustache turning grey.

They gathered around Lou, his mother and grandmother smothering him with kisses. His father stepped forward and hugged him, after hanging back awkwardly. They both became embarrassed. Lou turned to Jeb and shook his hand and embraced him. True, they'd all gotten older, especially Father. His shoulders were rounded and his thinning, grey hair had receded more and gone white over the ears. His deep blue eyes, under white, straggly eyebrows, were as piercing as ever, though sunken. His sallow face was gaunt, cheeks hollow. Lou was shocked. His dad had the air of a beaten man. His mother was still a pretty woman with the same wonderful smile, big, bright eyes and soft, brown hair.

They stepped inside and Lou immediately caught that familiar smell of furniture polish, tobacco and wood smoke from the bluestone fireplace, lingering from previous winters. He glanced around the room, appreciating the dark wood paneling and oak flooring, like a shadowy cave—cosy in winter, oppressive in summer. His eyes fell on a shotgun propped in the corner by the door. It jarred him for a moment. Above all else, this place was home—more home to Lou than the Fairfax house had ever been.

On one wall were a few yellowing pictures in frames: General Lee and Stonewall Jackson and a photo of Gran and Granddad taken in the 1880s. Beside them, photos of Lou: one in Marine dress uniform taken just before being shipped off to France, and the other, full of promise in his Navy uniform before leaving for England as an airshipman.

Gran scurried off to the kitchen to bring refreshments. Everyone sat down in the living room in the old, but comfortable, easy chairs. It was hard at first. Where to start? Father sat packing tobacco onto a cigarette paper. He licked the edge and rolled it.

"Tell us about the journey here, son. They say you flew the airship," Mother said.

"It was okay, Mom. Nothing spectacular really. Pretty boring most of the time."

"To read the newspapers and hear your mom tell it, you'd think he'd flown the damned thing to Canada all by himself," Lou's father said, flicking a brass lighter under his cigarette. It flamed, filling the room with smoke. He began to cough—a nasty, hacking cough. Gran came out from the kitchen with lemonade and iced tea. Everyone helped themselves except Father. Gran brought him coffee.

"We had plenty of experienced officers on board. I was just one of them."

"No, you were an officer aboard His Majesty's Airship *Howden R100* based at the British Government's Royal Airship Works in Cardington and Special Adviser to the Director of Airship Development, as well as being the Official American Observer. It says it all right here in the paper," Anna said, holding up the *Washington Post*.

"Sis—"

"Don't play it down, Lou. We're all very proud of you," Anna said. "Even Dad!"

Father remained impassive. He took a gulp of coffee and put his cup back in the saucer on the table beside him. Tom sat in an upright chair against the wall, arms folded across his chest, lips pursed, staring out the window.

"I don't know why you couldn't have settled down here and married a nice, American girl, one of your own kind, instead of going off and marrying *some hoity-toity British dame*," Father said. He stopped to cough and clear his throat. His voice was weak and hoarse."Julia sat around here waiting for you to come home in that silly damned airship. She would've been perfect. You broke that poor girl's heart, that's what you did. *Jilted!* That's what she was. She was devoted to you. And still is! She comes round here to see your mother every week and Mother treats her like a daughter. She'll die an old maid!"

Everyone sat silent. Lou felt bushwacked. That was *Father.* Nothing had changed and Tom was turning out just like him. The old animosity was alive and well. This was not exactly *The Return of the Prodigal Son.*

Mother dabbed her eyes with a handkerchief. "Cliff, you can't say that," she said. "He's got to lead his own life. Maybe it's lucky he's over there. At least he's working."

"I had every intention of coming back. After the crash, everything changed."

"Yeah, he got the hots for his nurse," Father sneered, glaring at Mother.

"It's true, Dad, I did fall for a wonderful girl, but that wasn't the only reason."

"They always fall for the nurse," Father said.

"What else was it, son?" Mother asked.

"I don't want to talk about it right now, Mom."

"He doesn't want to talk about it right now, Mom," Father scoffed in a whiny voice. He began to cough again and pinched out his cigarette in the dirty ashtray.

"Josh came to see us, you know," Mother said.

"He said he would."

"He was such a nice young man," Gran said. "Anna and Tom brought him to see me."

"He thought the world of you, Lou," Mother said.

"Anna was very taken with him. He was *so* good looking," Gran said.

Anna had become wistful and was tearing up. "He was a lovely guy," she whispered.

"It was a tragedy," Mother said.

"It was *inevitable!* That's what it was! Riding around in the air in a balloon filled with gas—you're asking for it. It defies logic. Common sense'll tell you that sooner or later you're gonna be blown to smithereens. It's the law of physics. Any damned fool could figure that out," Father said coldly.

No one said anything for a long time and Gran got up to get more refreshments. "Louis, how long are you staying for?" she said.

"I'll be here until August the eleventh—if you don't mind, Gran."

"You can stay as long as you like, my darlin' boy."

"I wish I could stay longer."

"But he's got to get back to the 'little wifey' in merry old England," Father said, smirking.

"Dad, *stop it!*" Anna cried.

Father got up and disappeared through the front door. Gran went round clearing things away.

"Don't be too upset by your Dad, Lou. He's had a rough time. He's been longing for the day when you walked through that door," Mother said. Lou looked skeptical.

"It's true," Anna said.

"You're all he thinks about," Mother said.

"You're his favorite," Anna said.

"I don't know about that ..."

Lou watched as Tom got up and went upstairs.

"Your dad worries himself sick about you, son," Gran said.

A few minutes later, someone tapped on the front door.

"It'll be Jeb," Mother said. "Come in."

Jeb stepped into the living room. "Shall I bring up anything special for dinner, ma'am?"

"Bring up a nice, plump chicken, Jeb, and some beans and carrots. Oh, and some squash, please," Gran said.

"Jeb, is my husband down there with you?" Mother asked.

"He's sitting on his seat by the crick as usual, Mrs. R."

Lou strolled down the pathway past the old barn to the paddock. He paused to pat the draft horse before moving past rows of lettuces and carrots in a small adjacent field. It was getting hot and insects were buzzing around. His movements were followed by three blackbirds wheeling overhead. He continued along the well-trodden path down to the creek, passing Jeb's shack on the right-hand side, among the trees. Lou stopped to inspect it. Though basic, Jeb had done a nice job. It had a small verandah across the front and window boxes full of yellow flowers. The wood siding was painted white and the roof was clad in corrugated iron sheeting. On each side sat a painted wooden barrel under a downspout. Everything seemed perfect and in its place. Instinctively, Lou got the impression that Jeb was a happy man, or at least he would be if the KKK left him alone. A plume of blue smoke came from the chimney.

Jeb's wife must be inside.

Mother had written to say that Jeb had got married late in life to a younger woman. He'd asked if he could bring her to Remington's Farm. The three blackbirds swooped down and landed on the roof and began to strut along the ridge, cawing noisily, heads bobbing, their eyes beady and wicked. The door opened and a big woman, about thirty, wearing a full-length, bright blue dress and a white turban emerged. She held a boy in her arms, a towel in her one hand. A little, brown-eyed girl peeped from behind a clutched handful of her mother's skirt. The woman gave Lou a stunning white smile. "You must be Mr. Lou. It's good to see you, sir," she said, standing above him on the edge of the porch.

"It's *Alice*, right? My mother told me all about you. How are you?"

"I's fine. Everybody's bin lookin' forward to seein' *you*, Mr. Lou."

"It's good to be home," Lou said.

But the blackbirds were causing a distraction. Alice looked up at them, vexed. "Ah don't know what's got into them darn birds. Carryin' on an' fussin' like 'at. She waved the towel at them. "Go on shoo!" The startled crows took off and circled the shack before flying off toward the river.

"Perhaps they're welcoming me home," Lou said.

"No, they're bad luck—a warning more like. I don' like 'em on our roof. Yer daddy shoots 'em when he has a mind to."

"Now, who are *these* little people?" Lou asked, peering at the children.

"This is Doris, she's four and this guy is Benjamin, he'll be three next week." Alice looked down at the kids. "Say hello to Mr. Lou."

The girl smiled, but was too shy to speak.

The boy was more bold. "Hello Mr. Lou-Lou," he said, giggling.

"How long is you stayin'? You stayin' for good, ain'tcha?" Alice asked.

" 'Fraid not."

"Yer daddy's down there by the crick. He sits there most of the time these days—thinkin' 'bout you I reckon."

"How do you know?"

"Oh, I jus' do."

"I'll go on down."

"He ain't bin too well lately."

Lou walked along the pathway past a chicken run with about fifty chickens clucking and carrying on, and then on past more plots where vegetables were thriving. His dad was sitting on a bench on the dock. Lou went over and eased himself down, trying not to disturb him.

"Dad, I'm so pleased to see you. You don't know how much."

Father said nothing—as if he hadn't heard. He looked away across the creek, took out his lighter and re-lit a half-smoked roll-up, exhaling a cloud of smoke that hung in the still, humid air. Two ducks splashed into the water and swam past them. Finally, Father nodded as if Lou's words had just sunk in. He wiped the sweat off his forehead with his hand and rubbed it on his checked shirt.

"I'm sorry about the house, Dad. I didn't know."

"How *would* you know?"

This stung, but Lou tried to ignore it. "It's *terrible*," he said.

"It really doesn't matter," Father said, staring at the dark water.

"I was shocked when I heard about it this morning."

"Well, you needn't concern yourself."

"I want to help."

"We'll manage."

"I'll help some way."

"How?" Father said his lip curling into that old familiar sneer.

"I'll find a way."

"Don't worry. *Tom'll* look after things. He's a good boy."

"He's a wonderful son and wonderful brother."

"As long as *he's* around, you can do your thing. You don't need to give us a second thought."

"Dad, I love you, you know. I love you all. I've been a rotten son. You're right."

Father didn't argue. He raised his eyebrows as if to say, '*It really doesn't matter.*'

"Dad, Tom told me you've been having trouble with the Klan."

This irritated Father. His eyes narrowed. Now he was mad at Tom.

"Goddammit! I told him not to tell you about them fools."

"What do they want?"

"You know what they want. Don't pay 'em no mind. I got the twelve. I'll deal with 'em. I'll have them sons o' bitches in the ground faster'n you can spit."

Lou exhaled and looked away. He didn't doubt his father on that score. No point in arguing. "I'm going back to sort a few things out." He got up and moved away. "See you later, Dad." Father nodded without turning his head, continuing his gaze into the creek. Lou walked back up the path past Jeb, who was weeding one of the vegetable gardens.

Lou called to him, "Jeb, you okay?"

"Yep, Mr. Lou. I'm fine."

"No, *really?*"

"Yeah, everything's good."

"What about them damned night riders?"

"Nah! They ain't nothin'. Don't you worry about *them* none. We got it covered, sir."

Back at the house, Gran served a ham salad at the massive kitchen table. Lou loved this room with its old, wood-burning range and huge, white porcelain sink. He opened the pantry door and looked inside. Lots of jars and homemade stuff. He looked at Gran.

"We don't buy much. We grow everything."

"What about things like toilet paper and milk?"

"We get the local newspaper once in a while," Gran replied, with a little smirk.

"We trade with Jonesie up the road; he's got Jerseys at his place," Mother said.

"You'd be surprised how much bartering goes on around here," Gran said.

"We're very blessed," said Anna, putting her arm around Lou's neck and kissing his cheek. "Oh, my darlin' brother, it's *so* good to have you home."

That first evening, a Saturday, the family gathered around the big oak table in the rarely-used dining room and ate the roasted chicken and vegetables Jeb had brought up. Gran took out a bottle of elderberry wine she'd made a year before—said she'd been keeping it for a special occasion. Anna poured some out and they raised their glasses.

"Here's to you, Lou—to your safe return in your airship," Anna said.

"And the rest of your flights," Mother added.

Father lifted his glass and took a sip, saying nothing. Tom did the same. Dinner was over by nine. Father said he was tired and went to bed, waving a hand to Lou as he left the room.

Well, at least that's something.

"Tom, can you take me into Georgetown on Monday morning?" Lou asked.

Tom frowned at first and then said, "Sure."

"I've a few errands to run. Wanna come, Sis?"

"I want to be with you every moment you're here, Lou."

"Do you still have the guitar and banjo somewhere? Or did the bank get them, too?" Lou asked, looking at Tom. But Mother seemed ready for this question.

"No, I hid them away and brought them here. I dug them out of one of the attic bedrooms and cleaned them up last week. I knew you'd be looking for them."

"So many times I've thought of how Dad and I used to play together, on good days."

"You should get him to play with you," Gran said in a whisper as though her son upstairs might hear. "Since you left, he hasn't played a note."

When Lou went to his bedroom, he saw Mother had stood the guitar and banjo against the wall in the corner. He undressed and fell asleep in his old bed, wishing Charlotte was there.

The next day, they all went to church, except for Father. He said he didn't feel like it. He used to go regularly, but his churchgoing, like his faith, had dropped off. Mother said she was surprised Julia wasn't in church—she'd kept up her attendance at this church after her family had moved away.

On Monday morning, Lou went with Tom and Anna in the pickup back along the river and over the recently completed Key Bridge, into Georgetown.

"This is all new," Lou said as they passed a streetcar gliding its way over the river.

"There's a lot of stuff round here you ain't seen," Tom said.

Lou turned and faced Tom and spoke across Anna who sat in the middle. "You still mad at me, little brother? What's eatin' you, huh?" Lou said. Tom paused, mulling things over. "Come on Tom, *spit it out!*"

"You show up here like you're '*the man*'. Giving money to the poor. Who the hell do you think you are? Some big shot!"

"Tom, I was just tryin' to help my—"

"And to tell you the truth, Louis, it irritates me, how everyone's had to suffer because of *you! Virginia's Favorite Son—my ass!*"

"Who?"

"Dad, and Mum, although *she* won't admit it—"

"I'm sure Dad doesn't care that much—"

"He does so! It tears him up worrying over you."

Lou was surprised, but glad it was all coming out.

"And then there's *Julia*," Tom added.

"*Julia?*"

"Yes, *Julia!* She believed, and the family thought, it was a foregone conclusion you'd come back and marry her."

"It's true, Lou. Tom's right," Anna said.

Lou glanced at Anna.

Not you, too, Sis.

"Now you show up like the big hero and we're supposed to fall at your feet, while you act all surprised at what's been going on in this country."

They traveled along M Street in silence for a time. It was getting busy with private cars and trucks on the road. Lou had brought Charlotte's photo, wrapped in the newspaper he'd read on the train. Lou asked Tom to stop outside a glass and mirror shop and went in. Ten minutes later, he was back with a smile on his face. He climbed back into the pickup.

"Look guys, I'm sorry. I really am. I don't know what to say. I'd fully intended to come home, believe me." He unwrapped the package. "Look at this," Lou said, as if it might explain things a bit. He handed the frame to Anna. "It fell down and got smashed on the airship."

"How did that happen?" Anna said.

"It just fell off my bedside table."

"Oh my, she's gorgeous. I can understand why you never came home!" Anna said. "Although, you did hurt poor Julia somethin' fierce."

The next stop was the post office. Lou went in and sent a wire to Charlotte telling her he'd arrived in Virginia and wished she were here. They drove on to Riggs Bank, parked and went inside. The bank building was cool under its domed, copper roof. The interior was ornate with hardwood and marble finishes. Lou found a sub-manager and explained they needed to open a joint account in their three names. This was done and Lou deposited ninety seven dollars and thirty-cents into the account after converting the bank draft he'd brought with him from the Midland Bank. Lou told them he'd be sending money to the account as an emergency fund. After Lou had drawn out thirty-five dollars, they climbed back into the pickup. Tom had become irritated again. "What are you doing all this for? We don't need your damned money! You think you can just pop back into everyone's lives, leave some money and go flying off again, huh! What the hell d'you think we are?"

"Tom, please don't be like that, brother, I just want to help. Seriously I do," Lou said.

"Well, we don't need your help. We've done all right without you for the last ten years."

"Oh, Tom—" Anna said.

"I need to call in at Fort Myer," Tom said.

"Okay, Tom. After that, I'd like to run by Anacostia Flats to see my army buddy, if you don't mind."

"Right," Tom answered.

They retraced their route and re-crossed Key Bridge. Fort Myer formed part of Arlington Cemetery. They passed white gravestones on their left and wove their way up the steep hill to the top, where stately, red brick buildings stood and pin oaks lined the street on the plateau. The place had the feel of a college campus and the smell of horses in the air. They slowed to a walking pace as a flag-draped caisson drawn by six white horses approached, on its way to a new grave down the hill. Four soldiers in blue rode four of the horses.

Tom drove past the officers' club to the morgue at the end of the street and around the back to an adjoining building. He unlocked the door and he and Lou entered. It was dark inside. When his eyes adjusted, Lou made out an old coffin on the floor. Tom took out a key and unlocked the padlock, opened the hinged lid and propped it against the wall. He went back to the pickup and threw back the canvas, revealing six cardboard boxes full of booze. Without speaking, Tom and Lou carried them inside and placed them in the coffin. Tom closed the lid and locked the padlock. They came outside into the sunshine and Tom relocked the door.

"That'll keep the fellas at the officers' club happy for a day or so," Anna said with a smile and a wink.

36

TENT CITY

Monday August 4, 1930.

om drove them down through Rosslyn back to the George Washington Parkway, then crossed the river again into the city. They motored along Constitution Avenue, passing the George Washington Monument, toward the back of the Capitol Building. Scenes on the street were much the same as before, with mounted police keeping a watchful eye on the poor wretches lining up for food or carrying placards. They crossed the Anacostia River into Anacostia Flats, where another miserable scene greeted them.

Hundreds of ragged, makeshift tents and shanties had been set up. At the moment, the ground was hard and rutted. Lou knew that after a rainstorm this place would be an unpleasant mud hole. Anna was visibly appalled at the squalor. Tom parked the pickup in the first open space he found. The place looked like a slum settlement in some distant country and smelled as bad. The conditions reminded Lou of the Front. Human misery! Although, due to his war experience, he perceived some semblance of order in all this chaos.

The camp was divided into rows, with street names daubed on wood slats nailed to posts: Ypres Row, Argonne Avenue, Somme Street, Verdun Road, Belleau Wood Boulevard. Saint-Mihiel Street. They watched kids playing in the dirt and blacks and whites together, chatting. They nodded as the Remingtons walked by, as if they were sitting on their old front porch.

Lou stopped a man passing by and asked where he could find Henry Faulkner. The man was polite and took them to a shack fifty yards away and called through the doorway.

"Henry, folks here to see you."

Faulkner appeared. His weary face broke into a warm smile and he ushered them inside, where there was a table consisting of packing case boards nailed together, old 4 x 4 legs and planks each side for seats. Two men were seated at the table—one black, one white, ill-kempt and dirty, faces glistening with sweat, their body odor overpowering. Lou regretted bringing Anna. The two men jumped up and stood erect when Lou entered. Tom looked surprised at the respect shown to his brother.

"This is Sergeant Terry of the 307th and this is Gunny Jackson of the New York 369th. This, gentlemen, is Commander Remington, formerly of the United States Marine Corps," Henry said. They all shook hands.

Lou spoke directly to Sgt. Terry. "You were in the Lost Battalion?"

"Yes, sir. Now I'm lost in Tent City," Terry said bitterly.

"Can I get you coffee or water?" Henry asked.

To be polite, Lou said he'd have coffee. Anna and Tom declined.

"What's going on, Henry?" Lou said.

"We've set up this camp as the First Expeditionary Force of army vets. We need the money they promised us. We need it bad and we need it now."

"How long can you last?"

"We've nowhere to go. We'll be here 'til we get the money—or until we starve or freeze to death, I guess."

"How many of you are there?" Anna asked.

"Right now, ten thousand. We expect that number to increase to fifty thousand. Hundreds are pouring in every day."

Sgt. Terry poured out coffee from a pot into a tin mug and gave it to Lou.

"It'll be a public health nightmare," Lou said, taking a sip. The coffee was lukewarm and bitter. He'd had worse in the trenches—*much worse.*

"We're pretty disciplined—we're running this place like an army camp, as we were trained. We have latrines dug and supervised, and kitchens of sorts."

"I'm here for a week. Tell me what I can do to help."

"You're well known, sir. Could you write or meet with a congressman or two? And write to the President on our behalf?"

Lou saw Tom looking at him with new-found respect, with perhaps a hint of remorse in his eyes. Anna and Tom couldn't believe what they were hearing.

"If I can help, I will. There must be a lot of things you need."

"What about medicines and food and stuff like that?" Anna said.

"Yes, all of that, and water, and soap. We need doctors and nurses, and some decent tents. We could use some lumber."

"What about the people here? Are they peaceful?"

"We've been trying to establish good relations with the police. There are elements trying to stir up trouble—they want a full-blown revolution."

"*Communists?*"

"Yes. But there are only a handful."

"It's important no one makes trouble, or your cause will be lost," Lou said. He pulled out his wallet and put twenty-five dollars on the table.

"Take this. It's not much, but it'll help a little," he said.

Henry was humble, but delighted. "Thank you, Lou. You don't know what it means to have your support," he said.

Lou finished his coffee and stuck out his hand. "We must go now. I'm staying with my folks in Virginia. Let me think about this."

They drove away from the camp depressed.

"We must help those poor people. Did you see those kids?" Anna said. "We must take food over there."

"They need more food than you've got, Sis," Lou said.

Tom remained deep in thought. It was his turn to be speechless.

Back at the farm, they found a black Ford sedan parked near the house, a driver at the wheel. A woman in her early thirties stood on the porch talking to Mother.

"This is Helen Smothers from the *Washington Post*. She wants to talk to you, Lou," Mother said.

The lady looked more like a fashion model than a reporter, her face exquisitely made up. She wore a white, wide-brimmed hat with a blue band, slightly cocked to one side, and a white jacket with wide lapels. Her skirt, to just below the knee, pinched at the waist, accentuated her graceful figure. She stepped forward, a perfectly manicured hand outstretched, her French perfume overpowering. Intense brown eyes held him in her gaze.

"Commander Remington, I'm so pleased to make your acquaintance," she announced, in a distinct Chicago accent. This woman was a *go-getter*.

Lou took her hand. He looked around at Tom and Anna who signaled that they'd leave him to it.

"Please, sit down," Lou said, pointing to the couch and easy chairs on the porch.

Mother reappeared. "Can I get you some iced tea?" she asked.

"A pitcher would be nice, with lemons, if you have any, Mom," Lou answered. He turned back to his visitor. "How can I help you, Miss Smothers?"

"Commander, there are so many questions our readers have about you. First, I'd like to ask you about the *ZR-2/R38* crash. Are you over that now?"

"Yes, completely, but I don't talk about it anymore."

"Of course. You have been in England for ten years now. Will you stay there? You're married to an English lady, I believe?"

"I'm pretty well settled, but you never know what tomorrow will bring. I love England almost as much as I love my wife, Charlotte."

Helen Smothers pressed Lou with questions for half an hour. He answered them carefully, taking his time while she took notes on a stenographer's pad. He thought this woman could be helpful.

"I was a marine before I went to England," he said finally.

"Ah, yes, you were in France, I believe?"

"Yes. I went to see some of our veterans today."

Helen Smothers stopped scribbling for a moment and sat back. He had her full attention. Lou knew this'd add dimension to the piece she'd write.

"What was your impression?" she asked.

"I was deeply saddened by their plight and the appalling conditions they've been reduced to live in. I was *totally stunned*, if you want to know the truth, Miss Smothers."

"You feel they should get the money?"

"Have you been to Anacostia Flats?

"No, not personally."

"Then you should. I think the country should do everything in its power to help and protect the men who faithfully served this nation and made great sacrifices."

"Perhaps I'll do that, Commander."

"Please write down this name: Henry Faulkner. Ask for him when you go. Sit down with him and have a cup of coffee," Lou said. "And please, *don't* go dressed as you are now."

"I understand."

"Prepare yourself, Miss Smothers. It isn't pleasant," Lou said.

Lou answered a few more questions and Helen Smothers thanked him for the interview. There would most certainly be something in the paper tomorrow and a feature article in the Sunday issue, she told him. She also intimated that she'd like to meet him again in the future—perhaps in more '*unofficial capacity*'.

37

JULIA

Monday August 4, 1930.

Lou spent the rest of the day helping Tom and Anna work on the vegetable gardens. He found it enjoyable and relaxing. Father, in his old, straw sunhat sat in a deck chair contentedly watching them and smoking cigarettes. Mother and Gran toiled in the kitchen making jam and bottling fruit. Later, they decided to have a quiet night, although Mother did warn Lou that Julia usually came by on Monday evenings. He sincerely hoped she would.

Julia had lived next door to Gran's place until she moved away twelve years ago with her parents to a big house in Georgetown. Over the years, her father had made a lot of money in business with his brother. Julia's father died of leukemia three years after moving to Georgetown. She now worked with her uncle, attempting to take over her father's shares in several businesses, including the largest lumber yard in Fairfax County—Tyson's Lumber & General Hardware Corp.

After dinner, Julia arrived in her burgundy Chrysler Imperial. They heard the sound of her tires on the driveway and the car door slam.

"That'll be Julia. She's later than usual," said Mother. "Why don't you kids sit on the porch and catch up."

The three siblings went out as Julia was climbing the wooden steps. She wore a simple beige cotton dress in the latest fashion, tight at the waist with short sleeves.

Lou was taken aback. She'd blossomed into an exceptional woman, exuding class and style. Her blond hair fell to her shoulders and across her face, causing her to toss her head every so often. Her almond-shaped, hazel eyes radiated wisdom, confidence and patience. She wore a hint of blush, accentuating high cheekbones and perfect skin.

"Well, look at you!" Lou said. "You're *so* beautiful, Julia." While Tom and Anna looked on, they embraced, holding each other tightly. Lou kissed her cheeks. She'd never been one to show much emotion—always calm and collected, but for her, he sensed this was a big moment.

"Look at her, Tom—isn't she *absolutely gorgeous!*" Lou said.

He saw a flash of jealousy in Tom's eyes.

"She's the most beautiful girl I know," Tom replied.

Lou knew instantly his brother was in love with her. Father stepped out onto the porch and smiled at Julia. He pointed at her.

"Now *that's* the girl you should have married—*that girl right there!* But what do you do—*you* go off to become a big shot with your uppity *British* friends. They don't make 'em like this one anymore. You made a *big* mistake, boy!"

Lou was mortified. He glanced at Tom and saw both acquiescence and annoyance in his eyes. But Tom had already made his feelings plain earlier in the day. Father looked at Tom and turned around and went back inside the house, shaking his head in disgust. Everyone continued without comment, but Father's words hung in the balmy air like a bad odor on this hot, still night. Julia's eyes glistened.

"Let's sit down, shall we?" Anna said.

Lou sensed Julia and Anna were close and suspected they confided about most things. Mother appeared with lemonade on a tray and put it down on the table in front of them.

The four chatted long after dark. Lou went over the events of his life since he'd seen Julia in 1920. Lou expressed sympathy about her father's death and she was grateful. His passing had been a blow and now, according to Anna, her uncle had seized control of everything, including most of the family fortune. Lou got the impression Julia wasn't all that fond of Uncle Rory.

A full moon had risen, casting a pleasant light across the drive, paddock and river beyond. The noise of the night insects and cicadas started up all around them in the trees, some with an overpowering ratcheting sound, accompanied by a loud purr. This subtropical racket was hypnotizing, coming and going from area to area as the swarms took their turns. Anna made excuses, saying they'd things to do, and got up, silently signaling to Tom. Tom reluctantly followed her into the house. Lou realized he'd been set up. Well, it didn't matter. He loved Julia very much. *Always had.*

"We used to have a swing under that tree, remember?" he said, gesturing toward the large oak on the edge of the paddock.

Julia nodded and smiled. "You kissed me there as the darkness fell."

He detected animosity in her voice. "Yes, I did."

"I remember it well, Remy," Julia said flatly. "That was the day I fell in love with you … the day I made up my mind to have your children."

This came as a serious blow. He was being pummeled from all sides. He sensed Julia had a lot more to say and was mulling things over. This was going to be a serious reprimand.

"Lou, when you went off and joined the Marine Corps, I was devastated."

"It was a dumb thing to do," Lou said.

"I decided to wait for you."

"Julia, I'm …"

She held up her hand to silence him. "No. I want to tell you—so you fully understand."

Feeling small, Lou sat silently, worried about what was to follow.

"I knew you'd joined up under age and thought for a long time you wouldn't be sent to war, and then I heard you were on a ship bound for France. I prayed to God He would return you home safely."

"And He did," Lou said.

"Yes, and I thanked Him for it. I was truly grateful. And I waited. Then you joined the Navy." She rolled her eyes and laughed sarcastically. Lou felt horribly guilty, appreciating the extent of her bitterness and his perceived betrayal. She hadn't shown these feelings at the time—or had he been too blind and dumb to notice? .

"You went off to England and I was happy for you. You were doing exactly what you wanted and you'd soon come back in a new airship. I longed to see you. I went over everything time and time again. I'd be waiting at the hangar in New Jersey and watch you descend from the heavens—and later, I'd become the proud wife of an airshipman."

Lou's mind was racing. Had he lead her on when he'd last seen her? Surely not. At least not to that degree. *She* obviously thought so. And so did his family.

"Julia, I'm so sorry."

She held up her hand again and went on, her breast heaving with uncharacteristic emotion as she relived events. "And then came the accident over the river in England. I went to church that day—it was a Wednesday—and lit a candle and prayed to God. I begged, 'Please, God, spare Lou's life again and I will never ask for anything—I will have no claim on him. I promise You'. And He did. Miraculously, you lived and you stayed and I was happy."

"Julia, after the crash, I couldn't face coming home. I was riddled with guilt," Lou said.

"I understand completely. It was God's will. He kept you from me."

Julia was calming down as if God had truly spoken to her. Lou felt wretched. She'd squandered her young life on him—such a magnificent girl. It was as though he'd left her at the altar. It felt strange and bizarre as he remembered thinking of her briefly at his wedding in St. Cuthbert's. All the things his family had said about her spilled over him.

What a heel!

"Julia, what can I say?"

"There's nothing to say. God kept His bargain and so will I."

Lou looked at her. She was so different from Charlotte—so un-needy. He dreamed of what might have been for a moment and caught himself. They sat in silence with nothing more to be said. Lou admired her candor, her acceptance. She appeared to be at peace with her agreement, without self pity, at least on the surface.

Suddenly, above the roar of the cicadas, they were disturbed by a commotion down in the trees on the path from the creek. In the flickering shadows, Lou could make out three horsemen riding toward the house. He stood up. Julia sat motionless.

The riders were led by a squat, heavy-set figure on a striking Appaloosa, its head and front half jet black, its rear, black and white leopard-spotted. They were clad in white sheets, fluorescent in the moonlight, with pointed hoods over their faces, their narrow eye slits, satanic. The last Klansman, on a black quarter horse, had a rope attached to his waist, the other end knotted around Jeb's neck. Jeb stumbled along behind, the whites of his eyes projecting his terror.

Alice followed, carrying their two wailing children, all of them crying hysterically.

"Please, don't hurt him!" she screamed. *"Please! Please! I beg you."*

The other Klansman rode a chestnut mare. He stopped about twenty yards from the porch and planted a cross in the ground lashed to a spike. Lou smelled diesel. The ten-foot cross went up with a whoosh as it was lit. The flames accentuated the whiteness of their robes, making them more phantom-like—calling up the fires of hell. The first Klansman, stopping at the porch steps, spoke in biblical tones with the cadence of the South. While he delivered his ultimatum, the shining Appaloosa fidgeted with its feet, swishing its tail, nickering softly, the bit clinking between his teeth.

"It's come to our attention an illegal still is operating on this here property. The making of moonshine and the distribution of liquor is prohibited by federal law and will not be tolerated!" He lifted his arm like Moses, pointing at Lou. "You there, boy, tell this here nigger to lead us to that still right now, or tonight he'll be hung by the neck from that tree over yonder, until he is dead!"

He pointed to the oak tree where Lou had kissed Julia years ago. Alice let out a bloodcurdling scream, *"Aaaaah, no! Please don't! ... No, no, please!"*

Jeb fell down on his knees, sobbing. At that moment, the two frenzied dogs came rushing from behind the house barking ferociously. Lou figured Father or Tom had let them out the back door. Lou eased his way along the porch and down the steps. The Klan could see clearly in this light, he was unarmed. He stared up at them—all high and mighty on their horses. The old black mutt kept barking up at the leader.

"You shut this mangy flea bag up, right now!" the Klansman yelled at Lou.

"Moonshine, shut up!" someone called. Lou wasn't sure who.

"Moonshine!" the Klansman shouted in a fury.

He drew a silver six-shooter and shot the dog through the head. Her bark trailed off into a scream as she fell down dead.

"A dog with a name like that deserves to die," the Klansman roared.

Lou ran round to the back of the last Klansman and grabbed the rope, yanking it hard. The horse rose high in the air on her hind legs.

The Klansman rolled backwards over the mare's rump into a heap at Lou's feet. Lou leapt onto the man's back and pulled his wrist up over his head tugging the arm out of its shoulder socket. The man screamed in agony. The first Klansman raised his gun to shoot, but was shaken by a deafening shotgun blast. Now, the Appaloosa reared up with a snorting scream.

"Keep those guns lowered," Father shouted from the open front door.

The two Klansmen sat still on their horses. "So what you gonna do now, mister? You got one left. My friend here an' me, we'll finish all a yer, including this punk down here."

Another voice screamed from a bedroom window. "Keep still, mister." It was Anna. "I got two in this here twelve to blow both yer heads clean off."

"And I got another two, right here, you demons from hell," Gran yelled from a ground floor window.

"Go home, Uncle Rory," Julia said calmly. "Go home right now."

"You don't know who we are," the leader shouted back.

"It's not hard to figure, Uncle Rory. You're on my damned horse. Now go!"

Lou untied the noose from Jeb's neck and lifted the third whimpering Klansman from the ground and laid him over his horse on his stomach. He took the rope and lashed his feet and hands under the horse's belly. He tugged on the man's hood, and yanked his head up by the hair, exposing his young face.

"Why you hiding that pretty little puss, huh?" Lou said. "Best be on your way now, boys, and don't let the bogeymen getcha on the ride home." He gave the horse's rump a hard slap, making her start forward violently. While the fiery cross crumpled and smoked and its light diminished, the three Klansmen rode off into the night without further threats. Lou took Jeb back to the shack with his wife, who had settled down some.

"They'll come back. I just know they will," she kept saying over and over.

Lou went back to the house where Julia was getting ready to leave. He put his arms around her and gently kissed her lips. She closed her eyes with pleasure. Tom watched silently.

"You must take care," Lou said.

"Don't worry. I'll be fine."

"I *am* worried about you, Julia."

"Who's the young one?" Father asked.

"He's my cousin, Israel, Uncle Rory's son. He's just as crazy as his father."

They walked Julia to her car.

"Make sure you come to us if you need help," Father said.

The next day, Tom and Jeb loaded the pickup with three consignments of whisky. Jeb had the appearance of a man whose spirit had been crushed—overnight his hair seemed to have become more grey. Lou, today in uniform, rode with Tom and Anna in the pickup to make deliveries, first to the Navy Yard across the river from the tent city, the second to the Capitol Building and the third to Fort Myer. At Fort Myer, above Arlington Cemetery, Lou reluctantly decided there was another place he really needed to visit.

"I need to find Captain Maxfield's grave," he said.

Anna smiled, realizing why Lou put on his uniform.

"I know exactly where it is," Tom said.

"How come?"

"Jeb and me dug that grave, amongst others. We all went to the funeral. Dad insisted he was going, so we all went."

"For God's sake! He didn't tell me."

"It changed Dad," Anna said. "Made him ill."

They drove round the circular gravel road flanked by thousands of white gravestones. Tom pulled up abruptly. They climbed out of the pickup and Lou stood in silence at the grave with a tombstone bearing the captain's name. Anna put her arm through his and they stood in the sunshine in silence, facing the new Lincoln Memorial across the river in the distance. Before leaving, Lou stood rigidly to attention and saluted the tombstone. Tom looked on in stunned silence.

That night, Lou dreamed he was aboard *R38*. Capt. Maxfield's voice came through loud and clear in the darkness.

Remington, look to your crew!

The ship was on fire and breaking up. Lou came round. He opened his eyes in a daze. The room was brightly illuminated. He leapt out of bed, realizing he was in Gran's house and ran to the window. The sky was lit by orange flames rising down by the creek. He understood immediately. He pulled on his pants and boots and ran out onto the landing as his whole family spilled out of their bedrooms.

"They're back. Come on," Lou shouted. "They got Jeb's place."

"You stay with Gran," Father yelled to Mother and Anna, grabbing his shotgun.

When they got down to the shack, the roof was falling in. There was nothing they could do. Jeb, his wife and two children sat under a tree in tears, safe from the flames, watching their home burn.

"I tol' yer they was comin' back. ... I tol' yer," Alice sobbed. "They got the still. They held a gun to my baby's head. Threatened to blow his brains out."

Lou glanced at Jeb who kept nodding, unable to speak. Everyone stood in silent disbelief until Father spoke. "Jeb, Alice, bring the kids. Come up to the house. Nothing we can do here."

The following morning Lou, Father, Tom and Anna went down with Jeb to inspect the smoldering ruin. Jeb led them to what was left of the still. It would've been hard to find. Jeb had constructed a huge dugout with a roof covered with dirt, grass and shrubbery. The barrels, copper piping and all parts had been smashed beyond repair.

In the afternoon, a military vehicle drew up outside Gran's house. Anna came out. A sailor in uniform leapt out and stood at attention.

"Pardon me, ma'am," he said. "I'm looking for Commander Remington. We understand he's visiting the family."

Anna went in and got Lou. The two men exchanged salutes.

"Chief Petty Officer Brown, sir, at your service. Commander, I've been ordered to bring you to the Navy Yard at your *earliest* convenience, sir."

"Like *right now?*"

"*Yes, sir!*"

"Give me five minutes."

Forty minutes later, Lou was escorted into a room in one of the Navy Yard Buildings in Washington, D.C., where he was introduced to a Capt. Yates. Lou sat down and they made small talk. The captain was familiar with Lou's history. They talked about the Canada flight in

Howden R100 and his upcoming voyage to India. After a few minutes, the captain cocked his head on one side, choosing his words carefully.

"This brings me to a rather delicate matter," he said coyly.

"It's come to my attention from different quarters that the source of the finest whisky in Virginia has just dried up!"

The captain looked mischievous, raising his hands in the air as if to say 'How could such a thing happen?' Lou was dumbfounded. The captain went on. "I've been asked to intercede, as this situation is going to have a severe impact on a few people—from a *medicinal standpoint*, you understand."

"I do indeed, sir."

"There's been some sort of a fracas, I hear."

"News travels fast, sir. Some gentlemen in white hoods paid my family a visit."

"*Bastards!* Anyone hurt?"

"No, but they terrorized my folks and did substantial damage."

"If you require any help in that regard, you must tell me."

"I could use a few good men, sir," Lou said.

"'*A few good men*'—I like that! Nice ring to it! On your way back to Virginia, tell Chief Brown exactly what assistance you need."

"I'll *do* that, sir."

"Now, as important as that issue is, *that* wasn't the main purpose of asking you here—although I know the folks in the Officer's Club will be pleased we had this conversation. The Army Chief of Staff, General Luby, is coming to talk with you about what's going on in Hooverville."

Lou gulped. "The Army Chief of Staff! …. Hooverville, sir?"

"Tent City, across the way." The captain waved his hand in the general direction of Anacostia. "Don't worry about the general. He's paying an informal visit. Wants to meet you."

Just then, the door swung open and they were joined by an imposing two star general in khaki, a briar pipe clenched between his teeth. Both Lou and Capt. Yates jumped up, snapped to attention and saluted. The general gave a casual return salute.

"At ease," he said. He removed his hat and pipe, and when he spoke he reminded Lou of a Shakespearean actor. He extended his hand to them both.

"Commander, I'm Ray Luby. Congratulations on your historic flight—well done, son. You make all of us proud!"

"Thank you, General."

"Sorry we've called you here at such short notice. Across the river here, we have a huge potential crisis."

"Yes sir. I visited the camp as soon as I got here."

"We know you did, and we don't have a problem with that. Maybe you can be of assistance to us."

"How, sir?"

"The situation must be kept under control."

"We know you met with one of their leaders," the captain said.

"I served with him in battle at Saint-Mihiel and then the Verdun sector, sir."

Respect showed in the officer's faces.

"We're anxious this camp doesn't turn into a festering sore, rife with violence and disease. I'd like to hear your views on the subject, since you were in the place and you know some of them personally," the general said.

"These people are desperate, sir, and it's going to get much worse," Lou said.

The two senior men looked startled.

"They're poverty-stricken, hungry, without medical help, and they've no place to go. They were *better* taken care of at the Front. This winter, they'll freeze to death."

The officers shifted uncomfortably in their chairs and Lou caught fleeting glimpse of compassion in the general's eyes.

"Do you have any suggestions, Commander?" Capt. Yates asked.

"Yes, sir, I do. Set up food banks within the camp. Send them decent tents and lumber they can use. Build temporary medical facilities in the camp. Send in medical supplies and assign them army doctors and nurses. Supply them with clean water and plenty of soap. Assign liaison officers to work with them and with the city's police chief on a *daily* basis. Most important of all—make sure these men are *not* forgotten!"

The two men stared at Lou. He'd given them more than they'd bargained for—so much to think about. But there were other factors to consider.

"There're people in this town who are concerned we have communist agitators in this camp fermenting revolution, encouraged by Marxist bastards from Britain and Russia," General Luby said.

"I understand, sir. Right now this is a public relations nightmare. I'm concerned if things aren't handled properly, you may have an unmitigated disaster on your hands—perhaps a full blown revolution."

"Yes, yes, but if there is the slightest hint of violence, they'll be cleared out, ruthlessly, without hesitation. We'll send tanks in there and flatten that place if necessary. Ex-military or not—traitors will not be tolerated! Make sure they understand that, Remington. This is the Army's mess. We own it, and we'll deal with it as we see fit," General Luby warned.

"There's a small element of trouble makers, sir.   Ninety-nine percent of those men are patriots—true-blue Americans."

"There're blacks and whites in that camp living together—all getting along like pigs in shit. That's making a lot of people around here mighty nervous. Seems unnatural to them!" the captain said.

"There is racial harmony—something many of them learned at the Front in the Army, which could be seen as a positive thing, sir."

The general relit his pipe and puffed out some smoke.

"So, Commander, how come you went to the camp?" he asked.

"They met me at Union Station and asked for my help, sir."

"What are you going to do?" the captain asked.

"I thought about writing my congressman and perhaps even the President."

"I strongly advise you not to get political," General Luby said. "I read your comments in the *Post*. That's already raised a lot of hackles up on that hill."

"Even though it's not due, I'd give them the damned money," the captain said.

"You're getting into politics," the general said, standing up. "I've a meeting. I must go." He shook hands with Lou. "I like what you said just now. Your advice is sound. Good luck on your flight back to England."

"The Commander here," the captain said, smiling at Lou, "has kindly agreed to look into that '*other matter*' we talked about."

The general broke into a broad grin. "*Excellent!* He's a good man, this one," he said.

The three officers saluted before the general left. When he'd gone, the captain asked Lou to sit down again.

"Your progress in England has been followed by some of the top people here, including Admiral Moffet himself. I should tell you, your name's come up in connection with the *Akron* and the *Macon* being constructed in Ohio, but more importantly, they've been following your work with the British engineer Barnes Wallis and, of course, with the Royal Airship Works. They see you as a potential player in our own program. I thought you might like to know that, Commander. There could be a bright future for you here."

Lou wasn't sure if this excited him or not. He tried to look pleased —it was inevitable the Navy would want him back sooner or later.

38

A FEW GOOD MEN

Thursday August 7, 1930.

The following morning Lou pulled up on the dirt road outside Tyson's Lumber & General Hardware with a truck full of marines. This was Vienna, seven miles from Remington's Farm, ten miles from Washington. They were all in fatigues, including Lou. The marines jumped down from the truck and moved into position with planned precision. The site was a sprawling fifty-acre compound surrounded by woods. It contained concrete products, pipe and lumber in a huge, fenced-in yard bordering the road. A buzz came from a sawmill way off in the distance at the back of the property.

Lou had planned this operation with these men at the Navy Yard after reconnoitering the premises the previous afternoon. He hoped serious violence wouldn't actually be necessary. His distaste for that hadn't changed. Permanent behavioral modification in a few individuals was the goal, as well as the negotiation and procurement of some serious compensation for damages. For the sake of his own family, for Jeb's and for Julia, he needed to make this count—not to mention the matter of keeping the brass in Washington happy— another major concern relating to family business.

Lou, carrying a rolled-up newspaper and a bullhorn, strode into the huge metal building, which was sectioned off and included an enclosed general hardware store within the shed itself. A rough wood stairway led up to a complex of offices high up near the roof, with windows overlooking the contractor's sales areas. The marines spread themselves out between stacks of lumber and architectural millwork. Lou nodded to one of them who blew a whistle. The staff of four yardmen and a handful of customers eyed them nervously. Lou stepped into an open area and raised a bullhorn to his mouth.

"Attention! Attention! Everybody, listen up! This business has been closed down. This is a danger zone. Leave these premises immediately. I repeat, this business has been closed down."

"What's the matter?" a concerned storeman asked.

"Everybody out!" Lou shouted.

Startled employees and customers obeyed, sensing trouble. They moved quickly to the entrance doors. Lou collared the last employee before he left.

"Bring me six lengths of chain about four foot long and six padlocks. Right now!"

The man scurried off as fast as he could without asking questions. He was back with the items in a few minutes. "Okay, get out. And speak to no one," Lou ordered, and then to his marines, "Get going, men!"

The marines started pulling down the stacks of lumber and architectural millwork into disorganized piles. There was a shout from the top of the stairs. Two men, red-faced and angry, were peering down, having heard the commotion.

"What the hell's goin' on dun 'ere?"

The one doing the shouting was built like a little bull, his voice familiar. Lou put on his pleasant face and smiled. He raised the bullhorn.

"This business has been closed down. Store's being evacuated, sir. This is a danger zone."

"What are you talkin' about? For what?"

"On account of the fire, sir."

"What fire?"

"The fire that's gonna gut this place ten minutes from now."

The man came racing down, tripping and struggling to regain his balance.

"You crazy bastard. Get the hell off my property, you son of a bitch!"

"Take this man into custody," Lou ordered, handing a pair of chains to two marines.

"*Yes, sir! Yes, sir!*"

The marines grabbed the man by the arms and forcefully backed him into a steel column, making him yelp and knocking the wind out of him. Another marine wrapped the chain around his neck and padlocked it snuggly. A second chain was wrapped around his ankles and locked. The other man was also grabbed and chained in the same fashion. Both were now terrified.

"Uncle Rory! Remember me? I'm the punk with the black dog."

Lou took another chain and gave it to another marine.

"Chain the back doors," Lou said. "We don't need anyone coming to the rescue."

The marine marched off to the rear entrance doors. Lou held up and swung the last piece of chain from side to side.

"This one's for the front doors, for when we leave."

Four more marines came in carrying tanks of gasoline. The Klansman's eyes protruded from his head. "What you gonna do?" he screamed.

"Give everything a good dowsing, men," Lou ordered. The marines spilled the gas over the piles of lumber and across the concrete floors. Lou took one of the cans and held it over their heads, thoroughly dousing them from head to toe. They quaked with terror.

"Sorry we don't have a cross, boys. I know you like to have one for this type of occasion."

"What are you gonna do?" Uncle Rory wailed his hair and face glistening with gasoline, the smell overpowering.

"Notice we don't use diesel. Gasoline burns *so* much better, don't you think?" Lou said.

"Please, mister. Please, don't. I'm begging you," the Klansman screamed.

The second man was blubbering and wailing, too.

"I'll make it right. I'll make it right!" the Klansman yelled.

"What are you gonna do about my family's dog, huh? Oh, how they *loved* that dog!"

"I'm sorry. I'm *so, so* sorry, mister."

"You're sorry! Sorry for *what?*"

"I'm sorry. I'm sorry," he wept. His pants had become saturated with urine and gasoline. A pool formed at his feet.

"Sorry for *what?*" Lou screamed into his face, his nose almost touching the Klansman's.

"I'm sorry for what I did, sir." The little bull screwed up his eyes and tears flowed down his cheeks, like a child.

"*What* did you do?" Lou shouted. He stepped back, took the newspaper, lit the end and held blazing it in the air. "I asked you, *what* did you do?"

"I burned your place down! And I killed your dog. Oh, please, please, no."

The marines stood glaring, their faces emotionless.

"You burned Mr. Jeb's place down. That man helped raise me, *by God!*"

"I'm so sorry, sir."

"How's it gonna feel to see *your* place burn down—with *you* cooking inside, fat boy?"

"Bad, bad …Oh, please, no …have mercy, sir."

"And what *else* did you do?"

"I destroyed stuff."

"You've made a lot of people in this town mad as hell. And when *they* get upset, bad things happen—property gets destroyed, *people die!*"

"I'll make it right. I beg you. Give me a chance. Please … please …"

The Klansman broke down, weeping uncontrollably. Lou handed the burning newspaper to a marine who took it outside and stomped out the flames.

"So *what* are you going to do? *How* are you gonna make things right?"

"I'll rebuild the house and send all the materials you need. I'll pay for everything and for labor. I'll rebuild the still."

"Let's recap. I just heard you say, you will send every scrap of material to rebuild Mr. Jeb's house, *bigger and better*, along with the other thing—right? Is that what you said?"

He nodded his head up and down vigorously, "Yes, yes, sir, I promise …bigger and better."

"Did I hear you say you would pay Mr. Jeb the sum of one thousand dollars—no make that two thousand dollars—compensation for pain and suffering you caused him and his family?"

"*Absolutely*, yes, *absolutely*."

"And deliveries will begin tomorrow morning?"

"Yes, sir. Yes, sir. Tomorrow."

"You will send laborers and carpenters on Monday morning at 6:00 a.m. sharp."

"*Absolutely*—anything, sir."

"You got three months to rebuild that house to his satisfaction— *bigger and better!*"

"Yes, sir, *bigger and better*."

 "I don't wanna hear any bitchin' or squawkin'."

"No, sir, you won't, I promise you."

"You know Anacostia Flats—Tent City?"

"Yes, I know it."

"You're to donate and deliver six—no, make that twelve—loads of lumber to that location by tomorrow."

"Yes, sir. No problem at all."

"2x4's—2x6's—2x8's with nails and a hundred sheets of canvas," Lou said.

"I don't have any canvas."

"Then *find* some dammit! And fifty paraffin heaters. Deliver it all to Henry Faulkner. Got that?"

"Yes, absolutely. To Henry Faulkner, sir."

"Another thing. Your niece. She's family to me. If you harm her in any way, I will come down here and I will kill you. I'll *roast* you alive like a pig on a spit!"

"I won't. I won't, I promise you."

"I'll be looking into her finances. You'd better not be stealing her father's fortune. See to it she and her mother are cut in fair and square, *fifty-fifty*. I want audited accounts *every year* and details of who owns what including all previous records. Do you understand?"

"Yes, yes, sir, *every year*. I'll see to it."

The Klansman had begun to relax. Sensing they were off the hook.

"We'll be talkin' again. Okay, men, let 'em loose." Lou handed the various keys to the marines. He turned to one. "Marine, find me a long-axe and some rope."

The marine strode into the hardware section and re-appeared a few minutes later with the axe and rope.

"This brings us to the matter of the family dog," Lou said, uncoiling the rope.

Uncle Rory began quaking again.

"Bring him over here," Lou said. Lou tied the rope around the fat man's wrist and laid him face down on his belly on a pile of lumber. The marines held him down and Lou lashed his right hand into position.

"This is the hand you used to shoot the dog. The *right* hand, wasn't it?"

"Oh no, no, no. Please no. Not my hand!"

The Klansman screamed and blubbered for a few moments and then gave up and put his head down. Lou took the axe and swung it over his head, bringing it down full force, but twisting it at the last moment, smashing the Klansman's hand with the blunt head. Uncle Rory screamed in agony and terror, believing his hand had been severed. When he opened his eyes, the bones were well and truly crushed, but his hand still remained attached to his wrist.

"Now you think about '*Moonshine*' every time you raise that hand, mister," Lou said. And then, leaning forward he whispered in the Klansman's ear, "I'll be watching you—don't make me come back again ...And remember ...*mum's the word*."

39

GOODBYE MY FATHER

Friday August 8 through Monday August 11, 1930.

The day after his lawless actions at Tyson's Lumber & General Hardware, Lou went with Tom and Anna to visit the city police chief. They found him to be warmhearted and sympathetic to the veterans. Lou spoke of the meetings in Tent City and at the Navy Yard. It turned out to be a worthwhile exercise in public relations. Lou assured the chief the men in the camp wanted to cooperate with him.

From the police station, they went to Tent City to update Henry. They also delivered a load of vegetables from the farm. Lou told the veterans he'd urged the general to give them support. Three truckloads of lumber had already been delivered. Henry was thrilled and very touched by the generosity of Tyson's Lumber & General Hardware. Helen Smothers had visited the camp and planned to write a feature article for Sunday's newspaper. Lou wished them good luck, urging them to keep the peace, relaying the general's warning. He promised he'd write to the President and the Congress on his return to England.

On Saturday, the first consignments of lumber began arriving at Remington's Farm for the reconstruction of Jeb's home. The truck driver confirmed Julia's uncle would be sending men to start the work on Monday. Anna and Tom sketched some drawings on sheets of paper with Jeb and Alice. Father had taken an interest and promised Lou he'd keep an eye on the construction. The new place would be bigger, with four bedrooms, a nice living room, a decent kitchen and a wrap-around porch with aspects over both the creek and the river—more a real home than a shack.

Lou spent much of the day with Anna, Tom and Jeb, cleaning up and removing the old parts of the building and making a junk pile for burning. They'd need to build some new piers for the extended sections. The driver from Tyson's Lumber was told to be sure to bring plenty of red brick and cement on Monday morning and, of course, bricklayers to lay them.

On Sunday, Lou's last day, spirits were low. Lou was torn; being in England away from family, was rough. Before leaving for church, Tom asked Lou to walk with him and Anna down to the river, just beyond the creek. There was something they needed to tell him. With the sound of overpowering birdsong surrounding them and the smell of charred wood in the air, they ambled down, past the remains of Jeb's shack to the misty river. Lou had a bad premonition.

"Lou, we're not supposed to tell you, but we decided you should know," Anna said.

"What is it?"

"Dad."

Lou realized immediately. He stared across the water at the distant Maryland shore. Lenny's face filled his mind.

The cough. How did I not see this?

"He's dying," Tom said.

Lou's throat became dry and tight.

"Cancer."

"What type is it?" Lou whispered.

"Lung cancer. It's spreading all over his body."

"How long?"

"Three months, maybe four," Anna said.

Everything became clear—his appearance, his attitude, his bitterness, his sadness.

"God, I wish I could be here with you all. Damn it!"

"We thought it important you knew tonight, as it'll be special," Anna said.

"Probably my last night with him on this earth," Lou whispered. He closed his eyes, grief already taking its toll and understanding Tom's irritability.

Anna put her arm through his. "Yes, Lou, 'fraid so."

Julia arrived in the Chrysler, and Mother, Gran and Father (all in their Sunday best) climbed in with her. Lou, Anna and Tom followed in the pickup. Jeb and Alice and the children were already in the church, nicely dressed in many colors, when they arrived. Throughout the service, Lou could think of nothing but Father, regretting he'd not spent more time with him. He looked at Julia standing at his side holding a hymnal. Did she know? Sympathy showed in her eyes when she returned his stare. *Yes, she knew.* All week they'd not told him—protected him. He felt like a spoiled brat.

He glanced across at his dad standing next to Mother. Dad never sang hymns, but he was valiantly doing his best, in his blue serge suit, his wife clinging to his arm. Lou looked around the church. He saw it clearly. They'd bring in his coffin and lay him down on trestles in the center aisle and say prayers for him. His mother, grandmother, Tom and Anna would hold on to one another, weeping—and *he* wouldn't be here to comfort them. He closed his eyes and tears flowed down his cheeks. Julia squeezed his arm to comfort him. He looked into her eyes and they held each other's gaze for a few moments.

What an incredible woman she is.

She had his profound and absolute respect.

After the service, the vicar stood at the door. He told Lou the community was proud of him and wished him well. After that, the congregation made a big fuss over Lou, gathering around him, while his family, including Father, watched with pride. Lou felt numb.

In the early afternoon, Mother came up to Lou's bedroom to get his uniform. "How long have you been married now, son?"

Lou thought for a moment. "Eight years."

"Eight years and no children?"

"Unfortunately no, Mom—but all that's about to change."

Mother picked up Lou's uniform from the chair and put it over her arm. "You must try and bring Charlotte to see us …before he goes."

That evening, they had a special dinner of roasted venison prepared by Gran and Alice—a farewell feast with nearly everyone in the world Lou cared about, including Julia, Jeb and Alice and the children. They made a feeble attempt at jollity.

At the end of the meal, Father rose from his seat at the head of the table. "I'm not one for speeches, but I want you all to know this." His eyes rested on Lou. "I've said things I shouldn't have said, *especially* when you were growing up. I pushed you hard, son. And I drove you out. I want to say in front of all of you—I'm truly sorry. I was out of line—but only because I cared about you. I haven't always made that plain. I want you to know, no father could be more proud of his son than I am of you. I wish you well on your journey. Good luck and may God bless you and protect you, *always.*"

Lou was stunned. This had come out of the blue. Everyone had tears in their eyes. Anna hurriedly got up and poured more elderberry wine. She sat down and raised her glass.

"Safe trip, my darling brother."

Everyone drank to that. After dinner they moved to the porch where Lou and Father played the guitar and banjo together. It was like those rare good old days, except those days were gone, forever.

The next day, Lou got up before dawn, put on his uniform, expertly steamed and pressed by Mother. He went down to breakfast as the first rays of sunshine poured into the kitchen. Outside, a lumber truck arrived along with a dozen workmen. Tom went out and directed them down to Jeb's ruin. Father said he'd go down, too.

A few minutes later, Julia appeared. Lou rushed down to his father who was directing the men. They shook hands and Father gave Lou a long hug goodbye and kissed him. Father looked at the activity going on and the piles of delivered materials and then back at Lou.

"You did Jeb mighty proud, son."

"I love you Dad."

"I love you, too, son."

Lou walked back up to the house and Father followed him. He embraced and kissed Mother and Gran and then his father again. Before climbing into Julia's car, Lou had them pose for some photos including Jeb and his family. They drove off, with Anna and Tom following in the pickup. Lou was barely able to look at them standing there waving. Lou and Julia traveled in silence to Union Station, slowed by demonstrators on Constitution. There were no words to be said.

At the station, they walked to the barrier where they said more hurried goodbyes—they were late. Lou kissed Anna and shook Tom's hand, but Tom grabbed him and gave him bear hug. Lou put his arms around Julia and held her tight. She closed her eyes as he kissed her cheek.

"I'll continue to pray for your safety," she said. "And I will always love you."

Calls echoed through the station. 'All aboard that's going aboard!'

Lou went back to Tom and cupping his hand, whispered a message in his ear. He grabbed his kit bag and ran for the train.

"Come back soon," Anna called after him.

"I will, I promise—*very soon!*" Lou yelled back.

Lou reached the train. Ezekiah Washington was standing by the door. "Ah bin waitin' here for you, my dear sir," he said.

Lou glanced back at the barrier. Tom stood with one arm around Anna and the other around Julia. All three were in tears. The two women waved sadly as he boarded the train.

"This *is* a coincidence," Lou said.

"If you *believe* in coincidences, sir," Ezekiah said.

Lou smiled.

"Got your same suite, Commander."

"I got you all figured out," Lou said.

"How's that, sir?"

"You're my guardian angel."

"Maybe I is, sir. Maybe I is."

Lou didn't protest this time. He followed Ezekiah down the corridor to the suite where the *Washington Post* lay on the table. He looked forward to reading what Helen Smothers had to say. He sat down and the train pulled away.

"I went to the camp," Lou said.

"Yes, I heard you did. That's good. I also heard you put a little hurt into our brethren under the sheets."

"How the hell—"

"Oh, you'd be surprised what I get to hear, sir. Now, here's a nice cup o' coffee. Nice and black, just the way you like it."

"Thank you, Ezekiah. Thank you very much."

"Not at all, sir. It's my pleasure."

END OF VOLUME TWO

Continued in the conclusion.

London

The Ritz Hotel, London, 1906.

House of Lords, Westminster Palace, London.

The Launching of Cardington Airship R101

October 12, 1929.

St. Mary's Church, Cardington.

Cardington R101 passes over Midland Road Bedford, 1929.

Cardington R101 Dining Room.

Cardington R101 Promenade Deck.

Artist's impression of *Cardington R101* Promenade Deck

Artist's impression of *Cardington R101* Smoking Room.

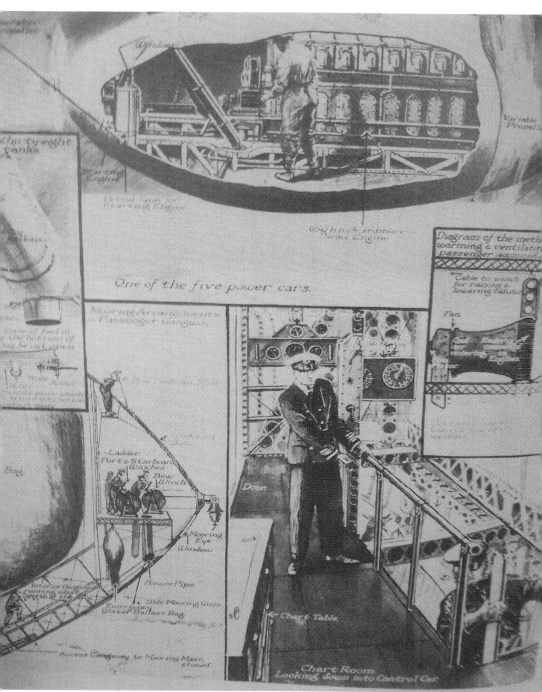

Artist's impression of working areas of *Cardington R101*.

The Launching of Howden Airship R100

Howden R100 is launched December 16, 1929 and flies to Cardington.

Howden R100 flies over farm workers on her maiden voyage.

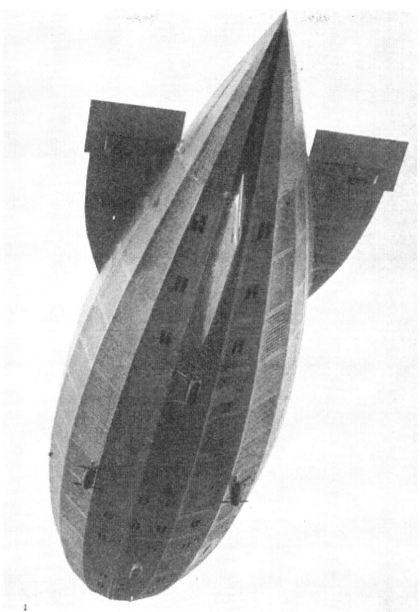

Howden R100 passes overhead.

Howden R100 arrives at Cardington and moored at the tower.

Howden R100 with collapsed tail after a test flight.

Howden R100 with her rebuilt, shortened tail.

Howden R100 Promenade Deck.

Howden R100 Dining Room.

1928 drawing by S W Clatworthy showing the accommodation aboard the R100 (The Sphere)

Howden R100 isometric interior.

Howden Airship R100 Officers & Crew

Sqdn. Leader Booth, Captain of *Howden R100.*

Captain George Meager, 2nd Officer of *Howden R100.*

Officers of *Howden R100*: Johnston, Scott, Booth, Steff, Giblett and Meager.

Howden R100 crewmen.

Howden Airship R100: Voyage to Canada.

The Saguenay River flowing into the St. Lawrence.

Sunset over the Saguenay River, St. Lawrence Marine Park.

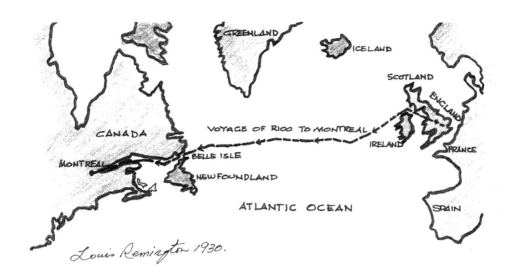

Voyage of *Howden R100* from Cardington to Montreal, Canada.

Howden R100 circling Montreal, Canada.

Howden R100 moored at the St. Hubert tower, Montreal, Canada.

Howden R100 at the St. Hubert Tower.

Thousands flock to see arrival of *Howden R100* at St. Hubert Tower.

Howden R100 over a Toronto bridge.

Commander Ralph S. Booth

The Great British Dirigible R-100

Postcard with Captain Ralph Booth and *Howden R100*.

Howden R100 over a Toronto skyscraper.

Canada celebrates the arrival of *Howden R100* with words and music.

Nestle's Milk advertisement, welcoming *Howden R100*.

Howden R100 over Toronto.

Howden R100 at the St. Hubert tower.

Howden R100 officer's cap badge.

1930: Scenes in America.

Hobos ride the rails in the USA during the Great Depression.

Veterans arrive in Washington to lobby to cash in their war service bonds.

A war veteran in search of work.

War veterans arrive in Washington in their thousands.

Union Station, Washington, D.C. 1929.

Union Station, Washington, D.C. 1929.

Newspapers report on the 1929 stock market collapse.

The hardship of unemployment.

Depression era street scene: photograph by Dorothea Lange.

Hungry men march in the streets.

Hopelessness: photograph by Dorothea Lange.

In search of work: photograph by Dorothea Lange.

The soup line.

Banks close around the country.

Bonus Army veterans gather at the Capitol demanding early payment for bonds issued for their war service.

The iconic image of the Depression: 'Migrant Mother' by Dorothea Lange.

Tent City, Anacostia: At first, relations between the veterans and police were excellent.

Homeless family: photograph by Dorothea Lange.

Despair in the camps: photograph by Dorothea Lange.

WORLD'S HIGHEST STANDARD OF LIVING

There's no way like the American Way

On the breadline.

Picketing for a job.

Lord Thomson welcomes Major Scott and the *Howden R100* crewmen on their return from Canada.

AUTHOR'S NOTES

This is a work of fiction—pure fantasy, if you like—based on actual events. It is not a historical nonfiction documentary written to 'set the record straight'. It is my hope that this novel piques the reader's interest in this dramatic era of aviation history. Some characters are based on real people, others are fictional. Some events in the novel took place, others did not. After some years of research, I took what I thought was the essence of the characters involved and built on those qualities for dramatic effect, with fictional characters woven into the story to take part and to witness events. In the end, Lou Remington and Charlotte Hamilton became as real to me as Brigadier General Christopher Birdwood Thomson and Princess Marthe Bibesco.

I did not see any real villains in this story and did not set out to portray anyone as such. But I did see all the characters as suffering with that one trying malady—being human. The myriad symptoms of this disorder include: unconditional love, passion, ruthless ambition, pride, megalomania, greed, spinelessness, jealousy, deviousness, murderous intent, loyalty, duty, trust, obedience, honor, patriotism and selflessness.

I took liberties for dramatic effect: Scott and McWade were *not* on Victoria Dock in Hull when the *R38* went down, as far as I know. Hull Infirmary is not on the waterfront. The scenes aboard *R38/ZR-2, Howden R100* and *Cardington R101* during their flights and crashes are painted mostly from my imagination with information drawn from many books (see bibliography). Actual events on board those ships, as well as the dialogue throughout the novel is, of course, conjecture. And no, as far as I know, Cardington R101 did not deviate from her route to India in order to show herself over the West End of London on that fateful night.

There is a great deal of truth in what I have written as a fictional account, but like the extraordinary Princess Marthe, the truth is elusive. Much I have taken from reading between the lines, exaggerating or emphasizing for dramatic effect. Some is pure speculation. The grand events are true, save for those actions carried out by fictional characters.

Lord Scunthorpe, the Tyson family and Tyson's Lumber & General Hardware Co. are fictitious entities, not based on any persons living or dead, any organization or corporation.

In order to help differentiate between airships *R100* and *R101*, I took the liberty of adding the prefix of the place of their birth, calling them *Howden R100* and *Cardington R101*.

ACKNOWLEDGMENTS

I have been blessed with a tremendous amount of help from many amazing people while researching and writing this book. Very special thanks are due to my consulting editor at LCD Editing (lcdediting.com) who has put many years into this project and kept me focused and on the straight and narrow. Thanks also to Steven Bauer at Hollow Tree Literary Services for his expert guidance and editing. Grateful thanks must go to Edith Schorah for additional editing and proofreading. My appreciation also goes to Kathryn Johnston and Jon Eig at the Writer's Center, Bethesda, Maryland for their patient and professional coaching during workshop sessions.

I am indebted to John Taylor, lighter-than-air flight test engineer and consultant and writer of *Principles of Aerostatics: The Theory of LTA Flight,* who conducted a technical review and spent many hours reading and critiquing this manuscript and offering a wealth of advice, not only regarding airships, but also on formatting and preparing this book for publication.

Special thanks to Eddie Ankers who worked tirelessly on book design and artwork, producing the cover for Volume One - *From Ashes.* Thanks also to Bari Parrott who created cover art for *The Airshipmen* and *Volumes 2 & 3.*

Deep gratitude is due to Katie Dennington who did a wonderful job of designing and setting up the website http://www.daviddennington.com (although she is not accountable for its content). Katie was also responsible for helping me get started in the realm of novel writing. Throughout this five year process, she gave me the spiritual fortitude and encouragement to see it through.

I am also very grateful to Frank Dene at Act of Light Photography who produced the website video and assisted Katie.

I owe a debt of thanks to the people at Cardington Heritage Trust Foundation for their kind help over the years, especially Dene Burchmore and Sky Hunt's son, Albert, who showed me around Shed No. 1. Thanks also to Alastair Lawson, Alastair Reid, C.P. Hall and to Dr. Giles Camplin, editor of *Dirigible Magazine, Journal of the Airship Heritage Trust,* who kindly assisted with contacts in the airship community and photographs for this book and for my website. Many thanks to Paul Adams of the British Airship Museum and Jane Harvey of Shortstown Heritage Trust, Christine Conboy of Bedfordshire Libraries, Paul Gazis of The Flying Cloud, Trevor Monk creator of Facebook pages relative to the sheds and airships, and John Anderson of the Nevil Shute Foundation, all of whom advised on or shared photographic information.

I would like to thank the following for their help and encouragement: my dear wife, Jenny (my own special Yorkshire lass), Lauren Dennington and Lee Knowles, Richard and Katie Dennington, Dawn and Nick Steele, Alan and Violet Rowe, John and Sandy Ball, Katya and Michael Reynier, Edith and Michael Schorah, Cliff and Pat Dean, Ray Luby, Chris and Jan Burgess, John and Sally Slee, Richard Lovell, Julie and Marty Boyd, Karel Visscher, Aaron Kreinbrook, Derek Rowe, David and Susan Adams, Commander Jason Wood,

Graham Watt, brothers Karl and Charles Ebert, Ruta Sevo, Harry Johnson, Alan Wesencraft of the Harry Price Library at the University of London, and Mitchell Yockelson at the U.S. National Archives. I am grateful to Isabelle Jelinski for consultation regarding French translation (any errors are mine).

And lastly, my sincere appreciation goes to the marine who helped distill into words what I thought it must be like to search for a reason to go on after surviving horrific events and having experienced your friends and brothers-in-arms dying all around you. He confirmed that 'survivor's guilt' is all too real. He told me how once home from the war in Vietnam, he was unable to speak of it to anyone, even to the woman he married after coming out of the VA hospital. He allowed his wife to believe for years that his wounds were the result of a traffic accident. This veteran's experiences and his reactions to them are, seemingly, not uncommon.

BIBLIOGRAPHY & SOURCES

Inspiration, information and facts were drawn from an array of wonderful books, as well as newspapers, magazines and documents of the period, including:

Report of the R101 Inquiry. Presented by the Secretary of State for Air to Parliament, March 1931.

Eleventh Month Eleventh Day Eleventh Hour. Joseph E. Persico. Random House, New York.

American Heritage History of WW1. Narrated by S.L.A. Marshall, Brig. Gen. USAR (ret). Dist. Simon & Schuster.

Icarus Over the Humber. T.W. Jamison. Lampada Press.

To Ride the Storm. Sir Peter Masefield. William Kimber, London.

Lord Thomson of Cardington: A Memoir and Some Letters. Princess Marthe Bibesco. Jonathan Cape Ltd., London.

Enchantress. Christine Sutherland. Farrar, Straus & Giroux. Harper Collins Canada Ltd.

Barnes Wallis. J. Morpurgo. Penguin Books, England. Richard Clay (The Chaucer Press) Ltd., England.

Howden Airship Station. Tom Asquith & Kenneth Deacon. Langrick Publications, Howden UK.

The Men & Women Who Built and Flew R100. Kenneth Deacon. Langrick Publications, Howden UK.

Millionth Chance. James Lessor. House of Stratus, Stratus Books Ltd., England.

Sefton Brancker. Norman Macmillan. William Heinemann Ltd., London.

The Tragedy of R101. E. F. Spanner. The Crypt House Press Ltd., London.

Hindenburg: An Illustrated History. Rich Archbold & Ken Marschall. Warner Bros. Books Inc.

My Airship Flights. Capt. George Meager. William Kimber & Co. Ltd., London.

Slide Rule. Nevil Shute. Vintage Books/Random House. William Heinemann, GB.

Chequers. Norma Major. Cross River Press. Abberville Publishing Group.

The Airmen Who Would Not Die. John Fuller. G.P. Putnam's Sons, New York.

R101 - A Pictorial History. Nick Le Neve Walmsley. Sutton Publishing, UK. History Press, UK.

Airship on a Shoestring: The Story of R100 John Anderson. A Bright Pen Book. Authors OnLine Ltd.

Airships Cardington. Geoffrey Chamberlain. Terence Dalton.

Dirigible Magazine: Journal of the Airship Heritage Trust, Cardington UK.

Aeroplane Magazine.

Daily Express, October 4, 1930 newspaper articles.

Daily Mirror, October 4, 1930 newspaper articles.

Daily Mail, October 4, 1930 newspaper articles.

Journal of Aeronautical History.

Documentary: Dorothea Lange, A Tribute.

Documentary: Survival Lessons from the Great Depression.

Documentary: Hobos of the 1930s.

Documentary: Hobos of the Great Depression.

Documentary: Survival Lessons of the Great Depression.

IMAGE SOURCES & CREDITS

<u>*Cover Art*</u> *'The Taj Mahal' by Bari Parrott.*

<u>*Front Material*</u>

Brigadier General Christopher Birdwood Thomson: Public domain

'Taj Mahal Painting': Art by Barri Parrott

<u>*Interior*</u>

Part One: Cardington R101 over London: Courtesy of Airship Heritage Trust.

Princess Marthe Bibesco Painting by Boldini: Public Domain.

Part Two: Howden R100 over York Minster: Courtesy of Gary Hodgkinson, Ima-gen Productions.

Part Three: Howden R100 approaching Toronto: City of Toronto Archives.

Part Four: Klansman with Horse: photographs and sketches by author.

End of Chapter 21: Howden R100 with cover billowing during her first tests. Courtesy of the Nevil Shute Foundation.

End of Chapter 32: Howden R100 at St. Hubert tower: City of Toronto Archives.

<u>*Back Material Images in order:*</u>

<u>*LONDON*</u>

Ritz Hotel, London, after opening in 1905: from John Mariani Virtual Gourmet website.

House of Lords, Westminster Palace, London. Attribution 3.0 Unported (CC BY 3.0).

<u>*THE LAUNCHING OF CARDINGTON AIRSHIP R101*</u>

Cardington R101 is launched and walked from her shed, October 12, 1929: Courtesy of Airship Heritage Trust.

St. Mary's Church, Cardington: from Northern Vicar's blog.

Cardington R101 passes over Midland Road Bedford 1929: Courtesy of British Airship Museum.

Cardington R101 Dining Room: Courtesy of Airship Heritage Trust.

Cardington R101 Promenade Deck: Courtesy of Airship Heritage Trust.

Artist's impression: Cardington R101 Promenade Deck: Courtesy of the Airship Heritage Trust.

Artist's impression: Cardington R101 Smoking Room: Courtesy of the Airship Heritage Trust.

Artist's impression: Cardington R101 Working areas: Courtesy of the Airship Heritage Trust.

THE LAUNCHING OF HOWDEN AIRSHIP R100

Howden R100 is launched December 16, 1929 and flown to Cardington:Courtesy of the Airship Heritage Trust.

Howden R100 flies over farm workers on her maiden voyage: From rarehistoricalphotos.com.

Howden R100 passes overhead. Reproduced by permission of Wonders of World Aviation.

Howden R100 arrives at Cardington and moored at the tower. Courtesy British Airship Museum.

Howden R100 at Cardington Tower with collapsed tail. Courtesy of the Nevil Shute Foundation.

Howden R100 at Cardington Tower with her rebuilt shortened tail: Courtesy of the Nevil Shute Foundation.

Howden R100 Promenade Deck: Courtesy of the Airship Heritage Trust.

Howden R100 Dining Room: Courtesy of the Airship Heritage Trust.

Howden R100 Isometric Interior: Courtesy of the Nevil Shute Foundation.

HOWDEN AIRSHIP R100 OFFICERS & CREW

Sqdn Ldr. Booth, Captain of Howden R100:Jane Harvey: britishairshippeople.org.uk.

Captain George Meager, 2nd Officer of Howden R100: Jane Harvey: britishairshippeople.org.uk.

Officers of Howden R100, Johnston, Scott, Booth, Giblett and Meager: Courtesy of the Airship Heritage Trust.

Howden R100 crewmen: Courtesy of the Airship Heritage Trust.

Howden R100 officer's cap badge: Courtesy of the Airship Heritage Trust.

HOWDEN AIRSHIP R100: VOYAGE TO CANADA

Saguenay River flowing into the St. Lawrence by J. Boulian Attribution Share Alike 3.0 Unported (CC BY-SA 3.0).

Sunset over the Saguenay River, St. Lawrence Marine Park, by Elena Tatiana Chis CC BY-SA 4.0.

Howden R100 circling Montreal: Toronto Archives.

Howden R100 moored at the St. Hubert Tower, Montreal, Canada: Toronto Archives.

Howden R100 at the St. Hubert tower: Toronto Archives.

Thousands flock to see arrival of Howden R100 at St. Hubert tower:Toronto Archives.

Howden R100 over a Toronto bridge: Toronto Archives.

Postcard with Captain Ralph Booth and Howden R100: Toronto Archives.

Howden R100 over a Toronto skyscraper: Toronto Archives.

Canada celebrates arrival of Howden R100 with words and music: Toronto Archives.

Nestle's Milk advertisement, welcoming Howden R100: Toronto Archives.

Howden R100 over Toronto: Toronto Archives.

Howden R100 at St. Hubert tower: Toronto Archives.

1930: SCENES IN AMERICA

Hobos ride the rails in America during the Great Depression: Documentary: Hobos of the Great Depression.

Army veterans arrive in Washington to lobby to cash in their war service bonds: Documentary: Hobos of the Great Depression.

War veteran in search of work: from Hobo Culture of the 1930s documentary.

War veterans arrive in Washington in their thousands: Documentary: Hobos in the 1930's by Simran Giri, Nicol Macan, Allyson Mark and Kevin Mendoza.

Union Station 1929 (ground level): Library of Congress: Public Domain.

Union Station 1929, from the air: Library of Congress: Public Domain.

Brooklyn Daily Eagle: 1929 US Stock Market collapses: Documentary: Survival Lessons from The Great Depression.

Santa Ana Register: 1929 US stock market collapses: Documentary: Hobo Culture of the 1930's.

The hardship of unemployment: Kid with billboard: Documentary: Survival Lessons from The Great Depression.

Depression era street scene: Photograph by Dorothea Lange, Library of Congress.

Hungry men march in the streets: Library of Congress.

Hopelessness: Photograph by Dorothea Lange, Library of Congress.

On the road in search of work: Photograph by Dorothea Lange, Library of Congress.

Soup line: Photograph by Dorothea Lange, Library of Congress.

Banks close around the country: Documentary: Survival Lessons from The Great Depression.

Bonus Army veterans gather at the Capitol demanding early payment for bonds issued for their service in the Great War: Library of Congress.

The iconic image of the 1930's, 'Migrant Mother' by Dorothea Lang: Library of Congress.

Tent City Anacostia: Library of Congress.

Homeless family: Photograph by Dorothea Lange, Library of Congress.

Despair in the camps: Photograph by Dorothea Lange, Library of Congress.

On the breadline: Documentary: Survival Lessons from the Great Depression.

Picketing for a job, men with billboards: Documentary: Survival Lessons from the Great Depression.

Lord Thomson welcomes home Major Scott and the Howden R100 crewmen on their return from Canada: Courtesy of the Airship Heritage Trust.

Every effort has been made to properly attribute images reproduced in these pages. If errors have occurred, we sincerely apologize. Corrections will be made in future issues.

ABOUT THE AUTHOR

As a teenager, I read all Nevil Shute's books, including *Slide Rule,* which tells of his days as an aeronautical engineer on the great behemoth *R100* at Howden and of his nights as an aspiring novelist. I was fascinated by both these aspects of his life. He inspired me to write and to fly (ignorance is bliss!). The writing was put on hold while I went off around the world assisting in the management various construction projects and raising a family. I picked up flying in the Bahamas, scaring myself silly, and sailing in Bermuda. This was all good experience for writing about battling the elements, navigation and building large structures.

Many years later, I read John G. Fuller's *The Airmen Who Would Not Die* and my interest in airships was rekindled. It was time to pursue my dream— writing. My daughter was in Los Angeles, trying to get into films. I thought, stupidly, I could help her by writing a screenplay.

I had done extensive research on the Imperial British Airship Program and attended many screenplay writing workshops at Bethesda Writer's Center. I wound up writing two screenplays which had a modicum of success. The experts in the business told me the stories were good and that I just *had* to write them as novels. So, back to the Writer's Center I went to learn the craft of novel writing. Five years later, with my daughter working as my editor and muse, *The Airshipmen* was finished and later turned into this trilogy.

CAST OF CHARACTERS FOR THE TRILOGY
(*Fictional)

A

*Alice—Jeb's Wife.

Atherstone, Lt. Cmdr. Noël G.—1st. Officer, *Cardington R101*.

B

Bateman, Henry—British Design Monitor, *R38/ZR-2*, National Physics Laboratory.

Bell, Arthur, ('Ginger')—Engineer, *Cardington R101*.

Bibesco, Marthe, ('Smaranda')—Romanian Princess.

Bibesco, Prince George Valentine—Princess Marthe's Husband.

Binks, Joe —Engineer, *Cardington R101*.

Booth, Lt. Cmdr. Ralph—Captain of *Howden R100*.

Brancker, Air Vice Marshall, Sir Sefton, ('Branks')—Director of Civil Aviation.

*Brewer, Tom—*Daily Telegraph* Reporter.

Buck, Joe —Thomson's Valet.

*Bull, John—Lou's Employer and Close Friend.

*Bull, Mary—John Bull's Wife.

*Bunyan, Fanny—Nurse at Hull Royal Infirmary and Charlotte's Best Friend.

*Bunyan, Lenny—Fanny's Husband.

*Bunyan, Billy—Fanny and Lenny's Son.

Burney, Dennistoun—Managing Director, Airship Guarantee (*Howden R100*).

*Brown, Minnie—Nurse at Hull Royal Infirmary.

C

*Cameron, Doug—Height Coxswain, *Howden R100 & Cardington R101*.

*Cameron, Rosie—Doug Cameron's Wife.

*Cathcart, Lady—A Friend of Brancker.

Church, Sam, ('Sammy')—Rigger, *Cardington R101*.

Churchill, Winston—Member of Parliament.

Colmore, Wing Cmdr. Reginald—Director of Airship Development (R.A.W.).

Colmore, Mrs.—Wing Cmdr. Reginald Colmore's Wife.

D

*Daisy—Thomson's Parlor Maid.

Disley, Arthur, ('Dizzy')—Electrician/Wireless, *Howden R100 & Cardington R101*.

Dowding, Hugh—Air Member of Supply & Research (AMSR), Air Ministry.

F

*Faulkner, Henry—WWI Veteran—Lou's Wartime Friend.

G

Giblett, M.A.—Chief Meteorologist at Royal Airship Works Met. Office.

*Gwen—Thomson's Housekeeper.

H

*Hagan, Bill—*Daily Mail* Reporter.

*Hamilton, Charlotte, ('Charlie')—Nurse at Hull Royal Infirmary.

*Hamilton, Geoff—Charlotte's Cousin.

*Hamilton, Harry—Charlotte's Father.

*Hamilton, Lena—Charlotte's Mother.

*Harandah, Madam—Gypsy Fortune Teller at Cardington Fair.

Heaton, Francis—Norway's Girl.

*Higginbottom, Peter, 'Pierre', Chief Steward, *Cardington R100 & Howden R101*.

*Hilda—Forewoman at the Gas Factory, Royal Airship Works, Cardington.

Hinchliffe, Emily—Wife of Captain Hinchliffe, MacDonald and Thomson's Pilot.

*Honeysuckle, Miss—Brancker's Pilot.

Hunt, George W. ('Sky Hunt')—Chief Coxswain, *Cardington R101*.

*Hunter, George—*Daily Express* Reporter.

I

Irene—Sam Church's Girl.

Irwin, Flt. Lt. H. Carmichael, ('Blackbird')—Captain of *Cardington R101*.

Irwin, Olivia—Captain Irwin's Wife.

Isadora—Princess Marthe's Maidservant

J

*Jacobs, John—*Aeroplane Magazine* Reporter.

*Jeb—Tenant and Friend Living at Remington's Farm.

*Jenco, Bobby—American Trainee Rigger, *R38/ZR-2,* Elsie's Boyfriend.

*Jessup, William, ('Jessie')—Charlotte's Ex Boyfriend.

*Jessup, Angela—William Jessup's Sister.

Johnston, Sqdn. Ldr. E.L. ('Johnny')—Navigator for *Howden R100 & Cardington R101.*

*Jones, Edmund—*Daily Mirror* Reporter.

K

*Knoxwood, Rupert—Thomson's Personal Secretary, Air Ministry.

L

Landsdowne, Lt. Cmdr. Zachary USN—Commander of *Shenandoah.*

Leech, Harry—Foreman Engineer (R.A.W.), *Cardington R101.*

*Luby, Gen. Raymond—U.S. Army Chief of Staff, Fort Myer, Arlington.

M

MacDonald, Ishbel—Daughter of Ramsay MacDonald.

MacDonald, Ramsay—British Prime Minister.

Mann, Herbert—Cardington Tower Elevator Operator.

*Marsh, Freddie—Cardington Groundcrewman, Joe Binks' Second Cousin.

McWade, Frederick—Resident R.A.W. Inspector, Airship Inspection Dept. (A.I.D.).

Maitland, Air Commodore Edward—British Commodore, *R38/ZR-2.*

*Matron No. 1—Matron at Hull Royal Infirmary.

*Matron No. 2—Matron at Bedford Hospital.

Maxfield, Cmdr. Louis H. USN—American Captain of *R38/ZR-2.*

Meager, Capt. George—1st Officer, *Howden R100.*

Mugnier, Abbé—Princess Marthe's Priest and Spiritual Advisor.

N

*Nellie—Worker at the Gasbag Factory, Royal Airship Works, Cardington

*'New York Johnny'—American Trainee Engineer, *R38/ZR-2.*

Norway, Nevil Shute, ('Nev')—Chief Calculator.

O

O'Neill, Sqdn. Ldr. William H.L. Deputy Director of Civil Aviation, Delhi.

P

Palstra, Sqdn. Ldr. MC, William, Royal Australian Airforce, Liaison Officer to the Air Ministry—representing the Australian Government.

*Postlethwaite, Elsie—Nurse at Hull Royal Infirmary, Bobby Jenco's Girl.

Potter, Walter—British Coxswain, Mentor of American Crewmen, *R38/ZR-2.*

R

Rabouille, Eugène—Rabbit Poacher, French eyewitness.

*Remington, Anna—Lou's Sister.

*Remington, Charlotte—Lou's Grandmother.

*Remington, Cliff—Lou's Father.

*Remington, Violet—Lou's Mother.

*Remington, Louis, ('Remy')–American Chief Petty Officer. *R38/ZR-2.*

*Remington, Tom—Lou's Brother.

Richmond, Lt. Col. Vincent—Head of Airship Design and Development (R.A.W.).

Richmond, Mrs. Florence, ('Florry')—Richmond's Wife.

*Robards—Ramsay MacDonald's Bodyguard.

*Robert—Charlotte's first love.

Robertson, Major—*Flight Magazine* Reporter.

*Ronnie—Works Foreman, Cardington Shed No. 1.

Rope, Sqdn. Ldr. F.M.—Asst. Head of Airship Design and Development (R.A.W.).

S

*Steel, Nick, ('Nervous Nick')—Rigger, *Howden R100.*

Scott, Maj. Herbert G. ('Scottie')—Asst. Director of Airship Development (R.A.W.).

*Scunthorpe, Lord—Member of the House of Lords, Opponent of LTA.

*Smothers, Helen—*Washington Post* Reporter.

Steff, F/O Maurice—2nd Officer, *Cardington R101 & Howden R100.*

*Stone, Josh—American Trainee Rigger, *R38/ZR-2 & Shenandoah.*

T

Thomson, Christopher Birdwood, ('Kit' or 'CB')—Brigadie General/Politician.

Teed, Philip—Chemist in Charge of Manufacture of Hydrogen, Howden.

*Tilly, Mrs. Queenie—Patient at Hull Royal Infirmary.

*Tyson, Julia—Lou Remington's first love.

*Tyson, Rory—Julia's Uncle, Proprietor, Tyson's Lumber and General Hardware Co.

*Tyson, Israel—Rory Tyson's Son.

W

Wallis, Barnes—Designer-in-Chief, *Howden R100.*

Wallis, Molly—Barnes Wallis' Wife.

Wann, Flt. Lt. Archibald —British Captain of *R38/ZR-2*.

*Washington, Ezekiah, II—Train Steward aboard *The Washingtonian.*

*Wigglesbottom, 'Moggy'—Owner of a 15th Century Cottage, Bendish Hamlet.

Y

*Yates, Capt. USN—Washington Navy Yard, Washington, D.C.

THE GHOST OF CAPTAIN HINCHLIFFE

Some characters in *The Airshipmen* also appear in *The Ghost of Captain Hinchliffe*. Available online at Amazon worldwide and at retail booksellers.

Millie Hinchliffe lives a near perfect existence, tucked away with her loving fighter-pilot husband in their picture-postcard cottage in the glorious English countryside. As a mother, artist, classical pianist and avid gardener, Millie has it all. But when 'Hinch' goes missing with a beautiful heiress over the Atlantic in a bid to set a flying record, her world is shaken to the core. Heartbroken and facing ruin, she questions the validity of messages she receives from 'the other side—messages that her husband is desperate to help her. In this suspenseful tale of unconditional love, desperate loss and wild adventure, Hinch charges Millie with an extraordinary mission: *Put a stop to the British Airship Program and prevent another national tragedy.*

PRAISE FOR *THE GHOST OF CAPTAIN HINCHLIFFE*

Another riveting tale from David Dennington, author of The Airshipmen. This time, he cleverly weaves together a couple's amazing love and the temptation it faces with the drama of a transatlantic flying record attempt and spine-tingling psychic connection from beyond the grave that becomes the only hope of preventing a horrific aviation disaster. It's an intriguing recipe that makes it hard to put down *The Ghost of Captain Hinchliffe*.
David Wright, Daily Mirror Journalist, London.

YouTube promo: The Ghost of Captain Hinchliffe

Available worldwide in paperback or Kindle from Amazon

Author's website: http://www.daviddennington.com

Printed in Great Britain
by Amazon